PLAUTUS: THE COMEDIES

Complete Roman Drama in Translation

David R. Slavitt and Palmer Bovie, Series Editors

PLAUTUS: THE COMEDIES

Volume I

EDITED BY

DAVID R. SLAVITT
AND PALMER BOVIE

THE JOHNS HOPKINS UNIVERSITY PRESS
Baltimore and London

© 1995 The Johns Hopkins University Press
All rights reserved. Published 1995
Printed in the United States of America on acid-free paper
04 03 02 01 00 99 98 97 96 95   5 4 3 2 1

The Johns Hopkins University Press
2715 North Charles Street
Baltimore, Maryland 21218-4319
The Johns Hopkins Press Ltd., London

Library of Congress Cataloging-in-Publication Data

Plautus, Titus Maccius.
   [Works. English. 1995]
   Plautus : the comedies / edited by David R. Slavitt and Palmer Bovie.
      p.   cm — (Complete Roman drama in translation)
   Includes bibliographical references.
   Contents: v. 1. Amphitryon / translated by Constance Carrier — Miles gloriosus /
translated by Erich Segal — Captivi / translated by Richard Moore — Casina /
translated by Richard Beacham — Curculio / translated by Henry Taylor . . . [etc.]
      ISBN 0-8018-5070-3 (v. 1 : alk. paper). — ISBN 0-8018-5071-1 (v. 1 : pbk. :
alk. paper)
      1. Plautus, Titus Maccius—Translations into English.   2. Latin drama
(Comedy)—Translations into English.   3. Greece—Drama.   I. Slavitt, David
R., 1935–   .   II. Bovie, Smith Palmer.   III. Title.   IV. Series.
PA6569.S55   1995
872'.01—dc20   94-45317

ISBN 0-8018-5056-8 (v. 2 : alk. paper). — ISBN 0-8018-5057-6 (v. 2 : pbk. : alk. paper)
ISBN 0-8018-5067-3 (v. 3 : alk. paper). — ISBN 0-8018-5068-1 (v. 3 : pbk. : alk. paper)
ISBN 0-8018-5072-X (v. 4 : alk. paper). — ISBN 0-8018-5073-8 (v. 4 : pbk. : alk. paper)

A catalog record for this book is available from the British Library.

Acknowledgments of prior publication appear at the end of this book.

CONTENTS

PREFACE

Roman literature begins with Plautus, at about the time of the Second Punic War that ended with Hannibal's defeat at the hands of Scipio at Zama (202 B.C.). It is not surprising, then, that arrogant generals, boastful military captains, and mercenary adventurers should jostle one another on Plautus's stages, or that his prologues may end with a wish for the audience's "good luck against your enemies." In *The Little Carthaginian*, Hanno is from Carthage and at one point speaks in Punic to the dismay of the Romans, one of whom volunteers to translate—and of course gets it totally wrong.

Born in Sarsina, in Umbria, in 254 B.C., Plautus came to Rome to work first as a stage carpenter and then, when he had earned a little money, to invest in his own business and leave Rome. The business failed, and Plautus returned to the city to work for a baker, grinding flour in a mill. It is at this time in his career that he began writing his plays. This is, at any rate, what we can infer from the texts, the point being that Plautus was not "literary," but a man of the world, even a man of the streets. He knew his way around—life and the Latin language, too. With considerable exuberance, he wrote many plays. Nearly 130 comedies had been attributed to him until a more conservative list was drawn up by the critic Varro (116–27 B.C.), whose canon lists the twenty plays that have survived to our day, which can still be read and performed and can still elicit lively chuckles and even peals of laughter.

Plautus is famous for his studies of mistaken identity, illustrated, for example, by twins. In the *Miles Gloriosus*, the braggart warrior's mistress impersonates her twin sister, to deceive him, one identity doing duty for both. In the *Amphitryon* Jupiter must impersonate the general if he is to seduce the chaste wife Alcmena. He also

vii

transforms Mercury into a twin Sosia, the general's servant, and at one wild moment the real Sosia meets the transformed figure: he confronts himself. When producing his version of the *Amphitryon* in the seventeenth century, Molière himself acted the part of Sosia, and ever since then the word for "stand-in" in French theater has been *un Sosie*.

The braggart warrior of the *Miles Gloriosus* is deceived twice: once by the supposed twin sister; later by a new female character, introduced expressly to entrap him. He ends up abjectly humiliated. Amphitryon, on the other hand, has been indeed victorious and deserves to be thought of as a *miles gloriosissimus*. By creating the illusion of being Alcmena's husband and so seducing her, Jupiter wreaks apparent havoc on both Alcmena and Amphitryon. She is filled with righteous indignation as well as being made pregnant with the twins Hercules and Iphicles. But after her momentary tragic disillusionment, Alcmena is hailed by Jupiter as the most glorious example of womanhood and honored as a model of steadfast virtue. The turn of events has produced, as Mercury announces in the prologue, a new form of drama, the tragi-comedy.

While all Plautus's comedies have a moral dimension, none is more earnest than his *Captivi*, with its all-male cast. This play studies not war but the victims of war and the enslavement of POWs. Ergasilus, the comic parasite, brightens things somewhat with his irreverence, but the play is serious throughout with a nervous awareness of avoidance of tragedy. John Wright has said that "there is morality enough for anyone in *The Captives*, but it is a morality colored by the usual fascinating combination of Plautine exuberance and irony."[1] I find this play deadly serious. The prologue presents the play in its new and unusual terms:

> . . . really, it will be worth your while to pay attention to this play. It is not written in the trite style and there are no off-color lines, as in other plays, that should not be spoken. Here you will not meet a lying procurer, a clever courtesan or a braggart warrior (miles gloriosus!).
>
> *The Captives*, ll. 54–58

---

[1]*Ancient Writers: Greece and Rome*, ed. T. James Luce (New York: Charles Scribner's Sons, 1982), 1:510.

And in the epilogue, the whole company comes forward to have the last word:

> Spectators, this play was founded on good behavior. . . . Dramatists find few plays such as this which make good men better. So, if we have brought you pleasure and not been boring, will you, who wish to see virtue rewarded, give us your applause.
>
> *The Captives*, ll. 1029–36

In the *Casina*, the desirable young slave girl for whom the play is named never appears. She is the drawing power for two slaves in the family. Both the father, Lysidamus, and the son want the girl, and each has proposed that his slave, serving as a "beard," marry the girl so that the master will have access to her. The revelation of these matched machinations is comic, and the spirit of the play is one of defiant and energetic naughtiness. This unraveling, a counterplot by Lysidamus's wife, is, as one of the neighbors says, the kind of thing a playwright might think up: "There never was a playwright invented a cleverer plot than this masterpiece of ours."

The word Plautus puts in the neighbor's mouth is *poeta*. All of the plays are in verse, after all, in varying meters, and they offer many passages in lyric measures that can serve—and probably did—as song material. Richard Beacham's translation is flexible enough to suggest both the lyrical and the obscene aspects of the Latin that the play requires.

There is similar connivance and contrivance in the *Curculio—The Weevil*—in which the eponymous manipulator is working to arrange things so that Phaedromus can buy the charming Planesium from her owner, Cappadox, the procurer. The machinations and double-dealings are real enough, and the insults are altogether in earnest—until the moment of revelation and resolution in which it turns out, against all odds, that the girl is not a slave but a free woman, a sister of the braggart soldier, Therapontigonus Platagidorus, who can confer her hand honorably on Phaedromus. Plautus is playing here as he often does with the general notion of fate and its extremely improbable instruments.

The scene is Epidaurus, A Greek never-never-land that is much like Shakespeare's conventional Italy. But at a significant point, the opening of what would be act 4, the Choragus, or Stage Manager, steps out to address the audience, worried about the return of the costumes he has loaned Curculio for his intrigues and masquerades. While he is waiting, the Choragus fills the audience in about the site, explaining exactly where they are; his descriptions of the place apply in perfect detail to Rome: forum; marketplace; the temple of Castor and Pollux in the forum; "Tuscan Street," the haunt of the hustlers; the Velabrum; the Old Shops; and the moneylenders' tables. The secret is out: call it Epidaurus, but what is happening is going on in Plautus's hometown. The new masters of the Mediterranean are a resourceful and imaginative group of people. As one of them remarks:

> Nec fallaciam astutiorem ullus fecit poeta atque haec est fabre facta a nobis. [There never was a playwright invented a cleverer plot than this masterpiece of ours.]
>
> *Casina*, ll. 860–61

Palmer Bovie

AMPHITRYON

Translated by Constance Carrier

INTRODUCTION

The *Amphitryon* is Plautus's most unusual drama. Mercury first calls the play a tragedy, then corrects himself; he acts puzzled. Doesn't he, a god, know what to call it? I'll make it both, he decides: "faciam ut commixta sit; sit tragicomoedia." Since it contains both gods and slaves, Mercury continues, it will have to be a tragicomedy.

Many previous dramatists had dealt with this story, but there is apparently no single source or predecessor of Plautus's comedy. The story of Zeus's love for Alcmena was a familiar one by the sixth century B.C.; later Sophocles and Euripides composed works based on it; there may well have been a comedy on the topic of "the long night" in Greek Middle Comedy; and Greek New Comedy would relish the double identity theme. Vase paintings show scenes from performances by vaudeville players in southern Italy, early in the third century B.C. Zeus, dressed as a character in farce, carries a ladder to climb up to the window from which Alcmena peers out. Plautus refers in the *Rudens* to a storm so terrific it was not a storm but "the tempest in Euripides' *Alcmena*." In the *Mercator* by Plautus, the maid casually says to the wife, "I hanc mecum ut videas simul tuam Alcumenam paelicem, Iuno mea" ["Come in, my lady Juno, and see your rival, his mistress Alcmena"] (ll. 689–90).

Like the other works he adapted from the Greeks, Plautus's *Amphitryon* emerged as a new, indelibly Roman creation. By making Mercury, the attendant of Jupiter, an identical twin of Sosia, Amphitryon's servant, Plautus doubled the confusion and divided it in different directions. Sosia, worried enough at being afloat in the streets of Thebes late at night, brave in tongue if weak in heart, feels his confidence slither away when confronted and robbed of his identity by the counterfeiting god. Mercury himself, patron saint of messages and money, ushers in the play appropriately for the audi-

3

ence of mercenary Romans. His prologue is a kind of messenger scene delivered by The Real Messenger—but Sosia's soliloquy is even more so when he strolls on stage to describe the great events of the battle he has just experienced—from a safe distance in the general's tent. The appearance of Mercury is enough to send Sosia reeling back to the harbor to report the mystery to Amphitryon.

The first action is rounded off with the touching farewell scene between Jupiter disguised as Amphitryon and Alcmena. The tragic note of the play is heard in Alcmena's words of affection and constancy. In the central scenes of the play, emotional turbulence gathers force, first in the touching but assured tones of the "parting." Then, as the real Amphitryon looms up, berating Sosia for seeing double, we hear the "greeting" scene and watch it develop into a confrontation between husband and wife that ends with denunciation and suspicion, on the brink of tragedy—dissolution. In the third part of the action Jupiter effects the reconciliation that Alcmena is generously inclined to grant; the "tragi" turns back into comedy. The ruffled dignity and severe confusion of the deceived husband ricochet off both Alcmena and Sosia. The slave has enough wonder and bruises to last him a good time, but insists on his claim to the truth that he saw things right even if he did see them double. When even the golden bowl seems to be in two places at once, Sosia can only mutter "omnes congeminavimus" ["we have all twinned"] (l. 786). Germane to the myth, the verb has capricious Roman overtones, for the Romans were fascinated by the idea of twins. Two legendary founders were better than one; two men named Scipio could finally take the measure of Carthage; two consuls should share the executive office. Rome herself was two things: *urbs et orbis terrarum*, the city and the inhabited world. The Amphitryon legend handily supplies the prized sibling cooperation for which Rome had so superstitious a regard. (Its aftermyth furnishes the twins Hercules and Iphicles with their double paternity.) At the end of the play Plautus risks another "tragic" sensation to bring the comedy to its crashing close. The nurse, like a messenger, reports the facts of Alcmena's effortless parturition brought on by Jupiter's obstetrical lightning. Promptly thereafter, she reports, Hercules strangled the two serpents (Plautus does not call them agents of Juno's jealousy) rustling toward the twins in their cradles. The happy ending is crowned by

Jupiter's appearance like the Greek tragic deus ex machina, while Amphitryon gazes up in wonder from below, in a very Roman way thanking his lucky stars for the cooperation of his heavenly double. The end of the legend of Amphitryon provides an auspicious omen for the saga of Rome, whose patron saint was Hercules, the great altruistic man of action.

Plautus not only invented a double term "tragicomedy," but decorated the plot as lavishly as he could with its elements. We have Amphitryon, whose name means "harassing on both sides," being harassed on both sides. Amphitryon, the romantic chevalier, wins the hand of his own bride in disguise. The spectacle shows a woman of unwavering merit and aplomb, seduced by her own husband. There are two slaves, one a capricious god, the other a craven mortal. There is the notorious long night, and rampant confusion as to its timeliness in the conception cycle of the new hero. There is the canonical battle description evocative of General Amphitryon's military prowess.

Jupiter's conduct on this errant night does not in Plautus's version invite reproach. Amoral as he is, he does no wrong. Like Penelope and Alcestis, furthermore, Alcmena is steadfast as well as attractive. Both Alcmena and Amphitryon find themselves in the puzzling predicament of being "harassed on both sides." Both are right, although Amphitryon thinks he is being wronged. Paradoxically, the Olympian *obligato* compromises Jupiter more than Alcmena. His very name originally was spelled in Latin "Diespiter" and meant Father of the Day, but here he must change into a father of the night to gain his conquest. The real Amphitryon survives this celestial put-on to recover his Roman credentials as the father of the day, the powerful husband, glorious in war, and at home assured of a wife he can love but not overwhelm.

Palmer Bovie

AMPHITRYON

CHARACTERS

MERCURY, a god
JUPITER, a god
SOSIA, a slave of Amphitryon
AMPHITRYON, a general
ALCMENA, wife of Amphitryon
BLEPHARO, a ship's pilot
BROMIA, maid of Alcmena

SCENE: *Thebes, before the mansion of Amphitryon.*

PROLOGUE

(Enter the god MERCURY; *he raises his hand for silence)*

MERCURY: Since every member of this crowd is eager
    For me to prosper all his business ventures
    And bring him luck in every trade and sale,
    Since all of you would have me guarantee
    Your least investment, near or far, a profit
    And flourishing returns on all transactions—
    Those you've embarked on, those you plan—forever;
    And since the only news you'd have me bring,
    Whether of public or private enterprise,

You'd choose to have encouraging in tone,　　　　　　10
(You know, of course, Olympus has assigned
To me control of messages and money):
Let me adjure you then, to the degree
You seek my favor, *settle down, shut up,*
And give this play we're acting a fair chance!
I'll tell you who sent me, and why I came,
And who I am, not beating 'round the bush.
Jupiter ordered it; I am Mercury.
I am supposed to ask a favor here—　　　　　　　　20
Our father knows that you, from proper awe
And reverence, would carry out his word,
As it is right you should when he has spoken.
At any rate, he has instructed me
To phrase this as a plea, not a command,
Worded most gently, spoken slow and clear.
(That Jupiter whose order sent me hence
Shivers like any man at punishment—
And why indeed shouldn't he fear the whip,
Born as he was of strictly human stock?
And I who am his son inherit this,　　　　　　　　30
As one inherits any weakness of his father.)
Peaceably, then, I come to bring you peace,
And ask no more fairness in return:
Justly I plead for justice from the just.
No one begs just men for unjust decrees,
And only fools think the unjust act justly,
Since these are ignorant of right and wrong.
Attention now, hear what I'm going to say.
What we wish, you should wish. This we deserve,
My father and I, from you and your republic.　　　40
No need that I remind you—like those gods
Whom I have seen playacted, Neptune, Virtue,
Victory, Mars, Bellona, listing all
Their kindnesses to men—you know what Jove,
Ruler of gods, has done for humankind.
It's not my father's custom to reproach

Good men with all the goodness he has shown;
He is content to see your gratitude,
And feels you're worthy to be treated well.
    Now first I'll tell you what I've come to ask,   50
Then what's the subject of this tragedy.
(He pauses. Audience groans at the prospect of a serious play.)
A god can change it, surely, and I shall.
Let it be comedy, and no line changed.
Would you like that? But what a stupid question—
As if I didn't know, being a god.
I understand your feelings perfectly:
We'll mix it up, half tragic and half comic.
Straight comedy can't deal with kings and gods—
That I shan't do; it's not correct. What, then?
Well, since it has a slave as character   60
Let's call it, as I said, a tragicomedy.
    Now here's the favor Jupiter would ask:
That you assign inspectors in each row
To hunt and mark down any hired claque—
And (as security) remove his toga—
Or one who's canvassed for his favorite
By letter, messenger, or word of mouth.
And if the aediles give the prize unfairly,
Jove would have these men punished just as those
Who seek an office for themselves or others.   70
How have you won your wars? By worth alone,
Not bought-votes or ambition. Let the same
High standard hold for actor as for army.
Not claqueurs but true artists should be crowned.
An honest audience gives its applause
Only to those who really live the role.
And Jove enjoined me further that by law
Inspectors check each member of the cast:
If one of these has hired his friends to clap
Or made another actor look a fool,   80
They'll cut to shreds his costume and his hide.
You're wondering why Jove loves players so?
It's no great marvel, not when you consider

That he himself will tread these very boards.
You're more astonished? But it's hardly new
For him, the king of gods, to play a part;
Just last year, when the actors called his name,
Suddenly he appeared upon the scene.
And so he will today, I promise you,
And I along with him. Attention now,   90
While I outline the comedy and its plot.
    We're in the city of Thebes. Amphitryon,
Argive by both descent and birth, lives there
In that house with his wife, Electrus's daughter,
Alcmena. Now her husband's off at war
Leading his troops against the Teleboans
And having left Alcmena pregnant by him.
Now I expect you know my father's ways—
How free he is, or can be, or has been,
And bound to have whatever takes his fancy.   100
Alcmena caught his eye, her husband elsewhere,
And, as he will, he had his will with her.
The net result, as you can guess quite clearly,
Is this: that she's with child by both of them,
Both by her husband and by Jove himself.
And as I speak, my father's in that house there,
Alcmena in his arms, and so the night
Goes on past dawn that he may have his pleasure—
Disguised (you've guessed it) as Amphitryon.
        So much for that. Don't wonder at my outfit,   110
My coming on the scene dressed as a slave, *mercury*
Since that's the part I play in this new version
Of a familiar folktale that you'll see.
I say again: Jove's in that house, remember—
But you would swear he was Amphitryon;
The very servants of the place accept him;
He can be a werewolf as well as a mere wolf.
And I'm no longer Mercury but Sosia,
Amphitryon's slave who's with him at the front—
My duty to assist my amorous father   120
And not be questioned by the family slaves

When I go busily about the household.
If they believe I'm one of them, nobody
Will ask me who I am or why I'm here.
      As I have said before, my father's in there,
His arms around his current light-o'-love,
Telling her how the enemy fled before him,
Describing to her the prizes he has won—
(We stole the genuine articles from her husband)
My father balks at nothing to convince.   130
Today Amphitryon comes home on leave,
And Sosia too, the slave I represent.
So that you may distinguish god from man,
Look for this little feather in my hat;
In Jove's a little golden knot, or tassel;
Nothing at all to mark Amphitryon's.
None of the household here will see these tokens,
But they'll be clear to you.
(*Looks offstage right, then points*)
Here's Sosia now;
He's coming from the harbor with his lantern.   140
My job's to keep him out when he gets here.
Watch closely now; it's worth your full attention
When Jupiter and Mercury perform a play.

ACT I

(*From stage right, enter* SOSIA, AMPHITRYON's *slave, scared of the dark, but trying to convince himself he's not*)

SOSIA: I'm a bold man, bolder than most, to walk
   Alone at night, with young fools out for trouble;
   What would I do if I got thrown in jail?
   Like something in a pantry, to be served
   Tomorrow—for a whipping—and nobody
   Let speak in my defense, me nor my master,

And everybody saying I deserved it.   · 150
Those eight strong-arms would pound me like an anvil—
A public welcome for the traveler.
     It's all my master's fault:
Why else would I be here, against my will,
Rushing from harbor into town? why not
By daylight? couldn't I do his errands then?
     The wealthy make bad masters;
      Don't envy a rich man's slaves—
"Do that!" "Say this!"—never a bit of rest.
And that spoiled master who never worked a day   160
Thinks you must satisfy his lightest whim—
This he expects, and who cares how you work?
Oh, slavery's the mother of injustice:
Take up your load and carry it—that's life.

MERCURY: (*Aside*) I am the one who ought to be complaining:
     This morning I was free;
     Now I'm my father's slave.
It's your born drudge who grumbles, like this one.

SOSIA: The kind of drudge I am deserves a beating—
     Fool, not to thank the gods I've got this far!   170
Lord, if they treat me as I should be treated,
They'll get some thug to lie in wait and jump me
Because I've seemed ungrateful for their care.

MERCURY: (*Aside*) Not many men know what the gods should
     grant them.

SOSIA: What I did not expect, nor any Theban,
     Has happened after all; we're safe and sound,
We've won the war, we'll be back home tomorrow,
The battle's over and the foe crushed.
Their town, where hundreds of our soldiers died—
That town's been taken by our strength and will.   180
Who led us on? My lord Amphitryon.
He's given us land and loot and lasting fame

And put King Creon on the throne of Thebes.
This news I bring his wife, straight from the harbor—
That his authority sets up our state.
I'd better practice what I'm going to say—
And if I lie a little, that's my failing.
The more the battle raged, the more I ran,
But I can't tell her that. I'll make things up,
But let me try it once before I start: 190
It's the details that count. Now then, let's see—
    First, when we'd got there, when we reached the shore,
Amphitryon picked out his bravest men
To go as legates and explain his terms:
The enemy must yield, return their plunder,
Give up the plunderers, recall the troops;
And then at once he would withdraw his men
And leave a land not ravaged but at peace.
If they refused, he said he had no choice—
He would attack the town with all his forces. 200
Our legates told this to the Teleboans.
You know those westerners; puffed up with pride,
Sure of themselves, they got on their high horse,
Swore they'd defend themselves and theirs with arms
And ordered every man of us to leave.
Amphitryon, at this news, drew up his troops,
And so did they—how all that armor shone!
Both sides marched out their men
Drawn up in proper rank;
Then we arranged our legions, 210
As usual, facing theirs.
The leaders met between them
In private conference:
The losers, they decided,
Must give up fields, homes, shrines,
And themselves, in surrender.
Agreed. The trumpets spoke;
Earth shook with cry and crash;
Both generals promised Jove
Rich votive offerings, 220

And urged their warriors on.
Each man lashed about him
With every ounce of strength,
Struck down, or was struck down.
Sky echoed back their screams,
Their panting made a cloud,
And strong men killed strong men,
At last the prayed-for victory was ours;
We forced our way through bodies heaped or sprawled,
And not one man of ours turned tail and fled,   230
But fought to keep what headway he had made,
Giving up his life rather than give way
And, falling, kept the lines where they had stood.
Amphitryon, seeing that the tide had turned,
Sent horsemen to attack them on the right;
The cavalry swooped down with devil yells,
And, plunging in, trampled them underfoot.

MERCURY: So far he hasn't spoken one false word:
    I, with my father, was an eyewitness.

SOSIA: Seeing the foe's ranks break, our men took heart   240
    And brought them shameful death, struck in the back;
    Amphitryon killed their king with his own hand.
    The fight went on all day, from dawn to dusk—
    Oh, I remember it well: I missed my lunch—
    But as the dark came down, the battle ended.
    Next day their leaders came to us in tears,
    Bearing olive branches, seeking peace
    And offering in surrender everything—
    Themselves, their holy shrines, town, families,
    For Thebans to dispose of as they chose.   250
    They gave Amphitryon a golden bowl
    Their king had drunk from.
                        There! That's what I'll say,
    Then with the master's orders done, go home.

(*He starts toward his master's front door*)

MERCURY: He's coming this way—now I've got to stop him.
    He won't get home tonight; I'll see to that.
    Easy to trick him now, since I'm his double
    In form and dress—I must be careful, though,
    To seem his twin in character as well—
    A good-for-nothing fellow, shifty, sly—
    And use those very traits to keep him here.   260
    Why is he looking at the sky? I'll watch him.

SOSIA: (*To himself*) Lord, if there's any truth I can believe,
    I'd say the god of night went drunk to bed;
    The Great Bear hasn't budged, not east or west;
    The moon's still in the same spot where it rose;
    They're standing still—the Pleiades, Orion,
    The evening star, they haven't moved at all. They're frozen
      up there, and no sign of dawn.

MERCURY: (*To the sky*) Night, for my father's sake now, stay
      stock-still—
    Best help to the best of gods in the best of causes.   270
    You'll be repaid.

SOSIA: (*To himself*) No night's gone on so long
    Except the one I spent, whipped and left hanging—
    And this one seems to me already longer.
    I'll bet the sun's asleep—asleep dead-drunk;
    Toasted himself too much at dinnertime.

MERCURY: You rascal, you think the gods resemble you?
    I'll entertain you: I'll teach you to be civil.
    Come here, you gallows bird; learn it the hard way.

SOSIA: Where are those nighthawks who won't sleep alone?
    This is a good night for some high-priced love.   280

MERCURY: (*Wryly*) Jupiter seems to have the same idea,
    Lying in there, Alcmena in his arms.

SOSIA: I'd better go deliver my master's message—
   (*Stops, notices the shadowy figure of* MERCURY)
   Who's that at midnight on the step, God help me?

MERCURY: Of all the cowards!—

SOSIA: Maybe all he wants
   Is just to take my cloak off and reweave it.

MERCURY: He's terrified. Let's have some fun with him—

SOSIA: Lord help me, but my teeth itch for a fight!
   He's got his welcome ready, with his fists.
   Good-hearted soul, he'll see I get my sleep   290
   After a night of running my master's errands.
   I'm done for, absolutely—the size of him!

MERCURY: (*To himself*) I'll speak out loud, so he can overhear.
   He's frightened now; this ought to make him faint.
   (*Calling in booming, stentorian tones*)
   Come on, fists! Give me something to feed on—
   Was it only yesterday you stripped four men
   And knocked them out?

SOSIA: Oh Lord, I have a feeling
   Sosia will have a new name very soon: The Fifth.
   He claims he's put four men away already;   300
   I see that I'm the next.

MERCURY: There now, let's go!

SOSIA: Let's go indeed! He's tightening his belt.

MERCURY: He won't get off this time!

SOSIA: But who's this "he"?

MERCURY: Whoever comes this way shall eat my fists.

SOSIA: I never eat at midnight; anyway,
I've had my meal. Find somebody who's hungry.

MERCURY: This fist must weigh ten pounds.

SOSIA: Good Lord, he
weighs them!

MERCURY: A slow stroke, lulling him to sleep?

SOSIA: Oh, great!
I haven't slept for three nights.   310

MERCURY: This is awful.
Why did I teach you, arm, to hit like that?
Remodel your victim with the merest graze!

SOSIA: He's going to give my face another shape?

MERCURY: Just skim it. What you hit has no bones left.

SOSIA: Oh God, he's going to bone me like a fish!
They shouldn't allow man-boning. Has he seen me?

MERCURY: I smell someone. He's out of luck.

SOSIA: Me? Me?

MERCURY: He may have been far off, but now he's not.

SOSIA: The devil's taught him.

MERCURY: See, my fists are up.   320

SOSIA: If I'm your sparring mate, try the wall first.

MERCURY: A voice flies to my ear.

SOSIA: What lousy luck—
   My birdlike voice—I should have had it clipped.

MERCURY: He says that I should whack his beast's back for him—

SOSIA: I don't own even a mule.

MERCURY: —a load of blows—

SOSIA: And me worn-out and seasick from the voyage—
   Could I walk with a load as I can't without one?

MERCURY: Someone is talking.

SOSIA: Saved! He doesn't see me.
   "Someone," he says, but my name's Sosia.   330

MERCURY: —comes from the right, this voice that strikes my
      ear—

SOSIA: I'm going to take a beating for my voice?

MERCURY: He's coming this way—good!

SOSIA: My legs won't move;
   If you asked me where I am, I couldn't tell you.
   My feet are blocks of wood, I'm cold as ice.
   There'll be no message and no messenger. . . .
   Take the bull by the horns, my boy. Speak out,
   Sound threatening, make him afraid of you.

MERCURY: (Approaching SOSIA, *still talking extra loud*)
   Where are you going, with Vulcan in a horn?   340

SOSIA: Why should I tell a man who bones men's faces?

MERCURY: Are you a freeman or a slave?

SOSIA: Whichever I choose.

MERCURY: Indeed?

SOSIA: Indeed.

MERCURY: You should be whipped.

SOSIA: You lie.

MERCURY: I'll teach you truth.

SOSIA: What need is there of that?

MERCURY: Who are you? Where are you going? Where are you
    from?

SOSIA: A slave his master's sent here. What does that tell you?

MERCURY: I'll violate your tongue—

SOSIA: You can't do that:
    It's guarded far too well.

MERCURY: Any more humor?
    What business have you here?   350

SOSIA: And what have you?

MERCURY: The king puts separate sentries here each night.

SOSIA: A good thing: when we're out, they guard the house.
    Now you can leave, though: say the family's home.

MERCURY: How do I know you're part of it? On your way:
    I don't give family slaves a family welcome.

SOSIA: I tell you my master lives here. I'm his servant—

MERCURY: I'll elevate you, if you stay.

SOSIA: You'll what?

MERCURY: They'll carry you out on their shoulders—
   You won't walk after I've hit you.   360

SOSIA: But I *am* a slave here—

MERCURY: Be off, or tell me when you want your bearing.

SOSIA: You're going to keep me put, just back from the war?

MERCURY: This is your home?

SOSIA: I've told you—

MERCURY: Who's your master?

SOSIA: Amphitryon, the Theban general.
   His wife's Alcmena.

MERCURY: Tell me your own name.

SOSIA: The Thebans call me son of Davus, Sosia.

MERCURY: Your luck ran out the minute you came back,
   You consummate scoundrel, with your patched-up lies—   370

SOSIA: There weren't any lies; I came with a patched-up tunic.

MERCURY: You came with your tunic, liar? You came with your
      feet.

SOSIA: Of course.

MERCURY: And of course you're going to be thrashed for
      lying.

SOSIA: Well, I object, of course.

MERCURY: As a matter of course, that's useless.
    My course is a solid fact, not a mere opinion.

(*He boxes* SOSIA'*s ears*)

SOSIA: Help! Help!

MERCURY: You dare to claim you're Sosia?
    I'm Sosia!

(*Hits again*)

SOSIA: Yours, by virtue of your fists.
    Help, Thebans, help!

MERCURY: Still screeching, troublemaker?   380
    Speak up: why are you here?

(*Hits again*)

SOSIA: For your fists to work on.

MERCURY: Your master—?

SOSIA: Is Amphitryon. I'm Sosia.

MERCURY: Another blow for that.
    (*Hits him*)
                              I'm Sosia.

SOSIA: I wish to God you were, and getting beaten.

MERCURY: Muttering?

SOSIA: No sir.

MERCURY: Who owns you?

SOSIA: Sir, you name him.

MERCURY: Good. And they call you—?

SOSIA: Anything you say, sir.

MERCURY: Sosia, the servant of Amphitryon?

SOSIA: I made a slip; I meant *associate*.

MERCURY: I knew there wasn't any Sosia but me.   390
   That *was* a slip.

SOSIA: I wish your fists had made one.

MERCURY: I'm Sosia, even though you thought you were.

SOSIA: Sir, could I speak a word without being whipped?

MERCURY: A truce, that's all. What do you have to say?

SOSIA: Nothing unless there's peace—your fists are too strong.

MERCURY: Go on. You won't be harmed.

SOSIA: You promise?

MERCURY: Yes.

SOSIA: If you don't mean it—

MERCURY: (*Ironically*) May Mercury punish Sosia.

SOSIA: Then listen. I can speak quite plainly now: 400
   I am Amphitryon's Sosia.

MERCURY: What? Again?

SOSIA: Remember your promise. . . . It's the truth.

MERCURY: Watch out—

SOSIA: Do as you please; you're far too strong for me.
   Whatever you do, I'll still stick to the truth.

MERCURY: You can't make me be anyone but Sosia.

SOSIA: You can't make me belong to another master;
   I'm the only Sosia he has, so help,
   The only one he took along to the war.

MERCURY: The man is out of his mind.

SOSIA: But you're the man,   410
   Not I. You devil, I swear I'm Sosia.
   Hasn't our ship just docked from the Port of Persis?
   Haven't I come from there with my master's message
   Here to our doorstep, my lantern in my hand?
   I'm talking, no? and awake? I've been beaten up?
   That I can prove: my jaws are aching yet.
   Why am I waiting? Why don't I go into our house?

MERCURY: You think this is your house?

SOSIA: I know it is.

MERCURY: You counterfeited each word you coined just now.
   I am so Amphitryon's slave, Sosia,   420
   And just this night we shipped from Persis port
   Where King Pterelas ruled, where we sacked the town
   And assaulted the legions of the Teleboans
   With our might, and Amphitryon himself cut down
   King Pterelas in the van of the fighting.

SOSIA: I believe
  I'm not myself when I hear that other me
  Recite all this. He knows just what took place,
  And narrates it religiously. Ah, but here's a question:
  What gift did the Teleboans give our general?

MERCURY: The royal golden bowl Pterelas drunk from   430

SOSIA: You said it. Where is it now?

MERCURY: It's in the chest,
  Safely sealed with Amphitryon's special seal.

SOSIA: What does that seal look like?

MERCURY: The orient sun,
  Four-horse-charioted. Think you can toy with me?

SOSIA: (To himself, perplexed)
  I can't refute evidence. I'll just go and look
  For another name for myself. Somehow or other,
  This character has seen it all. Oh, here's something
  That's bound to trip him up: what I did in the tent.
  I'm the only one who knows that—no one else
  Was anywhere around. He'll never be able to review   440
  That bit of action.
  (To MERCURY)
                      You so-called Sosia, see here:
  When the legions were locked in bitter battle, what
  Were you engaged in, in the tent? Tell me
  What you were doing there, and I'm really done for.

MERCURY: There was a jug of wine and I filled up my jug.

SOSIA: He's certainly starting off right.

MERCURY: I took the pure wine
  Just as it came from its mother.

SOSIA: That's how it was.
  Right there I drank a jug of unmixed wine:
  Wouldn't be surprised if he was hiding in the jug.

MERCURY: Are you convinced that you're not Sosia now?   450

SOSIA: You say I'm not?

MERCURY: How can you be? I am.

SOSIA: You're not, by Jove, I am, and that's the truth.

MERCURY: By Mercury, I swear Jove says you lie.
  He'll take my unsworn word against your oath.

SOSIA: But look: if I'm not Sosia, who am I?

MERCURY: Oh, you can have the name when I don't want it;
  I'm Sosia and you're nameless. Now get out!

SOSIA: (*To himself, panic mounting*)
  God help me, now that I look, he has my features—
  I've seen them in a mirror. We could be twins.
  My hat, my clothes—he's more like me than I am: 460
  Leg, foot, height, haircut, eyes, nose, even lips—
  Jaws, chin, beard, neck—no difference. I'm speechless.
  If his back's scarred he couldn't be more me.
  And yet I'm still the man I was:
  I know my master and my house; I'm sane.
  I won't be fooled by words. Why don't I knock?

(*Starts toward the front door*)

MERCURY: Where are you going?

SOSIA: Home.

MERCURY: Though you may mount
  Jove's four-horsed chariot, you can't escape.

SOSIA: Why can't I tell my mistress what I've come for?

MERCURY: Tell yours whatever you like; don't bother ours.   470
  And don't provoke me or I'll break your ribs.

SOSIA: (*Shrinking in terror*)
  Don't, don't—I'll go. . . . Gods, help me keep my wits:
  Where was I lost, transformed, made someone else?
  Did I forget and leave me at the harbor?
  He's moved in on my self. People will carry
  More death masks of me living than of me dead.
  Back to the port, now; I must tell my master—
  Unless he doesn't know me—why, by Jove,
  Then I could shave my head for a freedman's cap.

(*Runs offstage, frightened out of his wits*)

MERCURY: My little project's going very well.   480
  At last I've got that nuisance off the doorstep
  And given my father time for a last embrace.
  Now when my friend gets back there to the port
  He'll tell his master Sosia packed him off.
  Amphitryon won't believe a word of it—
  Will think he never went where he was ordered.
  I'll get them and Amphitryon's whole household
  So utterly bewildered and confused
  That Jove my father may have all the chance
  He wants for love. Then they may know the truth,   490
  But not till then. Afterward Jupiter
  Will see to it that harmony's restored;
  Amphitryon and Alcmena will quarrel,
  He'll say she's brought disgrace upon them both,
  And then my father will come in and calm them.
  Oh yes—Alcmena, as I've failed to mention,
  This very day is going to bear twin boys,

One being a seven-months child and one a ten.
One is Amphitryon's son, the other Jove's:
The younger one is fathered by the god.   500
You understand these curious complications?
Because he loves Alcmena, Jupiter
Has settled that both sons be born at once,
Two labors coming to a single birth
So that there'll be no rumor of any rape,
No thought of a clandestine love affair.
As I implied, he'll tell Amphitryon.
What difference will that make? Surely it's clear
No one will blame Alcmena. For a god
To let a mortal suffer for a sin   510
That is the god's—that would be most unjust.
Enough of this: I hear the door creak open.
Here comes the counterfeit Amphitryon
And with him Alcmena, his borrowed wife.

(*The front door opens; out come* JUPITER-*as*-AMPHITRYON, *followed by the lovely* ALCMENA)

JUPITER: Goodbye, my dear; take care of what concerns us—
　　Don't overdo; you know you're near your time.
　　I must leave now. Don't have the child exposed.

ALCMENA: But husband, must you leave so suddenly?

JUPITER: Don't think I'm bored with you or with our home;
　　But the commander's place is with his army: 520
　　More things go wrong than right if he's not there.

MERCURY: (*Aside*) Fit father for the patron saint of rogues!
　　Watch how his practiced hand will smooth her down.

ALCMENA: Lord knows you make it clear how much you love me!

JUPITER: The dearest woman on earth—isn't that enough?

MERCURY: (*Aside*) Don't let your wife up there
(*Pointing to the sky*)
                                                      Get wind of this—
Or you may wish you *were* Amphitryon.

ALCMENA: I'd rather have it happen than hear of it.
You're leaving before you've warmed your place in bed.   530
From midnight only to morning—is this right?

MERCURY: (*Aside*) I must back my father up like a parasite. . . .
(*Now "playing"* SOSIA, *he runs up to* ALCMENA)
A word to you, madam: there isn't a man alive
Who loves his wife as madly as yours loves you.

JUPITER: (*Angrily*) I know you, you troublemaker! Out of my
    sight!
It's not your business to interfere or chatter.
I'll take a stick to you—

ALCMENA: No! Don't!

JUPITER: . . . One word more—

MERCURY: Your helper's offers to help don't come to much.

JUPITER: As for what you say, little wife, you shouldn't be angry;
I deserted my post, I wangled this favor for you.   540
So you could hear from me how I've served my state.
I've told you it all. If I hadn't loved you, darling,
I wouldn't have come.

MERCURY: I told you he'd pacify her.

JUPITER: I must get to the troops before they know I've gone;
If I don't, they'll say my wife counts more than the war.

ALCMENA: You can watch me cry because you're leaving?

JUPITER: Now, love,
　Don't redden your eyes; you know I'll be back.

MERCURY: Years hence.

JUPITER: It's not my choice to go—

ALCMENA: Oh, how can you say that,
　Leaving the night you came!

JUPITER: Don't cling to me, sweetheart; 550
　It's time—I've got to get out of the city by dawn.
　(*Hands her a gift*)
　This bowl, which was given to me as reward for valor,
　The one King Pterelas, whom I killed, would drink from—
　Alcmena, this is for you.

ALCMENA: (*Gratefully*) You always do it:
　Choose a gift that exactly fits the giver.

MERCURY: Oh no, you're wrong. What it matches is the receiver.

JUPITER: (*Angrily*) You again, jailbird? Can't I get rid of you?

ALCMENA: Don't punish Sosia on my account, my dear.

JUPITER: Whatever you say.

MERCURY: What a savage Love has made
　him!   560

JUPITER: Nothing else?

ALCMENA: Only love me when we're apart.

MERCURY: Let's go, sir. It's getting light.

JUPITER: You go ahead.
  I'll follow. Nothing else?

ALCMENA: Only come back soon.

JUPITER: (Before you expect me, even.) Now cheer up!
  (*She reenters the house.* JUPITER *then addresses the sky.*)
  Let the night that has slowed for me yield to the dawn;
  Illumine the world again with the rays of the sun—
  A shorter day to balance that longer night.
  Let morning come. I follow now where Mercury leads.

(*He strides off regally, following "his slave"*)

ACT II

(*The stage is empty to indicate the passage of some time. Then enter
the real* AMPHITRYON, *followed by the real* SOSIA *carrying assorted
baggage.*)

AMPHITRYON: Come on there, hurry up!

SOSIA: I'm right here, sir.

AMPHITRYON: You're a worthless good-for-nothing.

SOSIA: Oh, sir, why?   570

AMPHITRYON: You've never told the truth, and you never will.

SOSIA: Just like you, sir—you never trust your slaves.

AMPHITRYON: What's that? Why, I'll be damned! Another word
  Like that and I'll cut your tongue out for you.

SOSIA: Sir,
  You own me, you can treat me as you choose.
  I'll tell you it all, exactly as it happened,
  And your worst threat won't make me change a word.

AMPHITRYON: Confound you—you expect me to think you're
    there
  At home, now, when I see you here?

SOSIA: Yes, sir.

AMPHITRYON: You'll get your punishment from me today   580
  And from the gods tomorrow.

SOSIA: I'm in your hands.

AMPHITRYON: You'd dare make fun of me, your master, you fool?
  You'd try to tell me something no one's seen
  Has happened, when it couldn't—that a man
  Is here and somewhere else at the selfsame time?

SOSIA: Exactly what I said, sir.

AMPHITRYON: Damn your tongue!

SOSIA: What have I done to make you say that, sir?

AMPHITRYON: You scoundrel, are you asking what you did?

SOSIA: You'd have a right to beat me if I lied.

AMPHITRYON: The man is drunk. He must be.   590

SOSIA: I wish I was.

AMPHITRYON: You are.

SOSIA: I am?

AMPHITRYON: Yes. Where's the wine?

SOSIA: I'm sober, sir.

AMPHITRYON: Good heavens,
  What sort of man *is* this?

SOSIA: I've told you ten times, sir,
  I'm at the house. Do you hear?
  And the same me is with you.
  Isn't that plain enough?

AMPHITRYON: Get away from me.   600

SOSIA: Why, sir?

AMPHITRYON: You've got the plague.

SOSIA: Sir, why
  Should you say that? I'm well,
  Perfectly well, my lord.

AMPHITRYON: You'll get what you deserve
  Once I am safe at home:
  You'll find you're not so healthy.
  Come on, march! And don't try
  To make a fool of me.
  I gave you orders; you never carried them out;   610
  And what's worse, you think you can make me think you did,
  With your talk of what's impossible and unheard-of.
  All your lies will come back to you as lashes.

SOSIA: Amphitryon, sir, for a good, truth-telling slave—
  It's hard for him to be threatened with the whip.

AMPHITRYON: Look, we'll go through it once more. How in the
    world
  Can you be at home and here, I ask you now?

SOSIA: I'm here and I'm there, and I'm not surprised that you're
    baffled.
  It's no less puzzling to me than it is to you.

AMPHITRYON: What did you say?

SOSIA: That neither of us can
    explain it.   620
  As Jove is my witness, I didn't believe myself
  (That's Sosia) until that other Sosia (that's me)
  Made this Sosia believe what that one said.
  He knows exactly what happened while we were fighting
  And he has not only my name but my face as well:
  We're just as much alike as two drops of milk.
  Why, hours ago when you sent me home from the harbor—

AMPHITRYON: Well?

SOSIA: There I was at home before I got there.

AMPHITRYON: What rubbish you talk! Do you still believe you're
    sane?

SOSIA: You can see that I am.

AMPHITRYON: You've been touched by the
    evil hand   630
  Since you left the camp.

SOSIA: And it beat me black and blue.

AMPHITRYON: Who beat you?

SOSIA: I did it myself—the self that's there at home.

AMPHITRYON: Now look here: answer my question, nothing more.
  Who is that other Sosia, first of all?

SOSIA: Your slave.

AMPHITRYON: I have one more of those than I want.
   The only one I've owned in my life is you.

SOSIA: Well, sir, watch out. I'll bet you find another
   Waiting for you as soon as you get home.
   He looks like me; he's my age; his father was Davus.   640
   What else can I say? I seem to have grown a twin.

AMPHITRYON: This is, I must say, strange. Did you see my wife?

SOSIA: He wouldn't let me go in the house.

AMPHITRYON: Who wouldn't?

SOSIA: The one I've been talking about. The one who beat me.

AMPHITRYON: Which Sosia was that?

SOSIA: I was. Sir, how many times
   Must I say—

AMPHITRYON: You didn't drowse off a bit?

SOSIA: Oh no, sir.

AMPHITRYON: You might have made up that Sosia in a dream—

SOSIA: I don't fall asleep when my master gives me orders;   650
   I've been wide-awake both in camp and talking here;
   I was wide-awake when he hit me, and so was he.

AMPHITRYON: Who?

SOSIA: Sosia. The other one. Can't you understand it?

AMPHITRYON: Who could understand you, the way you babble?

SOSIA: Well, you'll know what I mean as soon as you have met
    him.

AMPHITRYON: Follow me, then. I've got to look into this.
    Go see that all I ordered is brought from the ship.

SOSIA: I'll be very careful to see that they do what you wish, sir;
    I haven't drunk up your orders along with the wine.

AMPHITRYON: I wish that the gods would cancel all that you've
    said.   660

(ALCMENA *enters, saddened by the departure of her "husband." She
thinks she is alone.*)

ALCMENA: How little there is of joy, compared to grief,
    In all our years and hours! No man escapes—
    The gods arrange that sorrow follows pleasure,
    A great delight precedes a greater woe.
    Here, in our home, I learn this, painfully,
    Given a glimpse of happiness, a few
    Short moments with my husband—and he is gone.
    My loneliness, my love, grow with his going:
    More pain to part than joy to have him near.
        But Oh, thank God   670
    That he is still alive, is even a hero!
        There's comfort here,
    If he must go, that he goes forth to fame;
    I can bear anything unflinchingly
    If at the end I hear him hailed as victor.
        Then I shall be content.
           Courage is all—
    Courage atones for any other fault.
    What else protects, preserves, our way of life,
    Our liberty, our families, our homes?   680

All these are in its hands,
And a brave man, as he ought to be, is blest.

AMPHITRYON: How pleased she'll be that I am coming back,
The long-awaited husband whom she loves—
And the unconquered Teleboans conquered
By men whom he led on to victory.
She will run out to meet me, her arms wide—

SOSIA: Someone will welcome me the same way, sir.

ALCMENA: (*Notices* AMPHITRYON) My husband's back again?

AMPHITRYON: (*To* SOSIA) Come on!

ALCMENA: (*To herself*)   —But then   690
Why did he leave? Is this a test, to see
Whether I'm faithful to him when he's gone?
Could he think I'd object to his return?

SOSIA: We'd better go back to the ship, sir.

AMPHITRYON: Why?

SOSIA: Nobody's going to give us breakfast here.

AMPHITRYON: What made you think of that?

SOSIA: Well, we're too late.

AMPHITRYON: What of it?

SOSIA: There's my mistress waiting for us;
She looks well-fed to me, and satisfied.

AMPHITRYON: When I left, I hoped she might be
          pregnant—

SOSIA: Hang it!—

AMPHITRYON: What?

SOSIA: I'm back again in time to draw the
   water—   700
It's ten months since we went, as I count it, sir.

AMPHITRYON: Cheer up.

SOSIA: I'm cheerful, sir. If I get a bucket,
   Don't ever trust my sacred word again, sir,
   If I don't drain that well, once I've begun.

AMPHITRYON: Come on. That job can go to someone else.

ALCMENA: (*To herself*) I suppose, as a dutiful wife, I should go to
   meet him.

AMPHITRYON: Amphitryon is happy to welcome his wife,
   Whom he thinks the best and most charming in all of Thebes,
   And whose virtue every Theban is quick to praise.   710
   Are you well? Are you glad to see me?

SOSIA: (*Aside*)   Nobody more so:
   She welcomes him the way she'd welcome a dog!

AMPHITRYON: Pregnant and well—you couldn't have pleased me
   more.

ALCMENA: I don't understand. Why do you mock me so,
   With greetings as though we'd been parted a long, long time
   And you had just this moment come from the war?

AMPHITRYON: But this is the first time in months that I've seen
   you, darling!

ALCMENA: You deny you've been back?

AMPHITRYON: I'm a truthful man. I
   deny it.

ALCMENA: What truth you've learned you've forgotten. Is this a
   test
  To try my affection? Why are you back so soon?   720
  Was it bad omens or weather that detained you,
  From going back, as you said you must, to your troops?

AMPHITRYON: How long since I said that?

ALCMENA: A little while. Just now.

AMPHITRYON: How *can* it be both *just now* and *a while ago?*

ALCMENA: Well, how do you think? I'm the one who's teasing
   now,
  Like you, pretending you hadn't been here for so long.

AMPHITRYON: (*To* SOSIA) I think she's delirious.

SOSIA: Give her a minute
   or two
  To finish her dream.

AMPHITRYON: You mean she's awake and sleeping?

ALCMENA: I'm certainly not asleep, and was not when it
   happened.
  It was just before dawn that I saw the two of you.

AMPHITRYON: Where?   730

ALCMENA: Here in our house.

AMPHITRYON: I don't believe it.

SOSIA: Oh hush, sir!
  Maybe the ship brought us up from the port while we slept.

AMPHITRYON: You're siding with her?

SOSIA: Well, what do you want me
    to do?
  You don't go arguing with a frenzied Bacchante—
  You'll make things worse. She might even beat you senseless,
  But humor her and all you'll get is a tap.

AMPHITRYON: What humor I have is bad after such a welcome
  To one just home.

SOSIA: It's a hornet's nest—

AMPHITRYON: Be quiet.
  I must ask you something, Alcmena.

ALCMENA: Whatever you choose.

AMPHITRYON: What's making you act this way? some foolishness?
    pride?   740

ALCMENA: How can my husband ask me such a thing?

AMPHITRYON: Because till today you've always rejoiced at my
      coming;
  You've given me the greeting that good wives give—
  But today I find you've dropped the custom entirely.

ALCMENA: Goodness, I certainly welcomed you yesterday—
  Ran to meet you, asked how you were, at once,
  Caught at your hand and gave you a wifely kiss—

SOSIA: You welcomed him yesterday?

ALCMENA: And you with him, Sosia.

SOSIA: I'm afraid it isn't a son she's going to give you,
If I'm any prophet.

AMPHITRYON: What, then?

SOSIA: Insanity.   750

ALCMENA: Certainly not, and I'm praying the child is a boy.
Amphitryon, do your duty and punish this wretch—
Give him the reward he should have for such prophecies.
Make him ache.

SOSIA: But aches are for pregnant ladies, madam—
Aches, and lots of apples, a barrel of apples,
To nibble on in case she's feeling seedy.

AMPHITRYON: You saw me here yesterday?

ALCMENA: Must I tell you ten
more times?

AMPHITRYON: In a dream?

ALCMENA: We were both awake.

AMPHITRYON: Oh Lord, this is
terrible!

SOSIA: What's the trouble?

AMPHITRYON: (To SOSIA) She's raving.

SOSIA: She's probably only bilious.
Nothing brings on delirium like black bile.   760

AMPHITRYON: Alcmena, tell me: what was the first symptom?

ALCMENA: Heavens above, I've never been healthier.

AMPHITRYON: But you saw me yesterday? We docked just last
    night;
  I ate at the harbor and spent the night on the ship.
  Not once have I set foot in this house since I left
  To lead my army against the Teleboans.

ALCMENA: Indeed! You had dinner here, and we went to bed.

AMPHITRYON: What's that?

ALCMENA: The truth.

AMPHITRYON: No—not about going to bed;
  The rest—I don't know.

ALCMENA: And at dawn you went back to the
  troops.

AMPHITRYON: Now wait—

SOSIA: It's all quite true, sir, except she was
  dreaming.   770
  But you should have offered some cakes or incense to Jove
  This morning, madam—he's in charge of marvels.

ALCMENA: (*To* SOSIA) The devil take you!

SOSIA: That wouldn't help you,
  madam.

ALCMENA: He goes on insulting me and no one stops him!

AMPHITRYON: (*To* SOSIA) Sosia, keep still.
  (*To* ALCMENA)
                            I left you at sunrise this
  morning?

ALCMENA: Who else could have told me how the battle had gone?

AMPHITRYON: You know?

ALCMENA: You told me yourself how you captured
    the city
And single-handedly killed King Pterelas.

AMPHITRYON: I told you?

ALCMENA: Yes, and Sosia was standing right here.

AMPHITRYON: Have you heard me say this?

SOSIA: Where would I have
    heard you?   780

AMPHITRYON: Ask her.

SOSIA: You never said it with me there.

ALCMENA: What slave contradicts his master?

AMPHITRYON: Sosia, look at me.

SOSIA: Yes, sir.

AMPHITRYON: Now tell me the whole truth, and don't hedge.
    Have you ever heard me say what she says I said?

SOSIA: If you ask that, sir, I think insanity's catching.
    I'm seeing her now for the first time, here with you.

AMPHITRYON: Well, madam, you hear him.

ALCMENA: Yes, I do, and he lies.

AMPHITRYON: You won't believe him? You won't believe your
    husband?   790

ALCMENA: I believe myself. I know that it happened so.

AMPHITRYON: You believe I came yesterday?

ALCMENA: You deny that
   you left
This morning?

AMPHITRYON: Of course I deny it. I've just come home.

ALCMENA: Deny this, then, if you can: that this very morning
  You left with me the golden bowl you said was their gift.

AMPHITRYON: By God, I neither said it nor left it. I'd meant,
   though,
To give it to you, and I will. But who told you of it?

ALCMENA: You told me—you even gave me the bowl yourself!

AMPHITRYON: Wait, wait, I beg you! Sosia, I cannot see
  How she knew I'd been given a golden bowl
  Unless you came back here and told her of it.   800

SOSIA: I give you my word I've only been here with you.

AMPHITRYON: What kind of creature—

SOSIA: Shall we look at the
  bowl, sir?

AMPHITRYON: Yes.

ALCMENA: (*Opens house door, calls inside*)
  Very well. Thessala, the bowl my husband brought me
  Yesterday—bring it out at once.

AMPHITRYON: Sosia, a word—
  It's going to be even harder to explain
  If she has the bowl.

SOSIA: But she hasn't.
  (*Picks up piece of luggage*)
                          It's in this chest,
  The one that you sealed.

AMPHITRYON: And the seal's unbroken?

SOSIA: (*Shows him*)   See, sir—

AMPHITRYON: It's just as I left it.

SOSIA: Master, I really think
  A doctor should be called.

AMPHITRYON: By Jove, you're right.   810
  If we can get rid of those evil spirits she's filled with—

(*The maid brings the bowl from inside, curtsies, and exits*)

ALCMENA: More proof, sir? Here is your bowl.

AMPHITRYON: (*Reaching for it*)   Let me see.

ALCMENA: Look
  at it.
  Those who deny their actions must be refuted.
  Is this the bowl you received?

AMPHITRYON: Great Jupiter, help me,
  What do I see? It's the same one. Sosia, I'm lost.

SOSIA: Well, either she's a greater magician than Circe
  Or your bowl is still in the box.

AMPHITRYON: Unseal it and see.

SOSIA: Open it? Why? It's all right; the seals are unbroken.
You beget an Amphitryon, I a Sosia.
The bowl begets a bowl. We're all being doubled. 820

AMPHITRYON: No, I've made my mind up. Open it.

SOSIA: Check the
seal, sir.
I don't want to be blamed later on.

AMPHITRYON: Just open the box
Before she drives the three of us mad with her talk.

ALCMENA: If you didn't give this to me, then who did?

AMPHITRYON: I shall find out.

SOSIA: (*Opening box*) Oh holy gods of Olympus!

AMPHITRYON: What now?

SOSIA: There's no bowl here at all.

AMPHITRYON: What's that?

SOSIA: It's true.

AMPHITRYON: I'll put you to torture unless it's there.

ALCMENA: Well, this one is here.

AMPHITRYON: Who gave it?

ALCMENA: The one who's
asking.

SOSIA: I see your trick, sir. You took another road   830
    Here from the ship, ahead of me, on the sly—
    Took the bowl out, gave it to her, and sealed the chest.

AMPHITRYON: My God, are you crazy now too, trying to help her?
    (*To* ALCMENA)
    It was yesterday that we came?

ALCMENA: And the moment you entered
    We greeted each other, and I gave you a kiss.

SOSIA: I don't like that beginning: a kiss.

AMPHITRYON: Go on.

ALCMENA: You bathed.

AMPHITRYON: And after I bathed?

ALCMENA: We dined.

SOSIA: Well,
    splendid!
    Cross-question her.

AMPHITRYON: (*To* SOSIA) Don't interrupt.
    (*To* ALCMENA)
                    Go on with your story.

ALCMENA: Dinner was served, and I took my place beside
    you.   840

AMPHITRYON: Beside me?

ALCMENA: Of course.

SOSIA: (*Aside*) I don't care much for that dinner.

AMPHITRYON: (*To* SOSIA) She's speaking; don't break in.
   (*To* ALCMENA)
                                                    And
      after you'd eaten?

ALCMENA: The table was cleared; you were sleepy; we went to
      bed.

AMPHITRYON: Where did you sleep?

ALCMENA: Why, with you, of course, in
      our room.

AMPHITRYON: My God!

SOSIA: What's wrong with you?

AMPHITRYON: I wish I
      were dead.

ALCMENA: Dear, what is it?

AMPHITRYON: Don't speak to me!

SOSIA: What's the matter?

AMPHITRYON: God
      help me,
   Someone's seduced her while I was away.

ALCMENA: My husband, how can you think such a horrible thing?

AMPHITRYON: (*Angrily*) Don't call me your husband. You lie;
      there's no truth in you.   850

SOSIA: Is he changed to a woman, that he isn't her husband?

ALCMENA: What have I done that you talk to me like this?

AMPHITRYON: You've told me yourself—and you ask me where
the harm is?

ALCMENA: But I am your wife; what harm if I stayed with you?

AMPHITRYON: You stayed with me? What absolute impudence!
If you have no shame of your own, then borrow some.

ALCMENA: My pride alone would keep me from what you charge;
Set all the snares that you care to—I won't be caught.

AMPHITRYON: By the immortal gods, do you know me, Sosia?

SOSIA: Sure.   860

AMPHITRYON: And didn't we eat at the port last night?

ALCMENA: I have witnesses to prove my story, too.

SOSIA: My guess is, there's another Amphitryon
Who's taking over the place when you're away
And doing your job at home while you're with the army.
It was a shock when I found I had a twin
But to find that you have a double—that's even worse.

AMPHITRYON: I think she must be under some wizard's spell—

ALCMENA: I swear to you by the realm of the king of gods
And by Juno, the mother goddess I reverence most: 870
No mortal man has ever touched my body
Except yourself.

AMPHITRYON: If that were only true!

ALCMENA: It is the truth, but what's the use? You won't believe it.

AMPHITRYON: Women swear rashly—

ALCMENA: If they are innocent
  They ought to be bold, to defend themselves with spirit.

AMPHITRYON: Bold!

ALCMENA: Innocence must be.

AMPHITRYON: Oh, your talk is chaste—

ALCMENA: (*With deep conviction*)
  There was a second dowry that I brought:
  Chastity, self-control, propriety,
  Love for my parents and our gods and you,
  And for you, all a wife's warmth and devotion.   880

SOSIA: You'd think, to hear her, she's the perfect helpmeet.

AMPHITRYON: (*Upset*) I'm so bewitched I don't know who I am—

SOSIA: Amphitryon, sir. Keep title to yourself;
  Too many people have been losing theirs
  Since we came back.

AMPHITRYON: We must investigate this matter, madam.

ALCMENA: With all my heart I hope you will.

AMPHITRYON: Tell me—
  What if I bring Naucrates from the ship,
  Your cousin and my shipmate; if he says
  Your story's false, what punishment for you?   890
  No reason why I should not end this marriage.

ALCMENA: No reason, if I've lied.

AMPHITRYON: So be it. Sosia.
  Send in the luggage. I'll bring Naucrates here.

(*He exits*)

SOSIA: (*To* ALCMENA) Now that we're here alone, speak freely,
    ma'am:
  Is there a twin of Sosia in the house?

ALCMENA: You're worthy of your master. Leave me!

SOSIA: Yes, ma'am.

(*He runs off into the house*)

ALCMENA: How could my husband come to such a state—
  Accusing me of wild, undreamed-of crimes?
  I pray my cousin may help us toward the truth.

(*She goes back into the house*)

ACT III

Scene 1

(*After a moment,* JUPITER *strides onstage*)

JUPITER: I am Amphitryon. I own a slave,   900
  Sosia, who sometimes turns to Mercury.
  As for my home, it's on the second floor,
  And now and then I change myself to Jove.
  Not in this neighborhood, however. Here
  You'd give your oath I am Amphitryon.
  (*To the audience*)
  Be honored now to recognize my godhead,
  So that the play won't seem to end half-finished.
  Besides, I have to rescue poor Alcmena

From all those charges that her husband makes;
What justice would there be for her to suffer   910
Grief from this little joke of my invention?
Now I'll take on her husband's guise again,
As I have done before, and leave them all
Most thoroughly confounded and confused.
Little by little, then, I'll clear things up,
See to it presently that she gives birth—
And easily—to the twins she's carrying,
One child her husband's and the other mine.
I've ordered Mercury to stay at hand
In case he's needed. Now I'll speak to her.   920

(*Enter* ALCMENA, *dressed for travel, followed by maids who carry luggage*)

ALCMENA: I will not stay in that house another hour,
Where my own husband calls me a disgrace,
Goes raving through the rooms, makes lies of truth,
Accuses me of things I've never done,
And thinks I'll take it all without protest.
Heaven help me, I will not! I won't endure
Such words, such wholly baseless accusations!
Either I leave this house and him, or he
Confesses that it's all some nightmare horror
And makes amends for all I've had to bear.   930

JUPITER: (*Aside*) It's I who'd better do as she demands
If ever I'm to have her love again.
Since what I've done offends Amphitryon
And since my love affair has made him suffer
Though he is guiltless, now I, guiltless too,
Must suffer when he upbraids my beloved.

ALCMENA: There he is, the man who calls me whore—
His wife!

JUPITER: My dear, I want to speak to you.
  Why do you turn away?

ALCMENA: I cannot help it
  Before an enemy.

JUPITER: You think me that?   940

ALCMENA: It's true, unless you judge this one more lie.

JUPITER: You're too quick-tempered.

(*He goes to embrace her*)

ALCMENA: Take your hands away!
  If you were sane at all, had any sense
  When you believe and call your wife untrue—
  Call her that to her face—that's the last word
  You'd say to her, unless you are a fool.

JUPITER: My words don't make it true, or prove I think it.
  Now I've come back to clear myself with you:
  I've never been more unhappy than I was
  At the report that you were angry with me.   950
  Why did I do it, you ask? I can explain.
  I never thought you anything but chaste—
  This was a test, to see how you would take it,
  What your reactions would be. Really, darling,
  Everything I said was just a joke,
  A bit of fun. Ask Sosia if it wasn't.

ALCMENA: Why don't you bring Naucrates as your witness
  To prove that you had not been here before?
  You went to get him.

JUPITER: What was said in jest
  Shouldn't be taken seriously, my dear.   960

ALCMENA: A jest that's left a scar upon my heart.

JUPITER: I beg, Alcmena, by this hand I hold—
Grant me forgiveness, let your anger pass.

ALCMENA: Surely my life disproves your allegations;
Now, since my heart knows its own innocence.
I shall not stay to be insulted further.
(*She begins to go*)
Farewell. Keep your possessions, give me mine.
Send my slaves after me.

JUPITER: You're mad—

ALCMENA: If not,
If you refuse, honor alone will guard me.

JUPITER: Wait. I will swear, in any terms you choose,   970
That I believe my wife is wholly chaste.
If this is less than truth, I call on Jove
To curse Amphitryon now and forever.

ALCMENA: No, no—pray for his blessing!

JUPITER: That I'm sure of;
I swore the oath to counter your accusations.
No longer angry, love?

ALCMENA: No.

JUPITER: Ah, that's splendid!
This kind of thing is always happening:
Men have their joys, and after these their sorrows;
Now they are quarreling, now they're reconciled.
But if a quarrel like ours comes up between them,   980
Once they've made up their differences, they feel
Much fonder of each other than before.

ALCMENA: You know you ought never to have said such things,
   But now you've explained them away, I must forgive you.

JUPITER: Then have the utensils ready for sacrifice
   So that I may honor those gods who granted the prayers
   I prayed for a safe return from the battlefield.

ALCMENA: I'll see that it's done at once.

JUPITER: (*To maids*)   Call Sosia out.
   I must tell him to go to the shore and summon Blepharo,
   The captain of my ship, to join us all at dinner.   990
   (*Aside*)
   Not only he'll be unfed but he'll look absurd
   As soon as I've thrown Amphitryon out of the house.

ALCMENA: I wonder what he's murmuring to himself—
   Oh, the door is opening. Here comes Sosia now.

(*Enter the real* SOSIA)

SOSIA: I'm here, sir; whatever you want, say the word and I'll
   do it.

JUPITER: You're the man I want to see.

SOSIA: Are things patched up, sir?
   I must say, to find you calm is a great relief—
   I think on the whole a slave should stick to this rule:
   Be as like your master as possible. If he looks sad,
   Pull a long face; if he's cheerful, be cheerful too.   1000
   But tell me sir—is everything right between you?

JUPITER: I don't care for your humor; you knew it was all a joke.

SOSIA: A joke, sir? I never suspected it wasn't real—

JUPITER: I've explained and she understands.

SOSIA: I'm glad of that, sir.

JUPITER: I must go to offer my thanks to the gods.

SOSIA: Of course, sir.

JUPITER: And you must run down to the port, as I said before,
    And invite Blepharo to lunch, when the rites are done.

SOSIA: I'll be back before you think I've got there.

JUPITER: Hurry!

ALCMENA: Do you need me now, or shall I go in to make ready?

JUPITER: Go see to everything, to the last detail.   1010

ALCMENA: Come in when you wish; I'll see there's no cause for
    delay.

JUPITER: You speak, my dear, like yourself, the best of wives.
    (*Alone*)
    It's working. They both believe
    I'm Amphitryon, and they're wrong.
    Sosia's double, come down—
    Or hear me, wherever you are:
    Keep Amphitryon out of this house
    By any pretext you choose,
    For Jove wants a little time more
    To spend with his borrowed wife.   1020
    Do exactly as I say—
    While I offer thanks to myself.

(*He exits.* MERCURY *dashes onstage, parodying the comic "running
slave."*)

MERCURY: Come on now, clear the streets! No loitering there!
    You'll ask for trouble if you block my path.
    (Can't a god threaten people when they crowd him?
    The meanest slave can do it on the stage
    Announcing the ship is safe or the villain approaches.)
    Obedient to Jove, I am here at his bidding:
    More reason, then, that men should make way for me.
    My father calls, and I obey him, always—   1030
    I'm a good son to him, as a son should be:
    Help in his love affairs, warn, stand by, rejoice.
    Jupiter's pleasure is what pleases me.
    In love he's wise to follow his inclination,
    As men should do—well, within certain limits.
    Now he wants Amphitryon fooled. I promise you
    Fooled he shall be, while you, the audience, watch.
    I'll put a wreath on my head and pretend I'm drunk
    And climb out on that roof; from there it's easy
    To drive him off; he'll be both soaked and sober yet high
        and dry.   1040
    Sosia, his slave, will get the punishment—
    Amphitryon will think he's done what I'll do.
    What's it to me? I must follow my father's will.
    But here's Amphitryon now. O what a fool
    I'll make of him! Watch now; don't miss a trick.
    I'll go inside the house, pretend I'm drunk,
    Climb on the roof, and make him stay outside.

(*He exits. Enter* AMPHITRYON.)

AMPHITRYON: I couldn't find Naucrates on the ship
    Or at his home; nobody knew where he'd gone.
    I've tramped through every street, gymnasium, store,   1050
    Perfume shop, market, school—even the forum;
    Gone to the doctor's, the barber's, all the shrines.
    The man has vanished, and I'm worn out searching.
    Now I'll go home and ask my wife about this—
    Find out from her for what man she's betrayed me.
    I'll kill myself unless I learn it soon . . .

(*Tries to open his front door*)
What? They have locked me out? Well done, well done!
That fits in very well with all the rest.
I'll knock then. Open up, someone! Let me in!

(MERCURY *as* SOSIA *appears on the roof*)

MERCURY: Who's there?

AMPHITRYON: I am.

MERCURY: I am?

AMPHITRYON: *Yes!*

MERCURY: Jupiter   1060
And all the gods will get you, breaking doors—

AMPHITRYON: What do you mean?

MERCURY: I mean you're out of luck.

AMPHITRYON: Sosia!

MERCURY: That's me; do you think that I've forgotten?
What do you want?

AMPHITRYON: You wretch, you ask me that?

MERCURY: You're right, I ask. Ripping doors off their hinges—
Stupid, do you think we get our hardware free?
Who are you? What do you want? Stop staring, fool!

AMPHITRYON: You ask my name, you wearer-out of whips?
By God, I'll warm you with a scourge today.

MERCURY: You must have been a spendthrift in your youth.   1070

AMPHITRYON: How, pray?

MERCURY: The way you beg for trouble now.

AMPHITRYON: I'll make you eat those words, you slave-from-birth!

MERCURY: I make you an offering now.

AMPHITRYON: Of what?

MERCURY: Disaster.*   1074

AMPHITRYON: I'll have you beaten, good-for-nothing—tortured—

MERCURY: My master—that's Amphitryon—is busy . . .
      But still you have a chance to get away . . .
      I ought to break an ash-pot on your head . . .
      Would you like a pail of water poured upon you? . . .
      (MERCURY empties a bucket on AMPHITRYON)
      Bewitched! Too bad for you; go find a doctor . . .

ALCMENA: Why, you denied it, claimed it was a joke . . .
      For heaven's sake, get treatment right away . . .
      No doubt of it, you're either hexed or mad . . .
      If all that's happened isn't as I say,
      You have the right to claim that I betrayed you . . .

AMPHITRYON: Whose? When I'm gone she's free to take a
      lover! . . .
      What did you threaten if I broke the door? . . .
      Then you'll dig more than sixty ditches daily . . .
      Don't ask my pity for that rascal . . .

---

*Disaster: Here there is a gap of 272 lines in the manuscript. The few remaining fragments can be arranged to indicate the following sequence of events. "After the scene with Mercury, Alcmena expostulates with Amphitryon; Blepharo is brought in, but cannot decide which is the real Amphitryon" (Sedgwick, Plautus' Amphitruo [Manchester: Manchester University Press, 1960], 126).

BLEPHARO: Quiet!

JUPITER: I've got him, caught in the act and by the neck . . .

AMPHITRYON: No, Thebans, I've caught him, the Prince of Lust
   Who in my own home has seduced my wife . . .
   Aren't you ashamed, you villain, to be seen? . . .
   . . . in secret . . .
          You cannot tell which Amphitryon is which.

Scene 2

(BLEPHARO *the shipmate is on stage, already embroiled in the confusion*)

BLEPHARO: I've things to do. Divide the wife between you;   1075
   (*Aside*)
   I never saw such goings-on before!

AMPHITRYON: Blepharo, stay! I need you! Help me out!

BLEPHARO: I can't help when I don't know which one I'm
   helping.

JUPITER: (*Aside*) Alcmena's ready to give birth; I'll go to her.

AMPHITRYON: (*Despairing*) What shall I do, now everyone has
   left me?   1080
   Whoever he is, that mocker shan't go free.
   I'm off to the king; I'll tell him the whole story.
   I swear I'll catch that Thessalonian wizard
   Who's turned my household into an asylum,
   But where's he gone? Inside, to find Alcmena?
   I'm the unhappiest man in Thebes, and helpless,
   Humbugged at will, the whole town's favorite dupe.
   I'll break in, I'm determined, and anyone

I meet, maidservant, slave, my wife, her lover,
My father, or my grandfather—I'll murder,   1090
And neither Jupiter nor any god will stop me
From doing what I've set myself to do.

(*Just as he turns to enter the house, thunder roars and he faints on
the spot. From out of the house rushes* BROMIA, *the maid, in a panic.*)

BROMIA: No hope of getting out of this alive.
    Whatever confidence I had is lost!
    Everything—sea, land, sky—has its mind made up
    To kill me, crush me. Oh tell me what to do!
    Such things are happening in that house! Poor me!
    I'm fainting; give me water! Oh, I'm gone—
    My head is splitting, I can't hear or see.
    You won't find anyone worse off anywhere.   1100
    And my poor mistress! As her time comes near,
    She calls on all the gods to help her through—
    And then what happens? rumbles, crashes, bangs—
    And then, right in the room, a clap of thunder.
    We all fell where we stood, and a great voice cried:
        "Alcmena, help is near;
        Let trust dispel your fright.
        The dweller in the sky
        Comes down to bless your house.
        Let those who fell before me   1110
        Rise up now, unafraid."
    I did, and the room was so bright I thought it was burning.
    Just then Alcmena called me; I was still shaken,
    But afraid of her too, so I ran to see what was wanted,
    And found her with newborn twins—in the excitement
    No one had come to her while she was giving birth.
    (*Notices the stricken* AMPHITRYON)
    Oh! Who's this old man lying in front of our door?
    Has he been struck by lightning? I do believe it—
    He looks as though he were dead and buried already.
    I'll go look. Oh God, it's my master Amphitryon!   1120
    Master!

AMPHITRYON: (*Coming to*)
>Help!

BROMIA: Get up.

AMPHITRYON: I'm dead.

BROMIA: Take my hand.

AMPHITRYON: Who are you?

BROMIA: Bromia, your maid, sir.

AMPHITRYON: Jove's blast—I'm still terrified:
>It's as though I'd come back from the dead. But why did you
>>come out?

BROMIA: The same thing that struck you, sir, struck us all
>Inside the house. O sir, the things I've seen
>I don't know when I'll get my wits again.

AMPHITRYON: I *am* Amphitryon? You're sure of that?

BROMIA: Of course, sir.

AMPHITRYON: Look more closely.

BROMIA: Yes, you're he.

AMPHITRYON: (*Aside*) Well, not quite all the household is
>insane.   1130

BROMIA: Nobody is, sir.

AMPHITRYON: My wife will drive me mad
>Acting so strangely—

BROMIA: Sir, don't talk like that.
I'll make you see how virtuous she is;
If you need proof, I've got it for you, sir;
First off, she's had the baby, and it's twins.

AMPHITRYON: Twins?

BROMIA: Twins.

AMPHITRYON: The gods are with me.

BROMIA: Wait. There's
    more
To prove that all the gods protect this house—

AMPHITRYON: Tell me.

BROMIA: Well, as her time came closer, sir,
    And the pains began, she called upon the gods
    For help, as women do, her head well veiled,   1140
    Her hands washed. And before she'd said the prayer
    There was an awful crash and a strange light,
    So that the whole house shone as though it were gold.

AMPHITRYON: Oh stop your foolishness; come to the point!

BROMIA: Well, in the midst of all this no one heard
    Your wife cry out or groan or call for help—
    Those twins were born that easily.

AMPHITRYON: Thank God
    For that, no matter how she's acted.

BROMIA: Listen,
    There's more, sir. Then she ordered us to bathe them,
    But the one I held—he was so big and strong, sir,   1150
    We couldn't wrap him in the swaddling clothes.

AMPHITRYON: I almost can't believe it. If it's true,
  It was the divine assistance that she had.

BROMIA: There's still more, sir. When he was in his cradle,
  Two great snakes slipped out of the atrium fountain,
  Slid over the floor and lifted up their heads—

AMPHITRYON: Good Lord!

BROMIA: Don't worry, sir. They glared around
      at us,
  Then made like lightning for the babies' cradle.
  I backed away and pulled the cradle with me,
  Frightened to death. The snakes came hissing after—   1160
  But I swear, sir, the minute that child sees them
  He jumps out of the cradle, rushes toward them,
  And grabs their necks before I've got my breath.

AMPHITRYON: Marvelous! wonderful!—but it's frightening, too;
  The more I think of it the more I'm chilled.
  What next?

BROMIA: Why, sir, he chokes them both to death,
  And while he's choking them, he calls your wife—

AMPHITRYON: Who does?

BROMIA: Jove, sir, the ruler of us all.
  He says that secretly he's shared her bed,
  And that this is his son who's killed the serpents—

AMPHITRYON: So
      help me,   1170
  I'm honored to have shared my goods with a god.
  Quick, in with you! Make ready for an offering
  To Jupiter, a reconciliation—
  I'll call in the interpreter Tiresias,
  And, when I've told him all, ask what to do.

(*A sudden thunderclap*)
Thunder again? Gods, keep me safe, I pray!

Scene 3

JUPITER: (*Appearing on the roof*)
    Amphitryon, have no fear; I bring you aid—
    All will be well. Dismiss the soothsayers;
    I shall describe your future and your past
    Better than any seer, for I am Jove.   1180
    It was I, Jove, who lay with Alcmena,
    It was on her that I begot a son
    Though when you left she was with child by you.
    These two, my own and yours, she bore together,
    And mine will bring your house undying fame.
    Live as you used to live with Alcmena,
    In love and mutual trust. She did no wrong—
    It was my strength. Now I return to heaven.

AMPHITRYON: It shall be done, I give my word—give yours,
    I pray. Now I'll send old Tiresias packing,   1190
    And go inside to my Alcmena . . .
    (*To the audience*)
    And now for Jupiter's sake, applaud!

THE
BRAGGART SOLDIER

(MILES GLORIOSUS)

Translated by Erich Segal

INTRODUCTION

The Braggart Soldier does not begin with a prologue. It opens instead with one of the touchstones of comic literature: the hero discussing himself (who else?) with a hired admirer. This is a classic confrontation between *alazon* and *eiron*, the quintessential comic opposites originally described by Aristotle in the *Nicomachean Ethics*.[1] The *alazon* is the overstater, the bluffer, the great balloon of hot air. *Alazoneia*, braggadocio, has been aptly described as the comic counterpart of *hubris*, tragic pride. In contrast, the *eiron* is, as the word suggests, the *ironic* man, the understater, the needle of "I know nothing" that pricks the balloon of the *alazon's* "I know everything."[2] In all of ancient literature, the greatest *eiron* is Plato's Socrates; the greatest *alazon* is Plautus's Pyrgopolynices.

In a scene of but seventy-nine lines, the Braggart Soldier's outrageous character is exposed to an audience who will wait anxiously through more than half the play until he reappears. Pyrgopolynices ("terrific tower taker")[3] boasts of such mammoth exploits as having crushed (exactly) seven thousand men in a single day (l. 45), and of punching an elephant to smithereens—a behemoth exploit (l. 28). He is vain about his attractiveness to women. When his slave suggests that one of his female admirers may be compared in beauty to himself, the soldier can only remark, "Oh, how gor-

---

[1]Aristotle, *Nicomachean Ethics* 4.7.

[2]In discussing this comic process, we are reminded of Shaw's *Man and Superman*, where Ann punctures the pomposity of Jack Tanner, who, at one point (described by Shaw in a stage direction) "collapses like a pricked balloon."

[3]There may be a pun on the soldier's (Greek) name in l. 1055: "noble king-killer, *sacker of cities.*" As for his boast of killing exactly seven thousand of the foe in a single fray, he is outdone by another of Plautus's boastful warriors, who (in the *Poenulus*, ll. 470ff.) claims to have done away with sixty thousand "flying men" (*homines volatici*). He must have had an especially good day.

geous" (l. 968).[4] He is also a bit of a parvenu, anxious to drop names
of such friends as King Seleucus (cf. ll. 75, 77, 948–51). In his own
way, Pyrgopolynices is the ancestor of Molière's Monsieur Jourdain.

As the soldier struts off to the forum, the tricky slave Palaestrio
enters to deliver a long and complicated expository prologue. A fine
trick of Plautus it was to give the audience five minutes of funny
dialogue before inflicting on them the convolutions of plot. Not that
Plautus originated the delayed prologue (although he uses it again in
his *Cistellaria*); the technique was also practiced by Menander.[5]
Palaestrio has lots of complicated story to convey. In "good old Athens," the Braggart Soldier kidnapped his master's girlfriend.[6] Loyal
slave that he was, Palaestrio set out in pursuit, only to be kidnapped
by pirates and given as a gift to none other than the Braggart himself,
who had by this time rented a mansion in Ephesus, to set up
hausfrau-keeping with the kidnapped girl. By chance, the soldier's
mansion is right next door to that of an old family friend of Palaestrio's Athenian master. Clearly, the long arm of Fate has a board-
inghouse reach. Greek New Comedy dealt constantly with the
chance workings of Chance. In this prologue, Plautus mocks the
convention.[7]

The *Braggart* is an early play, and Palaestrio is the prototype for
such tricky Plautine servants as Pseudolus and Tranio (in the
Mostellaria). In the prologue he outlines but one of two "mighty
machinations" he will set working. This "architect"[8] has cut a passage
in the common wall between the two houses, and thus Pleusicles,
his Athenian master (newly arrived in Ephesus), can meet in secret
with his beloved—kidnapped—sweetheart. This particular hole-in-
the-wall is much more satisfying than the one that accommodated

----

[4]This splendid egotism is caught by Stephen Sondheim in one of his lyrics to *A Funny
Thing Happened on the Way to the Forum*, when he has a character named Miles Gloriosus
sing, "I am my Ideal."

[5]For example, in *The Shearing of Glycera*.

[6]"Girlfriend" is both anachronistic and inaccurate. "Mistress" is rather Victorian and
does not suit a lovely young thing like Philocomasium. But *she is not your sister either*. Since
she can be "owned," she is clearly some sort of slave. She is not a pay-as-you-go courtesan like
Acroteleutium. We have problems of vocabulary here, not of sociology. I trust the reader will
make the necessary adjustments of sensibility.

[7]The prologue to the Menander comedy mentioned in n. 5 constantly repeats, "It just
happened by chance that . . ."

[8]Cf. ll. 901, 902, 915ff., 1139.

Pyramus and Thisbe. As her name suggests, the young girl—
Philocomasium, "lover of revelry"—is the pleasure principle per-
sonified. She and Pleusicles are constantly hugging and embracing.
In fact, their tireless urge to neck almost undoes them in the finale.

When one of the soldier's slaves happens to spy the young
lovers, Palaestrio must convince this thick-witted bondsman that he
did not see Philocomasium, but her sister, who just happened to
arrive in Ephesus the night before. To substantiate this claim, Palaestrio trains the girl to impersonate her own twin sister; by dashing
through the hole-in-the-wall, she can appear from either doorway.
The twin joke proved successful for Plautus; he presents it again in
the *Menaechmi*, where two brothers unwittingly play one (here one
girl plays two), and in the *Amphitryon*, where Mercury becomes the
slave Sosia's twin and "steals" his identity.

All this masquerading scares off the silly slave who had spied
on the lovers, but does nothing toward getting Philocomasium away
from the soldier. And so Palaestrio needs a second machination.[9]
With the help of the old man next door, a zany codger who goes
to absurd lengths to prove that he thinks young,[10] he dresses up
a courtesan to pretend she is the old man's wife, desperately in
love with the soldier and willing to go to any length—and expense—
to get his amatory attentions. Pyrgopolynices will then hurriedly get
rid of his present mistress and devote himself to a more profitable
amour. The clever slave's scheme has a second purpose as well: to
deflate the soldier's gargantuan ego and show the "hero" to be a
groveling coward when confronted with the penalty for adultery—
castration.

Palaestrio knows his military master. And so he brilliantly
couches his proposition in terms that appeal to the soldier's greatest
source of pride: not his valor, not even his beauty, but his wealth (cf.
ll. 1063ff.). The slave feeds the soldier with ambiguous promises of
"profit" from this new affair, which he describes as "condicio nova et

---

[9]Much scholarly ink has flowed over the fact that Plautus has combined two plots in this
play, perhaps derived from two different Greek originals. This process is known as *contam-
inatio*, a term that has a pejorative connotation. See, for example, the prologues of Terence,
for very defensive defenses against this charge. If combining two unrelated plots from different sources be an artistic shortcoming, however, all of Elizabethan drama is in terrible
jeopardy.

[10]Cf. ll. 627ff.

luculenta" (l. 952), a phrase that could be understood either as a new love or business affair. He further stokes the fire of the soldier's *alazoneia* by presenting him with a ring that he calls the "first deposit on a love account" (l. 957). Moreover, Pyrgopolynices is later offered payment for his sexual services (ll. 1059–62). But ironically *he* pays a great deal. He ends up giving away not only his present mistress, but "all the gold and all the jewels and all the things you dressed her up with" (l. 981).

On every field of battle, the clever slave emerges victorious over the allegedly undefeated and unbeatable warrior. The farewell scene, in which the girl, her many trunks of baggage, and Palaestrio himself are all about to be given away by the soldier, is truly a masterpiece of irony. And there are some very interesting similarities between this ironic leavetaking and the finale of Euripides' *Helen*.[11] This may not prove any direct Euripidean influence, for Plautus himself has a predilection for trickery-by-masquerade. There are, in fact, three masquerades in *The Braggart Soldier*: Philocomasium as her own twin sister; the courtesan as the amorous wife; and Pleusicles, the young lover, as a ship's captain. Needless to mention, Palaestrio wrote all three scripts.

The *miles gloriosus* is by no means a Plautine invention, although the boastful officer is one of the Roman comedian's favorite characters, and appears in a half-dozen of his extant plays. Certainly General Lamachos in Aristophanes' *Acharnians* is a blustering military man of much the same ilk. But the type must have had a very special appeal for the Roman audience, almost all of whom were themselves soldiers.[12] And Plautus has added certain Roman innuendoes: private jokes for general laughter.

The Braggart Soldier has a long heritage on the comic stage. Even Terence's Thraso—in *The Eunuch*, his most successful play— owes quite a debt to Plautus. We see the same characterization in the

[11]In Euripides' play, Helen is departing from Egypt in the company of Menelaus, who is disguised as a sailor, as is young Pleusicles here. The Euripidean protagonists have bamboozled King Theoclymenos into giving them not only permission to leave the shore, but rich gifts as well. There are even striking similarities in the dialogue. Compare, for example, *Helen*, ll. 1419–20, with *Braggart*, ll. 1321–25.

[12]In describing the Roman character, the historian Polybius (6.37) observes that they considered boasting of military valor—even if true—to be bad form, a bad show, as it were. This may explain why they considered Plautus's comedy such a good show.

various captains of the *commedia dell'arte*, in Corneille's *L'Illusion Comique*, in *Ralph Roister Doister*, in Captain Bobadil of Ben Jonson's *Everyman in His Humor*, and, of course, in Falstaff, who is the greatest *alazon* of all time and also bids fair to be the best *eiron* as well![13] If nothing else, the Braggart Soldier has commanded a legion of imitators.

Erich Segal

[13]Cf. Falstaff's famous (and true) self-characterization: "I am not only witty in myself, but the cause that wit is in other men" (*Henry IV, Part II*, I, ii, 10).

THE BRAGGART SOLDIER

CHARACTERS

PYRGOPOLYNICES, a soldier
ARTOTROGUS, his parasite
PALAESTRIO, slave to the soldier (formerly to Pleusicles)
PERIPLECTOMENUS, an old man of Ephesus
SCELEDRUS, slave to the soldier
PLEUSICLES, a young man from Athens
LURCIO, slave to the soldier
PHILOCOMASIUM, a girl abducted by the soldier
ACROTELEUTIUM, a courtesan
MILPHIDIPPA, her maid
A SLAVE BOY
CARIO, Periplectomenus's cook

SCENE: *The entire action takes place on a street in Ephesus, before the adjoining houses of* PYRGOPOLYNICES *and* PERIPLECTOMENUS.

(*Enter* PYRGOPOLYNICES, *followed by his parasite* ARTOTROGUS *and several minions who carry his monstrous shield*)

PYRGOPOLYNICES:
(*Posing pompously, declaiming in heroic fashion*)
Look lively—shine a shimmer on that shield of mine
Surpassing sunbeams—where there are no clouds, of course.
Thus, when it's needed, with the battle joined, its gleam
Shall strike opposing eyeballs in the bloodshed—bloodshot!
Ah me, I must give comfort to this blade of mine

73

Lest he lament and yield himself to dark despair.
Too long ere now has he been sick of his vacation.
Poor lad! He's dying to make mincemeat of the foe.
(*Dropping the bombastic tone*)
Say, where the devil is Artotrogus?

ARTOTROGUS: He's here—
By Destiny's dashing, dauntless, debonair darling,   10
A man so warlike, Mars himself would hardly dare
To claim his powers were the equal of your own.

PYRGOPOLYNICES: (*Preening*) Tell me—who was that chap I saved
     at Field-of-Roaches,
Where the chief of staff was Crash-Bang-Razzle-Dazzle,
Son of Boom-Boom-Smash, you know, Neptune's nephew?

ARTOTROGUS: Ah yes, the man with golden armor, I recall.
You puffed away his legions with a single breath
Like wind blows autumn leaves or straw from thatch-roofed
     huts.

PYRGOPOLYNICES: A snap—a nothing, really.

ARTOTROGUS: Nothing, indeed—
     that is,
Compared to other feats I could recount—
(*Aside*)
                                   as false as this.   20
(*To the audience, as he hides behind the soldier's shield*)
If any of you knows a man more full of bull
Or empty boastings, you can have me—free of tax.
But I'll say this: I'm crazy for his olive salad!

PYRGOPOLYNICES: Hey, where are you?

ARTOTROGUS: (*Popping up*)   Here! And then that
     elephant in India—
The way your fist just broke his arm to smithereens.

PYRGOPOLYNICES: What's that—his *arm*?

ARTOTROGUS: I mean his leg, of
   course.

PYRGOPOLYNICES: I gave him just an easy jab.

ARTOTROGUS: A jab, of course!
   If you had really tried, you would have smashed his arm
   Right through his elephantine skin and guts and bone!

PYRGOPOLYNICES: No more of this.

ARTOTROGUS: Of course. Why bother to
      narrate   30
   Your many daring deeds to me—who knows them all.
   (*Aside, to the audience*)
   It's only for my stomach that I stomach him.
   While ears are suffering, at least my teeth are suppering.
   And so I yes and yes again to all his lies.

PYRGOPOLYNICES: What was I saying?

ARTOTROGUS: Oh, I know precisely what.
   It's done, by Hercules.

PYRGOPOLYNICES: What's done?

ARTOTROGUS: Well, something is.

PYRGOPOLYNICES: Have you—

ARTOTROGUS: Your tablets? Yes, of course, a
      stylus too.

PYRGOPOLYNICES: How expertly you suit your mind to know my
   own.

ARTOTROGUS: I ought to know your habits well-rehearsedly
And see to it I sniff your wishes in advance.   40

PYRGOPOLYNICES: How good's your memory?

ARTOTROGUS: It's perfect, sir. In
  Cilicia,
A hundred fifty. In Saudi I-robya, hundreds more.
Add thirty Sardians, those Macedonians, and there's
The total men you've slaughtered in a single day.

PYRGOPOLYNICES: "The total men," your final sum is—

ARTOTROGUS: Seven
  thousand.

PYRGOPOLYNICES: I believe you're right. You're good at your
  accounts.

ARTOTROGUS: I didn't even write it down; it's all by heart.

PYRGOPOLYNICES: My God, you've got a memory!

ARTOTROGUS: Food feeds it.

PYRGOPOLYNICES: Well, if you keep behaving as you have, you'll
  eat
Eternally. I'll always have a place for you at dinner.   50

ARTOTROGUS: (*Inspired by this*)
And then in Cappadocia, you would have slain
Five hundred with one blow—except your blade was dull.

PYRGOPOLYNICES: Just shabby little soldiers, so I let them live.

ARTOTROGUS: Why bother to repeat what every mortal knows—
    There's no one more invincible in all the earth
    In duties or in beauties than—Pyrgopolynices!
    Why, all the women love you—who can blame them, either—
    Since you're so . . . so attractive? Why, just yesterday
    Some women grabbed me by the tunic—

PYRGOPOLYNICES: Yes, what said they?

ARTOTROGUS: They badgered me with asking—"Isn't that
    Achilles?"   60
    "No," said I, "it's just his brother." "Ah," said one.
    "That's why he looks so beautiful and so genteel!
    Just look at him—that handsome head of hair he has!
    Oh, blessed are the women that can sleep with him!"

PYRGOPOLYNICES: They really said all that?

ARTOTROGUS: And then they
    begged me
    To parade you by today so they could see you.

PYRGOPOLYNICES: How wretched to be such a handsome
    man.

ARTOTROGUS: How true.
    They are a bother, screeching and beseeching me
    For just one little look at you. And sending for me!
    That's why I can't give all my time to serving you.   70

(*Suddenly, duty calls*)

PYRGOPOLYNICES: Now is the hour. Fall in! On to the forum
    To seek the mercenaries I conscripted yesterday.
    I must distribute salaries to all enlisted.
    King Seleucus has urgently appealed to me
    To gather fighting men for him and sign them up.
    Today shall be devoted to the king's demands.

ARTOTROGUS: Then off we go!

PYRGOPOLYNICES: Faithful fellows—follow!

(PYRGOPOLYNICES *leads his minions off. Enter* PALAESTRIO.)

PALAESTRIO: (*To the audience*) Now, folks, if you'll be kind
    enough to hear me out,
  Then I'll be kind and tell you what our play's about.
  Whoever doesn't want to listen, let him beat it   80
  And give a seat to one of those in back who need it.
    I'll tell you why we've gathered in this festive spot,
  What comedy we will enact, its name and plot.
  This play is called the *Alazon* in Greek,
  A name translated "braggart" in the tongue we speak.
  This town is Ephesus; that soldier is my master
  Who's just gone to the forum. What a shameless, crass
    bombaster!
  He's so full of crap and lechery, no lies are vaster.
  He brags that all the women seek him out en masse.
  The truth is, everywhere he goes they think he's just an ass. 90
  The local wenches claim they've tired out their lips,
  But not from kissing him—from making nasty quips.
    Not very long have I been slaving as his slave.
  I want you all to know how I became his knave,
  And whom I slaved for prior to this slavish lot.
  So listen very closely, folks, here comes the plot!
    My master back in Athens was a fine young man.
  In good old Athens, he was crazy for a courtesan.
  She loved him too. Yes, that's the kind of love that's best.
  Then he was sent to Naupactus—a governmental quest   100
  Of great importance. While my master served the state,
  The soldier came to Athens—by some trick of Fate.
  He made advances to my master's little friend.
  He played up to her mother and began to send
  Cosmetics, costly catered cookery, and wine—
  The soldier and the bawd were getting on just fine.
  Right when the soldier saw his chance for something shady

He bamboozled the old bawd—the mother of the lady
(That's the girl my master loved). He took her daughter
In secret on a ship, and made for open water.   110
To Ephesus—against her will—is where he brought her.
    Now when *I* learn he's kidnapped Master's concubine,
As fast as possible, I get a ship of mine.
I head for Naupactus to tell him of the fact,
But just when we get out to sea we are attacked—
And pirates take the ship. Fate's will is done,
And I was finished, though I scarcely had begun.
    The pirate made the soldier here a gift of me
And when the soldier took me home—what do I see?
The girl from Athens—my old master's concubine—   120
Who, when she saw me, winked and gave a sign
Not to address her. Later, when the coast was clear,
She wept and told me how unhappy she was here.
She longed to flee to Athens—in a phrase:
She loved my master from the good old days
And hated no one as she did this military guy.
On learning of the woman's inner feelings, I
Compose a letter, sign and seal it secretly
And get a merchant to deliver it for me
To my old master—he who still adored   130
This girl here. And my note to come was not ignored!
He came! He's staying with a neighbor right next door—
A wonderful old man his family knew before,
Who's been a blessing to my amorous young man,
Promoting our affair in every way he can.
    Now here within I've started mighty machinations
To make it easy for the lovers' . . . visitations.
The soldier gave the girl a bedroom of her own.
No one but she can enter it, it's hers alone.
So in this bedroom I have tunneled through the wall.   140
Right to the other house in secret she can crawl.
Our neighbor knows of this—in fact, he planned it all!
    So good for nothing is this fellow slave of mine—
The one the soldier picked to guard the concubine—
That with our artful artifice and wily ways

We'll coat this fellow's eyeballs with so thick a glaze,
We'll make him sure he doesn't see what's really there!
Don't *you* be fooled: one girl today will play a *pair*.
And so the girl that comes from either house will share
A single face, the same one claiming to be twins.   150
We'll fool that guard of hers until his head just spins!
But wait—I hear the creaking of our neighbor's door.
Here comes that nice old fellow I described before.

(Old PERIPLECTOMENUS *comes out of his house, still shouting back
angrily at the slaves within*)

PERIPLECTOMENUS: After this, by Hercules, if you don't beat the
     daylights out of
Anyone who's on our roof, I'll make your raw sides into
     rawhides!
(*In exasperation, to the audience*)
Now my neighbors see the show of all that happens in my
     house—
Looking right down through my skylight!
(*Back to his slaves*)
                                        Listen, I command
     you all:
Anyone you see on our roof, coming from the soldier's house—
That's excepting for Palaestrio—throw 'em down into the street!
Should they claim to be pursuing monkeys, pigeons, or the
     like,   160
You'll be finished if you don't just pound and pummel 'em to
     pulp!
Make it so they won't be able to infringe upon our gambling
     laws.
See to it they won't have even bones enough for rolling dice!

PALAESTRIO: Someone from our house has done a naughty thing,
     from what I hear—
The old man's commanded that my fellow slaves be beaten up.
Well, he said except for me—who gives a hoot about the rest?
I'll go see him.

(PALAESTRIO *steps into view*)

PERIPLECTOMENUS: Isn't this Palaestrio now coming toward me?

PALAESTRIO: How are you, Periplectomenus?

PERIPLECTOMENUS: There aren't many
    men I'd
Rather meet right now than you, Palaestrio.

PALAESTRIO: What's going on?   170
    Why are you in such an uproar with our household?

PERIPLECTOMENUS: We're all
    through!

PALAESTRIO: What's the matter?

PERIPLECTOMENUS: It's discovered!

PALAESTRIO: What's discovered?

PERIPLECTOMENUS: On
    my roof—
Someone from your household has been spying on us, through
    the skylight,
Where he saw Philocomasium in my house, with my guest—
Kissing.

PALAESTRIO: Who saw this?

PERIPLECTOMENUS: A fellow slave of yours.

PALAESTRIO: But which,
    I wonder.

PERIPLECTOMENUS: I don't know, the fellow got away too
     fast.

PALAESTRIO: Oh, I suspect—that
   I'm a dead man.

PERIPLECTOMENUS: As he fled, I cried, "Why are you on my roof?"
   He replied, still on the run, "I had to chase our little monkey."

PALAESTRIO: Pity me—I'll have to die—all for a worthless animal!
   But the girl—is she still in your house?

PERIPLECTOMENUS: She was when I came
     out here.   180

PALAESTRIO: Quick—have her cross back to our house, so the
     slaves can see her there.
   Make her hurry—that's unless she'd rather see her faithful
     slaves
   Just for her affair become fraternal brothers—on the cross!

PERIPLECTOMENUS: She'll be told.
   (*Going off*)
                                    If that is all . . .

PALAESTRIO: It isn't.
     Also tell the girl to
   See to it she doesn't lose her woman's ingenuity.
   Have her practice up her tricks and female shrewdness.

PERIPLECTOMENUS: What's
     this for?

PALAESTRIO: She must force the fellow who found her into full
     forgetfulness.
   Even if he saw her here a hundred times, have her deny it.
   She has cheek, a lot of lip, loquacity, audacity,
   Also perspicacity, tenacity, mendacity.

If someone accuses her, she'll just outswear the man with
    oaths.   190
She knows every phony phrase, the phony ways, the phony
    plays.
Wiles she has, guiles she has, very soothing smiles she has.
"Seasoned" women never have to get their spices at the
    grocer's—
Their own garden grows the pepper for their sharp and saucy
    schemes.

PERIPLECTOMENUS: I'll convey this all to her, if she's still there.
(*Stops, amazed*)
    What's going on?
What are you debating there inside yourself?

PALAESTRIO: Some silence,
    please,
While I call my wits to order to consider what to do
In retaliation: to outfox my foxy fellow slave, who
Saw her kissing in your house. We've got to make the
    seen . . . *unseen.*   200

PERIPLECTOMENUS: (*Starts to head for his house*)
Cogitate—while I withdraw and go in here.
(*Turns*)
                    Well, look at him!
Standing pensive, pondering profundities with wrinkled brow.
Now he knocks upon his head—he wants his brains to answer
    him.
Look—he turns. Now he supports himself with left hand on his
    left thigh.
Now he's adding something with the fingers of his right hand.
    Now he
Slaps his right thigh—what a slap! What to-do for what to do!
Now he snaps his fingers, struggles, changes posture every
    second.
Look—he shakes his head. No, no, what he's invented doesn't
    please him.

He'll cook up a plan that's well done—not half-baked—I'm
   sure of that.
Look—he's going in for building—with his chin he crowns a
   column.   210
Cut it out! That type of building doesn't please me—not at all.
For I hear a foreign poet also has his face so columned—
But he has two guards to keep him columned like that all the
   time.
Bravo! *Molto bello,* standing slavewise and theatrically.
He won't rest at all today until he finds the plan he's seeking.
Now I think he has it. Hey—get busy, man, don't slip to sleep.
That's unless you'd rather be on guard right here and
(*Points to his back*)

                                                             scarred

   right here.
Hey, have you been drinking? Hey, Palaestrio, I'm talking to
   you.
Rouse yourself! Wake up, I say; it's dawn, I say.

PALAESTRIO: (*Still rapt in thought*)   I hear you, sir.

PERIPLECTOMENUS: Don't you see the enemy is threatening that
   back of yours? *Think!*   220
Get us aid and reinforcements. No more napping; let's get
   scrapping!
Ready an offensive for the foe; prepare defenses too!
Cut the enemy's supply line, then we'll fortify our own.
So our rations and equipment get to you and to our legions
Safely: do it quickly. What we need is instant action!
Tell me that you'll take command yourself and then I'll rest
   secure,
Knowing we can crush the foe.

PALAESTRIO: (*Magnanimously*)   I do accept the office and do
Take command!

PERIPLECTOMENUS: I think you'll win the prize you seek.

PALAESTRIO: (*Paternally and gratefully*)   May Jupiter
  Shower blessings on you.

PERIPLECTOMENUS: Won't you share your plans?

PALAESTRIO: Be silent, sir,
  While I show you through the landscape of my "plot," so you'll
    be sharing   230
  Equally in all the plans.

PERIPLECTOMENUS: I'll guard them as I would my own.

PALAESTRIO: Master hasn't normal skin—it's thicker than an
    elephant's.
  He's about as clever as a stone.

PERIPLECTOMENUS: That much I know myself.

PALAESTRIO: Here's the whole idea, here's the notion that I'll set
    in motion:
  I will say Philocomasium has got a real twin sister
  Who has just arrived from Athens with a young man she's in
    love with.
  These two "sisters" are as alike as drops of milk. We'll say the
    lovers
  Stay at your house, as your guests.

PERIPLECTOMENUS: Bravo—it's a brilliant plan!

PALAESTRIO: Should this fellow slave of mine make accusations to
    the soldier,
  Claiming that he saw the girl there kissing someone else, why
    then   240
  I'll accuse my fellow slave of having spied on you and seen the
  Sister with her lover, kissing and embracing.

PERIPLECTOMENUS: Oh, that's fine!
　　If the soldier questions me, I'll back you up.

PALAESTRIO: Remember that the
　　Sisters are identically alike. Remind the girl as well, so
　　When the soldier asks her, she won't foul it up.

PERIPLECTOMENUS: A perfect ploy!
　　(*Suddenly*)
　　Wait—what happens if the soldier wants to see 'em both
　　　　together?
　　What do we do then?

PALAESTRIO: It's easy; there are thousands of excuses:
　　"She's not home, she took a walk, she's sleeping, dressing,
　　　　washing,
　　Dining, drinking, busy, indisposed, it's just impossible."
　　If we start this on the right foot, we can put him off forever. 250
　　Soon he'll get to thinking all the lies we tell him are the truth.

PERIPLECTOMENUS: This is just terrific.

PALAESTRIO: Go in—if the girl is there,
　　then have her
　　Hurry home. And train her, make things plainer and explain
　　　　her all.
　　She must fully comprehend our plan, the web we're weaving
　　　　with her
　　New twin sister.

PERIPLECTOMENUS: You shall quickly have a girl who's very quick.
　　What else?

PALAESTRIO: Be off.

PERIPLECTOMENUS: I'm off.

(The old man rushes off into his house, leaving PALAESTRIO *to ponder his next move)*

PALAESTRIO: Now I myself must go back home
  And by secret subterfugitive investigation find out
  Who of all my fellow servants chased that monkey on the roof.
  Surely he'll have shared the secret with the other household
    slaves,
  Whispering of Master's mistress, telling people how he
    saw her   260
  Here—within our neighbor's house—embracing some
    unknown young man.
  "I can't keep it secret; I'm the only one who knows," he'll say.
  When I find the man who saw her, my equipment will be
    ready.
  All is ready; I'm resolved to storm and take the enemy.
  If I can't discover him, I'll sniff just like a hunting dog
  Till I can pursue the little fox by following his footprints.
  Wait—our door is creaking—I had better quiet down for now.
  Look—here comes my fellow slave, the one they picked to
    guard the girl.

(Enter SCELEDRUS, *one of the soldier's household slaves. Normally a nervous nail-biter, he is now completely bewildered.)*

SCELEDRUS: If I wasn't walking in my sleep today up on that
    roof, I
  Know for sure, by Pollux, that I saw Philocomasium,   270
  Master's mistress, right here in our neighbor's house—in
    search of trouble.

PALAESTRIO: *(Aside)* There's the man who saw her kissing. I can
    tell from what he said.

SCELEDRUS: Who is that?

PALAESTRIO: Your fellow slave. How goes it, Sceledrus?

SCELEDRUS: Palaestrio!
   I'm so glad to see you.

PALAESTRIO: Why? What's up? What's wrong?
   Please let me know.

SCELEDRUS: I'm afraid—

PALAESTRIO: Of what?

SCELEDRUS: Today I fear we slaves are
   really *leaping* into
Trouble and titanic tortures!

PALAESTRIO: So leap solo, you yourself—
   I don't care the slightest bit for any leaping—up or down.

SCELEDRUS: Maybe you don't know the crime committed in our
   house today.

PALAESTRIO: Crime? What sort of crime?

SCELEDRUS: A dirty one!

PALAESTRIO: Then keep it
   to yourself.
I don't want to know it.

SCELEDRUS: Well, I won't allow you *not* to
   know it!   280
Listen: as I chased our monkey over our neighbor's roof
   today—

PALAESTRIO: Sceledrus, I'd say one worthless animal pursued
   another.

SCELEDRUS: Go to hell!

PALAESTRIO: *You* ought to go—on with your little tale, I mean.

(SCELEDRUS *glares at* PALAESTRIO, *then goes on with his story*)

SCELEDRUS: On the roof, I chanced by chance to peek down
    through our neighbor's skylight—
And what do I see? Philocomasium! She's smooching with some
Utterly unknown young man!

PALAESTRIO: (*Horrified*) What scandal, Sceledrus, is this?

SCELEDRUS: There's no doubt of it, I saw her.

PALAESTRIO: Really?

SCELEDRUS: With my own
    two eyes.

PALAESTRIO: Come on, this is all illusion; you saw nothing.

SCELEDRUS: Look
    at me!
Do my eyes look bad to you?

PALAESTRIO: Ask a doctor; don't ask me!
(*He now becomes the friendly adviser*)
By the gods, don't propagate this tale of yours so
    indiscreetly.   290
Now you're seeking trouble head-on, soon it may seek you—
    head off!
And unless you can suppress this absolutely brainless banter,
Double death awaits you!

SCELEDRUS: What's this "double" death?

PALAESTRIO: Well, I'll
   explain it:
  First, if you've accused our master's mistress falsely, you must
   die.
  Next, if what you say *is* true, you've failed as guard—you die
   again.

SCELEDRUS: I don't know my future, but I know I'm sure of what
  I saw.

PALAESTRIO: Still persisting, wretch?

SCELEDRUS: Look, I can only tell you
  what I saw. Why—
  She's inside our neighbor's house right now.

PALAESTRIO: (*With mock surprise*)   What's that, she's
  not at home?

SCELEDRUS: You don't have to take my word. Go right inside and
  look yourself.

PALAESTRIO: Yes, indeed I will!

(*He strides with severity into the soldier's house*)

SCELEDRUS: And I'll wait here and ambush
  her, the   300
  Minute our young filly trots from pasture to her storehouse
   stall.
  (*He reflects a moment, then groans*)
  What am I do to? The soldier chose me as her guardian.
  If I let this out—I die. Yet if I'm silent, still I die,
  Should this be discovered. Oh, what could be wickeder than
   women?
  While I chased the monkey, she just left her room and went
   outside!

Bold and brazen badness, by the gods! If Master learns of this,
Our whole household will be on the cross, by Hercules. Me
   too!
(*Resolves himself*)
Come what may, I'll shut my mouth. Better stilled than killed,
   I say.
(*Exasperated, to the audience*)
I can't guard a girl like this who's always out to sell herself!

(PALAESTRIO *marches out of the soldier's house, a very stern look
on his face*)

PALAESTRIO: Sceledrus! Is there a man more insolent in all the
   earth, or   310
Born beneath more angry of unfriendly stars—

SCELEDRUS: What's wrong?
   What's wrong?

PALAESTRIO: You should have your eyes dug out for seeing what
   was never there.

SCELEDRUS: Never where?

PALAESTRIO: I wouldn't give a rotten nut for your whole life!

SCELEDRUS: Tell me why—

PALAESTRIO: You even dare to ask me?

SCELEDRUS: Well, why can't
   I ask?

PALAESTRIO: You should really have that tattletaling tongue of
   yours cut off.

SCELEDRUS: Should I—why?

PALAESTRIO: My friend, the girl's *at home*—the
   one you said you saw
 In our neighbor's house with some young man, hugging and
   kissing him.

SCELEDRUS: It's amazing you don't eat your carrots. Why, they're
   cheap enough.

PALAESTRIO: Carrots, why?

SCELEDRUS: To aid your eyesight.

PALAESTRIO: Gallows bird! It's
   you who needs 'em.
 You're the blind man. My sight's perfect—and I'm sure the
   girl's at home.   320

SCELEDRUS: She's at home?

PALAESTRIO: At home she is.

SCELEDRUS: Oh, cut it out; you're
   fooling with me.

PALAESTRIO: Then my hands are very dirty.

SCELEDRUS: Why?

PALAESTRIO: Because I fool
   with filth.

SCELEDRUS: Damn your hide!

PALAESTRIO: No, Sceledrus, it's *your* hide that is
   now at stake.
 That's unless you make some changes in your visions and
   derisions.
 Wait—our door is creaking.

SCELEDRUS: (*At the old man's door*)
   I shall stay right here and block *this* door,
   For it's sure she can't cross over if she doesn't use the door!

PALAESTRIO: What's caused all this scurvy scoundrelism,
   Sceledrus? She's *home*.

(SCELEDRUS *keeps blocking the old man's door, looking straight
ahead and trying to reassure himself*)

SCELEDRUS: I can see . . . I know myself . . . I trust myself
   implicitly.
   No one bullies me to make me think she isn't in this house.
   (*He spreads his arms across the doorway*)
   Here—I'll block the door. She won't sneak back and catch me
   unawares.   330

PALAESTRIO: (*To the audience*) Now I have him where I want him.
   One small push and—he goes over.
   (*To* SCELEDRUS)
   Do you want me to convince you of your stupi-vision?

SCELEDRUS: Try it!

PALAESTRIO: And to prove that you don't know what eyes or
   brains are for?

SCELEDRUS: Well, prove it!

PALAESTRIO: Now . . . you claim the concubine's in there.

SCELEDRUS: Why,
   I *insist* she is,
   And I saw her kissing some young man as well—a perfect
   stranger.

PALAESTRIO: There's no passage from this house to our house,
   you know that—

SCELEDRUS: (*Impatiently*) I know it.

PALAESTRIO: There's no balcony or garden, just the
    skylight—

SCELEDRUS: I know *that*, too!

PALAESTRIO: Well . . . if she's in *our* house and I bring her out so
    you can see her,
    Would you say you're worthy of a whipping?

SCELEDRUS: (*Nods*)   Worthy.

PALAESTRIO: Guard the
    door—
    See she doesn't sneak out on the sly and slip across to our
    house.   340

SCELEDRUS: That's my plan.

PALAESTRIO: I'll have her standing in the street
    here right away.

(PALAESTRIO *dashes into the soldier's house*)

SCELEDRUS: (*Muttering to himself*)
    Go ahead and do it! I'll soon know if I saw what I saw.
    Or if—as he says he will—he'll prove the girl is still at home.
    (*Tries to reassure himself*)
    After all, I have my eyes. I never borrow someone else's. . . .
    (*Having second thoughts*)
    Yet he's always playing up to her—and he's her favorite:
    First man called to dinner, always first to fill his face with food.
    And he's only been with us about three years—not even that.
    Still I tell you, no one's slavery could be savory.

Never mind, I'd better do what must be done, that's guard this
    door.
Here I'll stand, by Pollux. Never will they make a fool
    of me!   350

(SCELEDRUS *stands with his arms spread across the doorway to the
old man's house.* PALAESTRIO *enters from the soldier's house, leading the girl* PHILOCOMASIUM.)

PALAESTRIO: Remember your instructions.

PHILOCOMASIUM: I'm astonished I'm
    admonished so.

PALAESTRIO: I'm worried you're not slippery enough.

PHILOCOMASIUM: What? I
    could make
A dozen decent damsels devils with my surplus shrewdness!

PALAESTRIO: Now concentrate on trickery. I'll slip away from you.

(*Strides jauntily up to* SCELEDRUS, *who is still blocking the old
man's door with all possible concentration*)

How are you, Sceledrus?

SCELEDRUS: (*Staring straight ahead*)
                        I'm on the job. Speak—I have ears.

(PALAESTRIO *looks at* SCELEDRUS's *pose, amused*)

PALAESTRIO: You know, I think you'll travel soon in that same
    pose—beyond the gates
With arms outstretched—to bear your cross.

SCELEDRUS: Oh yes? What for?

PALAESTRIO: Look to your left. Who is that woman?

SCELEDRUS: Oh—by all
    the gods—
  That girl—she's the master's concubine!

PALAESTRIO: You know, I think
    so too.
  Well, hurry, now's your time—

SCELEDRUS: What should I do?

PALAESTRIO: Don't
    dally—*die!*   360

PHILOCOMASIUM: Where is this "loyal" slave who falsely brands an
    honest woman
  With unchastity?

PALAESTRIO: (*Points to* SCELEDRUS)
              Right here! He told me all the things I
    told you.

PHILOCOMASIUM: You say you saw me—rascal—kissing in our
    neighbor's house?

PALAESTRIO: And with an unknown man, he said.

SCELEDRUS: By Hercules,
    I did.

PHILOCOMASIUM: You saw me?

SCELEDRUS: With these eyes, by
    Hercules.

PHILOCOMASIUM: You'll lose them soon—
    They see more than they see.

SCELEDRUS: By Hercules, I won't be
    frightened
    Out of seeing what I really saw!

PHILOCOMASIUM: I waste my breath
    Conversing with a lunatic. I'll have his head, by Pollux!

SCELEDRUS: Oh, stop your threats! I know the cross will be my
    tomb.
    My ancestors *all* ended there—exactly like my forefathers—
        and five-fathers.   370
    And so these threats of yours can't tear my eyes from me!
    (*Meekly motioning* PALAESTRIO *to one side*)
    But—could I have a word with you, Palaestrio? . . . Please tell
    me:
    Where *did* she come from?

PALAESTRIO: Home, where else?

SCELEDRUS: From home?

PALAESTRIO: (*Checking* SCELEDRUS's *eyes*)
    You see me?

SCELEDRUS: Sure.
    But it's amazing how she crossed from one house to the other!
    For certainly we haven't got a balcony, no garden,
    Every window's grated.
    (*To* PHILOCOMASIUM)
                            Yet I'm sure I saw you here inside.

PALAESTRIO: What—criminal—you're still accusing her?

PHILOCOMASIUM: By
    Castor, now
    I think it must have been the truth—that dream I dreamed last
    night.

PALAESTRIO: What did you dream?

PHILOCOMASIUM: I'll tell you both, but please
    pay close attention:
    Last night it seemed as if my dear *twin sister* had arrived   380
    In Ephesus from Athens—with a certain man she loved.
    It seemed as if they both were staying here next door as guests.

PALAESTRIO: (*Aside*) Palaestrio dreamed all this up.
    (*To* PHILOCOMASIUM)
                                 Go on—
    continue, please.

PHILOCOMASIUM: It seemed—though I was glad my sister
    came—because of her,
    There seemed to be a terrible suspicion cast upon me.
    Because it seemed that, in my dream, one of our slaves accused
    me,
    (*To* SCELEDRUS)
    Just as you're doing now, of having kissed a strange young man,
    When really it was my *twin sister* kissing her beloved.
    And so I dreamt that I was falsely and unjustly blamed.

PALAESTRIO: What seemed like dreams now happen to you wide
    awake!   390
    By Hercules—a real live dream!
    (*To* PHILOCOMASIUM)
                      Go right inside and pray!
    (*Casually*)
    I think you should relate this to the soldier. . . .

PHILOCOMASIUM: Why, of course!
    I won't be falsely called unchaste—without revenge!

(*She storms into the soldier's house.* PALAESTRIO *turns to* SCELEDRUS.)

SCELEDRUS: I'm scared. What have I done? I feel my whole back
    itching.

PALAESTRIO: You know you're finished, eh?

SCELEDRUS: Well, now at least I'm
    sure she's home.
    And now I'll guard our door—wherever she may be!

(SCELEDRUS *plants himself astride the soldier's door in the same
position he used to block the old man's doorway*)

PALAESTRIO: (*Sweetly*)   Sceledrus—
    That dream she dreamt was pretty similar to what went on—
    Even the part where you suspected that you saw her kissing!

SCELEDRUS: I don't know what I should believe myself. I thought
    I saw
    A thing . . . I think . . . perhaps . . . I didn't see.

PALAESTRIO: You're
    waking up—   400
    Too late. When Master hears of this, you'll die a dandy death.

SCELEDRUS: I see the truth at last. My eyes were clouded by
    some fog.

PALAESTRIO: I knew it all along. She's always been inside the
    house.

SCELEDRUS: I can't say anything for sure. I saw her, yet I
    didn't . . .

PALAESTRIO: By Jupiter, your folly almost finished us for good!
    In trying to be true to Master, *you* just missed disaster!
    But wait—our neighbor's door is creaking. I'll be quiet now.

(*Enter* PHILOCOMASIUM *again, this time from the old man's house*)

PHILOCOMASIUM: (*In a disguised voice*)
> Put fire on the altar; let me joyfully give thanks
> To Diana of Ephesus. I'll burn Arabian incense.
> She saved me in the turbulent Neptunian territory,   410
> When I was buffeted about, beset by savage seas.

SCELEDRUS: Palaestrio, Palaestrio!

PALAESTRIO: (*Mimicking him*)
>   O Sceledrus! What now?

SCELEDRUS: That girl that just came out—is that our master's
>   concubine,
> Philocomasium? Well—yes or no?

PALAESTRIO: It seems like her,
> Yet it's amazing how she crossed from one house to the other.
> If it is she . . .

SCELEDRUS: You mean you have your doubts?

PALAESTRIO: It seems like her.

SCELEDRUS: Well, let's accost her. Hey, what's going on,
>   Philocomasium?
> What were you doing in that house? Just what's been going on?
> Well, answer when I talk to you!

PALAESTRIO: You're talking to yourself—
> She doesn't answer.

SCELEDRUS: You! I'm speaking to you, wicked woman! 420
> So naughty with the neighbors—

PHILOCOMASIUM: (*Coldly*)   Sir, with whom are you
>   conversing?

SCELEDRUS: Who else but you?

PHILOCOMASIUM: Who are you, sir? What do you
     want with me?

SCELEDRUS: Asking me who am I?

PHILOCOMASIUM: Why not?—I don't know you,
     so I ask.

PALAESTRIO: I suppose you also don't know who *I* am.

PHILOCOMASIUM: Well, you
        and he—
     Are both a nuisance.

SCELEDRUS: You don't know us?

PHILOCOMASIUM: Neither one.

SCELEDRUS: I'm scared,
     I'm scared.

PALAESTRIO: Scared of what?

SCELEDRUS: I think we've lost our own identities
     somewhere—
     Since she says she doesn't know us!

PALAESTRIO: (*Very seriously*)   Let's investigate this
     further.
     Sceledrus—are we ourselves—or are we other people now?
     Maybe, unbeknownst to us, one of our neighbors has
       transformed us!

(SCELEDRUS *ponders this for a split second*)

SCELEDRUS: I'm myself for sure.

PALAESTRIO: Me too. Hey, girl—you're
   going after trouble.   430

(PHILOCOMASIUM *ignores him completely*)

PALAESTRIO: Hey, Philocomasium!

PHILOCOMASIUM: (*Coolly*) What madness motivates you, sir, to
   Carelessly concoct this incoherent name to call me?

PALAESTRIO: (*Sarcastically*)   Well now,
   Tell me—what's your real name, then?

PHILOCOMASIUM: My name is Dicea.

SCELEDRUS: No,
   you're wrong. The
  Name you're forging for yourself is phony, Philocomasium.
  You're not *de*cent, you're *in*decent—and you're cheating on my
   master!

PHILOCOMASIUM: I?

SCELEDRUS: Yes, you.

PHILOCOMASIUM: But I only arrived from Athens yesterday,
  With my faithful lover, an Athenian young man.

SCELEDRUS: Then tell me—
  What's your business here in Ephesus?

PHILOCOMASIUM: Looking for my dear
   twin sister.
  Someone said she might be here.

SCELEDRUS: (*Sarcastically*)   Oh, you're a clever girl!

PHILOCOMASIUM: No, I'm foolish, by the gods, to stand here
    chattering with you two.   440
    I'll be going. . . .

SCELEDRUS: No, you won't be—

(*He grabs her*)

PHILOCOMASIUM: Let me go!

SCELEDRUS: You're caught
    red-handed!
    I won't let you—

PHILOCOMASIUM: Then beware the noise—when my hand meets
    your cheek.
    Let me go!

SCELEDRUS: (*To* PALAESTRIO) You idiot, don't stand there. Grab
    her other arm!

PALAESTRIO: I don't want to get my back involved in this. Who
    knows—
    Maybe she's our girl . . . or maybe someone else who *looks* like
    her.

PHILOCOMASIUM: Will you let me go or not?

SCELEDRUS: You're coming home,
    no matter what!
    If you don't, I'll drag you home.

PHILOCOMASIUM: My home and master are
    in Athens—
    Athens back in Attica. I'm only staying as a guest here.
    (*Pointing to the soldier's house*)
    I don't know and I don't care about that house—or who you
    are!

SCELEDRUS: Go and sue me! I won't ever let you go unless you
    swear that   450
  If I do you'll come inside.

PHILOCOMASIUM: Whoever you are, you're forcing me.
  All right, if you let me go, I give my word to go inside.

SCELEDRUS: Go then.

(*He releases her*)

PHILOCOMASIUM: Go I shall . . . goodbye!

(*She dashes into the old man's house*)

SCELEDRUS: That's typical: a
  woman's word.

PALAESTRIO: Sceledrus, you let the prize slip through your
    fingers. No mistaking—
  She's our master's mistress. *Now*—you want to be a man of
  action?

SCELEDRUS: (*Timidly*) Tell me how.

PALAESTRIO: (*Boldly*) Bring forth a sword for me!

SCELEDRUS: (*Frightened*)   What will you do
  with it?

PALAESTRIO: (*Imitating his master's bombastic manner*)
  I'll burst boldly through these portals and the man I see inside
  Kissing Master's mistress, I shall slash to slivers on the spot!

SCELEDRUS: (*Meekly*) So you think it's she?

PALAESTRIO: There's no two ways
  about it.

SCELEDRUS: What an
    actress—
  So convincing . . .

PALAESTRIO: (*Shouts*) Bring me forth my sword!

SCELEDRUS: I'll do it right
    away.   460

(SCELEDRUS *dashes headlong into the soldier's house.* PALAESTRIO, *convulsed with laughter, addresses the audience.*)

PALAESTRIO: All the king's horses and all the king's men could
        never act with such great daring,
    Never be so calm, so cool, *in anything*, as one small *woman!*
    Deftly she delivered up a different accent for each part!
    How the faithful guard, my foxy fellow slave, was fully
        flimflammed!
    What a source of joy for all—this passage passing through the
        wall!

(PALAESTRIO *laughs gleefully as* SCELEDRUS *peeks out of the soldier's house, then sheepishly approaches*)

SCELEDRUS: Say, Palaestrio . . . forget about the sword.

PALAESTRIO: What's
    that? Why so?

SCELEDRUS: She's at home . . . our master's mistress.

PALAESTRIO: Home?

SCELEDRUS: She's
    lying on her couch.

PALAESTRIO: (*Building up in a frightening crescendo*)
   Now it seems you've found the trouble you've been looking for,
   by Pollux!

SCELEDRUS: Why?

PALAESTRIO: Because you dared disturb a lady who's our
   neighbor's guest.

SCELEDRUS: Hercules! How horrible!

PALAESTRIO: Why, there's no question,
   she must be the   470
   Real twin sister of our girl— and *she's* the one that you saw
   kissing!

SCELEDRUS: Yes, you're right. It's clearly she, just as you say. Did
   I come close to
   Getting killed! If I'd said a word to Master—

PALAESTRIO: Now, be smart:
   Keep this all a secret. Slaves should also know more than they
   tell.
   I'll be going. I don't want to get mixed up in all your mischief.
   I'll be at our neighbor's here. I don't quite care for your
   confusions.
   If when Master comes he needs me, he can send for me in
   here.

(PALAESTRIO *strides into the old man's house*)

SCELEDRUS: At last he's gone. He cares no more for Master's
   matters
   Than if he weren't slaving here in slavery!
   Well, *now* our girl's inside the house, I'm sure of that;   480
   I personally saw her lying on her couch.
   So now's the time to pay attention to my guarding.

(SCELEDRUS *paces before the soldier's door, concentrating on his guarding.* PERIPLECTOMENUS *rushes out angrily from his own house.*)

PERIPLECTOMENUS: By Hercules, those men must take me for a
    sissy—
  My military neighbor's slaves insult me so!
  Did they not lay their hands upon my lady guest—
  Who yesterday arrived from Athens with my friend?
  (*Indignantly to the audience*)
  A free and freeborn girl—manhandled and insulted!

SCELEDRUS: Oh, Hercules, I'm through. He's heading to behead
    me.
  I'm scared this thing has got me into awful trouble—
  At least that's what I gather from the old man's words.   490

PERIPLECTOMENUS: (*Aside*) Now I'll confront him.
  (*To* SCELEDRUS)
                              Scurvy
  scoundrel Sceledrus!
  Did you insult my guest right by my house just now?

SCELEDRUS: (*In a near panic*)
  Dear neighbor, listen please—

PERIPLECTOMENUS: *I* listen? *You're* the slave!

SCELEDRUS: I want to clear myself—

PERIPLECTOMENUS: How can you clear yourself,
  When you've just done such monstrous and disgraceful things?
  Perhaps because you're used to plundering the foe
  You think you're free to act here as you please, scoundrel?

SCELEDRUS: Oh, please, sir—

PERIPLECTOMENUS: May the gods and goddesses not
    love me
  If I don't arrange a whipping for you—yes,
  A good long-lasting lengthy one, from dawn to dusk   500
  For one, because you broke my roof tiles and my gutters,
  While you chased another monkey—like yourself.
  And then for spying on my guest in my own house,
  While he was kissing and embracing his own sweetheart.
  And *then* you had the gall to slander that dear girl
  Your master keeps—and to accuse me of atrocious things!
  And *now* you maul my lady guest—right on my doorstep!
  Why, if I don't have knotted lashes put to you,
  I'll see to it your master's hit by more disgrace
  Than oceans are by waves during a mighty storm!   510

(SCELEDRUS *trembles with fright*)

SCELEDRUS: I'm so upset, Periplectomenus, I just don't know
  Whether I'd better argue this thing out with you,
  Or else—if one is not the other—she's not *she*—
  Well then, I guess I should apologize to you.
  I mean—well, now I don't know *what* I saw at all!
  Your girl looks so much like the one we have—that is,
  If they are not the same—

PERIPLECTOMENUS: (*Sweetly*) Look in my house; you'll see.

SCELEDRUS: Oh, could I?

PERIPLECTOMENUS: I insist. Inspect—and take your time.

SCELEDRUS: Yes, that's the thing to do.

(*He dashes into the old man's house*)

PERIPLECTOMENUS: (*Calling at the soldier's house*)
   Philocomasium, be quick!   520
   Run over to my house—go at a sprint—it's vital.
   As soon as Sceledrus goes out, then double quick—
   Run right back to your own house at a sprint!
   (*Getting a bit excited himself*)
   Oh my goodness! Now I'm scared she'll bungle it.
   What if he doesn't see her? Wait—I hear the door.

(SCELEDRUS *reenters, wide-eyed and confused*)

SCELEDRUS: O ye immortal gods, there never were two girls more
   similar,
   More similar—and yet I know they're not the same.
   I didn't think the gods could do it!

PERIPLECTOMENUS: Well?

SCELEDRUS: I'm whipped.

PERIPLECTOMENUS: Is she your girl?

SCELEDRUS: It is and yet it isn't her.

PERIPLECTOMENUS: You saw . . . ?

SCELEDRUS: I saw a girl together with
   your guest,   530
   Embracing him and kissing.

PERIPLECTOMENUS: Was it yours?

SCELEDRUS: Who knows?

PERIPLECTOMENUS: You want to know for sure?

SCELEDRUS: Yes!

PERIPLECTOMENUS: Hurry to your
   house
And see if your girl's there within. Be quick—

SCELEDRUS: I will.
   That's good advice. Wait—I'll be back here right away.

(SCELEDRUS *rushes into the soldier's house*)

PERIPLECTOMENUS: By Pollux, never was a man bamboozled
      better,
   More wittily, in wilder or more wondrous ways.
   But here he comes. . . .

(SCELEDRUS *reenters, on the brink of tears, and throws himself at*
PERIPLECTOMENUS's *feet*)

SCELEDRUS: Periplectomenus, I beg of you,
   By all the gods and men—by my stupidity—
   And by your knees.

PERIPLECTOMENUS: What do you beg of me?

SCELEDRUS: Forgive
   My foolishness and my stupidity. At last   540
   I know that I've been thoughtless—idiotic—blind!
   (*Sheepishly*)
   Philocomasium . . . is right inside.

PERIPLECTOMENUS: Well, gallows bird—
   You've seen them both?

SCELEDRUS: I've seen.

PERIPLECTOMENUS: Would you please call your
   master?

SCELEDRUS: (*Beseeching*) I do confess I'm worthy of a whopping
    whipping,
  And I do admit that I abused your lady guest.
  But I mistook her for my master's concubine—
  The soldier has appointed me her guardian.
  Two drops of water from a single well could not be drawn
  Much more alike than our girl's like your lady guest.
  (*Quietly*)
  I also peeked down into your house through the skylight,   550
  I do confess.

PERIPLECTOMENUS: Why not confess? I saw you do it!
  And there you saw my guests—a man and lady—kissing—
  Correct?

SCELEDRUS: Yes, yes. Should I deny the things I saw?
  But, sir, I thought I saw Philocomasium.

PERIPLECTOMENUS: Did you consider me a man so vile and base
  To be a party to such things in my own house,
  And let my neighbor suffer such outrageous harm?

SCELEDRUS: At last I see how idiotically I've acted.
  I know the facts now. But it wasn't done on purpose.
  I'm blameless—

PERIPLECTOMENUS: But not shameless. Why, a slave should
    have   560
  His eyes downcast, his hands and tongue in strict control—
  His speech as well.

SCELEDRUS: If I so much as mumble, sir,
  From this day on—and even mumble what I'm sure of—
  Have me tortured. I'll just give myself to you.
  But now I beg forgiveness.

PERIPLECTOMENUS: (*Magnanimously*) I'll suppress my wrath
  And think you really didn't do it all on purpose.
  So—you're forgiven.

SCELEDRUS: May the gods all bless you, sir!

PERIPLECTOMENUS: Now, after this, by Hercules, you guard your
    tongue
  And even if you know a thing, *don't* know a thing—
  And *don't* see even what you see.

SCELEDRUS: That's good advice.   570
  I'll do it. Have I begged enough?

PERIPLECTOMENUS: Just go away!

SCELEDRUS: Do you want something else?

PERIPLECTOMENUS: Yes—*not* to know you!

(PERIPLECTOMENUS *turns away from* SCELEDRUS *in disgust and
walks aside*)

SCELEDRUS: (*Suspiciously*) He's fooling me. How easily he just
    excused me.
  He wasn't even angry. But I know what's up:
  The minute that the soldier comes home from the forum,
  They'll grab me in the house. He and Palaestrio,
  They want to sell me out. . . . I've sensed it for a while now.
  By Hercules, I won't snap at their bait today.
  I'll run off somewhere, hide myself a day or two,
  Till this commotion quiets and the shouting stops.   580
  I've earned myself much more than one man's share of
    troubles.

(SCELEDRUS *runs off*)

PERIPLECTOMENUS: Well, he's retreated. Now, by Pollux, I'm
    quite sure
A headless pig has far more brains than Sceledrus.
He's been so gulled he doesn't see the things he saw.
His eyes, his ears, his every sense has not deserted him
To join our cause. Well, up to now, so far so good.
That girl of ours came up with quite a fine performance.
Now to our little senate, for Palaestrio
Is there inside my house and Sceledrus is gone.
We now can have a meeting with the whole committee.   590
I'd better go inside before they vote without me!

(*He goes into his own house. The stage is empty for a moment. Then*
PALAESTRIO *tiptoes out of the old man's house.*)

PALAESTRIO: (*Motioning to the others who are still inside*)
Pleusicles, have everybody wait inside a little longer.
Let me reconnoiter first to see if there are spies around to
Stop the meeting we're about to have. We need a place that's
    safe,
Someplace where no enemy can plunder any plans we've made.
What you plan out will not pan out, if your enemy can use it.
Useful things for enemies become abuseful things for you.
Clearly, if the enemy should somehow learn about your plans,
    they'll
Turn the tables on you, shut your mouth and tie your hands.
    And so
Whatever you had planned to do to them, they'll do to you
    instead!   600
Now I'll peek around, look right and left, to see there's no one
    here, no
Hunter using ears for nets so he can "catch" our secret plans.
(*Looks to either side*)
Good—the coast is clear all up and down the street. I'll call
    them out.
Hey, Periplectomenus and Pleusicles, produce yourselves!

(*They come out eagerly*)

PERIPLECTOMENUS: Here—at your command.

PALAESTRIO: Commanding's
    easy when your troops are good.
    How about it now—that plan we figured out inside—shall we
        now
    Carry on with it?

PERIPLECTOMENUS: We couldn't do it better.

PALAESTRIO: What do you think,
    Pleusicles?

PLEUSICLES: (*Mindlessly devoted*)
    What could be fine with you and not be fine with me?
    No one's more my friend than you are.

PALAESTRIO: Nicely and precisely put.

PERIPLECTOMENUS: That's the way he should be talking.

PLEUSICLES: Yet it
    makes me miserable; it   610
    Troubles and torments me too—

PERIPLECTOMENUS: What troubles you? Speak up,
    my boy!

PLEUSICLES: That I burden someone who's as old as you with
    childish trifles.
    These concerns are so unworthy of your noble qualities—
    Asking you for so much help in what is really my concern:
    Bringing reinforcements to a lover, doing different duties,
    Duties that most men of your age would prefer to dodge—not
        do!
    I'm ashamed to bring annoyance to you in your twilight years.

PALAESTRIO: You're a novel lover if you blush at doing anything!
   You're no lover—just the palest shadow of what lovers should
     be.

PLEUSICLES: Troubling a man of his age with a youthful love
    affair?   620

PERIPLECTOMENUS: What's that? Do I seem so six-feet-under to
    you—is that so?
   Do I seem to be so senile, such a coffin candidate?
   After all, I'm barely fifty-four years old—not even that.
   I've got perfect vision still, my hands are quick, my legs are
    nimble.

PALAESTRIO: Maybe he's white-haired on top, but not inside his
    head—that's sure.
   All the qualities that he was born with haven't aged a bit.

PLEUSICLES: I know that, by Pollux, what you say is true,
    Palaestrio.
   He's been absolutely youthful in his hospitality.

PERIPLECTOMENUS: Try me in a crisis, boy. The more I'm pressed
    the more you'll note how
   I'll support your love affair—

PLEUSICLES: No need to note—I know it
   well.   630

PERIPLECTOMENUS: (*Casually boasting*)
   Experience, experience . . . the only way of finding out.
   Only he who's loved himself can see inside a lover's soul.
   Even I still have a little lively loving left in me.
   All my taste for joy and pleasure hasn't dried up in me yet.
   I'm the perfect party guest—I'm quick with very clever quips.
   And I never interrupt another person when he's talking.
   I refrain from rudeness, I'm restrained with guests and never
    rowdy.

I remember to contribute just my share of conversation.
And I also know to shut my mouth when someone else is
    talking.
I'm no spitter, I'm no cougher, and I'm not forever
    sneezing.   640
I was born in Ephesus; I'm not an Animulian.

PALAESTRIO: Mezzo-middle-aged at most, with all the talents he
    describes!
Certainly a Muse has shown this man how to be so amusing.

PERIPLECTOMENUS: I can show you that I'm even more amusing
    than you say:
Never at a party do I screw around with someone's girl,
Never do I filch the food or take the goblet out of turn.
Never do I let the wine bring out an argument in me.
Someone gets too nasty? I go home and cut the conversation.
Give me love and loveliness and lots of laughter at a party.

PALAESTRIO: All your talents seem to tend toward charm and
    graciousness, by Pollux.   650
Show me three men with such talents and I'll pay their weight
    in gold!

PLEUSICLES: Never—you won't find another man as old as he
    who is so
Thoroughly delightful and so good a friend to anyone.

(PERIPLECTOMENUS *is enjoying the compliments, but he doesn't
like being called an old man*)

PERIPLECTOMENUS: I'll make you admit I'm really just a
    youngster in my way.
Wait until you see the countless splendid services I'll render:
Do you need a lawyer—one that's fierce and angry? Here I am.
Do you need a mild one? I'll be smoother than the silent sea.
I'll be oh so softer than the southern breeze in early spring.
I can also be the most lighthearted of your dinner guests,

Or the perfect parasite, or else supply a super supper.   660
As for dancing—even fruity fairies haven't got *my* grace.

(*Acting very impressed,* PALAESTRIO *turns to* PLEUSICLES)

PALAESTRIO: (*To* PLEUSICLES) What else could you wish for if
 you'd even wish for something else?

PLEUSICLES: Just the talent to express my gratitude for
 everything.
Thanks to you
(*To* PERIPLECTOMENUS)
                and thanks to you for taking such good care of me.
I must be a burdensome expense to you—

PERIPLECTOMENUS: You silly boy!
 What you spend for enemies or for a nasty wife's expense,
 What you lay out for a guest, a real true friend of yours, is
  *profit!**
 Thank the gods I can afford to entertain you as I'd like to.
 Eat! Drink up! Indulge yourself, let laughter overflow the brim!
 Mine's the house of freedom—I am free—I live my life
  for me.   670
 Thank the gods, I'm rich enough. I could've married very well,
 Could've led a wealthy wife of high position to the altar.
 But I wouldn't want to lead a barking dog into my house!

PALAESTRIO: Yet remember—children can be pleasant—and it's
 fun to breed 'em.

PERIPLECTOMENUS: You can breed 'em. Give me freedom! *That,*
 by Hercules, is fun!

PALAESTRIO: You're a good adviser—for yourself as well as other
 people.

---

*Line omitted.

PERIPLECTOMENUS: Sure it's sweet to wed a *good* wife—if there's
 such a thing on earth.
 I'd be glad to marry someone who would turn to me and ask
  me,
 "Dearest husband, buy some wool, so I can make some clothing
  for you,
 First a tunic, soft and warm, and then a cloak for winter
  weather,   680
 So you won't be cold." You'd never hear a wife say things like
  that!
 Why, before the cock would crow, she'd shake me from my
  sleep and say,
 "Husband! Give me money for a New Year's gift to give my
  mother!
 It's Minerva's festival, so give to give the fortuneteller,
 Dream interpreter, diviner, sorceress, and soothsayer!
 She tells fortunes from your eyebrows—it's a crime to leave her
  out!
 How about the laundry girl? She couldn't do without a gift.
 Look how long it's been since we have tipped the grocer's
  wife—she's angry with us.
 And the midwife has complained—we didn't send her quite
  enough!
 What! Will we send nothing to the one who's nursed our
  household slaves?"   690
 These and other ruinations that a woman brings have kept me
 Single, so I'm not subjected to this sort of sordid speeches.

PALAESTRIO: All the gods have blessed you, for, by Hercules, if
 you let go of
Freedom just one second, it's no easy thing to get it back.

PLEUSICLES: Don't you think it's noble for a man of wealth and
 high estate to
Bring up children as a sort of monument to his good name?

PERIPLECTOMENUS: I have relatives aplenty, so what need have I
      of children?
   I live happily and well. I suit myself, do what I please.
   When I die, my relatives can split the money that I leave 'em.
   Now they're up at dawn to come and ask me if I've slept all
      right.   700
   When they sacrifice, they give me bigger portions than their
      own.
   And they take me out to banquets, have me home for lunch, for
      dinner.
   They're so sad if they can send me only something small and
      simple.
   They compete in giving, as I secretly repeat inside:
   "Let them chase my money; they're all eagerly supporting me!"

PALAESTRIO: Ah, you really know the way to live; you know what
      life is for.
   If you're having fun, it's just as good as having twins or triplets.

(PERIPLECTOMENUS *seems anxious to talk on any topic, so he now
pursues this one*)

PERIPLECTOMENUS: If I really had 'em, I'd be miserable because
      of them—
   Worrying about their health. Why, if my son had fever, I would
   Think he's dying. If he drank too much or tumbled off his
      horse,   710
   I would always be afraid he broke his neck or broke a leg.

PALAESTRIO: Here's a man who rightfully has riches. He should
      live forever.
   He keeps wealthy, ever healthy—and he's out to help his
      friends.

PLEUSICLES: What a charming chap! By all the gods and
      goddesses above,
   Gods should all decide how long we live by a consistent system.
   Just as the inspector fixes selling prices in the market,

Merchandise of quality is priced according to its merits,
Merchandise that's rotten gets a price that makes its owner
    poorer,
That's the way a person's life should be determined by the
    gods.
Men with charm and lots of talent should have long and
    lengthy lives;   720
Rotten men and rogues should be deprived of life without
    delay.
We'd be minus many scoundrels if the gods would use this
    system,
And the dirty deeds committed would be fewer. Furthermore,
Men would be of quality—and life would be a better bargain.

(PERIPLECTOMENUS *is flattered, but he playfully chides the young*
man)

PERIPLECTOMENUS: Only silly fools find fault with what the gods
    above decree.
    Only fools would scold the gods. Let's stop this stupid stuff for
    now.
    (*He starts to go off*)
    Now I'll buy the groceries to entertain my guest with
    something
    Worthy of us both, a welcome of good wishes *and* good dishes!

PLEUSICLES: Please—I've been a terrible expense to you already.
    Surely
    No guest can accept such friendly treatment as you've offered
    me and   730
    Not become an inconvenience after three days in a row.
    After *ten* days, he becomes an *Iliad* of inconvenience!
    Even if his host is willing, still the servants start to mutter.

PERIPLECTOMENUS: I've instructed servants in this house to stick
    to serving me,
    Not to give me orders or to have myself depend on them.
    Why, if

What I want displeases them—too bad! I'm captain of the ship.
Willy-nilly, they'll do what they're ordered—or be beaten up.
Now I'd better get on with the groceries. . . .

(*He starts to amble off*)

PLEUSICLES: Well, if you
    must—
Please don't buy extravagantly—anything is fine for me.

(PERIPLECTOMENUS *now stops to discuss this topic*)

PERIPLECTOMENUS: Stop that kind of talk. That stale cliché is
    older than the hills.   740
Really, now you're talking like the hoi polloi—you know the
    kind, who
When they're at the table and the dinner's set before 'em say,
"Did you go to all this trouble just for *me*—you shouldn't have.
Hercules, it's madness. Why, there's food enough for ten at
    least!"
Much too much for them! But while they're frowning, they are
    downing it!

PALAESTRIO: That's the way it is exactly.
    (*To* PLEUSICLES)
                                He speaks soundly and
    profoundly.

PERIPLECTOMENUS: Never will you hear these people, when a
    feast if set before 'em,
Say, "Remove this . . . take this plate away . . . take off the
    ham . . . I simply couldn't.
Take this bit of pork away . . . this eel would be much better
    cold."
"Take" . . . "remove" . . . "be off" are words you'll never hear
    from one of them.   750
No, they leap to reach the food, with half their bodies on the
    table.

PALAESTRIO: Bad behavior well described.

PERIPLECTOMENUS: I haven't told the
    hundredth part of
What I could expound upon if only we had time to talk—

(PALAESTRIO *seizes this opportunity to cut* PERIPLECTOMENUS's
monologue short)

PALAESTRIO: Right! But we had better turn our thoughts to what
    we're doing now.
Listen closely, both of you.
(*To* PERIPLECTOMENUS)
                              I'll need your services in this,
Periplectomenus. I've figured out a lovely scheme to help us
Take our curly-headed soldier to the barber's for a trimming.
And we'll give our lover here the chance to get his sweetheart
    back, and
Take her off from here for good!

PERIPLECTOMENUS: Now there's a plan I'd like
    to hear!

PALAESTRIO: First, I'd like to ask you for that ring of yours.

PERIPLECTOMENUS: (*Suspiciously*) How will you use it?   760

PALAESTRIO: When I have the ring you'll have the reason—and
    my whole invention.

PERIPLECTOMENUS: Here's the ring.

PALAESTRIO: And here's your reason in
    return, the little scheme that
I've been setting up.

PLEUSICLES: We're listening to you with
    well-washed ears.

PALAESTRIO: Master is the wildest wenching wanton man who
    ever was—
Or who ever will be for that matter.

PERIPLECTOMENUS: I believe it, too.

PALAESTRIO: He supposes he surpasses Paris in his
    handsomeness.
He thinks all the women here just cannot help pursuing him.

PERIPLECTOMENUS: I know several husbands here who wish that
    statement were the truth!
But proceed. I know too well he's what you say, Palaestrio.
Get on to the point, be brief, don't beat around the bush,
    my boy.   770

PALAESTRIO: Could you find a woman for me—someone beautiful
    and charming,
Someone full of cleverness and trickery from tip to toe?

PERIPLECTOMENUS: Freed or freeborn girl?

PALAESTRIO: It doesn't matter, just
    be sure and get me
One who's money-loving, and who earns her keep by being
    kept.
One who's got a mind—she doesn't need a heart—no woman
    has one.

PERIPLECTOMENUS: Do you want a . . . green one . . . or a ripe
    one?

PALAESTRIO: Just be sure she's juicy.
Get the freshest, most appealing girl you possibly can find.

PERIPLECTOMENUS: Say—I have a client—luscious, youngish
    little courtesan!
But—why do you need her?

PALAESTRIO: Bring her home to your house,
    right away.
Have her in disguise, so she'll look like a married woman— 780
Hair combed high, with ribbons and the rest. She must
    pretend that
She's your wedded wife. Now train the girl!

PERIPLECTOMENUS: I'm lost. What's all
    this for?

PALAESTRIO: You'll soon see. Now, does she have a maid?

PERIPLECTOMENUS: A very
    clever one.

PALAESTRIO: We'll have need of her as well. Now tell the woman
    and her maid the
Mistress must pretend that she's your wife—who's dying for
    the soldier boy.
We'll pretend she gave her little maid this ring—to give to me.
I'll give it to him, pretending I'm the go-between.

PERIPLECTOMENUS: I hear you—
Don't assume I'm deaf. I know my ears are both in fine
    condition.

PALAESTRIO: I'll pretend it's been presented as a present from
    your wife so
She could . . . get together with him. I know him—he'll be
    in flames!   790
Nothing gets that lecher more excited than adultery!

PERIPLECTOMENUS: If you asked the sun himself to find the girls
    you've asked me for,
He could never find a pair more perfect for the job. Relax!

(He exits)

PALAESTRIO: Fine. Hop to it then. We need 'em right away. Now,
    Pleusicles—

PLEUSICLES: At your service.

PALAESTRIO: When the soldier gets back home,
        remember *not* to
    Call your girl Philocomasium.

PLEUSICLES: What should I call her then?

PALAESTRIO: Dicea.

PLEUSICLES: Yes, of course, the name we just agreed upon.

PALAESTRIO: Now go.

(PLEUSICLES *remains stationary for a moment, "memorizing" the
name*)

PLEUSICLES: I'll remember.
    (*To* PALAESTRIO)
                          But I'd like to ask you *why* I should
        remember.

PALAESTRIO: When you have to know, I'll tell you. For the
        moment, just keep still,
    While the old man does his part—and very soon you'll play
        your role.   800

PLEUSICLES: Then I guess I'll go inside.

(*He starts to walk off*)

PALAESTRIO: (*Calling after him*)   And follow orders carefully!

(PLEUSICLES *walks slowly into the house, rehearsing to himself*)

PALAESTRIO: (*To the audience, with a broad smile*)
    What storms I'm stirring up—what mighty machinations!
    Today I'll snatch that concubine back from the soldier—
    That is, if all my troops remain well disciplined.
    Now I'll call him. Hey, Sceledrus! If you've got time
    Come out in front. Palaestrio is calling you.

(*A pause. Not* SCELEDRUS, *but another slave,* LURCIO *by name,
appears at the door, extremely drunk.*)

LURCIO: He's busy now.

PALAESTRIO: At what?

LURCIO: He's pouring . . . as he sleeps.

PALAESTRIO: Did you say "pouring"?

LURCIO: "Snoring" 's what I meant
        to say.
    But snoring, pouring—isn't it about the same?

(LURCIO *starts to reel offstage.* PALAESTRIO *stops him.*)

PALAESTRIO: Hey—Sceledrus inside asleep?

LURCIO: Except his nose.   810
    That's making quite a noise.
    (*Confidentially*)
                            He took some secret snorts
    'Cause he's the steward and was spicing up the wine.

(LURCIO *again turns to go;* PALAESTRIO *again stops him*)

PALAESTRIO: But wait, you scoundrel, you're the guy's
        substeward—wait!

LURCIO: Your point?

PALAESTRIO: (*Indignantly*) How could he let himself just go to
    sleep?

LURCIO: He closed his eyes, I think.

PALAESTRIO: I didn't ask you that!
    Come here! You're dead if I don't know the truth at once!
    Did you serve him the wine?

LURCIO: I didn't.

PALAESTRIO: You deny it?

LURCIO: I do, by Hercules. He told me to deny it.
    I also didn't pour four pints into a pitcher.
    He also didn't drink 'em all warmed up at dinner.   820

PALAESTRIO: You also didn't drink?

LURCIO: Gods blast me if I did.
    I wish I'd drunk.

PALAESTRIO: How come?

LURCIO: Because I *guzzled* it instead.
    The wine was overheated and it burned my throat.

PALAESTRIO: Some slaves get drunk, while others get weak
    vinegar!
    Our pantry has some loyal steward and substeward!

LURCIO: You'd do the same, by Hercules, if you had charge.
    You're acting jealous now 'cause you can't copy us.

(*He once again turns to go*)

PALAESTRIO: Wait, wait, you scoundrel! Has he drunk like this
   before?
  And just to help your thinking, let me tell you this:
  If, Lurcio, you lie, you'll suffer horribly.   830

LURCIO: Oh, really now? Then you can tattle what I've told
  To get me kicked out from my storeroom stuffing job,
  And pick a new substeward when *you're* put in charge.

PALAESTRIO: By Pollux, no, I won't. Come on. Be brave and
  speak.

LURCIO: He never poured a drop, by Pollux. That's the truth.
  He'd order me to do it—and I'd pour for him.

PALAESTRIO: That's why the jars were always standing on their
  heads!

LURCIO: By Hercules, that isn't why the jars were jarred.
  Inside the storeroom was this very slippery spot.
  A two-point pot was leaning on the casks nearby;   840
  It often would get all filled up—ten times or so.
  I saw it filled and emptied. Mostly it got filled.
  And then the pot danced wildly and the jars were jarred.

PALAESTRIO: Get in! You held that storeroom bacchanal
  yourselves.
  By Hercules, I'll go bring Master from the forum.

(PALAESTRIO *takes a few steps toward the forum, then stops to listen
to* LURCIO's *lament*)

LURCIO: I'm dead. Master will crucify me when he comes
  And finds out what's been done because I didn't tell him.
  I'll run off somewhere so I can postpone the pains.
  (*To the audience*)
  Folks, please don't tell Palaestrio, I beg of you.

(*He starts to tiptoe off.* PALAESTRIO *scares him with a shout.*)

PALAESTRIO: Hey—where are you going?

LURCIO: (*Nervously*)   I'll be back. I'm on an
     errand.   850

PALAESTRIO: For whom?

LURCIO: Philocomasium.

PALAESTRIO: Go—rush right back!

LURCIO: Do me a favor, will you? If while I'm away
     There's punishment distributed . . . please take my share.

(LURCIO *scampers off*)

PALAESTRIO: (*To the audience*) Ah, now I understand our young
        girl's strategy.
     With Sceledrus asleep, she sends his underling
     Off on some business while she sneaks across.
     (*Looks offstage to his left*)
     But here's our neighbor with the girl I requisitioned—
     And, oh, is she good-looking! All the gods are with us.
     She's dressed so finely—most unprostitutishly.
     This whole affair now seems most charmingly in hand!   860

(PERIPLECTOMENUS *enters with a girl on either arm. One is the
courtesan* ACROTELEUTIUM, *a reasonably young old pro, and the
other is her maid* MILPHIDIPPA.)

PERIPLECTOMENUS: (*To the girls*) Now I've explained this whole
        thing to you both from start to finish,
     Acroteleutium and Milphidippa. If you haven't grasped
     This artful artifice as yet, I'll drill you once again.
     But if you understand it all, then we can change the subject.

ACROTELEUTIUM: Now don't you think I'd be a stupid idiot to
    undertake
An unfamiliar project or to promise you results,
If I were unacquainted with the whole technique—the art of
    being wicked?

PERIPLECTOMENUS: Forewarned's forearmed, I say.

ACROTELEUTIUM: Not to a
        real professional—
A layman's words are little use. Why, didn't I myself,
The minute that I drank the smallest drop of your proposal, 870
Didn't *I* tell *you* the way the soldier could be swindled?

PERIPLECTOMENUS: But no one ever knows enough. How many
    have I seen
Avoid the region of good sense—before they even found it.

ACROTELEUTIUM: But when it's wickedness or wiles that's wanted
    of the woman,
Why, then she's got a monumentally immortal memory.
It's only when it comes to something fine or faithful
That suddenly she's scatterbrained—and can't remember.

PERIPLECTOMENUS: Well, that's what I'm afraid of. Here your job
    is double-edged:
For when you do the soldier harm, you're doing *me* a favor.

ACROTELEUTIUM: Relax, you're safe as long as we don't know
    we're doing good.   880

PERIPLECTOMENUS: What mangy merchandise a woman is.

ACROTELEUTIUM: Just
        like her customers.

PERIPLECTOMENUS: That's typical. Come on.

PALAESTRIO: I ought to go ahead
    and meet them.
    It's good to see you, sir, so charmingly accompanied.

PERIPLECTOMENUS: Well met, Palaestrio. Look—here they are—
    the girls
    You ordered me to bring—and in their costumes.

PALAESTRIO: (*Pats him on the back*)   You're my man!
    Palaestrio salutes Acroteleutium.

ACROTELEUTIUM: Who's this
    Who speaks to me as if he knew me?

PERIPLECTOMENUS: He's our . . . architect.

ACROTELEUTIUM: My greetings to the architect.

PALAESTRIO: The same to you.
    Has he
    Indoctrinated you?

PERIPLECTOMENUS: The girls I bring are well rehearsed.

PALAESTRIO: I want to hear how well. The fear of failure
    frightens me.   890

PERIPLECTOMENUS: I didn't add a thing to those instructions that
    you gave me.

(ACROTELEUTIUM *approaches* PALAESTRIO *and speaks to him in a
very blasé manner*)

ACROTELEUTIUM: Now look. You want the soldier to be swindled,
    right?

PALAESTRIO: That's right!

ACROTELEUTIUM: Neatly, sweetly, and completely—everything's
   arranged.

PALAESTRIO: I want you to pretend to be his wife—

ACROTELEUTIUM: I *am* his wife.

PALAESTRIO: Pretend that you're enamored of the soldier—

ACROTELEUTIUM: So I
   will be.

PALAESTRIO: Pretend that I'm the go-between for this—with
   Milphidippa.

ACROTELEUTIUM: You should have been a prophet—all you say
   will soon come true.

PALAESTRIO: Pretend this ring was given by your little maid to
   me
  To offer to the soldier with your compliments.

ACROTELEUTIUM: That's true!

PERIPLECTOMENUS: Why bother to remind the girls of things
   they know?   900

ACROTELEUTIUM: It's good.
  Remember if you're dealing with a first-rate architect,
  And if this man designs a ship with well-drawn plans,
  You'll build the ship with ease if everything's laid out and set.
  Now we've a keel that's accurately laid and nicely set,
  Our architect has helpers who are not exactly . . . amateurs,
  So if our raw material is not delayed en route,
  I know our capabilities—we'll have that ship in no time.

PALAESTRIO: (*To* ACROTELEUTIUM) I guess you know my military
   master—

ACROTELEUTIUM: What a question!!
  How could I *not* know such a public menace, such a bigmouth,
  Fancy-hairdoed, perfumed lecher?!

PALAESTRIO: Hmm—does he know
  you?   910

ACROTELEUTIUM: He never saw me, so how could he?

PALAESTRIO: Ah, that's
  lovely talk.
  I'm sure the action will be lovelier.

ACROTELEUTIUM: Now just relax—
  Leave him to me. If I don't make a fancy fool of him,
  Then put the blame on me completely.

PALAESTRIO: Fine, now go inside
  And concentrate completely on this project.

ACROTELEUTIUM: (*Going*)   Just relax.

PALAESTRIO: Periplectomenus, take them inside. I'm for the
  forum.
  I'll find my man, I'll offer him this ring, and I'll insist
  That it was given to me by "your wife," who's dying for him.
  (*Pointing to* MILPHIDIPPA)
  As soon as we get back from the forum, send her out,
  Pretending she was sent to him in secret.

PERIPLECTOMENUS: Fine—relax.   920

PALAESTRIO: Just keep on the alert. I'll bring him here already
  stuffed.

(PALAESTRIO *rushes out toward the forum*)

PERIPLECTOMENUS: Now walk and talk successfully! Oh, if we
    work this out,
And if my guest gets back the soldier's concubine today,
I'll send you such a gift—

ACROTELEUTIUM: (*Casually*) Say—is the girl cooperating?

PERIPLECTOMENUS: Absolutissimo, bellissimo.

ACROTELEUTIUM: (*Facetiously*)   Swellissimo.
    When all our roguery is pooled together, I'm convinced,
    We'll never meet defeat by any trickier deceit.

PERIPLECTOMENUS: Let's go inside and then rehearse our parts
    with care.
We all must follow our instructions nicely and precisely,
So when the soldier comes, there'll be no blunders.

ACROTELEUTIUM: You're
    the slow one.   930

(PERIPLECTOMENUS *leads the two women into his house. The stage is
empty for a brief moment [musical interlude?], then enter* PYR-
GOPOLYNICES, *smiling with pleasure at his accomplishments of the
morning.* PALAESTRIO *follows at his heels, trying to get his master's
attention.*)

PYRGOPOLYNICES: (*Smiling smugly*)
    What a pleasure when affairs go well—exactly as you planned
        them.
    I've already sent a parasite of mine to King Seleucus,
    Leading mercenaries I conscripted for His Majesty.
    While they guard his kingdom, I shall have a little relaxation.

PALAESTRIO: Come now. Think of your affairs, not King
    Seleucus's. Why, look, a
Promising new venture has been proposed to me as go-
    between.

PYRGOPOLYNICES: (*Condescendingly*) Well, I'll put the other
　　things aside and give you my attention.
　Speak—I now surrender both my ears to you and to this
　　venture.

PALAESTRIO: (*Suspiciously*) Reconnoiter first—is there a snare to
　　catch our conversation?
　I'm commanded to pursue this business with all secrecy.　　940

(PYRGOPOLYNICES *"scouts" the area, then whispers to* PALAESTRIO)

PYRGOPOLYNICES: No one.

PALAESTRIO: (*Gives the ring*) Take this—it's the first deposit on a
　　love account.

PYRGOPOLYNICES: What's this? Where'd you get it?

PALAESTRIO: 　　From a
　　lovely and a lively lady
　Who adores you and who longs to have your handsome
　　handsomeness.
　She has had her maid give me this ring to forward on to you.

PYRGOPOLYNICES: But who is she—is she freeborn or some
　　manumitted slave?

PALAESTRIO: Feh! How could I dare negotiate for you with
　　freedwomen—
　You're already swamped with offers from the well-born girls
　　who want you!

(PYRGOPOLYNICES *smiles and continues his questions*)

PYRGOPOLYNICES: Wife or widow?

PALAESTRIO: Wife *and* widow.

PYRGOPOLYNICES: Tell me
    how a woman can be
    Both a wife and widow?

PALAESTRIO: Easy: she is young, her husband's old!

PYRGOPOLYNICES: Goody!

PALAESTRIO: She's delectable and dignified.

PYRGOPOLYNICES: Tell
    me no lies—   950

PALAESTRIO: She alone could be compared to *you* in beauty.

PYRGOPOLYNICES: Oh,
    how gorgeous!
    Who is she?

PALAESTRIO: The wife of old Periplectomenus, next door.
    How she's dying for you, longing to escape—she hates the old
       boy.
    I've been asked to beg you—to beseech you—let her have a
       chance to
    Give herself completely.

PYRGOPOLYNICES: Hercules, why not? If she is willing—

PALAESTRIO: Willing? *Thrilling!*

PYRGOPOLYNICES: (*Suddenly remembering*) Say—what shall we
    do about the girl at home?

PALAESTRIO: Let her go—wherever she would like to. *And it just
    so happens*
    Her twin sister and her mother have arrived to fetch the girl.

PYRGOPOLYNICES: What—her mother's come to Ephesus?

PALAESTRIO: Those
   who saw so say so.

PYRGOPOLYNICES: Hercules—the perfect chance for me to kick
   the woman out!   960

PALAESTRIO: Yes, but you should do it in the "perfect" way.

PYRGOPOLYNICES: All
   right, what's your advice?

PALAESTRIO: Don't you want to have her hurry from your house
   with no hard feelings?

PYRGOPOLYNICES: Yes yes yes.

PALAESTRIO: Here's what to do: you're rich
   enough, so let the girl have
All the gold and all the jewels and all the things you dressed
   her up with.
Better not upset her; let her take the stuff where she would
   like.

PYRGOPOLYNICES: That sounds good. But watch out when I let
   her go this other woman
Doesn't change her mind!

PALAESTRIO: Oh, feh! Don't be absurd—the girl
   adores you!

PYRGOPOLYNICES: (*Preening*) Venus loves me!

PALAESTRIO: Quiet now—the
   door is open—hide yourself.
   (MILPHIDIPPA *enters from the old man's house*)
That one coming out is Madam's clipper ship, the go-between
   who
Brought the ring that I just gave to you.

PYRGOPOLYNICES: By Pollux, she's not
    bad, not   970
Bad at all!

PALAESTRIO: A chimpanzee—a harpy set beside her mistress!
    Look at her there—hunting with her eyes and using ears as
      traps.

MILPHIDIPPA (*To the audience*) There's the circus where I must
    perform my little act right now.
    I'll pretend that I don't see them—I won't even know they're
      there.

PYRGOPOLYNICES: (*Whispering to* PALAESTRIO)
    Shh . . . let's listen in to see if there's a mention made of *me*.

MILPHIDIPPA: Are there men about who care for others' business,
    not their own,
    Idlers who don't earn their supper, who might spy on what I'm
      doing?
    I'm afraid of men like these, lest they obstruct me or delay
      me—
    If they come while Mistress crosses over—burning for *his* body.
    How she loves that man—too beautiful, too too magnificent,
      the   980
    Soldier Pyrgopolynices.

PYRGOPOLYNICES: (*Aside*) This one's mad about me too!
    She just praised my looks.

PALAESTRIO: By Pollux, her speech needs no
    further rubbing.

PYRGOPOLYNICES: How is that?

PALAESTRIO: Because her words are bright enough—already
    polished.
  And why not? She speaks of you—she has a shining subject,
    too!

PYRGOPOLYNICES: Say, her mistress surely is a gorgeously
    attractive woman.
  Hercules, I'm getting sort of warm for her already, boy.

PALAESTRIO: Even when you haven't seen her yet?

PYRGOPOLYNICES: (*Ogling* MILPHIDIPPA)   I take your
    word for it.
  Meanwhile, "clipper ship" here whets my appetite for love.

PALAESTRIO: No,
    you don't, by Hercules!
  Don't you fall in love with her—that girl's engaged to *me*. If you
    should
  Wed the mistress, *she* becomes my bride at once.

PYRGOPOLYNICES: (*Impatiently*)   Then speak
    to her.   990

PALAESTRIO: All right, follow me.

PYRGOPOLYNICES: I'll be your follower.

(*They approach* MILPHIDIPPA, *who still pretends not to see them.
She gets even more melodramatic.*)

MILPHIDIPPA: Would I
    could find him—
  Find the man I've left the house to meet. O heaven, grant me
    this!

PALAESTRIO: All you dreamed will appear, you can be of good
      cheer—there is certainly no cause for fearing,
   For the person that's speaking knows just who you're
      seeking—

MILPHIDIPPA: My goodness—who is this I'm hearing?

PALAESTRIO: Of your council a sharer—and also a bearer of
      counsel, should you be confiding it.

MILPHIDIPPA: Oh no! Heaven forbid! What I'm hiding's not
      hid!

PALAESTRIO: Well, you may or may not still be hiding it.

MILPHIDIPPA: Tell me how that can be.

PALAESTRIO: It's not hidden from me—
      but I'm trusty, a tacit and mum one.

MILPHIDIPPA: Can you give me a sign that you know our
      design?

PALAESTRIO: Let us say that a woman loves someone.

MILPHIDIPPA: There are hundreds who do—

PALAESTRIO: Ah, but ever so few
      send a gift given straight from their finger.

MILPHIDIPPA: Ah, now I understand I've the lay of the land
      now—and no more uncertainties linger.   1000
   Are there spies hereabouts?

PALAESTRIO: (*Pointing to the soldier*) We're both with and
without.

(MILPHIDIPPA *motions* PALAESTRIO *to one side*)

MILPHIDIPPA: I must see you alone, so I beckoned.

PALAESTRIO: Well, for many or few words?

MILPHIDIPPA: I only want two words.

PALAESTRIO: (*To the soldier*) I'll be back with you in a second.

PYRGOPOLYNICES: What of me—hey, explain—must I stand here
in vain, looking fiery, fierce . . . fascinating?

PALAESTRIO: Yes, sir, stand there in view—I'm just working for
you.

PYRGOPOLYNICES: (*In great heat*) But I'm wasting away with this
waiting!

PALAESTRIO: But it's best to go slow, for I'm sure you well know of
the kind of low mind that her stock has.

PYRGOPOLYNICES: Yes yes yes—on with your quest—do what you
think best.

PALAESTRIO: (*Aside to* MILPHIDIPPA)
This man has no more brains than a rock has!
Now I'm back here with you—ask me.

MILPHIDIPPA: What shall I do?
What's your method for storming our Troy here?
Can you give me a plan?

PALAESTRIO: Just pretend if you can, that you're
    dying with love—

MILPHIDIPPA: (*Nodding*) For our boy here!

PALAESTRIO: Don't forget when you speak, praise his face and
    physique—and his courage in every endeavor.   1010

MILPHIDIPPA: Now you don't have to harp, I've got everything
    sharp. As I showed you before, I'm quite clever.

PALAESTRIO: In respect to the rest, you resolve what is best—
    hunt a hint in whatever I'm saying.

PYRGOPOLYNICES: (*Chafing at the bit*)
    Well, I wish we would start and you'd tell me my part in all
    this—come back here—you're delaying!

(PALAESTRIO *scampers back to the soldier's side*)

PALAESTRIO: Here I am. Don't be nervous; I'm back at your
    service—

PYRGOPOLYNICES: Tell me what she has said—

PALAESTRIO: It's her mistress—
    Why, the poor dear's been sighing and crying—near dying—in
    short, she's in terrible distress.
    For she's crazy about you and can't live without you, so she sent
    out her maid on this mission.

PYRGOPOLYNICES: Let her come—

PALAESTRIO: Why so pliant? Do act more
    defiant, disdainful of this proposition.
    Shout—why did I annoy you, debase, hoi-polloi you?—pretend
    that this whole affair piques you.

PYRGOPOLYNICES: Say, there is something to that; I'll certainly do
    that.

PALAESTRIO: (*Aloud*) Shall I call this woman who seeks you?

PYRGOPOLYNICES: Let her come if she wants something.

PALAESTRIO: Come if
    you want something, woman.   1020

MILPHIDIPPA: (*Hurling herself at the soldier's feet*)
                    O beauty so beaming!

PYRGOPOLYNICES: What a clever young dame—she remembers
    my name.
  (*To* MILPHIDIPPA)
          May the gods grant whatever you're dreaming—

MILPHIDIPPA: Why, to live out this life as your own wedded
    wife.

PYRGOPOLYNICES: That's too much!

MILPHIDIPPA: Oh, it's not *my* desire—
    It's for Mistress I woo—she's just dying for you.

PYRGOPOLYNICES: My dear girl,
    there are thousands on fire.
    And there just isn't time—

MILPHIDIPPA: Oh, by Pollux, sir, I'm quite aware
    that you've so high a rating.
    You're a man so attractive, in action so active—and "fiery,
      fierce . . . fascinating."
    (*Aloud to* PALAESTRIO)
    And there could be no one more godlike than he—

PALAESTRIO: He's *not*
   human—you're right, no debating.
   (*Aside*)
   Why, it couldn't be plainer—a vulture's humaner than he is.

PYRGOPOLYNICES: (*Not hearing this*)
   I'll act more imposing. I must put on a show since she's praising
   me so—

PALAESTRIO: (*Aside to* MILPHIDIPPA)
            What an ass—will you look at him posing!
   (*Aloud, to the soldier*)
   Will you deign a reply to her mistress's cry? You remember, I
   spoke a while back of it.

PYRGOPOLYNICES: I don't quite understand—from *which one*?
   The demand is so great that I cannot keep track of it.   1030

MILPHIDIPPA: Well, she took from her hand something grand,
   something handsome, to hand you in elegant fashion.
   Look—you're wearing the ring I was bidden to bring—from a
   woman who's burning with passion.

PYRGOPOLYNICES: All right, what's her request—speak out,
   woman, I'm pressed.

MILPHIDIPPA: How she wants you—oh, please don't reject her!
   She lives only for you—who knows what she may do—she's
   near death—but *you* could resurrect her!

PYRGOPOLYNICES: What's her wish now?

MILPHIDIPPA: To touch you, to clasp
   you, to clutch you—she cries for complete consummation.
   And unless you relieve her, I truly believe her to be very near
   desperation.
   O Achilles so fair, won't you answer my prayer—save this
   pretty one all the world pities.

Oh, produce something kind from your merciful mind—noble
    king-killer, sacker of cities!

PYRGOPOLYNICES: Ah, these girls who adore me do nothing
    but bore me.   1040
(*To* PALAESTRIO)
You shouldn't be letting me near all this.
Do you think it's your job—giving me to the mob?

PALAESTRIO: (*To* MILPHIDIPPA)   Hey there,
    woman, I hope that you hear all this!
Look, I've told you before—must I tell you once more? This
    great stud always must be rewarded.
He can't give out his seed to just any old breed—it's too
    valuable not to be hoarded!

MILPHIDIPPA: Let him make his demand; we have cash here on
    hand.

PALAESTRIO: Well . . . one talent—not silver, but golden.
    And he never takes less—

MILPHIDIPPA: By the gods, I confess that he's
    cheap at that price; we're beholden!

PYRGOPOLYNICES: Oh, I'm not one for greed, I've got all that I
    need. To be frank, I've got wealth beyond measure:
Golden coins by the score—by the thousands and more—

PALAESTRIO: Not
    to mention a storehouse of treasure!
Silver, too, not in pounds, no, not even in mounds, but in
    mountains, like Aetna—or higher.

MILPHIDIPPA: (*Aside*) Oh, ye gods, how he's lying!

PALAESTRIO: (*Aside to her*)   And how I'm
    supplying him fuel—   1050

MILPHIDIPPA: And I'm stoking the fire!
  But do hurry, I pray, send me back right away.

PALAESTRIO: (*Aloud*)   Will you deign,
    sir, to give her an answer?
  Say you do or you don't, say you will or you won't—

MILPHIDIPPA: Save a
    suffering wretch while you can, sir!
  Why torment her so long? She has done you no wrong.

PYRGOPOLYNICES: (*Magnanimously*) Have her come back to me
    for a viewing.
  You may say that I'm willing; I'll soon be fulfilling her dreams—

MILPHIDIPPA: (*Excitedly*) Just as you should be doing!
  Being very astute you will do what is mutual—

PALAESTRIO: (*Waving her off*)   Experts need
    no further cuing.

MILPHIDIPPA: You're so kind to be heeding my passionate
    pleading, and letting me speak to your soul myself!
  (*Aside to* PALAESTRIO)
  Well, speak up—how's my act?

PALAESTRIO: (*Aside to* MILPHIDIPPA) As a matter of fact, I have
  all I can do to control myself!

MILPHIDIPPA: That's why I turned aside. I was trying to
  hide—

(*She breaks into giggles*)   1060

PYRGOPOLYNICES: (*Completely involved in self-praise*)
  Do you know this occasion is stellar?
  Do you know the great honor I lavish upon her?

MILPHIDIPPA: I know, and I'll
    certainly tell her.

PALAESTRIO: The demand is so great I could ask for his weight in
    pure gold—

MILPHIDIPPA: By the gods, you'd receive it!

PALAESTRIO: And the women he lies with he fecundifies with real
    heroes—and would you believe it—
    The children he rears live for eight hundred years—

MILPHIDIPPA: (*Aside*)   Oh please
    stop it, you joker—I'm crying!

PYRGOPOLYNICES: My dear boy, there are many who live a
    millennium—from age to age without dying!

PALAESTRIO: Oh, I knew it but hid it—and I underdid it so she
    wouldn't think I was lying.

MILPHIDIPPA: Oh, I'm simply aghast—why, how long will *he*
    last—if his sons are of such great duration?

PYRGOPOLYNICES: Jove was born of the Earth just preceding my
    birth—I was born one day after Creation.

PALAESTRIO: And what is more—had he been born before, *he*
    would be in the heavens now, reigning!

MILPHIDIPPA: (*Aside to* PALAESTRIO)
    Please—one more and I'll crack! By the gods, send me back—
    let me go with some breath still remaining.   1070

PALAESTRIO: (*Aloud*) Don't stand lazily by—go—you've got your
    reply.

MILPHIDIPPA: Yes—I'll go and I'll bring back Madam now.
How her spirits will soar!
(*To* PYRGOPOLYNICES)

Do you want something more?

PYRGOPOLYNICES: To be
no handsomer than I am now.
It is so aggravating to be devastatingly handsome. . . .

PALAESTRIO: Go on,
girl!

MILPHIDIPPA: I'm going.

PALAESTRIO: Now remember. Be smart—use your head and your
heart.
Have *her* heart fairly dance, have her glowing!
(*Aside to* MILPHIDIPPA)
And if our girl's in there, have her cross and prepare—say the
soldier's returned to his station.

MILPHIDIPPA: She's with Mistress inside; they found someplace to
hide where they took in our whole conversation.

PALAESTRIO: That was smart—what they're hearing will help
them in steering their own course with good navigation.

MILPHIDIPPA: Come—you're holding me back—

PALAESTRIO: I'm not holding
you actually, nor am I—
(*Gives a knowing glance*)
no further mention now.

(MILPHIDIPPA *exits*)

PYRGOPOLYNICES: Have your mistress make haste, I have no time
  to waste. I shall give this my foremost attention now.
  (*Paces back and forth, deep in thought, then turns to* PALAES-
    TRIO)
  Palaestrio, you're my adviser, what about   1080
  My concubine? For clearly it's impossible
  To ask the new one in before the other's out!

PALAESTRIO: Why ask me for advice on what to do? I've told
    you
  How to do it gently—with the most compassion:
  Let her keep the jewels and fancy clothes you gave her.
  Tell her to prepare 'em, wear 'em, bear 'em off.
  Say the time is ripe for her to go back home—
  Her mother's here with her twin sister—say that too.
  It's fitting she go home accompanied by them.

PYRGOPOLYNICES: (*Worried*) How do you *know* they're
    here?

PALAESTRIO: Why, with these very eyes   1090
  I saw our lady's twin.

PYRGOPOLYNICES: And have the sisters met?

PALAESTRIO: Yes.

PYRGOPOLYNICES: (*Lecherously*) How's the twin—good-
    looking?

PALAESTRIO: Sir! You want
  To grab at everything!

PYRGOPOLYNICES: (*Lecherously*) Where did you say the mother
    was?

PALAESTRIO: Aboard the ship, in bed with swollen and infected
    eyes.
    The skipper told me—that's the man who brought 'em here.
    He happens to be staying as our neighbor's guest.

PYRGOPOLYNICES: How's *he*—is he good-looking?

PALAESTRIO: Cut it out!
    Indeed—
    You really have been quite the model stud—
    Pursuing both the sexes—male and female!
    Enough of this!

PYRGOPOLYNICES: (*A bit cowed, changing the subject*)
                Now this advice you've given me—   1100
    I would prefer your speaking to her of the matter.
    You seem to get on well with her in conversation.

PALAESTRIO: What better than to go yourself; it's your affair.
    Just say that it's imperative you take a wife.
    Say your relations tell you and your friends compel you.

PYRGOPOLYNICES: You think so?

PALAESTRIO: Would I tell you what I didn't
    think?

PYRGOPOLYNICES: I'll go inside. Meanwhile, you stay before the
    house
    And guard. As soon as *she* appears, you call me out.

PALAESTRIO: (*Confidently*) Just do your own part well.

PYRGOPOLYNICES: Consider it
    as done!
    If she's unwilling, then I'll kick her out by force!   1110

PALAESTRIO: Oh, do be careful. It's much better that she leave
   With no hard feelings. So just give her what I told you—
   The gold, the jewels, and all the stuff you dressed her up with.

PYRGOPOLYNICES: Ye gods, I hope she'll go!

PALAESTRIO: I think that you'll
      succeed.
   But go inside—don't wait.

PYRGOPOLYNICES: I'll follow your advice.

(PYRGOPOLYNICES *dashes into his house.* PALAESTRIO *smiles
broadly as he watches his master, then turns to the audience.*)

PALAESTRIO: Well, folks, did I exaggerate a while ago
   In what I said about this concupiscent captain?
   Now I need Acroteleutium, or else
   That little maid of hers, or Pleusicles. By Jupiter!
   My luck is coming through for me at every turn!   1120
   For just the ones I wanted most of all to see,
   I see—coming together from the house next door!

(*Enter* ACROTELEUTIUM *from the old man's house, leading* MIL-
PHIDIPPA *and* PLEUSICLES)

ACROTELEUTIUM: (*To the others*) Follow me and look around to
   see there's no one spying on us.

MILPHIDIPPA: I see no one here—except the man we want to
   see.

PALAESTRIO: Well met!

MILPHIDIPPA: How're you doing, architect?

PALAESTRIO: Feh, I'm no
      architect.

MILPHIDIPPA: What's that?

PALAESTRIO: Why, compared to you, my talent couldn't bang two
  boards together.

MILPHIDIPPA: Come now, don't exaggerate—

PALAESTRIO: (*Smiling*)   Why, you're a filly
  full of felony!
And you polished off the soldier charmingly.

MILPHIDIPPA: We haven't
  finished.

PALAESTRIO: Smile a little; this affair is well in hand—at least
  for now.
  Simply keep on giving helpful help as you have done so
    far.   1130
  Soldier boy is there inside, beseeching her to go away:
  "Please go back to Athens with your mother and your
    sister!"

PLEUSICLES: Great!

PALAESTRIO: And he gave her all the gold, the jewels, the stuff he
  dressed her up with
  As a gift—to go away. He's following the plan I gave him!

PLEUSICLES: It looks easy: he is all insistence—she gives no
  resistance.

PALAESTRIO: Don't you know that when you're climbing upward
  in a well that's deep,
  You're in greatest danger of a fall when nearest to the top?
  We have almost drawn this from the well, but if he gets
    suspicious,

We'll get nothing out of him—so now's the time to be our
    sharpest.
We have raw materials aplenty for the job, that's clear.   1140
Three girls,
(*To* PLEUSICLES)
                you're a fourth, and I'm a fifth—the old man is
    a sixth.
We six have a large reserve of rogueries to draw upon.
Name a city—we could storm and conquer it with all our
    tricks.
Pay attention now—

ACROTELEUTIUM: That's why we've come—to find out what
    you want.

PALAESTRIO: Nice of you to say. Now I'll command you in your
    line of duty.

ACROTELEUTIUM: You'll command commendably. I'll do my best
    for your request.

PALAESTRIO: Lightly . . . brightly . . . and in spritely fashion—
    fool the soldier boy.
I command it.

ACROTELEUTIUM: Your command's a pleasure.

PALAESTRIO: You've got the way?

ACROTELEUTIUM: I pretend I'm torn apart for love of . . . him,
    that I've divorced my present husband,
Since I'm burning so to marry . . . him.

PALAESTRIO: (*Smiling*)   It's all in order now.   1150
One more thing—this house is *yours*—since it was in your
    dowry. Say the
Old man has gone off already, since the separation's final.
We don't want our man afraid to enter someone else's house.

ACROTELEUTIUM: Well advised.

PALAESTRIO: When he comes out, be
    hesitant—don't come too close.
  Act as if you're too ashamed to place your beauty near his own.
  Be in awe of all his riches; lavish praise upon his looks, his
  Splendid face and figure, charm, his personality, et cetera.
  Have you been rehearsed enough?

ACROTELEUTIUM: Of course. Won't it be quite
    enough to
  Render you a polished piece of work? I know you'll find it
    flawless.

PALAESTRIO: Fine.
  (*To* PLEUSICLES)
                    It's your turn now to be commanded in your
    line of duty.
  When what we've discussed is done, and she goes in—you
    come at once.   1160
  Get yourself disguised the way the skipper of a ship would
    dress:
  Have a wide-brimmed hat—rust-brown—and on your eye a
    woolen patch.
  Also have a rust-brown cloak—since that's the color sailors
    wear.
  Fasten it to your left shoulder; tie it round with one arm bare.
  One way or another, you must seem the master of a ship.
  All these clothes are there inside—the old man owns some
    fishing boats.

(PLEUSICLES *nods, having taken great pains to memorize all this*)

PLEUSICLES: Well, when I am here . . . all dressed up like you
    just described . . . what then?

PALAESTRIO: Come here—and pretend you're fetching
     Philocomasium for her mother.
   Say that if she's going to Athens she must hurry to the harbor.
   Also have them carry all the things she wants to take on
        board.   1170
   (*Affecting an old-salt accent*)
   If she doesn't come, you'll cast off anyway—the wind is fair.

PLEUSICLES: Pretty picture—please proceed.

PALAESTRIO: Then right away
        he'll urge the girl to
   Hasten, hurry—don't keep Mother waiting.

PLEUSICLES: (*Admiringly to the others*)   He's poly-
        perceptive!

PALAESTRIO: I'll have her request my aid in taking luggage to the
        harbor.
   He'll command me to escort her. When I'm there, be sure of
        this—
   Straightaway I'll be away, straight . . . back to Athens.

PLEUSICLES: When
        you're there,
   You won't be a slave for three days longer. I'll release you.

PALAESTRIO: Quickly now, and dress yourself.

PLEUSICLES: There's
        nothing else?

PALAESTRIO: Just don't forget.

PLEUSICLES: I'll be going . . . .

(*He goes*)

PALAESTRIO: (*To the women*) You two hurry in as well, since any
     minute
He'll be coming out again, I know.

ACROTELEUTIUM: (*Taking leave*)   Your wish is our
     command.   1180

PALAESTRIO: Everybody go—retreat!
(*Turns*)
                              And just in time—our door is open!
(*To the audience*)
Here he comes—so chipper—he's "succeeded"! Fool—he
     gapes at nothing!

(PYRGOPOLYNICES *bursts out, overjoyed with himself*)

PYRGOPOLYNICES: I've succeeded! I got what I wanted as I
     wanted it—
Sweetly and completely she agreed.

PALAESTRIO: What took so long in there?

PYRGOPOLYNICES: Never was I loved as madly as that little
     woman loves me.

PALAESTRIO: Oh?

PYRGOPOLYNICES: I needed countless words; she was the
     toughest nut to crack.
Finally, I triumphed. Did I give her gifts! I gave her
Everything that she demanded.
(*Sheepishly*)
                              I even had to give her . . . you.

PALAESTRIO: (*Mock shock*) Even me! How could I live away from
     you?

PYRGOPOLYNICES: Stiff upper lip.
   I would like to have you back, and yet there was no other
      way. I   1190
   Couldn't get the girl to go without you—I tried everything, she
   Overwhelmed me.

PALAESTRIO: (*Dramatically*) Well, I trust the gods—and you, of
      course. I know that
   After this, though 'twill be bitter, parted from the best of
      masters,
   This at least will comfort me: that your surpassing beauty will
      have—
   Through my humble efforts—won that lady. I will now arrange
      it.

PYRGOPOLYNICES: Ah, what need of words. If you succeed, you'll
      be a free man—
   And a rich man.

PALAESTRIO: I'll succeed.

PYRGOPOLYNICES: (*Impatiently*) I'm bursting—hurry!

PALAESTRIO: Self-control!
   Take it easy, don't be so . . . hot-blooded. Wait—she's coming
      out.

(PALAESTRIO *pulls the soldier aside, as* MILPHIDIPPA *leads* ACRO-
TELEUTIUM *from the old man's house*)

MILPHIDIPPA: (*Aside to* ACROTELEUTIUM)
   Oh, Mistress, there's the soldier.

ACROTELEUTIUM: Where?

MILPHIDIPPA: Right to your left.

ACROTELEUTIUM: I see.

MILPHIDIPPA: Take just a hasty glance so he won't know we're
    looking at him.   1200

ACROTELEUTIUM: All right, by Pollux, now's the time for bad girls
    to be worse girls.

MILPHIDIPPA: You take the lead.

ACROTELEUTIUM: (*Melodramatically*) Please tell me—did you see
    the man in person?
    (*Aside*)
    Don't speak too softly—let 'im hear.

MILPHIDIPPA: (*Proudly*)   I spoke to him myself,
    Quite calmly, easily—and just as long as I desired.

PYRGOPOLYNICES: You hear?

PALAESTRIO: I hear. She's overjoyed just to have
    talked to you.

ACROTELEUTIUM: Oh, what a lucky woman!

PYRGOPOLYNICES: How they love me.

PALAESTRIO: You
    deserve it.

ACROTELEUTIUM: What a miracle—you got to him and begged
    him to submission.
    I heard one needed letters, or a page—like for a king.

MILPHIDIPPA: Indeed, it took a bit of effort getting through to
    him.

PALAESTRIO: You're legendary, sir.

PYRGOPOLYNICES: I bear it—it's the will of Venus.

ACROTELEUTIUM: (*Picking up a cue*)
I give my thanks to Venus and I beg her and beseech   1210
That I may be successful with the one I love and long for.
May he be kind to me and not deny me my desire.

MILPHIDIPPA: I hope so too. And yet so many women long for
    him.
He spurns them all, despises them—except for you alone.

ACROTELEUTIUM: I'm terribly tormented, since he's so
    discriminating,
That, seeing me, his eyes will make him change his mind.
Why, his own splendidness will spurn with speed my plain
    appearance.

MILPHIDIPPA: He won't. Be of good cheer.

PYRGOPOLYNICES: (*Taken—and taken in*)
                                       How she disparages
    herself.

ACROTELEUTIUM: I'm frightened you exaggerated my good looks
    to him.

MILPHIDIPPA: Oh, I was careful—you'll be prettier than I
    described.   1220

ACROTELEUTIUM: If he won't take me for his wife, then I'll
    embrace his knees
And I'll implore him. Otherwise, if I can't win him over,
I am resolved to die. I know I cannot live without him.

(PYRGOPOLYNICES *starts toward her with open arms*)

PYRGOPOLYNICES: I must prevent that woman's death. I'll
    go—

PALAESTRIO: (*Restraining him*) Oh, not at all!
   You're cheapening yourself to give yourself so liberally.
   Do let her come unbidden, sir: to yearn, to burn, to wait her
      turn.
   Now, do you want to lose your reputation? Don't do that!
   No man was *ever* loved by woman thus—except for two:
   Yourself and Phaon, Sappho's lover on the Isle of Lesbos.

ACROTELEUTIUM: Dear Milphidippa, call him out—or I'll go
   in myself!   1230

MILPHIDIPPA: Let's wait at least till someone else comes out.

ACROTELEUTIUM: But I
      can't wait—
   I'm going in!

MILPHIDIPPA: The doors are locked.

ACROTELEUTIUM: I'll break 'em.

MILPHIDIPPA: (*Rushing to the soldier's door*)   You're insane!

ACROTELEUTIUM: But if he's ever loved, or if his wisdom match
      his beauty,
   Then he'll forgive whatever I may do because of love.

PALAESTRIO: (*To the soldier*) The poor girl's burning up for love
   of you.

PYRGOPOLYNICES: (*Trembling*) It's mutual!

PALAESTRIO: (*Hushing him*) Don't let her hear!

MILPHIDIPPA: You're standing
      stupefied—why don't you knock?

ACROTELEUTIUM: The man I love is not inside.

MILPHIDIPPA: How do
  you know?

ACROTELEUTIUM: I smell.
  My nose would sense it if he were inside.

PALAESTRIO: A prophetess!

PYRGOPOLYNICES: She loves me; therefore Venus gave her powers
  of prophecy.

ACROTELEUTIUM: He's near—somewhere—the man I long to
  see. I smell him!   1240

PYRGOPOLYNICES: She sees more with her nose than with her
  eyes.

PALAESTRIO: She's blind with love.

(ACROTELEUTIUM *begins an elaborate fainting act*)

ACROTELEUTIUM: Oh, hold me!

MILPHIDIPPA: Why?

ACROTELEUTIUM: I'm falling!

MILPHIDIPPA: Why?

ACROTELEUTIUM: Because I
  can't stand up!
  My soul's retreating through my eyes—

MILPHIDIPPA: By Pollux, then you've
   seen
The soldier!

ACROTELEUTIUM: Yes!

MILPHIDIPPA: I don't see—where?

ACROTELEUTIUM: You'd see him if you
   loved him!

MILPHIDIPPA: What's that? Why, if you'd let me, I would love him
   more than you do!

PALAESTRIO: It's obvious that every woman loves you at first
   sight.

PYRGOPOLYNICES: (*Confidentially*) I don't know if I told you, but
   my grandmother was . . . Venus.

ACROTELEUTIUM: Dear Milphidippa, please go up to him.

PYRGOPOLYNICES: (*Preening*)   How she
   reveres me!

PALAESTRIO: Well, here she comes.

MILPHIDIPPA: I want you—

PYRGOPOLYNICES: (*Aside*)   I want *you*!

MILPHIDIPPA: As you
   commanded,
   I've brought my mistress out.

PYRGOPOLYNICES: I see.

MILPHIDIPPA: Well, tell her to
    approach.   1250

PYRGOPOLYNICES: Your pleas have forced me not to hate her as I
    do the others.

(PYRGOPOLYNICES *starts toward* ACROTELEUTIUM, *but* MILPHIDIP-
PA *suddenly blocks his way*)

MILPHIDIPPA: If she approaches nearer you—she couldn't speak a
    word.
    For when she simply looks at you, her eyes cut off her tongue.

PYRGOPOLYNICES: I'll cure milady's malady.

MILPHIDIPPA: Oh, how she shaked
    and quaked
    When she beheld you.

PYRGOPOLYNICES: Mighty men in armor do the same—
    I do not wonder that a woman does. What does she want?

MILPHIDIPPA: She wants to live a lifetime with you, so—come to
    her house.

PYRGOPOLYNICES: (*Hesitantly*) I—to her house? She's married—
    why—her husband—he might catch me!

MILPHIDIPPA: But, sir, for love of you, she's thrown her husband
    out.

PYRGOPOLYNICES: How could she?

MILPHIDIPPA: (*Smiling*) This house was in her dowry.

PYRGOPOLYNICES: Yes?

MILPHIDIPPA: Yes, sir.

PYRGOPOLYNICES: Then take her home—   1260
   I'll be there in a second.

MILPHIDIPPA: Please don't keep her waiting long—
   Don't break her heart.

PYRGOPOLYNICES: I won't—of course. Be off!

MILPHIDIPPA: We're off.

(MILPHIDIPPA *helps her "fainting" mistress back into the old man's*
house)

PYRGOPOLYNICES: (*Looking offstage*) What do I see?

PALAESTRIO: What do
   you see?

PYRGOPOLYNICES: Someone's approaching, dressed
   In sailor's clothes.

PALAESTRIO: He's heading for our house—it's clear he
   wants you.
   Why, that's the skipper—

PYRGOPOLYNICES: Come to fetch the girl,
   no doubt.

PALAESTRIO: No doubt.

(*Enter* PLEUSICLES, *looking very uncomfortable in his elaborate*
sailor's costume. Among other items of apparel, he has a large patch
over his left eye.)

PLEUSICLES: If I were not aware how many others have
    Done awful things because of love, I'd be afraid
    To march around dressed up like this to win my love.
    Yet, since I know of many others who committed things
    Both shady and dishonest for the sake of love . . .   1270
    Why mention how Achilles let his Greeks be killed? . . .
    But there's Palaestrio—he's standing with the soldier.
    I'd better change my language to a different style.
    (*Affecting the accent* PALAESTRIO *demonstrated earlier*)
    Why, woman's born the daughter of Delay herself.
    For any other plain delay of equal length
    Seems less of a delay than waiting for a woman.
    I really do believe it's in their constitution.
    But now to fetch this girl Philocomasium.
    I'll knock. Hey—anybody home?

PALAESTRIO: (*Rushing up to him*)   Young man—what's up?
    What are you knocking for?

PLEUSICLES: I want Philocomasium.   1280
    Her mother sent me. If she's coming, let her come.
    The girl's delaying everyone—we're anxious to set sail.

(PYRGOPOLYNICES *dashes over nervously*)

PYRGOPOLYNICES: Oh, everything's all ready. Go, Palaestrio—
    Get helpers to transport her stuff onto the ship—
    The gold, the jewels, the clothes, and all the fancy things.
    The gifts I gave her are all packed. Now let her take them!

PALAESTRIO: I'm off.

PLEUSICLES: For heaven's sake be quick!

PYRGOPOLYNICES: (*Trying to placate him*)   He won't be long.
    But tell me, sir, what happened to that eye of yours?

PLEUSICLES: (*Pointing to his unbandaged eye*)
Why, this one's fine.

PYRGOPOLYNICES: I mean your left one.

PLEUSICLES: It's like this:
The *ocean* caused me to use this eye less. And yet   1290
Were it not for *dev*-otion, I could use it now.
But they're delaying me too long—

PYRGOPOLYNICES: Ah—here they come!

(PALAESTRIO *leads a tearful* PHILOCOMASIUM *out of the soldier's house*)

PALAESTRIO: Will there ever be an end to all this weeping?

PHILOCOMASIUM: (*Woefully*)   Can
    I help it?
I must leave this beautiful existence. . . .

PALAESTRIO: This man's come
    for you
From your mother and your sister.

PHILOCOMASIUM: Yes, I see.

PYRGOPOLYNICES: (*Impatiently*)   Palaestrio!

PALAESTRIO: Yes!

PYRGOPOLYNICES: Command that all the stuff I gave the girl be
    carried off!

PLEUSICLES: Greetings, Philocomasium.

PHILOCOMASIUM: The same to you.

PLEUSICLES: Mother
   and sister
Also bade me tell you . . . greetings.

PHILOCOMASIUM: Greetings to them both as
   well.

PLEUSICLES: (*Delivering his carefully memorized speech*)
   They beseech you . . . come ahead . . . the wind is
   fair . . . the sails are full.
If your mother's eyes were better, she'd have come along
   with me.   1300

PHILOCOMASIUM: Though I long to stay, one must obey one's
   mother.

PLEUSICLES: Very wise.

PYRGOPOLYNICES: (*Confidentially to* PLEUSICLES)
   If she hadn't lived with me, she'd be a half-wit to this day!

PHILOCOMASIUM: That's what pains me so—the separation from
   so great a man.
Why, with your abilities, you could . . . enrich . . . most
   anyone.

(*At this moment,* PALAESTRIO *appears from inside the soldier's
house, carrying a treasure chest*)

And because I used to be with you, I held my head up high.
Now . . . I have to lose that one distinction.

PYRGOPOLYNICES: Do not cry.

PHILOCOMASIUM: I must—
   When I look at you. . . .

PYRGOPOLYNICES: Stiff upper lip.

PHILOCOMASIUM: Oh, if you knew my
  feelings!

PALAESTRIO: I don't wonder, girl, that you lived happily with
    him, and that his
  Beauty's blaze, his noble gaze, his manly ways have held you
    rapt, for
  Even I—slave that I am—am brought to tears at leaving
    him.   1310

PHILOCOMASIUM: (*To the soldier*) May I hug you one more time
    before I go for good?

PYRGOPOLYNICES: You may.

(PYRGOPOLYNICES *readies himself for her embrace. She starts to-*
ward him with open arms, then staggers, wailing.)

PHILOCOMASIUM: Oh, my darling . . . oh, my soul . . .
    oh . . . .

(*She begins an elaborate faint.* PALAESTRIO *catches her "just in time"*
and hands her to PLEUSICLES.)

PALAESTRIO: Hold this woman please; she may do
    Damage to herself!

PYRGOPOLYNICES: What's going on?

PALAESTRIO: Because she has to leave
    you, the
  Poor girl's fainted dead away!

PYRGOPOLYNICES: Well, run inside and get some
    water!

PALAESTRIO: Never mind the water—she needs rest.
  (*The soldier starts toward her*)

                                                        No—

    don't come any closer!
  Please—let her recover.

(PYRGOPOLYNICES *eyes* PLEUSICLES *and* PHILOCOMASIUM *with suspicion*)

PYRGOPOLYNICES: Say—their heads are awfully close
    together!
  I don't like the looks of this. Hey, sailor—take your lips from hers!

PLEUSICLES: I just tried to see if she was breathing.

PYRGOPOLYNICES: Use your ear
    for that!

PLEUSICLES: If you'd like, I'll let her go—

PYRGOPOLYNICES: No no—hold on!

PALAESTRIO: (*Weeping*)   Oh,
    woe is me!

PYRGOPOLYNICES: (*Calling inside his house*)
  Men! Come out—bring forth her stuff—bring everything I
    gave the girl!   1320

(*Various lackeys enter with* PHILOCOMASIUM's *luggage and assorted gifts, as* PALAESTRIO *readies himself for an impassioned valedictory*)

PALAESTRIO: Ere I go . . . let me salute you once again . . . ye
    household gods.
  And to you, my male and female fellow slaves . . . hail and
    farewell.
  Please don't speak too badly of me 'mongst yourselves when I
    am gone.

PYRGOPOLYNICES: Come, Palaestrio, buck up!

PALAESTRIO: Alas, I cannot help
   but cry—
I must leave you.

PYRGOPOLYNICES: Take it like a man.

PALAESTRIO: Oh, if you knew my feelings!

(PHILOCOMASIUM *suddenly "regains consciousness"*)

PHILOCOMASIUM: What? Where am I? What's been going on.
   Who are you?
   (*Aside*)
               Hello, darling!

PLEUSICLES: Ah, you have revived,
   (*Aside*)
                      my darling.

PHILOCOMASIUM: Goodness! Who am I embracing?
Who's this man? I'm lost—I must have fainted.

PLEUSICLES: (*Aside*)   Never fear, my
   dearest.

(*She puts her head on* PLEUSICLES*'s chest*)

PYRGOPOLYNICES: What's all this?

PALAESTRIO: (*Trying to cover up*) It's nothing . . . nothing . . .
   just another fainting spell.
   Oh, I shiver and I quiver.
   (*To the lovers*)
             This is getting *far too public!*   1330

PYRGOPOLYNICES: What'd you say?

PALAESTRIO: Uh—carrying this stuff in
   public—through the city—
It might hurt your reputation.

PYRGOPOLYNICES: Well, it's mine to give and no one
   else's.
I don't care what others think. Now depart—the gods be with
   you.

PALAESTRIO: I was looking out for you.

PYRGOPOLYNICES: I know.

PALAESTRIO: Farewell.

PYRGOPOLYNICES: Farewell
   to you.

PALAESTRIO: (*Aside to* PLEUSICLES)
   Hurry, I'll be with you in a second.
   (*Aloud*)
                 Just two words with Master.
   (*He goes to the soldier*)
   Though you have thought other servants far more faithful than
      myself,
   Still and all, I'm very grateful to you, sir . . . for everything.
   And, if you'd seen fit to, I would rather have been slave to you
   Than a freedman, working for another.

PYRGOPOLYNICES: Come—stiff upper lip.

PALAESTRIO: (*Sudden burst of passion*)
   Fond farewell to following a fiery, ferocious fighter!   1340
   Now I'm flunky to a frilly female . . . fortitude forgot.

(*He breaks into sobs.* PYRGOPOLYNICES *pats him on the shoulder,
barely able to restrain his own tears.*)

PYRGOPOLYNICES: Good old fellow.

PALAESTRIO: Oh, I can't go on—I've lost
   my will to live!

PYRGOPOLYNICES: Go, go—follow them—no more
   delay.

PALAESTRIO: Farewell.

PYRGOPOLYNICES: Farewell to you.

(PALAESTRIO *turns to go, then whirls back toward the soldier*)

PALAESTRIO: Don't forget me, sir, for if perchance I should be
   freed someday,
   I will send you word. You won't forsake me?

PYRGOPOLYNICES: Ah, that's not my
   style.

PALAESTRIO: Always and forever think how faithful I have been to
   you.
   Then at last you'll know who's been a loyal slave and who has
   not.

PYRGOPOLYNICES: I'm aware. I've noticed often—never quite so
   much till now.

PALAESTRIO: Yes, today at last you'll know the kind of slave I
   really am.

(PALAESTRIO *turns and starts to walk slowly off*)

PYRGOPOLYNICES: I can hardly stop myself from keeping you—

PALAESTRIO: (*Frantically*) Oh, don't do that!   1350
  There'd be talk—they'd say you didn't keep your word—
    untrustworthy.
  They would say you had no faithful slaves at all—except for me.
  If I thought it could be done the proper way—why, I'd insist—
  But you simply can't—

PYRGOPOLYNICES: Be off then.

PALAESTRIO;   I shall bear whatever comes.

PYRGOPOLYNICES: So, farewell.

PALAESTRIO: I'd better hurry off.

PYRGOPOLYNICES: (*Impatiently*) All right—farewell already!

(PALAESTRIO *races offstage—with a broad smile*)

PYRGOPOLYNICES: (*Reflecting, to the audience*)
  Till today I always thought he was the very worst of slaves.
  Now I see he was devoted to me. When I think it over,
  I was foolish giving him away. But now I'll head inside,
  Now's the time for love! Wait—I perceive a sound—made by
    the door.

(A SLAVE BOY *enters from the old man's house*)

BOY: (*To those inside the house*)
  Stop coaching me, please. I remember what to do.   1360
  (*Getting melodramatic*)
  Wheresoever in the world he be, I'll find him.
  Yes, I'll track him down; I won't spare any effort.

PYRGOPOLYNICES: This one seeks me. I'll go up and meet the
  boy.

BOY: Aha, I'm looking for you. Hail, you gorgeous creature!
  O man of every hour, beyond all other men
  Beloved of two gods—

PYRGOPOLYNICES: Which two?

BOY: Venus and Mars.

PYRGOPOLYNICES: A clever boy.

BOY: She begs of you to go inside.
  She yearns, she burns, expectantly expecting you.
  Bring solace to the lovelorn, don't wait—go!

PYRGOPOLYNICES: (*Hungrily*)   I will!

(*He dashes full speed ahead into the old man's house*)

BOY: (*To the audience*) Well, now he's trapped himself, caught
    in his own devices.   1370
  The ambush is prepared: the old man's standing staunchly
  To attack this lecher who's so loud about his loveliness,
  Who thinks that every woman loves him at first sight,
  When really they detest him, men as well as women.
  Now I'll rejoin the uproar—there's a shout inside!

(*He runs back into the house. Sounds of a scuffle from within, then
enter* PERIPLECTOMENUS, *followed by his servants, who are carrying* PYRGOPOLYNICES. *Among them is* CARIO, *the cook, who has a
long, sharp knife.*)

PERIPLECTOMENUS: Bring 'im out! If he won't come, then pick
    him up and throw him out!
  Make a little seat for him—right in the midair. Tear him apart!

PYRGOPOLYNICES: Please—I beg—by Hercules!

PERIPLECTOMENUS: By Hercules, you
   beg in vain.
Cario, see to it that that knife of yours is sharp enough.

CARIO: Why, it's long been eager to remove this lecher's vital
   parts, 1380
And to hang 'em like a baby's string of beads—around his neck.

PYRGOPOLYNICES: Oh, I'm dead!

PERIPLECTOMENUS: Not yet—you speak too soon.

CARIO: (*Brandishing that knife*) Can I go at him now?

PERIPLECTOMENUS: First let him be pummeled by your clubs a
   little more.

CARIO: Much more!

(*The slaves pound* PYRGOPOLYNICES *much more*)

PERIPLECTOMENUS: So! You dared to make advances to another's
   wife—you pig!

PYRGOPOLYNICES: By the gods, she asked me first—she came
   to me!

PERIPLECTOMENUS: He lies—hit on.

PYRGOPOLYNICES: Wait a second—let me talk.

PERIPLECTOMENUS: (*To the slaves*) Why do you
   stop?

PYRGOPOLYNICES: Please—may I speak?

PERIPLECTOMENUS: Speak.

PYRGOPOLYNICES: The woman begged me—

PERIPLECTOMENUS: But you
    dared to go—hit him again!

PYRGOPOLYNICES: Stop—stop—stop—I'm pounded plenty.
    Please, I beg—

CARIO: When do I cut?

PERIPLECTOMENUS: At your own convenience. Spread 'im out and
    stretch 'im all the way.

PYRGOPOLYNICES: Please, by Hercules, I beg you, hear my
    words before he cuts!   1390

PERIPLECTOMENUS: Well?

PYRGOPOLYNICES: I didn't want to—Hercules—I thought
    she was divorced!
  I was told as much—her maid—that little bawd—she lied to
    me!

PERIPLECTOMENUS: Swear that you won't harm a single person
    for this whole affair, or
  For the pounding you've received today—and will receive—if
    we now
  Let you go intact—sweet little grandson of the goddess Venus.

PYRGOPOLYNICES: Yes! I swear by Jupiter and Mars, I'll never
    harm a soul.
  And my beating up today—I grant it was my just reward.
  As a favor, let me leave with testimony to my manhood!

PERIPLECTOMENUS: If you break your promise after this?

PYRGOPOLYNICES: Then
    may I live . . . detested.

CARIO: I suggest we wallop him a final time and let him go.   1400

PYRGOPOLYNICES: Thank you—may the gods all bless you, sir, for
    speaking up for me.

CARIO: Also give us gold—a hundred drachmas.

PYRGOPOLYNICES: Why?

CARIO: To let
    you go—
    Without giving testimony—grandson of the goddess Venus.
    Otherwise, you'll never leave.

PYRGOPOLYNICES: You'll get it.

CARIO: Now you're being
    smart.
    And you can forget about your cloak, your tunic, and your
    sword.
    (*To* PERIPLECTOMENUS)
    Should I pound or let him loose?

PYRGOPOLYNICES: Your pounding's made me
    loose already!
    Please—I beg of you—no more.

PERIPLECTOMENUS: Release the man.

PYRGOPOLYNICES: Oh, thank
    you, thank you.

PERIPLECTOMENUS: If I catch you after this, you'll never testify
    again!

PYRGOPOLYNICES: How can I object?

PERIPLECTOMENUS: Come, Cario, let's go
     inside.

(*The old man takes his slaves inside, just as* SCELEDRUS *appears,
with the soldier's lackeys, returning from the harbor*)

PYRGOPOLYNICES: Look now—I
   See my slaves. Quick, tell me, has the girl set sail—well, has
     she, has she?   1410

SCELEDRUS: Long ago—

PYRGOPOLYNICES: Damn!!

SCELEDRUS: If you knew what I know,
     that's not all you'd say. That
   Fellow with the woolen patch on his left eye . . . was no real
     sailor!

PYRGOPOLYNICES: What? Who was he?

SCELEDRUS: Your own
     sweetheart's lover.

PYRGOPOLYNICES: How'd you know?

SCELEDRUS: I know.
   Why, the minute they were past the city gates, right then and
     there, they
   Started kissing and embracing—constantly.

PYRGOPOLYNICES: Oh, pity me!
  Now I see I've been bamboozled. Oh, that rogue Palaestrio!
  He enticed me into this. And yet . . . I find the verdict's just.
  (*Philosophically*)
  There would be less lechery if lechers were to learn from this;
  Lots would be more leery and less lustful.
  (*To his slaves*)
                                    Let's go in!
  (*To the audience*)
                                              Applaud!

(*All exit into the soldier's house*)

THE CAPTIVES

(*CAPTIVI*)

Translated by Richard Moore

INTRODUCTION

Goethe remarked to Eckermann that Molière could take an idea that might serve a lesser dramatist for a line or two and spin a whole magnificent comic scene out of it. Molière learned to do that from his beloved Plautus—that and much more. And it is to his credit that he could respond to such a demanding teacher. Molière's "pieces," said Goethe, "border on tragedy; they are apprehensive; and nobody has the courage to imitate them." And in that, too, the inimitable Frenchman imitates his Latin original. When David Slavitt invited me to translate one of Plautus's comedies for the Johns Hopkins Roman drama series, I had been carrying about in my memory one of those magnificently spun-out Plautine scenes bordering on tragedy for the decades since I had encountered it in college: the farcical scene in the *Amphitryon* where the god Mercury, impersonating the servant Sosia, convinces Sosia with the help of a cudgel that he, Sosia, can't be Sosia because he, Mercury, is. "Where did I lose myself?" asks Sosia finally, bludgeoned into submission. "Where was I transformed? Where did I drop my shape? I didn't leave myself behind at the harbor, did I?" I had been taking another course in which the professor said that modern man had lost his identity—or misplaced it, I forget which—and it struck me that Plautus must have been pretty clever to have made the discovery two thousand years ahead of time.

Slavitt's offer was not of the *Amphitryon* but a choice of two other plays. I choose the *Captivi* almost blindly—a play of the mature Plautus, popular in the eighteenth century, said an account, but not much considered today because it has no female parts—and took the book, along with my Latin dictionary, to a writers' colony a few days later. When I read the play I was awed and excited to find another of those magnificent scenes, this one the pivot of the whole

183

play, in which one man blinded by his own self-righteousness unwittingly gets another condemned to a slow and agonizing death simply by telling the truth. And, as if this weren't irony enough, the audience knows it is the victim's father who does the condemning, banishing his own son to the horrors of the stone quarries while he himself feels virtuous and victimized.

Plautus is the only ancient author I know with anything much to say about slavery, that universal institution and foundation of all ancient economies. It makes one wonder what horror among us in the twentieth century might be so necessary, so universal, so obvious to all that no one ventures even to give it a thought—as Plautus ventured. The *Captivi* is a searching anatomy of slavery—or, if you wish to think about it in more general terms, of man's inhumanity to man. That is why there are no female parts. There were women slaves, of course, in classical times, but slaves of both sexes were a valued byproduct of that uniquely male occupation and source of male identity, war. (It was the women, of course, who invented war so that the men would have something to do.) The characters appear to have been chosen to represent all aspects of slavery and to give it form and immediacy. There is Hegio (whose name is related, one would suppose, to hegemony), the "commander," standing for all slave owners—not a bad man, but like most men, shallow, self-centered, and forever trying to think well of himself. Then there are the aristocratic captives, Philocrates, Philopolemus ("lovers" of "power" and "war"), and Aristophontes, the country-club hanger-on, whose name suggests that he "sounds nice." To balance this trio, we have Tyndarus, Stalagmus, and the Overseer, men who were slaves from birth (an important distinction, as the play makes clear).

Standing apart from these agents of the central action is that remarkable creation, Ergasilus (the "excluded" one), the glutton and parasite—a stock comic figure, to be sure, but here given a strikingly individual twist. As other critics have observed, his relation to the main action is tenuous at best. Why is he there at all, the reader (if not the spectator) wonders. His soliloquies, so full of gusto and a gayer kind of madness, are a necessary tonal contrast, one feels, and keep the play from sliding disastrously into terror and gloom. But mere "comic relief" will not explain him. His lack of relation to the action, his apparent "plotlessness," is functional—

integral to the play's structure, meaning, and manner of holding its audience in a way that some Chekhovian devices are. He is the one person in the play who is not part of the slavery scene. He is the man who owns nothing and is owned by no one, a kind of Rousseauian presence (if I may be permitted the anachronism) which allows us to glimpse man himself aside from his cruel institutions: a towering heap of appetites, verging on chaos; a figment, a kind of nothing which, like Lear's Fool, is—properly—not given an exit. Yet his speeches, introducing the acts and signaling the play's changes of direction, seem to show us the raw material out of which civilized, enslaved-and-enslaving man is made.

When I agreed to undertake the translation, my concern was whether my Latin would be equal to the task. I quickly realized that the primary demand would not be on my Latin, but on my theatrical imagination. My version is "accurate" in that it renders the original speech-for-speech. But that is only where true accuracy begins— and it need not even begin there. The real problem is best expressed, I think, by a Taoist story from ancient China. Confucius brags to Lao Tzu about the classics he has collected and codified. "Your classics, your histories," Lao Tzu replies, "are mere footprints in the dust. The foot that made them—and makes them interesting —is gone forever." If the past—the force, flesh, and reality of it— has vanished beyond recall, then scholarship is a useless activity; or if one shies from that conclusion, deciding that the essence of Taoist literary technique was overstatement, then one must conclude that the only way to see the foot again and touch it is to imagine it. There are several cases in point in this play. Perhaps the most striking is in the final scene, in which Hegio reencounters Stalagmus, the slave who ran off with his four-year-old son twenty years before. There was, I thought, a murkiness in the Latin text, an apparent pointlessness, to my modern ear at least, which I decided could best be resolved by supposing that the lines alluded to a sexual relationship twenty years before between the slave and the master. That would also explain how Stalagmus, entrusted with the boy and given considerable freedom, found the opportunity to escape, and why Hegio felt betrayed. (And it makes Stalagmus another example of a familiar character in late Classical poetry, found also, for example, in *Catullus* 25: the treacherous male prostitute.)

But had I "merely imagined" the whole relationship, I wondered. A few months later I had a conversation with a teacher of classics who specializes in Plautus. She knew the scene well. My interpretation, she said, was perfectly possible; classical scholarship had nothing to say about it. Yet, we agreed, it would be impossible to stage the play without making a decision on the point. The footprint was not enough. One needs the foot as well, which only the imagination can supply.

But inevitably in this process the present gets injected into the past: to understand the past in any meaningful way is to distort it. Thus it is with any metaphor: to understand something, we ask, "What is it like?" We can give any reply we wish because every thing is like every other thing in some way; and every answer we give will be wrong, too, because every thing in some way is *un*like every other thing. We escape from this dilemma by noting that some metaphors are better then others—profounder, more interesting. Our conclusions about history ultimately are esthetic judgments. There is, as Herodotus realized, no clear border between history and mythology.

The situation becomes beautifully clear when we glimpse people in some other age using their present, their unexamined assumptions, to understand their past, which is also our past. Thus, this play, in its eighteenth-century popularity, seems to have been taken as a representative of that wretched eighteenth-century genre and darling of the rising middle-class, sentimental comedy. Tyndarus (named evidently after the husband of Leda, who was also a manager and trickster) in generous devotion (as one would expect from a good slave) puts himself at risk to free his master and, when his plot is discovered, almost dies as the object of Hegio's wrath. Even as the quarry slave's chains are loaded upon him, he says he is glad to have been thus devoted to his master; and, sure enough, his virtue is rewarded and all ends happily—except, of course, for Stalagmus, who deserves what he gets. It is all very pat, a play that would, I believe—I hope!—be unplayable to a modern audience and would—can we doubt?—have been hooted from the stage by the tough pagan customers who first watched it.

The problem with this view of the play is that, once we allow ourselves to see it, Plautus's irony appears everywhere—from the opening prologue to Stalagmus's bitter final line. Tyndarus undertakes his plot with the simple aim of earning his own freedom—clearly just another unsentimental comic character intent on buttering his own parsnips. But when he is caught, there occurs what for me is one of the great transformations in comic drama: he enters a state that I think a psychiatrist (thank Heaven, there were none back then) would have to label masochistic ecstasy. He laughs at himself, at his torturer, and even at his oncoming tortures. It is all perfectly absurd and stunningly believable. People—men especially—often do things like that, perversely, madly, in the most incredible circumstances, maintaining their dignity, greatness, and style as human beings.

It may be that the time for another staging of the *Captivi* has arrived. With its brilliant characterization, its superbly paced scenes, its hilarious, almost surrealistic dialogue, and its terrifying concerns, it is one of Plautus's best.

Richard Moore

THE CAPTIVES

CHARACTERS

ERGASILUS, a glutton and parasite
HEGIO, a rich old man
OVERSEER, Hegio's slave and slave manager
PHILOCRATES, a young Elean captive
TYNDARUS, his slave, captured with him
ARISTOPHONTES, another young Elean captive
A PAGE, in the service of Hegio
PHILOPOLEMUS, Hegio's son
STALAGMUS, Hegio's slave

SCENE: *Stage in darkness. Spotlight reveals two young men with their wrists chained to the arms of a scaffold so that they can't sit down. The clothing of each is in a sorry state, but it is clear that* PHILOCRATES *was once the master,* TYNDARUS, *the slave. Behind them a house front is dimly visible.* PROLOGUE *enters forestage.*

PROLOGUE

Those two captives you see, standing right there—
the ones standing up, not the ones sitting down,
I mean, trust *me* to tell you people the truth!
Well, this old man Hegio (you'll see
a lot of him later; he lives back there)

is the father of this one.
(*Tweaking* TYNDARUS's *rags*)
                              How it happens
that he's his old man's slave, you'll just
have to let me explain. See, the old guy
had two sons, and a long time ago a slave
ran off and stole this one here, Tyndarus,   10
when he was only four years old. You
can get a very good price for four-year-olds—
they're *so cute*!
(*Putting his finger first on* TYNDARUS, *then on* PHILOCRATES)
                    That runaway slave
sold this little four-year-old to the father
of this fellow here—Philocrates.
Because, you know, a little boy slave
is just about the nicest thing in the world
for a little rich boy to have for his very
own—to play with. Get me? Play with.
You on the back bench there—you don't   20
understand? Just step right up and I'll show
everybody. Come on, sir, sit still or go
for a walk, and let's get on with the show.
We got a bunch of starving actors back there.
But listen to my story, all you respectable
property owners! There were these two kids
about the same age, one owning the other,
and they grew up and here they are,
both owned by somebody else now—captives in war.
(*Mysteriously*)
      And the slave boy's
back with his dad, but no one knows.   30
The gods are a playful lot, now aren't they?
(*Resuming his jaunty tone*)
Well, that's one son of old Hegio.
The other one—the son old Hegio
knows about—is off in the enemy city,
a captive too. And Hegio's been buying
enemy prisoners down at the slaver's

to get one he can trade back for his son.
That's how he bought his other son back, not knowing.
Lucky old man! And *this* young man here
(*Fingering* PHILOCRATES)
is a *real* plum, *rich*—he'll go for a lot.   40
But there's going to be some big problems
before all this works out. Because the rich one,
Philocrates here, and his childhood slave buddy,
Tyndarus, have grown—Oh so *fond* of each other.
So they've changed places: each is pretending
that *he* is the *other*. That way, Tyndarus,
the slave pretending to be the master,
is going to pull off a real clever trick
to get his master free. And that'll bring back   50
his brother too, home to his father for nothing,
and all of this with nobody knowing.
Oh those gods! No man knows what he's doing—
at least when he's doing good, he doesn't.
And this is all sober fact for the actors,
just crazy fun for you, the watchers.
(*Mockingly*)
We wouldn't *think* of playing anything
the *least* bit heavy! After all, this is comedy—
and such *nice* comedy: no whores, no pimps,
no braggarts, and all in the choicest style,   60
none of those filthy jokes that everyone
hates to repeat.
(*Stepping forward to the audience*)
                    And listen: if you want
a fight, go down to the bar on the corner,
get yourself a good bright nosebleed—on him
or on you. But here all the nastiness,
the dirt—man's cruelty, man's rage—
don't worry, dears: it'll all be offstage.

ACT I

(ERGASILUS, *a tall man, very fat and flabby, glances at the writhing young men, recoils in disgust, and walks up to the audience. He is much given to the grand manner.*)

ERGASILUS: The youth all call me "Campy"—that's short
    for "Camp Follower"—because at dinner,   70
    strictly by invitation, understand,
    that's when I'm on call, lapping it up.
    A dumb name? No, don't you believe it!
    Their whores are all there too, now, aren't they,
    egging them on? And he gives her a call,
    and she hears him call and comes running.
    'T's exactly what we "Stomachs" do,
    we poor little, helpless, starving mice
    forever nibbling at someone's goodies.
    Oh, and the wine! Just meal-to-meal, that's us.   80
    We feel the call to dinner too, dearies.
    Then when the summer vacation comes
    and everyone takes off to their country houses,
    our teeth take a summer vacation too,
    and don't we dwindle! Oh, it's depressing.
    While those fine young men are off in the country
    countrifying among the trunks and saplings,
    we poor saps just sit here, sipping . . . sap!
    We who were wolf-hounds, boar-hounds,
    beef-hounds, get skinny as greyhounds.   90
    And if a stomach (in this town anyway)
    objects when dishes get smashed on his head
    and the champagne splashed up his . . . Why, off he goes
    to the catering service and washes the dishes,
    and hangs, like those lads there, if he doesn't.
    That's my sad fate—I can feel it coming—
    now that my best provider of dinners
    has been "overpowered by the enemy."
    You see, friends, Aetolia and Elis

are at war, and this fine place is Aetolia,
and my lovely provider of lovelier dinners   100
is a prisoner there in Elis—my dear
Philopolemus. He's Hegio's son. Hegio
lives right here. What a miserable house it's become!
Just looking at it makes me queasy.
All thought of dinners forgotten, daily
off to the market he goes to buy more captives,
looking for one he can trade for his son.
Not exactly the sort of messy business
you'd look for in a nice old gentleman like that.
But I've only good wishes for his success.   110
Either that kid *comes* home, or I *go* hungry.
No hope for our youth nowadays, just endless love
for their own fat selves, but that lad there
was out of a kinder, a gentler time.
You never smoothed *his* feathers without a tidbit.
So maybe his father . . . Maybe I'll knock right now.
Why not? Haven't I rolled out over
this threshold stuffed with magnificent yummies
and roaring with wine? But look! It's opening!

(ERGASILUS *tiptoes into the shadows.* HEGIO *enters from his house,
an obviously wealthy man, superficially commanding and decisive,
but lacking in force and dignity. The* OVERSEER *and servants follow
him.*)

HEGIO: Now look, you. Pay attention! I want   120
those two fellows I bought at the spoils
commission yesterday—put them in the light
chains. Take off those heavy ones. It won't
hurt to let'em walk around a bit,
better inside, but outside too if they need to.

(*The crew release* PHILOCRATES *and* TYNDARUS [*who seem to come
to life*] *and lead them, groaning, into the house*)

HEGIO: But don't you take your eyes off of them.
    An unchained prisoner's worse than a wild bird.
    One little chance and *flit!* It's the last you'll see of him.

OVERSEER: Well I guess, sir, we'd all prefer to be free.
    Slavery's irksome.

HEGIO: (*Familiarly*) I never see you   130
    scrimping and saving to pay for your freedom—
    just eating whatever you get on the spot.

OVERSEER: (*Teasingly*) Poor master! What'll I give you? A run?

HEGIO: Give me that, and just see what you get for it.

OVERSEER: I'll be that wild bird that you told me about.

HEGIO: Then catch! Clap! In the cage! But enough now.
    Get on with your work—and remember my orders.
    I'll be checking the captives I have at my brother's—
    see what kind of ruckus they made *last* night.
    Prisoners, prisoners! I won't be long.

(*He begins to leave, passing in front of* ERGASILUS)

ERGASILUS:
    (*Cupping his hands around his mouth to make* HEGIO *hear*)
    Oh, how it grieves me to see this nice   140
    old man, mucking around in this slavery
    business!
    (*Turns to audience*)
            Well, if he can spring his son with it,
    he can be a hangman too, for all I care.

HEGIO: (*Pauses, looks around*)
    Who's talking?

ERGASILUS: (*Rushing up to* HEGIO)
        I, I worn by your misery—
undined, I am pining away in sorrow.
My bones grow brittle. My skin shrivels. Nothing pleases me,
    dining at home.
My beatitude lies in the morsels of others.

HEGIO: (*With a laugh, at ease*)
    Ah, Ergasilus!

ERGASILUS: May the gods love you,
    Hegio!

(*He bursts into tears and hugs* HEGIO)

HEGIO: Now, now, don't . . .

ERGASILUS: Not weep for him?
Not cry my eyes out for such a young man?   150

HEGIO: Well, I did always know that he—thought about you,
    and I knew you were a friend of his, but . . .

ERGASILUS: We mortal men appreciate our blessings
once they are torn from us, carried away.
For me, after your son was captured,
I understood, and my insides longed for him.

HEGIO: There, there! When a stranger feels such grief,
    think what a father must feel, his only . . .

ERGASILUS: A stranger! Me, a stranger to him? O Hegio,
    never utter, never allow such a thought!   160
    He was your only—but he was my *only* only!

HEGIO: (*His patience worn thin*)
    That's fine. You make his misfortune your own.
    Come on, now, buck up, man!

ERGASILUS: (*Rubbing his stomach*) Ooo. Here's where it hurts!
    The campaign to keep this filled's been disbanded.

HEGIO: You mean no one's turned up in the meantime
    to reorganize the campaign and lead it?

ERGASILUS: Would you guess it? They all fight shy of the office.
    Your dear son, the commander's, captured.

HEGIO: I can't say I'm surprised you find no recruits.
    You'd need a whole army—special services,   170
    juicy contingents—the Custardites,
    the Porkalines, the Beeflies,
    Saucy Dumplingers and Truffelates,
    the Zinfondellies and the Champagne Bubblies . . .

ERGASILUS: O genius! How often you lurk in obscurity!
    This modest man's a generalissimo.

HEGIO: That's it. Cheer up now. I'm confident
    the lad'll be back here in a day or two.
    I've got an Elean prisoner inside,
    prominent, looks like, and rolling in money.   180
    He could do as a trade for my son.

ERGASILUS: May the gods and goddesses second it! But say, are
    you dining at home tonight?

HEGIO: (*On his guard*)   I guess.
    But why, may I ask, do you ask?

ERGASILUS: (*With elaborate formality*) Today, sir,
    you see, is my birthday. I should like to invite you
    to the feast, to be served, if you please, in your home.

HEGIO: (*Laughing*)
  Choice phrasing! You're welcome—on the condition—
  can you make do with little?

ERGASILUS: None of your
  pusillanimous littles, your picayune littles,
  I hope; none of those detestable
  comestibles that I endure on my own?   190
  (*Embarrassed at* HEGIO'*s determined silence*)
  Well . . . now . . . a deal? Ah . . . sir . . . well—
  in the event that nothing more tasty affords
  my discriminating friends and myself
  shall appear, as tycoons at a mortgage auction,
  in dignity, bending the rules to our taste.

HEGIO: Leave your goons and tycoons at home. Your own
  vast emptiness is enough. And come on time.

ERGASILUS: As it happens—I'll come right now if you'd like.

HEGIO: (*Ironically*) No, great delectables beckon you. Try them!
  There's only a snack at my place. Rinds, crusts.   200

ERGASILUS: (*Menacingly*) You can't scare me off like that, Hegio.
  I'm coming famished with teeth at the ready.

HEGIO: My meals are bitter.

ERGASILUS: I'm a better biter.

HEGIO: My victuals are rough.

ERGASILUS: I'll gorge and stuff.

HEGIO: Nothing but vegetables.

ERGASILUS: That's going too far.
  Maybe I should . . .

HEGIO: Come on time!

ERGASILUS: No need
  to say that. Bye for now!

(*He exits left*)

HEGIO: Buy? Buy what?
  I'll check my money, and then to my brother's.

(*He exits right*)

ACT II

(*Enter* OVERSEER, *slaves, the two captives, who have exchanged clothes:* PHILOCRATES *in rags,* TYNDARUS *more elegantly dressed, pretending to be the master. Both in light fetters.*)

OVERSEER: (*In a sing-song*)
  Since the immortals all wish it
    and you're chained up like this,   210
  rest you content, my two laddies,
    and you'll have a soft time of it.
  Back home you were free men, no doubt,
    now slaves, as it happens.
  Gracefully, therefore, follow your masters.
    It's better that way.
  Rescue dignity out of indignity.
    Think all is "appropriate."
  Masters may utter the craziest nonsense.
    Applaud it as wisdom.   220

TYNDARUS and PHILOCRATES: Ooooooo!

OVERSEER: Blubbering and moaning won't help you at all,
  nor tears in your eyes. Just keep up your spirits.
  That helps.

TYNDARUS: (*Relishing the role of master, even overdoing it a bit*)
  But we're so *ashamed* of our chains!

OVERSEER: Well just think how *disgusted* your *master*'d be
  if he took off your chains and you flew the coop.
  Think of the *money* he's paid for you.

TYNDARUS: *We're*
  nothing to fear. We understand our *duty.*

OVERSEER: You'd run. I know it. There's footwork afoot.

TYNDARUS: Us run? Run where?

OVERSEER: To your country.

TYNDARUS: Get out!   230
  Us imitate *fugitives?* Oh, that's improper!

OVERSEER: (*Wistfully*)
  If you had the chance, I don't think I could blame you . . .

TYNDARUS: (*Pouncing on the opening*)
  Grant a request, then.

OVERSEER: Maybe. What is it?

TYNDARUS: Away from these goons here, give us a place
  where we can talk together a little.

OVERSEER: Done!
  (*To the slaves*)
  Off with you—and you! I can step back too—
  why not? Don't be talking all day, though.

TYNDARUS: Not my intention.
(*To* PHILOCRATES)

                                 Come over here.

OVERSEER: (*To the slaves*)
Leave 'em alone, you!

TYNDARUS: (*To the* OVERSEER *with elaborate politeness*)
                                 We are indebted
to you much, sir, for this most generous privilege,   240
the friendliness, decency you've shown us.

PHILOCRATES: (*To* TYNDARUS, *impatient to reassert his authority*)
Just come over here right now if it *pleases* you!
We don't want to be left with a leaked plan—
leaked out and down the drain—now do we?
(*Sententiously*)
A plot's no plot, improperly managed.
Once it goes public, it's a nasty business.
Now, if it looks like you are the master
and I—little I!—your obedient servant—
looks like it, I say—*still*, one must be
wary, one must be cautious, one must   250
take care that the plan is worked out carefully,
in silence, with discretion, with diligence.
It's a tough job. Let's not fall asleep at it.

TYNDARUS: (*Ironically*)
I shall be . . . just as you wish me to be . . .

PHILOCRATES: So I hope.

TYNDARUS: . . . for now you see, I think, *sir*,
me risking, for *your* sweet neck, *my* sweet neck
like a little cheap thing at your service.

PHILOCRATES: (*Chastened*)
                                 I know.

TYNDARUS: (*On the verge of crooning*)
   Then don't forget when you get your wish.
   Oh, men are such fine fellows when they *get*
      something for being fine!   260
      Then, once they have
   that, back they go with the spoils they wanted
   into their same old nasty habits.
   So now you know what *I* wish *you* to be.

PHILOCRATES: Heavens! I venture now to call you my—
   my father! You are the best, almost the real . . .

TYNDARUS: I hear you.

PHILOCRATES: (*Unaware of his empty rhetoric*)
         'T's why I keep reminding you:
   remember what the situation demands *now.*
   I'm not your master now; I am a slave.
   I only ask one thing—since we have proof,   270
   clear proof, that the immortal gods consent
   that I no longer am to be your master, but
   your fellow slave—that I, who at one time
   commanded you, now *humbly* entreat you,
   remembering the perils that surround us,
   mindful of Father's kindnesses to you
   and our captivity and the war's dangers—
   feel—please!—no less respect for my every wish
   than in those happy days when you were my slave!
   Remember always who you were—and are!   280

TYNDARUS: (*Dryly*) Yes, right. I'm you, you me, a little while.

PHILOCRATES: (*Buoyantly*)
   Good, then! Keep that in mind, and I'm quite sure
   our nifty plan will be a grand success.

(HEGIO *comes out of the house, calling back to those inside*)

HEGIO: I'll be back when I get what I want from these fellows.
(*To the* OVERSEER)
Those captives I left out in front here—where are they?

PHILOCRATES: My goodness, I don't think you'll have to look far
with all these hedges about us, these shackles and warders.

HEGIO: (*Sententiously*) Watching out for deception, one never can
watch out enough;
even while watching, the watcher gets diddled.
Indeed, lad, haven't I reason to keep you in focus,   290
who paid a huge price for you, cash on the table?

PHILOCRATES: (*Loftily*) True, sir, we can't find fault with you
holding us—
nor, you'll admit, that we'd flee if the chance came.

HEGIO: (*Suddenly in earnest*)
Just as you here, my dear son's held in your city.

PHILOCRATES: A captive?

HEGIO: Exactly.

PILOCRATES: (*Happily*)   Then others are cowards
also!

(HEGIO *takes* PHILOCRATES *by the arm and moves aside with him*)

HEGIO: Come here, let's talk for a moment—
and don't try to lie to me.

PHILOCRATES: No, sir—no, never!
What *I* know, *you*'ll know. When I *don't* know, I'll tell you.

TYNDARUS: (*Gazing after them*)
   Well there you are in the barber's chair, old man.
   And it's going to be clip, clip, clip till you're hairless.   300
   Not even a sheet to cover yourself, old dad.
   Hair down your neck. Oh, you'll itch for a good long while.

HEGIO: (*To* PHILOCRATES) You—would you rather be free now—
   or chained here?

PHILOCRATES: (*Grandly*) Maximal pleasure combined with the
   minimal pain, sir—
   that is my preference. Being a servant, however, 's
   never much bothered me: dined with my betters,
   treated no different than he, the true-born son there.

TYNDARUS: (*Aside*) Beautiful talking! By heaven, I'd rather have
   him than
   Socrates! All that excellent knowledge and wisdom.
   Hear how he goes on just like a bona fide lackey!   310

HEGIO: (*To* PHILOCRATES, *pointing to* TYNDARUS)
   What of his family—him there, Philocrates?

PHILOCRATES: Them? The
   Rich buggers? Gods! They're besotted with prominence,
   money.

HEGIO: Him in particular—what?

PHILOCRATES: Hobnobs with the highest.

HEGIO: Properties? Fruitful?

PHILOCRATES: Buckets of bucks for the old man.

HEGIO: Father's alive, then?

PHILOCRATES: Was, I believe, when we left him.
   Whether he's walking around on the earth at the moment,
   maybe you'd better go down there to Hades and ask them.

TYNDARUS: (*Aside*) Lovely! He not only lies; he patrols the whole
   cosmos.

HEGIO: What are his earned names?

PHILOCRATES: Vaultsfullo'dough Dollarbilly.

HEGIO: Names he acquired on account of his riches, I take it.   320

PHILOCRATES: No, on account of his being so greedy and
   grasping.

HEGIO: (*Anxiously*) What are you saying? The father's a skinflint?

PHILOCRATES: Sticky.
   When he makes offerings, sir, to his Guardian Spirit,
   you'd be surprised at the cheap plate silver he uses.
   He is afraid that the Guardian Spirit might swipe it.
   And you can gather from that what sort of a man he . . .

HEGIO: (*Embarrassed at hearing his own kind described*)
   Thanks! That'll do. Come along now.
   (*Aside*)
                             I'll get to the bottom,
   cross-check all this now with the master.

(HEGIO *leaves* PHILOCRATES *standing and trots back to* TYNDARUS)

HEGIO: (*To* TYNDARUS)   Your servant's
   told me about you, Philocrates—all—as is proper.
   You will agree, I hope; you will see that it's best to   330
   tell me your secrets yourself—though I know them already.

TYNDARUS: (*Sadly resigned*) Well, he has done what he had to,
    hasn't he?—told you
facts that I'd hoped to conceal of my lineage, status,
wealth . . .
(*In the tragic manner, imitating* PHILOCRATES)
       Ah, Hegio, he without liberty, country,
loses all claim on his servants. That fellow there fears you
more than he fears me. Who'd expect otherwise? War now
places us, equals, before you. But I can remember,
not long past, when he *dared* not—not as he does now—
anger me—dropped as I am from the high bright summits
into these depths. I, once an accustomed commander,   340
now to the careless commands of all others obsequious—
Hegio—if you'll allow me—one *small* admonition . . .

HEGIO: (*Overcome by this display of upper-class tribulation*)
    Speak, man!

TYNDARUS: I was as free as your son was once, when
fortunes of war bereft me of liberty. *He,* your
son, serves as *I* do—as if we'd agreed to change places.
Jupiter! Surely you hear, see all of our doings.
He will observe you, Hegio, treat your son there
just as you treat me here. Yes! Merit for merit.
Just as you long for your son, so my father for me so.

HEGIO: (*With false sympathy*)
    Oh, I know!
    (*Aside*)
          Are they true, though, these stories they
    tell me?   350

TYNDARUS: Yes, I admit it. My father is loaded with money.
    As for my pedigree—certainly grand and distinguished.
    But I beseech you, Hegio, *don't* get too greedy!
    Though he has one son only, my father might think it
    better for me to remain as your well-fed slave, than
    hungry at home because you have made him a pauper.

HEGIO: (*With a superior air*)
   I'm not one of those poor sick fools, for whom money's
   always a blessing. I know it can tarnish the spirit.
   Sometimes I think it's better to lose it than gain it.
   Vile gold!—leads men into ridiculous ventures.   360
   Please! Your attention: my son is a captive in Elis.
   (*With deep feeling*)
   Just get him back to me; that's—that's *all* I shall ask you.
   That, sir, and nothing else added—no, not a penny!
   That, that only, and then you can go—and your servant.
   Nothing to bargain. I'll make no other condition.

TYNDARUS: Well, you're a generous man. I accept
       your proposal. Whom
   do we deal with, though, for your son? Is he sold yet?
   Doubtless you've heard. What authority? Public or private?

HEGIO: Private. A Doctor Menarchus.

TYNDARUS: (*Aside*)   My God! He's my master's
   client.
   (*To Hegio*)
           Good going—as easy as rain when it's pouring.   370

HEGIO: Ah, you can ransom him?

TYNDARUS: Easy! But Hegio—promise!

HEGIO: Anything! Just so long as our interests . . .

TYNDARUS: Listen,
   judge for yourself. You can keep me here, but my servant,
   (under a forfeit, of course) ought to go to my city,
   talk to my father, arrange with Menarchus for ransom . . .

HEGIO: No, no, it would be better, I think, that another—
   after an armistice, maybe—is sent there to work out
   terms that we all can agree on.

TYNDARUS: A stranger can't do it!
Delicate matters! You'll just waste time with a stranger.
(*Pointing to* PHILOCRATES)
Send *him* back! He can work out everything. Trust me!   380
And he's reliable, more to the taste of my father certainly.
Why, I'd venture to say, there is no one
more on his mind these days. Sir, *you* can rest easy,
(*With a double sense for* PHILOCRATES)
I'll be responsible for him—for *he*—I am certain—
he will appreciate all of the kindness I've shown him.

HEGIO: (*Reluctantly*) Okay, *your* man—under a forfeit now, mind
   you.

TYNDARUS: Excellent!

HEGIO: *You'll* guarantee it?

TYNDARUS: Of course.

HEGIO: How much,
      then?
   Twenty-five grand?

TYNDARUS: I can live with it.

HEGIO: . . . that you will pay me
   if he should fail to return?

TYNDARUS: You got it—a bargain!

HEGIO: (*To a slave*) You there, take his—take both of their chains
   off.

(HEGIO's *slaves remove the chains from* TYNDARUS *and* PHILO-
CRATES)

TYNDARUS: (*To* HEGIO) Oh grand!
   All the immortals will bless you for this, good sir.   390
   (*Aside*)
   Oh, and it feels *quite nice* with these necklaces off me!

HEGIO: (*Proud of himself*)
   Ah, when a good man does good deeds, the result is . . .
   goodness! I feel so happy! Instruct him—that fellow—
   (*Pointing to* PHILOCRATES)
   What's-his-name: tell him—be clear!—what to say to your
     father.
   Listen, I'm going to call him over now.

TYNDARUS: Do that.

(HEGIO *gestures vigorously to* PHILOCRATES, *who comes trotting*)

HEGIO: (*To* PHILOCRATES) What a good thing for me, for my son,
   and for you, your new master wishes you to do—
   and your old one too—and faithfully!
   Under a 25,000 forfeiture bond,
   you are to go to his father and arrange   400
   for him to ransom my son and for me
   to trade his son to him for mine.

PHILOCRATES: Sir, I'll be happy to be of use.
   Just give me a whirl and a spin like a wheel
   this way and that, wherever you feel . . .

HEGIO: Well there's a fellow who knows what's good for him,
   accepts his servitude and makes the best of it.
   (*To* TYNDARUS)
   Come on, then. Here's your man.

TYNDARUS: Thank you,
   sir, for giving me this chance to tell
   my father that I'm safe and how he may   410
   ransom me by ransoming your son.

Tyndarus, this wise old man agrees
to send you to Father on my behalf
under a bond: twenty-five thousand—
my forfeit, if you disappear.

PHILOCRATES: Now that's a good idea, if you ask me.
I bet your father's heard you're safe
and he's expecting me, or someone.

TYNDARUS: Doubtless, and here's the message that you're
to take. Listen carefully. First—   420

PHILOCRATES: (*Ceremoniously, acting a part*)
First, you must know that I'll give, as I've always, my
     staunchest
(as I conceive it, Philocrates) help to your purpose,
following all of your wishes with diligence, wisdom . . .

TYNDARUS: (*Irritated by this unnecessary playfulness*)
Oh, that's lovely! Begin, then, by paying attention.
Go to my father and mother and tell them I'm safe here.
Then you'll inform all the others, my uncles and nephews—
friends, loves, playmates, whatever; assure them I'm healthy—
slave to this gentleman here, who accords me the utmost
kindness, the utmost decency—hard to believe it!

PHILOCRATES: (*Chafing at the bit*)
Yes, I'll remember all that. To proceed, then, to
     business . . .   430

TYNDARUS: (*Enjoying giving commands to his master*)
Really, except for my guard, I would think me a free man.
Father should hear next all the arrangements for ransom
Hegio stipulates here with regard to his son there . . .

PHILOCRATES: Isn't it silly to say what I've heard, sir, already—
that he's to ransom and send him back to redeem me?

TYNDARUS: Good, then.

HEGIO: But all that quickly as possible—of the
    highest importance to me.

TYNDARUS: (*To* HEGIO) Oh, don't, sir, imagine
    your son dearer to you than I to my father. .

HEGIO: Sons to all fathers are dear.

PHILOCRATES: (*To* TYNDARUS) Something more for your dad, sir?

TYNDARUS: Hmm, let me see. I'm in good health. Haven't we
    said that?   440
    (*Making a veiled appeal to* PHILOCRATES)
    Tyndarus! Speak up boldly to Father. Inform him
    how we have always been happy together and faithful,
    each to the other, in every adversity. Show him
    clearly—forget false modesty!—that you have never,
    even in servitude that has reduced us to equals,
    dreamed of disloyalty to me; and, once he has heard that,
    Tyndarus, he will be eager to grant you your freedom
    gratis. We both know *my* dad isn't a skinflint.
    Then, when I come, I also will urge him to free you,
    making him deeply aware, if you haven't already,   450
    that without *your* help, I might have vanished forever—
    for it was you who informed this gentleman that I'm
    wealthy and prominent. Wisely you gave him a motive—
    moved him to pity my fate by removing my fetters.

PHILOCRATES: (*Getting the message and answering in kind*)
    Right, good Philocrates. Witty of you to remind me.
    And how deserving you are of the good I have done you
    also! And were I to go on listing the kindness
    you as the *master* have shown me, why, we'd be here all
    day, and we'd never be finished. Had *you* been my servant,
    I *your* master, I think it could hardly be different.   460

HEGIO: (*To the audience*) Aren't these the noblest fellows I've
    listened to ever!
  Gods, what fidelity! Warm tears moisten my eyelids.
  How they adore each other!
  (*With unconscious irony*)
                        Were each one the other,
  would it be different? And who would imagine a bound slave
  praising his master like that?

TYNDARUS: (*Being deliberately confusing*)
                        Oh, he praises me, dear sir,
  hardly a tenth of the praises that *he* should be praised for.

HEGIO: Here's the occasion, then, Tyndarus, for you to crown now
  all of your noble achievements, and bring home your master.

PHILOCRATES: Oh, I shall do that! Yes, sir, you can be certain
  always when push comes to shove that I will hold highest,   470
  God be my witness, Philocrates, best of all masters!

HEGIO: There's a good fellow!

PHILOCRATES: . . . as precious to me as my own self!

TYNDARUS: (*Giving another concealed message*)
  Soon, I hope, you will back up your words with your actions,
  and, if I've said of your conduct less than I cared to,
  pardon my honesty now. Please don't be offended,
  but I must beg of you, dear friend, not to forget me
  once you are free of me, home safe under a forfeit.
  I *must pay* if you fail to return—I in my prison
  here among strangers, a hostage whose *life* is in danger,
  whom you must *free* by returning this gentleman's ransomed 480
  son and persuading my father to pay that ransom.
  He will be willing, I'm certain, and true to his duty.
  Keep me your friend! Keep Hegio's friendship with it.

(*They grasp each other's forearms*)

TYNDARUS: Now by this right hand grasping your arm, and yours
    mine,
  don't be less faithful to me than I to you always.
  Well, then—go now. Now you're my master and hold my
  fate in your hands, my protector, my patron—my father.
  Now I entrust to you—all.

PHILOCRATES:
  (*Torn by sympathy for* TYNDARUS *and eagerness to leave*)
                          Well enough of this, good friend.
  Is it enough that I do as I've promised?

TYNDARUS: Enough, yes.

PHILOCRATES: Good! So to you—
  (*Turning to* HEGIO)
                          and to you—I'll return—
    with the booty!   490
  Anything else?

TYNDARUS: Come as soon as you can!

PHILOCRATES: (*Smiling confidently*) But of course, sir!

HEGIO: (*To* PHILOCRATES) Come to the changer's. We'll get you
    some traveling money
  and from the praetor a passport.

TYNDARUS: (*Alarmed, almost betraying himself*)
                          Passport?

HEGIO: (*A little impatiently*)   Papers
  needed to get through the armies and get back safely.
  Now, sir, into the house!

TYNDARUS: (*Lingering in the doorway, to* PHILOCRATES)
                          Good journey!

PHILOCRATES: Good-bye, sir.

(TYNDARUS *goes into the house.* HEGIO *and* PHILOCRATES *go off-stage in slow motion.*)

HEGIO: (*Aside, to audience*)
    Gods, haven't *I* been lucky! To think that I almost
    passed up these two fellows for sale at the spoil-mart.
    How I debated about them—and gods, what they cost me!
    But if my luck holds, maybe I'll soon have my son back.
    (*Calls back to the house*)
    Don't let that prisoner out of your sight, you, ever!   500
    Keep him inside. When he has to go out, you watch him.
    Later I'll visit my brother and look at my others.
    One of them might be acquainted with my young man there.
    (*To* PHILOCRATES)
    Come, fellow, off to the changer's. We've things to attend to.

ACT III

(*A little while later. Enter* ERGASILUS, *working himself up into a grand lamentation.*)

ERGASILUS: Miserable man! Needs food, and he scarcely can
    find it.
    Yet more miserable man, when he needs it and finds none.
    Miserablest of all, when he pines and there's nothing.
    Gods, if you'd let me, I'd scratch both eyes out of daylight,
    since it has filled all mortals with malice against me.
    Hungrier hours, a day more blighted with famine,   510
    bloated with emptiness, stupidly, hopelessly scrounging,
    I in these drab years never have suffered, so help me!
    Oh, what a banquet of starving my innards are having!
    Pour down curses, ye gods, on this calling of stomachs!
    No one cares nowadays to invite great wits to their dinners,
    charmers of banquets, flashing our verbal stilettos.
    What do they want now? Boobs with return invitations.

Dreary exchanges of dinners for dinners ad nauseam.
Talk without cash is a faux pas, mere indiscretion.
Oh, but we helped with the shopping, we stomachs. What
    now, then?   520
Everyone shops for himself, picks groceries solus,
interviews streetwise pimps on his own with the same brash
manners he uses to question defendants in law courts.
Wit these days means nothing. Such egotists out there!
Why, just now in the forum I worked on a couple—
fellows I knew, young lawyers, and, "Going to lunch, then?"
I in my innocence ask. And a terrible silence
settles upon us. Does anyone say, "You come too!"?
Heads begin shaking. I tell them a nice little story,
one of my best. God knows how often it's fed me.   530
Laughter then? No. Smiles? No. Not one of them even
bares teeth. Dogs can do better than that when they're
    barking.
So, feeling foolish, it's off to the *next* group for Stomach.
There it's the same, and the same, and the same: same, same,
    same
all day long—a collusion against—decent eating!—
like the monopolists cornering markets in truffles,
pomegranates, piglets—a vile persecution of stomachs.
Others—more stomachs—were prowling around in the forum,
barren of fortune, as I was. We need legislation.
New laws. Make the world safe for us, punish offenders,   540
stop the conspiracy! Rights of all stomachs—protect them!
Fine the transgressors, the starvers, and pay us with dinners—
fifteen, twenty—and all at the times of our choosing—
which will be times when the prices of dinners are highest.
Yes! We will catch 'em and squeeze 'em. Now on to the harbor.
All gastronomical hopes now cling to the seaside.
(*Nodding to* HEGIO's *house*)
Failure brings *that* old man's indigestible pickings.

(*Exit* ERGASILUS *to one side, and from the other, enter* HEGIO, *leading* ARISTOPHONTES)

HEGIO: (*To the audience*) What's lovelier than working things
    properly
for public good, as I did yesterday,
buying those strapping lads for my uses?   550
Everyone stops me, praises my good fortune.
How it all held me up with pleasant chit-chat!
        Slaves are so interesting!
At last I escaped to the praetor's
and breathlessly asked for a passport.
Right away they produced it.
Now Tyndarus has it,
        heading for home.
        I, too, headed home, then, by way of my brother's—
asked all my prisoners: "Who knows Philocrates, well-known
townsman of Elis?"   560
(*Pointing to* ARISTOPHONTES)
                Then this fellow calls out, stands up,
wagging his bracelets—Philocrates, best of his buddies!
Begs me to take him along. So I had him unfettered.
(*To* ARISTOPHONTES)
Come, fellow, in with me. He'll be along in a moment.

(*They go into the house.* TYNDARUS *rushes out, stops, looks at the
audience.*)

TYNDARUS: Lucky the man who has been, and who is no longer!
    Hopes, helps, fountains of wit, why haven't you spouted?
    This is the day when I'll surely depart from the living.
    Done for, and nothing remains to be done now—nothing!
    Lies and inventions, resourcefulness, why do you flee me?
    Where are the elegant clothes you wear in performance?   570
    Is there no hostel, hotel, no miserable lodging
    hospitable to my trickery? Cover me, blankets!
    Oh, but they're threadbare, slip down, slide from my body,
    leaving me shivering, all my plotting apparent.
    Master, escaped, will be saddened perhaps—yes, and me too!
    Aristophontes, the friend of Philocrates, in there
    fans my perdition about like a pitiful ember.

How can I counter him? Nothing sufficiently clever
comes to me. What, then? Something? Anything? . . .
   Nothing!
Oh, I'm a simpleton!

(HEGIO *enters, looks about.* TYNDARUS *tries to hide.*)

HEGIO: My, he's elusive, that fellow.   580
   Where did he go, then, skittering out of the courtyard
   just as we entered?

TYNDARUS: (*Aside*)   It's over, then, finished, unless I—
   what can I think up? Quick now! Stratagem, story!
   Shall I deny that . . . maybe admit something. *Maybes*
   hedge me about like monsters! I'm trapped in confusion.
   Would that the gods had disposed of you, Aristophontes,
   on your way here, tripped you and smashed you to toothpicks.
   Why did you have to arrive?—you disrupter of sweet
      schemes—
   ruined—unless some ruse quintessentially clever . . .

HEGIO: (*To* ARISTOPHONTES, *catching sight of* TYNDARUS)
   Come along, fellow! It's *him* there. Go and address him.   590

(ARISTOPHONTES *advances toward* TYNDARUS *in slow motion, with*
HEGIO *following closely*)

TYNDARUS: Mortal more miserable—have the Fates ever made
   one?

(ARISTOPHONTES, *then* HEGIO, *stop short about six feet from* TYN-
DARUS)

ARISTOPHONTES: (*In his best country club accent*)
  Tyndarus! What do you *mean* by this, hiding away there,
  snubbing me, cutting me, shrinking away from our master?
  True, I'm a slave like you are now, but I *once* was
  free in our homeland. *You* were a slave from your boyhood.

HEGIO: (*Angry, anguished*) Rage of the gods! No wonder he shies
    from us both now.
  Tyndarus—that's what you call him—Philocrates vanished?

(TYNDARUS *rushes forward, gets between* HEGIO *and* ARISTOPHON-
TES)

TYNDARUS: (*Frantic*) Hegio, listen! This nincompoop's known for
    his raving.
  Back home—don't go polluting yourself with his nonsense!—
  once he . . . he threatened his father and mother at
    spearpoint.   600
  He is a known epileptic. Spit on him! Stop him!

(TYNDARUS *pushes* HEGIO *away from* ARISTOPHONTES)

TYNDARUS: Out of his reach! Quick!

HEGIO: (*Convinced again, a reed in the wind*)
                                Keep him away! Keep him
    off me!

(ARISTOPHONTES *follows them, as if drawn by them*)

ARISTOPHONTES: (*Incredulous, unaccustomed to being crossed*)
  What? Are you crazy? My father and mother at spearpoint?
  (*Like a pampered child*)
  Me with that ghastly disease that everyone spits on?

HEGIO: (*Soothingly, forgetting to retreat*)
  There, there, don't fret! Many men, otherwise decent,
  have that disease. Sometimes being spat on cures it.

ARISTOPHONTES: (*Backing off*)
   What? You believe him?

HEGIO: (*Confused*)
                              Believe what?

ARISTOPHONTES: Think I'm a madman.

(TYNDARUS *grasps* HEGIO, *pulls him away*)

TYNDARUS: (*To* HEGIO, *reestablishing the illusion*)
   Look at him! Look at his eyeballs! Look at him sweating!
   He's on the brink of a fit now, Hegio. Watch out!

(HEGIO *and* TYNDARUS *talk to each other while* ARISTOPHONTES
creeps closer, trying to overhear)

HEGIO: (*Convinced again*)
   I should have known it the minute he said, "Tyndarus."   610

TYNDARUS: And he can even forget his own name—have you
   noticed?

HEGIO: Strange! And he said he was intimate with you.

TYNDARUS: (*With heavy irony*)   For
      certain!
   Maddened Orestes, fleeing the furious sisters,
   foaming with guilt, was exactly as chummy as this one.

(ARISTOPHONTES, *overhearing this, rushes closer*)

ARISTOPHONTES: (*To* TYNDARUS, *enraged*)
   Gallows-food, eater of offal, you say I don't know you?

HEGIO: (*Retreating with* TYNDARUS)
   Clearly you don't, when you stupidly juggle that name so.
   Call him Tyndarus instead of Philocrates, will you?
   Him you can see, you deny. Stop naming the absent!

ARISTOPHONTES: (*Confused, but blustering*)
  He says he is who he isn't—and is, but denies it.

(TYNDARUS *advances toward* ARISTOPHONTES)

TYNDARUS: (*To* ARISTOPHONTES, *trying to make him understand*)
  You're here to *beat*, make it *hard* for Philocrates, are you?   620

ARISTOPHONTES: (*Self-righteously*) You, as I see it, are here to
  make *truth* into *falsehood*.

(ARISTOPHONTES *advances;* TYNDARUS *retreats to* HEGIO)

ARISTOPHONTES: Dammit now, look me straight in the eye.

TYNDARUS: Yes?

ARISTOPHONTES: Tell me:
  Do you deny that you're Tyndarus?

TYNDARUS: Certainly.

ARISTOPHONTES: *And* you
  claim you're Philocrates?

TYNDARUS: Certainly do.

ARISTOPHONTES: (*To* HEGIO, *having reached him*)
                                         You believe him?

HEGIO: (*Almost lapsing into senility*)
  How can I fail to? But can I believe what I'm saying,
  saying it? Didn't I send that fellow you tell me
  this fellow is to his home just now, where a father's
  eager to ransom this son?

ARISTOPHONTES: (*Brusquely*) Such ridiculous nonsense!
  Son, son? Who ever heard of a slave with a father?

TYNDARUS:
(*Making another attempt to make* ARISTOPHONTES *see*)
Well, look, aren't you a slave now too—and were free
    once?   630
As for myself, I was *also* and hope to *become so*
as my *repayment* for getting this gentleman's *son home.*

ARISTOPHONTES: Rascal, you say that at birth they called you a
    freeman?

TYNDARUS: (*Giving up*) Freeman was never my name. I'm
    Philocrates, nitwit.

ARISTOPHONTES: Oh, did you hear that, Hegio? Villain—he
    mocks us!
He is a slave. If he's not, there was never another.

TYNDARUS: (*Loftily*) Living in want and with nothing to eat in
    your kitchen
fills you with longing to find others like you. Of course, that's
typical. Poor beggars everywhere envy their betters.

ARISTOPHONTES: Hegio, since you insist on crediting
    cheaters,   640
watch it! You seem to be suffering from him already.
All this ransom-talk fills me with dreadful foreboding.

TYNDARUS: *You* may forebode as you will, but you'll soon see it
    happen.
(*Tries to get through with a clear explanation*)
I shall restore this man's son, who, in return, will
send me back to my father in Elis. Tyndarus
went to my father to . . .

ARISTOPHONTES: *You* are Tyndarus, impostor!
Other than you, there is no other slave who is named so.

TYNDARUS: On about slavery still? We were captured in
    battle . . .

ARISTOPHONTES: (*Losing patience*)
    I can't deal with this!

(TYNDARUS, *capitalizing on* ARISTOPHONTES' *anger, draws* HEGIO
away from ARISTOPHONTES)

TYNDARUS: (*Renewing the attack*)
                    Watch out, Master, he's twitching.
    Run! He'll be reaching for stones in a minute. Be careful!   650
    Help, help! Grab him!

ARISTOPHONTES: It's maddening!

TYNDARUS: Look at him twitching!
    Master, he's having one. Look at those spots on his body!
    Furies tormenting him!

ARISTOPHONTES: (*Addressing the heavens, then* TYNDARUS)
                    Gods! If he had any sense, this
    old man—hot-flaming pitch would be stuffed up your nostrils,
    making you shine like a beacon.

TYNDARUS: (*To* HEGIO, *drawing him away*)
                    Be careful, he's raving.
    Devils inhabit him, Hegio. Put him in shackles!

(*The slaves rush up to* ARISTOPHONTES *and look questioningly at*
HEGIO, *who motions them to pause*)

ARISTOPHONTES: Help, gods! Show me a stone I can pick up and
    smash him!
    Talk-talk's driving me wild.

TYNDARUS: Stones! Listen! He's looking.

ARISTOPHONTES: (*Suddenly calm, realizing that* HEGIO *has restrained the slaves*)
Hegio, listen to me for a moment—alone—please!

(ARISTOPHONTES *advances;* HEGIO *and* TYNDARUS *retreat*)

HEGIO: (*Tremulously*) Say it from there, if there's anything. . . .
Stop! I can hear you.   660

TYNDARUS: That's it. Be careful. He'd end up biting your nose off.

ARISTOPHONTES: (*Standing still, instinctively waiting for sanity to take hold, then, deliberately*)
Do not believe me insane; don't, Hegio, or that
I've ever had the disease he describes me as having.
Nevertheless, if you all are afraid of me, tie me.
Just put fetters on him there also.

TYNDARUS: I'll none of it, Master.
Fetter the fellow who wants to be.

(ARISTOPHONTES *advances.* TYNDARUS *steps forward as if to defend* HEGIO.)

ARISTOPHONTES: Shut up a moment,
can't you, you phony Philocrates? I can give *proofs* you're
Tyndarus. . . . What are you nodding about?

(TYNDARUS *tries to tell* ARISTOPHONTES *silently that there is a plot afoot*)

TYNDARUS: Me, nodding?

ARISTOPHONTES: (*To* HEGIO, *trying to look around* TYNDARUS)
What if you weren't here, Hegio? What would he do then?

HEGIO: (*To* TYNDARUS, *having heard* ARISTOPHONTES *imperfectly*)
What's that? What if I stepped right up to the madman?   670

TYNDARUS: (*Weakly, sensing the tide turning against him*)
   Well, if you want to feel foolish, get lost in the snakepit,
   jabber with jabberers . . . Look at him drooling and foaming.

HEGIO: (*Half to himself*) Maybe I'll have to.

(HEGIO *steps past* TYNDARUS *and up to* ARISTOPHONTES)

TYNDARUS: (*Aside*)   I think that the party
      is over.
   Who knows what's next? Now it's the rock and the hard place.

HEGIO: (*Overcoming his fright*)
   Aristophontes, I'm here to be open and listen.

ARISTOPHONTES: (*Soothingly, soberly, proud of himself*)
   You will decide that it's truth that was taken for falsehood.
   First, though, let me convince you: I'm sane and I'm healthy.
   Only captivity pains me. And now with the heavens'
   king and the earth's as my witness, I tell you that fellow's
   no more Philocrates, good sir, than you are or I am.   680

HEGIO: (*Almost dreamily, overcome by* ARISTOPHONTES' *simple
      earnestness*)
   Ah! . . . Can you tell me, then, who . . . who he *is?*

ARISTOPHONTES: He's exactly
      he, who I *said* he was, in the beginning. Discover
   that I'm mistaken, and I will forfeit my parents,
   homeland, liberty—slave to you here, sir, forever.

HEGIO: (*To* TYNDARUS, *turning to him in sudden anger*)
   Who are you?

TYNDARUS: (*Calmly, knowing that all is lost*)
                I am your servant, and you are my master.

HEGIO: Not what I wanted to hear. Say: were you a freeman?

TYNDARUS: Yes.

ARISTOPHONTES: He's a liar. Absurdities!

TYNDARUS: (*To* ARISTOPHONTES, *with genuine loftiness and a deep sense of superiority*)
                                   Tell me: my mother's
midwife, were you, to speak so confidently on the matter?

ARISTOPHONTES: (*To* TYNDARUS, *lamely*)
When we were children together, I *saw* you.

TYNDARUS: (*To* ARISTOPHONTES, *ironically*)   Mature years
seem to have *blinded* you. Where is your decency, poking   690
into my private affairs? Do I poke into yours, sir?

HEGIO: (*To* ARISTOPHONTES) Wasn't his father called
Vaultsfullo'dough Dollarbilly?

ARISTOPHONTES: (*To* HEGIO, *thoughtfully*)
No, sir, he wasn't. I *must* say that name's unfamiliar.
Theodoromedes—*that* is Philocrates' father.

TYNDARUS: (*Aside*) Oh be still, heart, thumping inside me so
loudly!
Yes, I am done for. Knees, stop turning to water!

HEGIO: (*To* ARISTOPHONTES) So it is true, then: *this* fellow—
always—the servant—
never Philocrates?

ARISTOPHONTES: (*With stupid iteration*)
                         No, never otherwise—never.
(*A thought entering his dimness*)
Tell me, though, where has Philocrates gotten to?

HEGIO: (*Grimly*)   Where I
  wouldn't have sent him, and where he desires.
  (*Pleadingly*)
                                  But can't you   700
  find some mistake?

ARISTOPHONTES: (*Growing sad, beginning to realize his blunder*)
                Not unless it's untrue that I stand here.

HEGIO: So you are certain, then?

ARISTOPHONTES: Certain.

HEGIO: How *can* you be?

ARISTOPHONTES: (*Mournfully*)   O sir,
  we three boys were inseparable playmates together.

HEGIO: (*Wheeling around and going up to* TYNDARUS, *angrily*)
  So! I've been rooted up, rifled and ripped, left bloody,
  torn by this scalawag's trickery, trimmed at his pleasure.
  (*Turning back to* ARISTOPHONTES)
  What's your Philocrates look like?

ARISTOPHONTES: Hair a bit reddish,
  wavy and curled, the complexion quite fair, and the face thin,
  nose sharp, eyes black.

HEGIO: That's him!

TYNDARUS: (*Aside, in a strange, almost ecstatic tone*)
                      That's me, roasting,
  dreadfully visible, peeled by hot whips as they stroke me.
  Poor little whip lashes, dying . . .

HEGIO: (*With angry self-pity*)
                    Oh, *yes!* I've been *cheated!*   710

TYNDARUS: (*Aside*) Come, little shackles! Advance to me, snugly
    embrace me!

HEGIO: (*With bitter anguish, unconscious of his own absurdity*)
    Haven't these wretches outwitted me, robbed me, blinded
      me . . .
    beaten me mad with their pretenses! Slave plays master,
    master—the *nut!*—and I keep *dry husk* for my ransom:
    stand here—fool!—with a faceful, smiling through garbage.
    Well now, but *this* one here won't laugh at me, *ever!*
    (*Turning to his house*)
    Box-em-up, Buffeter, Bangs! Out! Bring out the leather!

(BOX-EM-UP, BUFFETER, *and* BANGS, *three burly fellows with whips
and thongs, rush out of the house.* TYNDARUS *has a strangely superi-
or, detached air—seems almost ecstatic—which infuriates* HEGIO
even further.)

BOX-EM-UP, BUFFETER, and BANGS: What do we cut down, cut
    down, cut down, cut?

HEGIO: Mangle that fellow with manacles.   720

(*They seize* TYNDARUS)

TYNDARUS: What are you doing? What have I done?

HEGIO: Sower, hoer of nastiness—and the reaper!

TYNDARUS: Say "harrower" first. It comes before "hoeing."

HEGIO: You, Confidence, dare talk back to me?

TYNDARUS: (*Laying it on a bit thick*)
    Confidence springs from rectitude, decency.
    Peerless I stand up, confess to my master.

(*They strap him to the scaffold*)

HEGIO: Tie up his hands there! Tight. Good and tight.

TYNDARUS: Father, they're yours. Cut them off if it pleases you.
  But deign to explain, if you will, this fury.

HEGIO: (*Unconsciously farcical*) Me and my business as much
      as you could   730
  you demolished me, polished me. Your dodges have diddled
      me.
  Your fallacies falsified, ruined my fortunes,
  puddled my prospects, piddled my plans.
  You sprung Philocrates, spawning your fantasies.
  I believed him the servitor, you the enfranchised.
  You said so yourselves and out of your names
  made vile permutations.

TYNDARUS: (*Proudly, gaily*) I admit it, all of it,
  just as you say. Yes, I have swizzled you
  out of him, swished him away to his homeland
  all by my scheming and consummate trickery.   740
  Surely, sir, it is not *that* that incenses you!

HEGIO: (*Almost to himself*)
  It shall be done with torture and blood-letting.

TYNDARUS: (*In beatific self-righteousness*)
  If it is not for some ill deed, I can perish. It's little.
  And if I die, and he fails to return, as he promised,
  my act will be memorable long after my dying:
  I, who my captured master out of servitude
  among enemies caused to be led into liberty,
  home and homeland, and placed my head in peril
  rather than see him suffer . . .

HEGIO: (*Getting tough*)   My bleeding heart!
  Find it in Hades, your hero's welcome!   750

TYNDARUS: (*Primly*) Virtue, though put down, never shall perish.

HEGIO: Well, sonny boy, after I've tortured you good,
in all the nastiest ways I can think of,
and you have *roasted* for all the lies you have *cooked* up,
we'll send you below, and we'll see what perishes.
When you're dead, good and dead, we'll see what lives on.

TYNDARUS: (*Lightly, threatening*) You won't do that without
    punishment, good sir—
not when my master returns. I expect him.

ARISTOPHONTES: (*Suddenly igniting with understanding*)
Immortal gods! I see! I understand!
What cleverness! Good old Philocrates,   760
home free in his homeland! *Bully* for him!
Can't think of anyone I'd rather see out of this.
God, though, what a nasty business for this one—
through my stupidity—him, strapped there!

HEGIO: (*To* TYNDARUS, *as to a child*)
Didn't I pledge you to tell me no fibs?

TYNDARUS: You did.

HEGIO: (*Almost as though he is talking to his son—which, of
    course, he is*)
                    Then, bad boy, how could you dare to?

TYNDARUS: (*Like a good little boy*)
Truth would have *hurt* my true-pledged master.
My falsehood *saved* him.

HEGIO: (*Suddenly himself*) It'll hurt *you*, though.

TYNDARUS: (*Ecstatic*)   So be it!
I saved my master, and I'm glad that I saved him,
him that his father, my master, entrusted to me.   770
Really, do you think I did badly?

HEGIO: Evilly.

TYNDARUS: (*Primly*) Well *I* think it right, and I *beg* to differ.
    And consider: What if *your* slave did that
    for *your* child? What *gratitude* wouldn't *you* feel?
    I think you'd *free* him, now *wouldn't* you?
    Wouldn't he *just* be the darling of *all your slaves?*
    (*A pause*)
    Your answer?

HEGIO: (*Wavering*) Perhaps.

TYNDARUS: (*Soothingly, like a father*)
                            Then why this anger?

HEGIO: (*With childish petulance*)
    You were faithful to *him*. What about *me?*

TYNDARUS: *You?* You've only owned me a *day!* Do you suppose
        that a day would wipe away
    decades of loyalty felt for a master   780
    grown up with—together since boyhood?

HEGIO: (*With sudden anger, reminded of his own bereavement*)
    Then go ask *him* for thanks!
    (*To the slaves, who untie and hold* TYNDARUS)
                            To the quarries!
    Put him in shackles—heavy ones, thick ones! There—
    (*To* TYNDARUS, *going up to him*)
    while the others dig out their eight stones daily,
    you'll dig twelve, and we'll give you a new name.
    We'll call you "Sixhundredlashes Skinless."

ARISTOPHONTES: (*To* HEGIO, *going up to him*)
    By all the gods, I beseech you, Hegio,
    do not destroy this man!

HEGIO: (*To the world in general, ignoring* ARISTOPHONTES)
　　　　　　　　Yes, we'll see to it.
　　At night he'll be looked after, winched and strapped,
　　and by day underground he will hack stone.   790
　　We'll draw out the torture; it won't be done in a day.

ARISTOPHONTES: (*Awe-struck*) Are you fixed in this?

HEGIO: (*Dreamily*)   Fixed as death.
　　(*To the slaves, briskly, businesslike*)
　　March him off to the blacksmith. Have Hippolytus
　　forge him some good heavy foot-shackles,
　　then lead him out through the gates to my freedman,
　　Cordalus, in charge down there in the quarry,
　　and put him to work—and treat him, mind you,
　　just as well—*as well*—as the *worst*.

TYNDARUS: (*Matter-of-factly*) Since hate fills you, why ask you for
　　　　mercy? The danger you put me in, puts *you* in danger.
　　After death, death holds no fear anymore.
　　Though perhaps I must die slowly, lingering,
　　it is a brief space only that you menace me with.
　　(*Almost singing*)
　　Farewell! Health to you, sir—though you deserve other wishes!
　　You, Aristophontes, deserving as well, farewell.
　　It's from you that this has fallen upon me.

HEGIO: (*Frantic, losing control, to the slaves, who move
　　reluctantly*)
　　　　　　　　　　　　　　　　　　Take him, you!

TYNDARUS: I just ask one thing: if Philocrates comes back,
　　that I meet him, that you grant me the means.

HEGIO: (*To the slaves, beside himself*)
　　You'll die—or you'll get him out of my sight.

(*The slaves seize* TYNDARUS. *There is a crazy scuffle as they pull him about.*)

TYNDARUS: Well! This is real force—to be pulled—and pushed—
   at once!

(*The slaves take* TYNDARUS *off*)

HEGIO: (*To himself*) My lad, you'll be stuck in the hole that
      suits you,   810
   and I . . .
   (*Finding a reason for his actions*)
         It'll teach those others a lesson,
   so somebody else won't try such tricks.
   If it hadn't been for this one,
   (*Indicates* ARISTOPHONTES)
                     who pulled it all out
   in the open, why, they'd be riding me still.
   That's the last time *I* believe *anybody.*
   Once is enough . . .
   (*With sudden tender feeling, gazing after* TYNDARUS)
                  O my son, my lost son! I had such
      high hopes of getting you free!
   (*Bitterly*)
   So much for that. One son lost long ago,
   the four-year-old, when that runaway took him.
   Neither boy nor slave—no, not a trace.
   Now the other in enemy hands. What's my crime?—   820
   leading my own sons into destruction!
   (*Noticing* ARISTOPHONTES)
   As for you . . . back where you were! I'll never
   feel pity again, since none feel pity for me.

ARISTOPHONTES: (*Wistfully*) It seemed magic to get out of chains.
   It seems
   I'm to be magicked back into them now.

ACT IV

(Enter ERGASILUS, *ecstatic)*

ERGASILUS: Jupiter, serve me and minister unto my plumpness!
   Boundless abundance, abundance unbounded, you bring me.
   Joy, praise, profit; festivity, jollity, pleasure;
   banqueting, pompous with edibles, roaring with goodies.
   Never again shall I toady to mere human beings.   830
   Now I can praise friends, damn all my enemies freely,
   daylight's delighted me so with delights so delightful!
   Oh, I have landed a legacy, vast, unencumbered!
   Up to the old man, Hegio's, house I shall run now,
   bringing him happiness, more than he ever imagined.
   I shall unload all the heavens upon him, and more too.
   Here's how now: like the slave in the comedy—run, run,
   (Running in place, as on a treadmill)
   thus, with my cloak tucked under my chin. I will bring him
   news he shall never forget, be the first one to tell him,
   pleasing him so, he will stuff me with dinners forever.   840

(Enter HEGIO *from his house, miserable. He doesn't see* ERGASILUS.*)*

HEGIO: The more I roll this around in my head,
   the bitterer it makes me feel.
   To fool me like that, and I couldn't see through it!
   The whole city will laugh at me when it gets out.
   In the forum, as soon as they see me, they'll say,
   "Here comes that silly old man who got swindled."
   (Notices ERGASILUS*)*
   Look! Is that Ergasilus over there with his
   cloak tucked under his chin? What's he up to?

ERGASILUS: *(Still running)* Move! No delay now, Ergasilus. On to
      the business!
   Threats to all, direst threatenings! None shall obstruct me,   850
   (Stopping, punching the air)

none except those poor fools grown weary of living:
they shall be stood on their ear.

HEGIO: He's becoming a boxer!

ERGASILUS: Certain it is! Henceforth they shall mind their own
    business,
    quiet at home, not littering avenues, alleys.
    Now with this great siege-engine, my fist, and his forearm
    catapult, battering ram of a shoulder, I'll punch all
    into submission. I'll pick their teeth—from the gutter!

HEGIO: (*Forgetting his troubles*)
    Such bombast, such bluster! He *is* so amusing.

ERGASILUS: (*Still in his fantasy*)
    He shall remember this day and my doings forever.

HEGIO: What great work is the fool undertaking so loudly?   860

ERGASILUS: Publish my edicts, lest none through ignorance
    perish.
    Keep to your houses, preserved from my terrible anger.

HEGIO: Miracles gestate, confidence swells up inside him.
    (*Prophetically*)
    Woe to the wretch with this madman loose in his larder!

ERGASILUS: Pig-keeping millers, who fatten their porkers with
    refuse,
    making the landscapes near an offense to the nostrils—
    when I catch sight of those blundering sows in the roadway,
    out of their owners, with fists, I shall pummel the garbage.

HEGIO: Blasting pronouncements, pompous imperial edicts
    bloat him: indeed great confidence swells up inside him!   870

ERGASILUS: Mongers who peddle their festering fish to the
    public—
"Perch! Perch!"—jolting about on their miserable geldings,
clearing the forum with deadly basilisk odors—
them I shall thwack with their own fish baskets and teach them
what an offense they are to our citizens' noses.
Butchers as well, who will make poor sheep-mothers childless,
promise you young lambs fit for the slaughter, then give you
sick old doddering rams, more ancient than two such:
rammers like that, I shall render you miserably mortal.

HEGIO: Listen: he's issuing laws; he's the Warden of
    Foodstuffs.   880
He'll be promoted tomorrow to Market Inspector.

ERGASILUS: I am no parasite now, no "stomach." I reign here,
prince among eaters with harborfuls under my waistline.
But I must hurry! I'll load old Hegio here with
ecstasy. No old dotard alive is so lucky.

HEGIO: Ecstasy? Largess out of the ambling larder?

(ERGASILUS *walks past* HEGIO, *knocks on* HEGIO's *door*)

ERGASILUS: Who's home? Hey, come on now, somebody open!

HEGIO: Oh, he's come now to welcome himself to his dinner.

ERGASILUS: (*Shouting*) Open the doors there, before I reduce
    them to splinters!

HEGIO: Won't he be pleasant to talk to!
    (*To* ERGASILUS, *shouting*)
                                          Ergasilus!

ERGASILUS: Who calls   890
    doughty Ergasilus?

HEGIO: Look over here!

ERGASILUS: Over whom? Where?
   That's more than good luck does—or that old whore, Fortune.
   What's going on?

HEGIO: Look, stupid! It's Hegio, out here.

ERGASILUS: (*Seeing* HEGIO *finally, rushing up to him*)
   Best of the bless'd of the trodders of earth! You come timely.

HEGIO: Have you discovered a banquet? You're acting so mighty.

ERGASILUS: Give me your hand.

HEGIO: Hand?

ERGASILUS: Give it right now!

HEGIO: Well, here, then.

ERGASILUS: Joy to you!

HEGIO: Joy? Me? Why on . . .

ERGASILUS: Because I have said so.

HEGIO: O friend, grief beats all joy out of me these days.

ERGASILUS: I shall remove all griefs now, out of your person.
   (*With great intensity*)
   Boldly rejoice!

HEGIO: (*Weakly complying*) I'm rejoicing—but why? Please
   · tell me.   900

ERGASILUS: Good! Now I order you . . .

HEGIO: (*At the point of taking offense*)
                    Order me!

ERGASILUS: (*With authority*) Build a great fire,
    roaring, gigantic.

HEGIO: (*Wavering*) A fire, gigantic?

ERGASILUS: A big one.
    Haven't you heard me?

HEGIO: (*Coming to himself, removing his hand*)
                         Now listen, you vulture! You fancy
I'm gonna' burn my house down just for your pleasure?

ERGASILUS: (*Magisterially*) Calm, calm! Mustn't excite yourself.
    Order the cauldrons—
will you?—placed over the hearth and the pots in the oven.
After the platters are well washed, stack them with bacon,
chops, roasts, tenderloins, cutlets.

HEGIO: (*Aside, realizing that Ergasilus is mad*)
                              Dreams! . . . Poor fellow!

ERGASILUS: Send out servants to buy pork, lamb, spring
    chicken . . .

HEGIO: (*Ironically*) Knows his own pleasure, I guess.

ERGASILUS: . . . ham,
    fresh-water lamprey,   910
    mackerel, cheeses well-aged, fish pickled in sherry . . .

HEGIO: There is a greater abundance, Ergasilus, naming
    foods in my house than in finding them there.

ERGASILUS: (*Leaving his fantasy*)   Do you think I
    say things just for the pleasure of saying them?

HEGIO: Well, you
won't get *nothing* today—not much *more* than that either.
(*Virtuously*)
Bring me a stomach that's ready for *work-a-day* feeding.

ERGASILUS: (*Earnestly*) Sir, you shall long for great *feasts,* even
though I for*bid* them.

HEGIO: (*Taken aback*) Me?

ERGASILUS: You.

HEGIO: You are the master, then?

ERGASILUS: Only
your friend, sir.
Wish to be fortunate?

HEGIO: Rather than pine in my sadness.

ERGASILUS: Give me your hand.

HEGIO: (*Presenting his hand again*) Well?

ERGASILUS: (*Grasping and gazing at Hegio's hand*) Gods,
but you're lucky!

HEGIO: (*Dryly*)   I doubt it.   920

ERGASILUS: (*Sympathetically*) Poor man, still in the *thorns?* So
you're *bushed.*
(*Briskly*)
                              You must order
vessels of sanctified oil to be filled for the service,
lambs to be brought in, succulent, juicy, and fat.

HEGIO: Why?

ERGASILUS: So you may offer . . .

HEGIO: To someone among the immortals?

ERGASILUS: By the sweet heavens, to *me!* I am Jupiter to you:
　　Fortune, Salvation, and Light; Joy, Gaiety, Gladness—
　　all the same I, me! Let me be satisfied, then, with . . .

HEGIO: Food, it appears to me.

ERGASILUS: Food, but to *me*, not to *you*, sir.

HEGIO: (*Resigned*) Oh, as you wish: I permit it.

ERGASILUS: (*Suggestively*)   Permissive
　　in youth, eh?

HEGIO: (*Angrily*) Jupiter blast you!

ERGASILUS: (*Earnestly*)   You'd better be *grateful*
　　to me, sir,   930
　　now that I'm bringing you such good news from the harbor:
　　careful to please me.

HEGIO: (*Wearily, impatiently*)
　　　　　　　　　　Be damned with you finally; it's *late* now.

ERGASILUS: *Earlier* maybe you'd have some reason to say that.
　　(*With careful emphasis and rising intensity*)
　　Now, sir, accept this ecstasy that I convey: your . . .
　　son has arrived! Philopolemus, safe! And I saw him,
　　healthy and pleased with himself in the rowboat. With him
　　that young man that you sent. There was also Stalagmus,
　　slave of yours once, who, stealing your four-year-old ran off . . .

HEGIO: Go to the devil! You're mocking me!

ERGASILUS: Hegio, no, it's
 true, what I tell you—as Blessed Satiety loves me! 940
 There they . . .

HEGIO: My son?

ERGASILUS: Yes, him, by my Guardian Spirit!

HEGIO: Also my prisoner?

ERGASILUS: Yes, by Apollo!

HEGIO: And him too,
 wretched Stalagmus, who kidnapped my toddler and vanished?

ERGASILUS: Yes, by Poseidon!

HEGIO: But can I believe this?

ERGASILUS: By Hera,
 yes, sir!

HEGIO: He's come, then?

ERGASILUS: Yes, sir, by—Aphrodite!

HEGIO: Careful now!

ERGASILUS: Yes, now by Artemis!

HEGIO: Why are you naming
 ancient divinities like that?

ERGASILUS: They, like your dinners,
 so you have told me, are terrors.

HEGIO: Get on with you, wild man!

ERGASILUS: Those are my feelings exactly. Why can't you believe
   me
  since I am telling you earnestly, soberly? Tell me,   950
  what nationality was that Stalagmus when he
  ran off?

HEGIO: Sicily.

ERGASILUS: He's no Sicilian now, though.
  No, he's a Gaul now: galled by a collar, most wifelike.
  Oh, how she clings to him!

HEGIO: Look! Are you giving me straight
  fact?

ERGASILUS: Straight fact.

HEGIO: Great gods, goddesses! I am reborn now!
  Sure you're not lying?

ERGASILUS: My dear sir, how can you doubt me?
  Haven't I sworn? Well, Hegio, since my solemn
  oath won't do, trot down to the harbor yourself and
  see with your own eyes.

HEGIO: Just what I'm going to do now.
  You can go in there. Anything needed, just do it!   960
  Kitchen and storeroom—you be the butler.

ERGASILUS: The . . . Oh my!
  Gods! If I don't do well, you may comb me with cudgels.

HEGIO: If you have spoken the truth, I shall feast you forever.

ERGASILUS: Who gets the bill?

HEGIO: (*Bursting with joy*)   *I shall*—and my *son!*

ERGASILUS: On your word?

HEGIO: Yes.

ERGASILUS: He has arrived in the harbor, your son, sir. Go find
    him!

HEGIO: Care for things here!

ERGASILUS: Oh, yes, sir! Have a good walk now.

(HEGIO *runs off*)

ERGASILUS: (*Solus*) Gone! And this whole great house of
    digestibles open,
  bared to my loving attentions. Immortals of heaven!
  I shall strike smartly, and heads shall fly from their bodies.
  Ham's poor case shall be hopeless and bacon be battered.   970
  Pork shall be potted and sow's udder udderly done for.
  Lamb-butchers, pig-vendors, all who bring joy to the belly,
  how can I mention you all? To the glorious work, then!
  Hams hung high in suspense are awaiting the judgment.

(ERGASILUS *rushes into the house. A great commotion and banging
of pots and pans is heard. A young page runs out, as if propelled by
some overwhelming force.*)

PAGE: (*Calling back into the house*)
  Maddened Ergasilus, God take you and your belly!
  (*To the audience*)
  Perish all parasites! Punish the fools who would feed them!
  Thunder, calamity, shakes old Hegio's kitchen—
  hot wind, vast devastation. He lunged to me, howling,
  grinding his teeth, and his wild eyes rolled in their sockets.
  Then, with its carcasses swinging, he toppled the
      meat-rack,   980
  smashed it and, grabbing a huge knife, hacked away tidbits.
  Three choice porksides ruined! Then smashed all the pots there

smaller then cauldrons and turned over pickle-vats, laughing,
rifled the pantry and tore out the insides of cupboards.
(*Calling back into the house*)
Hey, you inside there, watch him! I'm off to the old man.
Maybe he'd better go shopping—or else go hungry.
Everything's gone, or it will be gone in a minute.

(*He exits*)

ACT V

(*Enter* HEGIO, PHILOPOLEMUS, PHILOCRATES, *and* STALAGMUS,
lightly bound)

HEGIO: (*To* PHILOPOLEMUS, *a bit silly, almost singing*)
        Jupiter merits our thankfulness,
bringing you home to me, happy,
ending my terrible sadness   990
day after day here without you.
(*Pointing to* STALAGMUS)
        Yes! and he caught this traitor;
(*Pointing to* PHILOCRATES)
        proved this man solid in honor.

PHILOPOLEMUS: (*Betraying a certain weary impatience with his
      father*)
Haven't we poured all bitterness out of our hearts now?
Father dear, haven't we finished recounting our sorrows?
(*Glancing at* PHILOCRATES)
On to the business . . .

PHILOCRATES: (*Cautiously*)
                Ah, yes! What's—now that your son's back,
happy in liberty, what's . . .

HEGIO: (*Interrupting in his eagerness and silly joy*)
         O, sir, you have done such
deeds! I shall never be able to thank you, my dear, my
splendid Philocrates!

PHILOPOLEMUS: (*With gentle impatience*)
         Father, you *are quite* able,
and you will always be able, as *I* will also,   1000
with the immortals to aid us, to render a kindness
back to this young man—just as this miserable slave here
soon shall receive his deserts.

HEGIO: (*Undaunted*)   Yes! Words are quite useless!
Sir, I could never refuse you, whatever you ask me.

PHILOCRATES: What's—what I ask you to do—that slave that I
    left here—
is he about, somewhere? Since youth, he has always
cared for me more than himself. I would like to reward him.

HEGIO: (*Sheepishly*) That you have done so well, sir, demands in
    repayment
this and all other requests—all—granted. But sir, please,
don't be incensed that, enraged, I . . . treated him badly. 1010

PHILOCRATES: (*Anxiously, menacingly*)
What did you do, then?

HEGIO: Had him confined to the quarries.

PHILOCRATES: (*Horrified*) Stone quarries?

HEGIO: Granite. I found that
he'd lied to me, tricked me.

PHILOCRATES: (*A little too virtuously*)
Gods in the heavens, forgive me! That wonderful person
suffering so! I—I was the cause.

HEGIO: (*Revealing his fundamental insensitivity*)
                    Well in that case,
sir, you shall have him back gratis. I won't take a penny.

PHILOCRATES: (*Distracted*) Hegio—yes, many thanks. Now,
     please, get him up here!

HEGIO: Right!
(*Calling in at his door*)
               In the house there: go get Tyndarus—quickly!
(*To* PHILOPOLEMUS *and* PHILOCRATES, *indicating* STALAGMUS)
Meanwhile, sirs—while I ask this collector of whippings
what he has done with my son, what he did when he stole
     him—
care for a swim now?

PHILOPOLEMUS: Come, dear Philocrates!

PHILOCRATES: Coming!

(PHILOPOLEMUS *and* PHILOCRATES *go into the house*)

HEGIO: (*To* STALAGMUS, *with too much familiarity*)
  Now, then, my good man, light little property—stand
     there!   1020

STALAGMUS: (*Effeminate, knows too much*)
  Well what—what's proper, when *such* fine masters are fibbers?
  I've been a lovely, a "light" one—never a "good man."
  Fruitless—no fruits out of *me*, love. Don't get your hopes up.

HEGIO: (*Dryly*) You have a good comprehension, I see, of your
     place now.
  Try to be truthful for once. It may lighten the damage
  whips will inflict. Just speak it out clearly—your story,
  shameful . . .

STALAGMUS: (*Interrupting*) Ashamed? Do you say so? Of what I'm
    admitting?

HEGIO: (*Angrily*) Oh, I will *make* you ashamed. You'll be one big
    blush, you!

STALAGMUS: (*Ironically*) *Well now*, I—such a *novice!*—I'm
    promised a *whipping*.
    Good old Master!
    (*Intimately*)
                    Just say what you want, and I'll do it.   1030

HEGIO: (*Still tempted after all these years*)
    Oh, he's a speaker, he is! But save that a moment.

STALAGMUS: Just as you wish.

HEGIO: (*After a pause, with calculation*) The compliance
    you showed in your boyhood
    charms in the man—not at all. So to business: and answer
    carefully just what I ask.

STALAGMUS: (*Impatiently, seeing there's no way out for him*)
                    This is pointless. You've made your
    mind up already—now haven't you?—
    (*Betraying his fear*)
                        what I have coming.

HEGIO: (*Enjoying* STALAGMUS*'s fear*)
    You could escape from a little, perhaps. True, not much.

STALAGMUS: (*Half ironic, half hoping to escape through
    compliance*)
    Not much I can escape—but of course, I have *earned* it:
    ran off, stealing your child, and then afterward sold him.

HEGIO: Sold him to whom?

STALAGMUS: (*Like a clerk, reading a bill of lading*)
　　　　　　　　　　One Theodoromedes, Elis,
　　two hundred quid.

HEGIO:　　　　　　　　Great heavens! Philocrates' father?　　　1040

STALAGMUS: Well I suppose that I *knew* the man, *didn't* I?—saw
　　him—
　　socially.

HEGIO: (*Excitedly*) Great God Jupiter, keep him and keep me . . .
　　(*Running to his house and calling inside*)
　　Hey there, Philocrates! Quickly! Come out here! I need you.

(*Enter* PHILOCRATES *from the house, wrapped in a towel*)

PHILOCRATES: Right here, Hegio. What can I do for you?

HEGIO: (*To* PHILOCRATES, *nodding to* STALAGMUS) *He* claims
　　that—for two hundred—he sold *my son*—to your father.

PHILOCRATES: (*To* STALAGMUS) How long ago did you do this?

STALAGMUS: Twenty years, maybe.

PHILOCRATES: Lies!

STALAGMUS: (*To* PHILOCRATES) As you wish. You, me . . . as a
　　matter of fact, sir,
　　didn't your father once buy you a boy for a playmate,
　　four years old? You yourself at the time were a youngster.

PHILOCRATES: (*Wavering*) What was his name? If you're telling
　　the truth, you will know that.　　　　　　　　　　　　1050

STALAGMUS: Paegnium when he was little, but later Tyndarus.

PHILOCRATES: (*Restraining an exclamation*)
Why don't I know you?

STALAGMUS: (*Ironically*) Because it's the custom to drop all
useless acquaintances just as their uselessness sets in.

PHILOCRATES: (*Ignoring* STALAGMUS's *sarcasm*)
Tell me: the boy that my father picked up from you—was he
given to me?

STALAGMUS: Yes, Hegio's son.

HEGIO: (*Eagerly, nonsensically*) He's alive still?

STALAGMUS: (*Nastily*) Gave me the money, now didn't he? Then it
was *o-ver.*

HEGIO: (*After a pause, to* PHILOCRATES)
What do you think?

PHILOCRATES: (*In measured tones, a little stupidly*)
It's Tyndarus himself. He's your son, sir.
How can we doubt such evidence?
(*Somewhat pompously*)
He was a slave, but
brought up properly, well into late adolescence.

HEGIO: (*Deeply troubled, without losing his shallowness*)
Misery, joy in me struggling!—*if* what you say is   1060
true! Oh, miserable—to have treated my *dear son*
badly! I did much more—maybe less!—than I should have.
Oh, such suffering! If I could only undo it . . .
Look there, he's coming! He shouldn't be dressed like *that,*
though!

(*Enter* TYNDARUS, *in rags, caked with dirt, hardly able to stand—
absurdly so*)

TYNDARUS: (*To the world at large*)
Paintings I've looked at, picturing Acheron's tortures,
never came close to depicting the anguish, the horror
down in those quarries. I'll tell you, the man who is weary
down there drives all weariness out of his body
easily, quickly, it won't take long. When I got there,
why, it was just like little rich boys being given   1070
sparrows or tame ducks for their amusement: for there they
thoughtfully gave me this nice little *crow*bar to play with.
(*Getting close enough to see the others*)
Look there! Master in front of his house—and my other
master returned!

HEGIO: (*Running and embracing him, though repelled by his filth*)
                    Joy, health to you, son that I've longed for!

TYNDARUS: What's this? Son? Ah, maybe you're mocking me.
    Father—
(*Dreamily*)
ah, yes! Out of the bowels of the earth—you have given
light to me.
(*Lightly*)
                    Thank you! Perhaps you'll permit me to stay here.

PHILOCRATES: (*Going up to him*)
    Health to you, Tyndarus!

TYNDARUS: (*Confused*)   You, sir, for whom I endure this . . .

PHILOCRATES: Free you shall *be* now, and wealthy, I promise you!
    Meet your
father!
(*Pointing to* STALAGMUS)
                    This slave when he ran off, stealing you, sold you,   1080
four years old at the time, to my family. My father
gave you to me as a present. Two hundred you cost him.
(*Unaware of the hollowness of his joke*)
You were a bargain, friend of my youth! The slave here

(*Nodding to* STALAGMUS)
gives clear evidence.

TYNDARUS: Hegio? What of his son, then?

PHILOCRATES: Just go look in the house and discover—your
   brother!

TYNDARUS: Good God, now I remember—or—cloudily—
   seem to:
there was a man called Hegio—also called—father.

HEGIO: Yes! Yes! Me!

PHILOCRATES: But those chains—you must *lighten* your
   son, sir!
(*Jocularly, indicating* STALAGMUS)
And you may make *him* heavier.

HEGIO: Yes, we must do that.
   Call for the blacksmith! Everyone inside!
(*Pointing to* TYNDARUS)
                              Free him!
(*Pointing to* STALAGMUS)
Give *him* new chains!

STALAGMUS: Since I have nothing now—thank you!

A FUNNY THING HAPPENED ON THE WAY TO THE WEDDING

(*CASINA*)

Translated by Richard Beacham

INTRODUCTION

The *Casina*, which is thought to be a late play by Plautus, is an unusual work. Although it would be misguided to ascribe great *gravitas*, or moral seriousness, to what is, ultimately, a comic farce contrived to entertain its audience, it does have serious undertones, and even something of a "message." The playwright in the end upholds the values of "hearth and home," and those who have sought to violate them are appropriately caught and humiliated. Women, who in Roman society could exercise little authority, commandeer the plot of the play and determine its outcome, cleverly and skillfully manipulating their would-be oppressors: the men. The latter are the objects of a great deal of unflattering animal imagery, as well as (through frequent references to food and hunger) the equation of their consuming and brutalizing sexual desires with mere physical appetite.

In the course of the play, the men are deprived first of their food, and then, by a highly ironic twist in the plot, of the object of their lust as well. They experience a shocking comic *anagnorisis*—a recognition scene unique in ancient drama for its bawdy humor. Its basis, the "bed trick," was adopted by a host of later writers. Although not shown, it is vividly conveyed in what is clearly a parody of the "messenger speech" so common in Greek tragedy.

Plautus's treatment of his subject is best appreciated when one considers the nature and values of the audience for which he wrote. Roman society of the second century B.C. was severely puritanical in its moral values and deeply conservative in its outlook. Men exercised enormous power not only over their slaves, but over their wives and sons as well. No sign of disrespect for a *paterfamilias* was tolerated; indeed, fathers could have their slaves or children executed for disobedience. Indulgence of the senses, frivolity, the taste for luxury, or any lapse of piety or morality was subject to severe disapproval and condemnation. Under such circumstances, comedy undoubtedly functioned as a sort of social "safety valve," indulging the relatively harmless vicarious enjoyment of vices and attitudes that would not have been tolerated in everyday life. Indeed, the prologue of the *Casina* points out that the occasion for performance is a holiday, and it invites the audience to set aside for a while their normal cares and decorum.

This invitation could be more easily taken up because of the useful convention, invariably employed by Plautus, that the characters, setting, and circumstances are not respectably Roman at all (and therefore not directly threatening or subversive) but are entirely Greek. Thus, as in the case of jokes right up to the present day, directed at familiar minority ethnic groups, the audience could safely enjoy and ridicule the outrageous antics of others, while remaining innocent of any taint or criticism themselves. In this sense, each of Plautus's plays is actually an extended "Greek joke."

Plautine comedy relies for much of its appeal on the convention of "the world turned upside-down"—the comic realm of "topsy turveydom," in which clever slaves usurp their masters, love-struck sons outwit their disapproving elders, and such authority figures as soldiers are shown (no doubt socially therapeutic) disrespect. But in the *Casina*, this formula is handled somewhat differently. The "hero" is not the usual male, saucy slave, but the woman of the house. The libidinous designs of the old man and his slave accomplice (of the sort for which Plautus often shows sympathy) are, in a most literal sense, rudely interrupted. The figure of the wife, usually treated as an unattractive shrew, is shown to have justice on her side, and a fair claim on the sympathy of the audience, even if in actual performance, the portrayal of her husband Lysidamus (however ridiculous and excessive his lust) is likely to exercise a subversive and anarchic appeal rather greater than that suggested to a reader of the play. Yet it is Cleostrata who controls and dominates this play, which in the end results in the triumph of the women (both genuine and surrogate!) over the men.

Finally, it is worth noting that the *Casina* we find one of the most tightly and coherently plotted of any Plautine play. The subplots, inconsequential interruptions of the flow of action, and extended verbal digressions (which the Romans evidently enjoyed, but which can prove tedious to a modern audience) are entirely absent. The play begins in a quick, energetic scene between the rival slaves in which the essential conflict is efficiently delineated, and never flags nor falters to its final manic moments. Plautus inherited the basic plot of the play, as the prologue makes clear, from a Greek original (by the playwright Diphilus), but he evidently made substantial changes. Indeed, the prologue hints at these by apologizing that Plautus has dropped the role of the son, who presumably played a prominent part in the original. "This son who went abroad won't make it back today. / Plautus changed his mind and dropped him from the play / by washing out a bridge that lay upon his way." And of course, the title role, Casina herself, never appears either. Unless Diphilus's lost play could legitimately be subtitled *Waiting for Casina,* some fairly drastic cuts must have occurred! Perhaps Plautus took only the initial situation and idea from the Greek original, and then developed that, without incorporating the rest of the plot, which most plausibly would have concluded with the son winning Casina.

It is commonplace to note that any translation is, inevitably, an adaptation—a compromise involving difficult choices between achieving literal accuracy on the one hand, and, on the other, capturing the spirit and allusive resonances of the original and wrestling them into English. This conflict is particularly acute in the case of Plautus. The translator has to consider not only these concerns, but also the need while striking a balance between them to strive to create stageworthy language, capable of standing up to the rigors of performance. The task is made more difficult still, in the case of the *Casina,* because of all Plautine comedies, it is the most complex metrically, with a large portion of its text devoted to "lyrical" non-prose, passages, which, as they develop, have frequent variations in meter, according to changes in mood or subject. Although there is considerable debate over the extent to which these sections, the *cantica,* were meant to be sung in the sense that we understand the term, there is no doubt that such passages are in some way to be "lifted" from the rest of the text: less realistic, more fanciful, and for want of a better word, more "theatrical."

In this context it is important to bear in mind, too, that the conventions of Plautine comedy are highly artificial: there is no attempt to establish or preserve anything approaching theatrical verisimilitude or fourth wall illusion. On the contrary, the audience is constantly reminded that they are participating in a performance, which, moreover, presents a far from realistic world. The action is interrupted; characters comment on its development, refer directly to the audience and to the play itself. This deliberate and self-conscious sense of "play" is constantly conveyed by the language of the characters as well. Puns, outrageous alliteration, assonance, the coining of fanciful words, and unbridled metaphors are all yoked together to achieve a dazzling verbal dexterity—the most charac-teristic (and inimitable) element of Plautus's style. The translator can, ultimately, only suggest the elements of this style, wherever possible finding equivalents in English.

In the case of this play, I attempted *first*, to keep the language as stageworthy as possible, while preserving at all times the tone, vitality, and sense of the original, and *then*, wherever practicable, to convey as much of the literal, word-for-word meaning, as these priorities would allow. In this context, it should be emphasized, there was no attempt to make either more explicit on the one hand, or more reticent and coy on the other, the passages of sexual innuen-do or reference which abound in this play. No coloring was added, nor was there any attempt at a whitewash!

The following two excerpts, each comprised of a literal transla-tion followed by the version actually used, are typical of the manner in which the play was translated. The first, from the opening "num-ber" of the husband, Lysidamus, has been translated into a meter commonly used by Plautus, *anapaestic septenarius*, which is some-times termed the Gilbertian meter because of its frequent use in Gilbert and Sullivan "patter songs." The second, because of its de-liberately mock-heroic context, has been conveyed through the Al-exandrines used in French neoclassical tragedy.

Lines 219–23: Indeed, I am surprised that cooks, with all their use of spices, should not use this one spice that excels them all. For when love is added, I believe it a pleasing taste for all;

nothing is either salty or sweet, without love being added: it will
make bitter gall into honey, and an elegant and pleasing man out
of a miserable one.

And I do think it odd, when a cook's at his job
giving dishes the very best flavor,
he can't use for a spice, what is *ever* so nice
just a sprinkling of *Love* to add savor!
Why, what more could you wish, a mouth-watering dish
neither salty nor cloying? How handy!
Love would transform it all, making honey from gall,
and a dirty old man to a dandy!

Lines 625–29: Such amazing deeds as I saw in there, so amazing
[*tanta factu modo mira miris modis intus vidi*]; such strange
unknown boldness. Take care, Cleostrata, keep away from her, I
pray, lest in her fury she do you an injury. Take away the sword,
she is out of her mind!

Such things I saw inside, can scarcely be conveyed.
Bold and brazen badness! Turmoil and alarm!
Be careful, Cleostrata! Lest she do you harm!
The woman's lost her senses—her mind has gone astray!
For goodness sake avoid her, but snatch the sword away!

In my experience the *Casina* is one of the most attractive and successful of Plautus's works for contemporary performance. Its humor
is easily accessible, its subject matter relevant, and its plot unusually
coherent. Like his other plays, it is meant ultimately for the *stage*,
not the *page*, and I urge would-be producers to place their trust in
the theatrical skill of the "father of farce." In doing so, they are likely
to discover that actors will enjoy breathing life into these vividly
drawn characters who long to take the stage once more, and that
audiences will be first surprised and then delighted, to find themselves laughing at jokes and situations still funny (and more than a
little crazy), after all these years.

                                                    Richard Beacham

A FUNNY THING HAPPENED
ON THE WAY
TO THE WEDDING

―――――――――――――――

CHARACTERS

OLYMPIO, slave and country foreman of Lysidamus
CHALINUS, city slave of Lysidamus and his absent son
CLEOSTRATA, wife of Lysidamus
PARDALISCA, maid to Cleostrata
MYRRHINA, wife of Alcesimus, neighbor to Cleostrata and
  Lysidamus
LYSIDAMUS, an elderly Athenian
ALCESIMUS, friend and neighbor of Lysidamus
COOK and ASSISTANTS

SCENE: *A street in Athens. The setting consists of an open stage
backed by a scenic façade. This has two doorways, each of which has
a small porch in front of it, with steps descending to the stage. The
door to the left represents the house of* LYSIDAMUS; *that to the right
belongs to* ALCESIMUS. *The actor—or possibly two actors—
representing the* PROLOGUE, *enter.*

PROLOGUE

Warm welcome, folks, you faithful jovial crew.
You trust in me, I'll place my trust in you.
If that seems fair, then give a little sign
to show you'll hear me with an open mind.
(*Waits for applause*)
Now wise men—men of taste, refined,
favor old farces, just like a vintage wine.
They love the works and wisdom of the good old days,
and fail to see the merit of these modern plays
so faulty, feeble, flaccid, and fickle
with less real value than a wooden nickel.   10

Now rumor has it—as people have their say,
you're longing to applaud a play by Plautus here today.
A titillating tale, to charm, amuse, and move;
the sort of stuff the older crowd approve.
You younger folks who don't remember Plautus
we'll also do our best to win your plaudits,
with such a play! The greatest glory of its age,
once more before you on a modern stage!
Those dedicated, decorated, dear-departed souls
those ancient comic playwrights shall inspire our roles.   20

Now let me *earnest-nestly* urge you pay us close attention.
Away with sorrowing, thoughts about your borrowing, not to
    mention
work! It's fun and games, so put your cares away,
Why even bankers get a holiday!
Now all is peaceful, quiet, sunken in repose,
the shops are shuttered, and the banks are closed.
They're calculating, bankers—no need to hinder us—
For while we take a break, they're taking interest!
So lend your ears and I'll your loan repay,
by telling you the plot and title of our play!   30
Once known as, *Clerumenoe* by the Greeks,

'twas titled, *Sortientes* in Latin speech,
(or, let's see now, that's *Lot-Drawers* to you)
when funny, punning Plautus fashioned it anew.

*(During the following passage, the characters appear "on cue" in
dumb show behind the* PROLOGUE)

A married gentleman, somewhat past his prime,
his son, and slave, live here, and once upon a time
—some sixteen years ago to be exact—
this slave, no knave, performed a kindly act.
A baby girl, abandoned by her mother—that's a fact!
—he saved, and gave her to the old man's wife,   40
begging that the baby spend its life
within this very house; the newfound foundling's home.
His mistress readily agreed and raised it as her own.

Now when the girl had reached that certain age,
when men begin to notice and to gauge
their chance for romance and to "have their way,"
the young man fell in love with her—he has it bad—
and strange to say, so does his dad. How *sad!*

Now each prepares his forces; summoning all hands,
while knowing nothing of his rival's plans!   50
The father told a slave, a rustic chap,
his farmyard foreman (something of a sap),
to make the girl his own,
so, later, his foreman having wed her, unbeknownst
to Mother, Dad himself can bed her.

Meanwhile, the son has told his slave, and right-hand man
to act for him, and seek the lady's hand
in marriage, knowing if the slave would keep his head,
he'll bow to master: and so to bed.

The old man's wife has stumbled on the plot.   60
To thwart her husband, she would throw her lot

in with the son, but then, the secret's out!
Dad learns of son's infatuation, and—the lout!—
sends him abroad while wily Mother, still party to the plan,
determines to assist her son in every way she can.

Oh, a minor point and rather sad to say,
that son who went abroad won't make it back today.
Plautus changed his mind and dropped him from our play,
by washing out a bridge that lay upon his way.

Now some may mutter 'mongst themselves, no doubt,   70
"By Hercules! But what's all this about?
Since when can slaves propose, or marriages take place?
Nowhere in all the world, can such things be the case."

And yet, *it is*, in Carthage, and Apulia—and the Greeks,
are prone, and have been known to celebrate for weeks
when slaves get wed. Who dares to disagree?
I'll bet a drink, but let the referee,
be Carthaginian, Apulian, or Greek.
Well, now's your chance. No takers? Come on, speak
up! Not got the nerve to bet or anything to say?   80
On second thought, I'll bet . . . you've drunk enough today!

Now don't forget, that foundling pet,
the girl I told you of.
The sweet young thing, whom, with a ring,
the men all long to love.
In fact she's free.
Well, don't blame me!
And, please, don't worry,
for she's in no hurry, to lose her . . . "way"
—not in our play at any rate. But just you wait,   90
till afterwards, to date her.
For a little money, she's anyone's honey,
and the marriage can wait till later!

That's all I know, enjoy the show,
be healthy, wise, and strong
to obtain what through valor you gain:
great victories, as ever.

(*Exit* PROLOGUE)

ACT I

(*Enter* OLYMPIO *from the right, followed closely by* CHALINUS. *The scene between them should be played with a good deal of slapstick, including physical bullying of* CHALINUS *by* OLYMPIO.)

OLYMPIO: Can't I talk as I walk, or use my mind to mind my own business without being overheard, *gallows bird*, by you? Why are you following me?

CHALINUS: You might as well know: I'm resolved to go wherever you go. Just like your shadow, I'll follow. Even if you're strung up on the cross, I'll string along. So just decide for yourself, whether as bride for yourself, you'd descend to taking my intended Casina— by tricking me!

OLYMPIO: Why bother with my business?

CHALINUS: What's that, you creep? Why are you creeping around the town, you oversized overseer?

OLYMPIO: I feel like it.   110

CHALINUS: Why aren't you back on the farm, on your own turf? Why not mind your own business, there, and leave city affairs to city folks? You've come to carry off Casina, you cur! Get back to the outback, clodhopper!

OLYMPIO: I am perfectly mindful of my duties, Chalinus; someone's
looking after the farm. And when I've got what I came for, and
marry that girl you swoon over, that fellow slave of yours—that
pretty, sweet, little Casina—when I've got her back with me on
the farm, you can bet I'll bed down with my bride, on my "own
turf"!

CHALINUS: You have her, you! Hang me, by Hercules, I'd sooner die
than let you get her!   121

OLYMPIO: Hang on! She's mine, my booty, baby! So your neck's for
the noose.

CHALINUS: You, *d-d-dug* from a *d-d-dungheap!* She's your booty,
booby?!

OLYMPIO: You said it; you'll see it.

CHALINUS: Damn you!

OLYMPIO: Oh, how I'll needle you at my nuptials! As sure as I
breathe.

CHALINUS: What'll you do to me?   130

OLYMPIO: What'll I do to you? First, I'll make you carry the torch for
my new bride. Then, you'll go back to being your usual good-for-
nothing nobody. And later, when you visit the villa, I'll give you
one pitcher, one path, one well, and eight enormous casks to fill.
And fill you will, or you'll be well full of welts! I'll bend you double
with trouble, till you look like a yoke—no joke! And further, when
you fancy some fodder, you'll eat dirt like a worm, compliments of
the compost heap. By Pollux, you'll eat up less than nothing; you'll
famish on the farm. And then . . . at the end of the day, when
you're hungry and hurting, I'll see that you spend the night, just
right.   141

CHALINUS: What'll you do?

OLYMPIO: I'll fasten you firmly in the frame of the window, where you can listen and *stew*, while I kiss and . . . "*hug*" Casina. And when she murmurs to me, "Oh, sweetie-pie! O Olympio, my darling, my little honey pot, my joy, let me kiss those cute little eyes of yours, my precious! Oh please, please, let me *love* you, light of my life, my little dickey bird, my lovey-dovey, my bunny-wunny! Well then, when she's cooing these things to me, you'll flutter, gallows bird, you'll shudder like a mouse shut up in the wall. And you can shut up now. I'm going in. I'm tired of talking to you.   152

CHALINUS: I'll follow you. By Pollux, you won't get away with anything! Not while *I'm* around!

(*They exit into* LYSIDAMUS's *house. Pause, then enter* CLEOSTRATA *from the same house, speaking within to* PARDALISCA.)

CLEOSTRATA: Lock up the pantry, and bring me the key. I'm going next door to the neighbor's. If my husband wants me, come and get me.

PARDALISCA: "Sir" is asking for his dinner.

CLEOSTRATA: Hush! Go away! Be quiet and be quick; I'll not do his dinner today! Not when he turns against his own dear son, and *me!* in order to appease his appetite, that monster of man! I'll wrack that rake with hunger and thirst, curses and worse. By Pollux, I'll torture him with torment from my tongue! I'll give him the life he deserves, that dungheap dandy, the haughty debauchee, that sink of sin! Oh, how wretched I am! I think I'll just go and tell my neighbor. Ah! I hear her door creaking, and there she is herself, coming out. Dear me, I think I've timed this visit badly.   167

(*Enter* MYRRHINA *from* ALCESIMUS's *house*)

MYRRHINA: Follow me next door, girls! Hey! You! Do you hear what I say? I shall be there if my husband or anyone wants me. Some-

how alone at home, I'm so drowsy I just keep drifting off. Didn't I
tell you to fetch me my distaff?

CLEOSTRATA: Oh, *Myrrhina!*

MYRRHINA: Why, hello! But why so miserable, Love?

CLEOSTRATA: It's the same with all unhappily married women. In-
doors or out, we're always down in the dumps. I was just coming
over for a visit.

MYRRHINA: How about that! I was on my way over to you! But what's
on your mind? When you're troubled, it troubles me too.

CLEOSTRATA: By Castor, but I believe it does! There's none of my
neighbors I like more than you; you're always such a comfort to
me.   181

MYRRHINA: I like you likewise, and I'm longing to know what's the
matter.

CLEOSTRATA: It's simply a scandal how I'm abused in my own home!

MYRRHINA: Goodness, how's that again? I don't quite get it.

CLEOSTRATA: My husband! It's perfectly scandalous how he treats
me, and as for justice, well, I can just forget about that.

MYRRHINA: If that's the case, it's very odd, since usually it's the *men*
who don't get what they deserve from their wives.

CLEOSTRATA: Here he is, to spite me, intending to give my maid to
his foreman on the farm—the maid whom I've reared myself—
because *he* fancies her!   192

MYRRHINA: Hush your mouth!

CLEOSTRATA: I'll say what I like; we're by ourselves.

MYRRHINA: So we are. Now how can she be yours? After all, a proper wife ought not to have any property apart from her husband. And if she does have things, in my opinion she got them improperly; she's guilty either of stealing or stealth, or . . . *hanky-panky!* In my opinion *all* that you have is your husband's.

CLEOSTRATA: Now there you go! Accusing and abusing your own dear friend.   201

MYRRHINA: Oh, do be still, you silly-billy, and listen to me! Now don't oppose your husband! Let him have his fling, and do what he wants, just so long as he looks after you properly at home.

CLEOSTRATA: Are you out of your mind? There you go again, speaking against me and your own interests!

MYRRHINA: You stupid woman! There's one thing you must always prevent your husband from saying.

CLEOSTRATA: What's that, then?

MYRRHINA: "Shove off, woman!"   210

CLEOSTRATA: Shh-h! Be quiet!

MYRRHINA: What's the matter?

CLEOSTRATA: Look over there! My old man's coming! Go inside quickly! Hurry, love!

MYRRHINA: Already, already, I'm going!

CLEOSTRATA: Soon as we've got a moment I want to have a proper chat with you. But bye for now.

MYRRHINA: *Ciao!*

(*Exit* MYRRHINA *into her house;* CLEOSTRATA *withdraws; enter* LYSIDAMUS, *garlanded, pleased with himself and more than a little inebriated as he sings his love song*)

LYSIDAMUS: You can take it from me: not on land or at sea
    is there anything finer than love.   220
    Nothing half so entrancing, everyday life-enhancing
    not on earth nor in heaven above.

    And I do think it odd, when a cook's at his job
    giving dishes the very best flavor,
    he can't use for a spice, what is *ever* so nice,
    just a sprinkling of *Love* to add savor!

    Why, what more could you wish, a mouth-watering dish
    neither salty nor cloying? How handy!
    Love would transform it all, making honey from gall,
    (*Aside*)
    and a dirty old man to a dandy!   230

    Now, I didn't just hear this; I speak from experience,
    for since Casina captured my heart,
    quite overpowered, I have utterly flowered:
    I've turned nattiness into an art!

    To become more alluring, I'm even procuring
    the very best scent that's available.
    Just a touch of perfume, to help her love bloom,
    for I do think her virtue's assailable!

(*Seeing his wife, glowering in the doorway*)

    Yet . . . I *am* at a loss. There's that old rugged cross,
    that I bear, while she lives, called my *wife!*   240
    And she's looking quite vile—soothing words—mustn't rile.
    Ah, how goes it, sweet light of my life?

CLEOSTRATA: Buzz off, and don't touch me!

LYSIDAMUS: Ah, now my Juno shouldn't be cross with her Jove. Where are you going?

CLEOSTRATA: Let me go!

LYSIDAMUS: But stay!

CLEOSTRATA: I won't stay!

LYSIDAMUS: Well, then, by Pollux, I'll follow you.

CLEOSTRATA: Good Lord, is the man mad?   250

LYSIDAMUS: Yes! I'm madly in love with you.

CLEOSTRATA: I don't want any of your love.

LYSIDAMUS: You can't avoid it!

CLEOSTRATA: You shall be the death of me!

LYSIDAMUS: (*Aside*) If only it were true!

CLEOSTRATA: (*Hearing*) Ah, now *that* I believe!

LYSIDAMUS: Please look at me, O darling, mine!

CLEOSTRATA: Right! Just like you're mine. Excuse me, love, but where is that smell coming from?

LYSIDAMUS: (*Aside*) Damnation! I'm afraid she's got me red-handed! I'd better wipe it off on my cloak. (*Looking up*) Mercury, be a good chap and destroy that perfumer who gave me this stuff.   262

CLEOSTRATA: Why, you lecherous old louse! I'm almost ashamed to tell you what I think of you. At your age, going about town all perfumed up, you worm!

LYSIDAMUS: Gosh, I was only assisting a certain friend of mine in choosing a scent.

CLEOSTRATA: Always ready with a smart answer! Have you no shame?

LYSIDAMUS: (*Humbly*) All you could want.   270

CLEOSTRATA: What fleshpots have you been stewing in lately?

LYSIDAMUS: *I*, in a *fleshpot?*

CLEOSTRATA: I know a lot more than you think I do.

LYSIDAMUS: How's that? What exactly do you know?

CLEOSTRATA: Of all the worthless old men, you're the worst of the worthless. Yell, where were you, thick-head? Where have you been wallowing about? And, soaking it up? By Castor, you're crocked! Here, just look at the state of your cloak.

LYSIDAMUS: May the gods not love me (*Aside*)—or you either—if a single drop of wine has passed my lips today.   280

CLEOSTRATA: Never mind! Please yourself! Go right ahead: eat, drink, waste your life!

LYSIDAMUS: Oh now, dear wife, *please,* that's enough. Come on, get hold of yourself. And that tongue of yours. Save a bit of abuse for tomorrow's row. Now, how about it? Instead of opposing him, can't you curb your temper long enough to do a little something nice for your husband? Hmmmm?

CLEOSTRATA: Like what?

LYSIDAMUS: Need you ask? Why, Casina of course. Don't you think we ought to marry her off to that fine fellow of a foreman of ours, Olympio, where she'll not want for food, fuel, warm water, or nice clothes and where she can bring up her babies? Instead of flinging her at that good-for-nothing slave, that worthless rascal, Chalinus, who hasn't got two pennies to rub together?   294

CLEOSTRATA: By Castor, you *disaster* of a man, you do amaze me! At your time of life, forgetting how to behave.

LYSIDAMUS: What now?

CLEOSTRATA: Well, if you acted properly and with propriety, you'd leave the maids to me; after all, they're my responsibility.

LYSIDAMUS: But, blast it, why do you want to give her to that lack-luster lackey?   300

CLEOSTRATA: Because we ought to do something nice for our only son.

LYSIDAMUS: Only son be damned! He's no more my only son, than I'm his only father! (*Realizing his slip of the tongue as* CLEOSTRATA *glares*) I mean I'm as much his only father, as he's my only son, of course! He ought to want to do something nice for me.

CLEOSTRATA: By Castor, dear boy, you're pushing your luck!

LYSIDAMUS: (*Aside*) I think she's on to me! (*To* CLEOSTRATA) *M-m-m-m-eee?*

CLEOSTRATA: Yes, you. Why are you stuttering? And why are you so mad about this match?   311

LYSIDAMUS: Why, I'd like to see her go to a worthy servant instead of to a rascal.

CLEOSTRATA: Supposing I persuade Olympio as a personal favor to let Chalinus have her?

LYSIDAMUS: And supposing I persuade Chalinus to give her to Olympio? (*Aside*) Which, I believe, I *may* just be able to do.

CLEOSTRATA: It's a deal. Shall I call out Chalinus for you? You work on him, while I deal with Olympio.

LYSIDAMUS: Good idea!   320

CLEOSTRATA: He's on his way. Then we'll see which of us is more persuasive.

(*She exits inside*)

LYSIDAMUS: By Hercules, I wish the gods would do something nasty to that woman! Is that too much to ask? Here I am, aching with love, while she's doing her worst to oppose me. She's definitely got wind of what I'm up to; that's why she's so keen on helping Chalinus. May the gods do their worst to him!

(*Enter* CHALINUS *from* LYSIDAMUS's *house*)

CHALINUS: (*Sullenly*) Your wife says you sent for me.

LYSIDAMUS: That's right.

CHALINUS: Well, go on, tell me what you want.   330

LYSIDAMUS: Well, for starters, put on a happy face when you speak with me; it's ridiculous for you to scowl like that when I'm the master and you're the slave! (*Winsomely*) For some time now, I've considered you an honest and upright fellow.

CHALINUS: Oh, I quite agree. In that case, how about setting me free?

LYSIDAMUS: Oh, I'd really like to. But my wishes don't count much, unless you do your part.

CHALINUS: Well then, let me know what you have in mind.

LYSIDAMUS: Listen, I'll speak frankly. I've given my word to marry Casina off to Olympio.   341

CHALINUS: Yes, but your wife and son gave me their words, both of them: *two* words!

LYSIDAMUS: (*Patiently*) I know. But now, which would you really prefer? To be single and *free;* or married, with you and your kids in slavery forever and ever? The choice is yours; choose whatever you prefer!

CHALINUS: If I were free, I'd have to look after myself; as it is, I live off you. As for Casina, I'm quite determined not to give her up to any man alive.   350

LYSIDAMUS: (*Furious*) Go right inside and summon my wife out here at once. And bring out an urn of water and some lots.

CHALINUS: That's okay with me.

LYSIDAMUS: By Pollux, I'll soon foil your little plot. If I can't win by persuasion, we'll draw lots. That's the way to confound you and your confederates!

CHALINUS: Fine. Except that the lots will go my way.

LYSIDAMUS: The only way you're going, by Pollux, is toward titanic torture.

CHALINUS: (*Teasingly*) You can curse and do your worse; the girl will marry *me!!*   361

LYSIDAMUS: Will you get out of my sight?

CHALINUS: Upset are we? Never mind! I'll live.

(*Exits inside*)

LYSIDAMUS: Was ever anyone more wretched than I? Now all things do conspire against me. Now I'm worried that my wife may have talked Olympio out of marrying Casina. If so, she's made an old man very unhappy. If not, there's still hope for me in the lots. If I lose the lots, I'll just lay down my life on my sword, and so, goodnight! But look! Here comes Olympio. There's hope!

(*Enter* OLYMPIO, *speaking to* CLEOSTRATA *within*)

OLYMPIO: By Pollux, madam, you could put me in the oven and turn me till I'm turned to toast, before I'd agree to what you're asking!

LYSIDAMUS: Ah! Salvation! While I hear, I hope!   372

OLYMPIO: Why are you trying to frighten me with threats about my freedom? Neither you nor your son, whether together or on your own, can keep me from being freed—for nothing!

LYSIDAMUS: Why, what's the matter, Olympio, who're you arguing with?

OLYMPIO: The same one you're always at it with.

LYSIDAMUS: My old lady.

OLYMPIO: Lady? Lady is it? You follow a real sporting life with that wife of yours: day and night with a baying bloodhound.   381

LYSIDAMUS: What's she been going on about with you?

OLYMPIO: Screeching and beseeching me not to marry Casina.

LYSIDAMUS: What'd you say?

OLYMPIO: I wouldn't give her up to Jove himself, not even if he begged me!

LYSIDAMUS: The gods preserve you! (*Aside*) For my sake!

OLYMPIO: She's really on the boil now—about to explode!

LYSIDAMUS: By Pollux, if only she'd have split right down the middle!   390

OLYMPIO: (*Leeringly*) Well, golly, as a good husband, you ought to know! But seriously, I've had it up to here with this love affair of yours. You wife's turned against me, your son, the whole household's turned against me.

LYSIDAMUS: So what's your worry? As long as old Jupiter here is on your side, these lesser deities can go flog themselves!

OLYMPIO: That's a load of litter! Don't you know how suddenly these mortal Jupiters can shuffle off? Tell me this: if old Jupiter here snuffs it, and your kingdom falls to the small fry, who's going to save my hide and cover my backside?   400

LYSIDAMUS: Oh, things will go better for you than you think. Just you and I cooperate, so Casina and I can . . . (*Softly*) copulate.

OLYMPIO: But, by Hercules, I don't see how, with your wife dead set against my getting her.

LYSIDAMUS: Here's what I plan to do. I'll put the lots in the urn, and you and Chalinus will draw. If it comes to it, we'll draw swords as well, and settle it by force.

OLYMPIO: And what if the lots don't go your way?

LYSIDAMUS: Don't even think such a thing! I trust in the gods. We'll just put our faith in heaven.   410

OLYMPIO: I wouldn't invest a penny up there. Why everyone alive trusts in heaven, but I've seen plenty of those faithful foolish folks flummoxed.

LYSIDAMUS: Shh! Just be quiet for a moment.

OLYMPIO: What's up?

LYSIDAMUS: Look over there! There's Chalinus coming out with the urns and lots. Now's the time to close ranks and fight!

(*Enter* CHALINUS *with urns and lots;* CLEOSTRATA *in the door*)

CLEOSTRATA: Now, Chalinus, what is it my husband wants me to do?

CHALINUS: Gosh, what he'd *most* like is to see you going up in smoke out by the crematorium!   421

CLEOSTRATA: By Castor, I think you're right.

CHALINUS: I don't think; I know!

LYSIDAMUS: (*Aside*) It appears I have more servants than I thought: we seem to have a mind reader on the staff. Well, then, shall we raise our standards and sally forth? Follow me. What are you two up to?

CHALINUS: Everything you commanded is here: wife, lots, urn, and yours truly.

LYSIDAMUS: I could do very well without that last item.   430

CHALINUS: By Pollux, I guess you could. I must really needle you. A right prick in your backside, as it were. I've got you in a real sweat, you old reprobate.

LYSIDAMUS: Shut up, Chalinus!

(LYSIDAMUS *pushes* CHALINUS)

CHALINUS: Hey! Get hold of this fellow!

OLYMPIO: Oh, no! Get hold of him. He loves it!

LYSIDAMUS: Put the urn there. (*With the urn in the center,* LYSI-
DAMUS *and* OLYMPIO *stand on one side, and* CLEOSTRATA *and*
CHALINUS *on the other*) Give me the lots. Now concentrate, both
of you. Now, my dear, I did hope, and indeed, still do hope to
persuade you, my wife, to make Casina my wife.   440

CLEOSTRATA: Give her to *you!?*

LYSIDAMUS: Oh, yes, please. To me . . . (*Realizing his "Freudian
slip"*) No! I take that back! What I *meant* to say was *me,* when I said
him. No, that's wrong. What I wanted was for me . . . Oh dear, I
seem to have become all muddled up.

CLEOSTRATA: Yes, indeed! You certainly are!

LYSIDAMUS: Let him . . . No, that is, on the contrary, let . . . Well
now . . . uhmmm. I think I'm on the right path at last.

CLEOSTRATA: By Pollux, you're always straying from it!

LYSIDAMUS: Well now, that's just the way it is, when one wants
something bad—uhh—*badly* enough! But, anyway, both of us—
Olympio and I, recognizing your rights in the matter, appeal to
you.

CLEOSTRATA: For what?   453

LYSIDAMUS: Just this, honey pot. To do a little favor for our foreman
here in this Casina affair.

CLEOSTRATA: By Pollux, I won't! I wouldn't dream of it.

LYSIDAMUS: I see. Well, in that case I think we should have them both draw lots at once.

CLEOSTRATA: What's stopping you?   460

LYSIDAMUS: That is, after all, in my considered opinion, the best and fairest thing to do. Later, if things go as we would wish, we'll celebrate; if not, we'll bear it with a tranquil mind. Take this lot. What's written on it?

OLYMPIO: One.

CHALINUS: Hey! It's not fair he should get his before me!

LYSIDAMUS: And you may take that one.

CHALINUS: Let's have it!

OLYMPIO: Wait a minute. I just thought of something. Make sure there isn't another one in there, underwater.   470

CHALINUS: You rascal! Do you think I'm like you?

CLEOSTRATA: No, there isn't. Now calm down, everyone.

OLYMPIO: May good fortune attend my lot!

CHALINUS: Misfortune will be your lot.

OLYMPIO: By Pollux! I know all about your pious ways! Just wait a second. Your lot isn't made of wood, is it?

CHALINUS: What's it to you?

OLYMPIO: I just don't want it floating on top of the water.

LYSIDAMUS: That's right! Be careful. Now both of you throw your lots in here. There we go. Check them, dear.   480

OLYMPIO: Never trust a wife!

LYSIDAMUS: Keep your pecker up!

OLYMPIO: By Hercules, I'm afraid if she touches them, she'll put a spell on them!

LYSIDAMUS: Be quiet.

OLYMPIO: I'm quiet. I pray the gods . . .

CHALINUS: . . . will fit you with a ball and chain . . .

OLYMPIO: . . . that the lots will let me . . .

CHALINUS: . . . be hung up by your heels, by Hercules!

OLYMPIO: No! Will have you blow your brains out through your nose!   491

CHALINUS: What are you worried about? The noose is all ready and waiting for you!

OLYMPIO: You're a dead man!

(*They square off to fight, but are restrained*)

LYSIDAMUS: Now pay attention, both of you!

OLYMPIO: I'll not say another word.

LYSIDAMUS: Now, Cleostrata, so you won't be suspicious or think I've tricked you, I'll let you draw the lots yourself.

OLYMPIO: You're killing me!

CHALINUS: He'll be better off for that.   500

CLEOSTRATA: Very well.

CHALINUS: I beg the gods—let your lot slip out of the urn!

OLYMPIO: You do, do you? Since you're so slippery yourself, you want everything to imitate you?

CHALINUS: Oh, if only your lot would dissolve, you dissolute cur!

OLYMPIO: And here's hoping you melt away yourself, soon. Warmed up with a whipping!

LYSIDAMUS: Pay attention, please, Olympio.

OLYMPIO: If only this outlaw would allow me!

LYSIDAMUS: May good fortune be with me!   510

OLYMPIO: Here here! And with me too!

CHALINUS: *No!*

OLYMPIO: Oh, yes! With *me,* by Hercules!

CHALINUS: Oh, no! By Hercules, *me!*

CLEOSTRATA: (*To* OLYMPIO) He's going to win, and you'll always be a loser!

LYSIDAMUS: Shut that man's mouth this minute! Go on, what are you waiting for?

CLEOSTRATA: Don't you dare raise a hand!

OLYMPIO: Shall I sock him or slap him, sir?   520

LYSIDAMUS: Whichever you prefer.

OLYMPIO: Take that!!

(*Hits* CHALINUS)

CLEOSTRATA: How dare you strike that man!?

OLYMPIO: My Jupiter here gave orders.

CLEOSTRATA: (*To* CHALINUS) Well, you hit him right back!

(*He does so*)

OLYMPIO: *Owwwwww!* He's pounding me to a pulp, Jupiter!

LYSIDAMUS: How dare you strike that man!?

CHALINUS: My Juno here gave orders.

LYSIDAMUS: We'll just have to put up with it. My wife's already
giving the orders even though I'm still alive.   530

CLEOSTRATA: Chalinus is just as much entitled to talk as Olympio!

OLYMPIO: (*Whining*) Why did he have to go and spoil my omen?

LYSIDAMUS: I warn you, Chalinus. Keep an eye out for trouble!

CHALINUS: Oh, that's kind of you! After my eye's been blackened!

LYSIDAMUS: Get on with it, wife. Draw the lots. Both of you pay
attention. Dear me, I'm so worried, I hardly know where I am!
I'm afraid I've got palpitations. My heart's pumping so it's pounding me to pieces!

CLEOSTRATA: Oh, I've got a lot!

LYSIDAMUS: Pull it out!   540

CHALINUS: (*Seeing the lot first*) Oh, I'm a goner!

OLYMPIO: Hold it up. Ah!! It's *mine!*

CHALINUS: Hell and damnation!

CLEOSTRATA: You've lost, Chalinus.

LYSIDAMUS: The gods are smiling on us, Olympio. Rejoice!

OLYMPIO: It's all due to the piety of me and my forefathers.

LYSIDAMUS: Go right inside, woman, and make way for the wedding!

CLEOSTRATA: Just as you say.

LYSIDAMUS: You do understand it's a long journey out to that country villa where he's taking her.   551

CLEOSTRATA: I know.

LYSIDAMUS: Well, go on in, even though you're upset, and start getting things prepared.

CLEOSTRATA: As you wish.

(*She exits*)

LYSIDAMUS: Let's us go inside, too, and make sure things hurry along.

OLYMPIO: Who's delaying?

LYSIDAMUS: I don't wish to say anything more in present company.

(*Indicating* CHALINUS. *They exit to* LYSIDAMUS's *house, leaving* CHALINUS *alone on stage.*)

CHALINUS: If I hanged myself now from a noose   560
    the effort would serve little use.
    Why pay out for a rope,
    and thus give my foes hope
    when I'm already dead from abuse?
    That I've lost the lots can't be denied.
    And Olympio's taken my bride.
    But what rankles me so, and I'd most like to know—
    why was Master so keen on his side?

    How it worried and wracked the old boy!
    When he won, how he capered with joy!   570
    Wait! They're coming outside;
    from my *kind* friends I'll hide,
    and learn what I can of their ploy.

(*Withdraws. Enter* OLYMPIO *and* LYSIDAMUS *from the house.*)

OLYMPIO: Just wait till he comes to the farm! I'll return him to you bent double like a coalman.

LYSIDAMUS: Just as you should!

OLYMPIO: I'll make certain of that!

LYSIDAMUS: If Chalinus were here now, I'd send him off shopping with you—to give our fallen foe even more misery and woe!

CHALINUS: I'll just creep back against this wall like a crab, and listen to what they're saying. (*Conceals himself along the wall of the scenic facade*) While one of them flails me, the other one nails me! Just look at how he struts about all dressed in white. That thing with horns! That thicket of thorns! That settles it. I'll postpone my passing: I won't perish till I've posted that pest off to purgatory!

OLYMPIO: I've certainly been a sensationally servile surrogate, helping you to help yourself to your lady love, without your spouse suspecting!

LYSIDAMUS: Be quiet! (*Seeing* CHALINUS, *they feign the following homoerotic scene to put him off the track. Alternatively, since such an interpretation is not actually suggested by the text,* LYSIDAMUS's *sudden passion for* OLYMPIO *may simply be an expression of his overheated state.*) May the gods not love me, if on account of it I'm able to keep myself from giving you a great big kiss, my dear!   591

CHALINUS: What's this!? "A great big kiss"? How's that again? "My dear"? Good Lord, I think Master intends to f-f-f-fondle the f-f-foreman!

OLYMPIO: You're just a little bit fond of *me* now, are you?

LYSIDAMUS: Oh, *no!* Far fonder than I am for myself. Won't you let me hug you?

CHALINUS: What!? "Hug" him?

OLYMPIO: Oh, I suppose so.

LYSIDAMUS: Oh, when I touch you it's like sucking sugar!   600

(OLYMPIO *pulls away and* LYSIDAMUS *is left clutching him from behind*)

OLYMPIO: Hey there, lover boy! Get off my back!

CHALINUS: There you have it! That's why he made that fellow his foreman! I remember now once when I was with him he offered to make me his "*butler*," on the spot.

OLYMPIO: Ah, how I've pampered and pleased you today!

LYSIDAMUS: Ah, what a friend I'll be to you all my life—even more
than I am to myself!

CHALINUS: I'm afraid, by Pollux, those two will soon be head over
bollocks in bed! Actually the old boy always did go for anything
with a beard!   610

(*Starts to leave*)

LYSIDAMUS: (*Possibly having seen* CHALINUS *earlier, and now be-
lieving him to have left*) Ah, how I'll kiss and cuddle Casina today!
What a life, what a lark! And my wife in the dark!

CHALINUS: (*Hearing this*) Ah, ha! Now, by Pollux, I'm on the right
path at last! He craves Casina for himself! I've got 'em!

LYSIDAMUS: By Hercules, I'm dying to kiss and caress her right now!

OLYMPIO: Not before *I've* got her! What's the rush, damn it?

LYSIDAMUS: I'm in *love*.

OLYMPIO: Well, I don't think you can bring it off today.

LYSIDAMUS: Oh, yes, I can. That is, if you'd like to be off tomorrow: a
free man.   620

CHALINUS: (*Still concealed*) Now's the time to prick up my ears.
What fun to capture two boars in one bush!

LYSIDAMUS: There's a place ready for me over there at the home of
my good friend and neighbor. I've told him everything about my
little love affair, and he's promised to let me use his place.

OLYMPIO: What about his wife? Where'll she be?

LYSIDAMUS: It's neatly and completely arranged. My wife will invite
  Myrrhina over for the wedding where she can hang about, make
  herself useful, and stay the night. I've told my wife to do it, and
  she's agreed. So Myrrhina will sleep there, (*Indicating his house*)
  and I can *promise* you, her husband won't be here! (*Indicating the
  other house*) You'll take your bride off to the farm, but the farm will
  be right here where Casina and I will enjoy our wedding night.
  Tomorrow, before dawn, you'll take her away to the country. Pretty clever, huh?   635

OLYMPIO: Brilliant!

CHALINUS: (*Concealed*) Go right ahead and plot a lot! By Hercules,
  you two will be screwed for being so shrewd.

LYSIDAMUS: Do you know what to do now?

OLYMPIO: Tell me.   640

LYSIDAMUS: Take this purse, and go shopping for the wedding feast.
  Be quick, but get something sumptuous since she's so scrump-
  tious.

OLYMPIO: Right!

LYSIDAMUS: Get some cockles; some cuddly cuttlefish, some little
  octopussies, and maybe a nice piece of ass.

CHALINUS: (*Concealed*) You mean a bit of bass, you ass!

LYSIDAMUS: And some sole.

CHALINUS: Sole? Why not get the whole damn shoe to smash your
  face with, you odious old man?!   650

OLYMPIO: How about a little snapper?

LYSIDAMUS: Who needs a little snapper when we've got "Jaws," that
    wife of mine at home who never closes her mouth?

OLYMPIO: Once I'm there I can decide what to buy from the fish-
    monger's stock.

LYSIDAMUS: Okay. Get on with it. But buy plenty; don't be selfish
    with the shellfish! Right now, I've got to meet with my neighbor to
    make sure he does what I've asked.

OLYMPIO: Can I go now?

LYSIDAMUS: You bet!   660

(*They exit separately, leaving* CHALINUS *on stage*)

CHALINUS: You could offer me freedom, nay offer it thrice,
    but you couldn't dissuade me, whatever your price,
    from cooking those two in a stew—and how?
    By spilling the beans to my mistress right now.

    Our rivals are cornered, and caught in the act.
    If she does her part, then we've won—that's a fact!
    We'll trap them but good; they won't get away.
    We victims are victors—it's our lucky day!

    How shameless our chef has cooked up his plan.
    It's flavored and simmering inside, in the pan.   670
    But I'll lend a hand, and give it a stir;
    the seasoning I use won't satisfy, sir!

    The tables are turned, so ready or not,
    he'll eat what *I* serve: thus thickens the plot!

(*Exits*)

ACT II

(*Enter* LYSIDAMUS *and* ALCESIMUS *from the latter's house*)

LYSIDAMUS: Now we'll see whether you'll play the friend or foe,
Alcesimus. The truth revealed, signed, and sealed! As for delivering lectures on my love life, you can dispense with "a man of your
age!" And "with your grey hair!"—you can cut that, too. And as for
"and you a married man!"—you can most certainly take that and
shove it!   680

ALCESIMUS: I've never seen anyone more lovesick than you!

LYSIDAMUS: Get everyone out of the house.

ALCESIMUS: All right, by Pollux. I'm sending all the servants over to
your house.

LYSIDAMUS: What a genuine genius you are! But make certain your
servants bring their own provisions. Just like in the birdie's song,
"to eat! to eat! to eat! to eat! to eat!"

ALCESIMUS: I'll keep that in mind.

LYSIDAMUS: That's right. There never was a more generous, inge-
nious genius than you. Keep an eye on things. I'm off to the forum;
be back soon!   691

ALCESIMUS: Have a nice day.

LYSIDAMUS: And see that you teach your house some manners.

ALCESIMUS: How's that?

LYSIDAMUS: So when I return it puts out a welcome (*Spelling*) M-A-
T- for me, alone. Get it? "*Em-pty!*" for me!

ALCESIMUS: *Yeaccch!* You really ought to be suppressed—you and
  your witticisms.

LYSIDAMUS: What's the use of being in love, if I'm not allowed to be
  wise and witty? Now make sure I don't have to go looking for you.

ALCESIMUS: I'll be here at home.   701

(*They exit, separately. Enter* CLEOSTRATA *from her house.*)

CLEOSTRATA: By Castor, now I know the reason why
  My husband's been so keen to have the neighbors by.
  With them all here, the house next door'd be free,
  where they could cuddle Casina, while conning me!
  Well now, I shan't invite them, or provide a spot
  for amorous rams to rut, however hot
  they are. But wait! My neighbor's coming out.
  Here comes that *bast*ion of the state, the lout!
  Who panders to my husband's fatal fault.
  Such men as he aren't worth a pinch of salt!   710

(*Enter* ALCESIMUS)

ALCESIMUS: I'm surprised no one's come to invite my wife over to
  next door. She's been waiting ages, here, all decked out, to be
  asked over. Ah! There's Cleostrata, coming to invite her now, I
  suppose. Good day, Cleostrata!

CLEOSTRATA: And to you, Alcesimus! Where's your wife?

ALCESIMUS: Right inside, waiting for your invitation. Your husband
  beseeched me to send her over to help you out. Shall I call her?

CLEOSTRATA: No, not if she's busy.

ALCESIMUS: Oh, she's not!   720

CLEOSTRATA: Never mind! I don't want to bother her. I'll catch her later.

ALCESIMUS: Aren't you arranging a wedding over there?

CLEOSTRATA: That's right.

ALCESIMUS: Well, couldn't you use a hand?

CLEOSTRATA: There's plenty at home. I'll come see her after the wedding. Well, *ciao* for now! And give her my regards.

(*Moves out of sight, in her doorway*)

ALCESIMUS: So what do I do now? What a dastardly deed I did! On account of that ruthless, toothless old goat, I'm offering my wife's services around like some sort of scullery maid. What a lying lout he is! Saying his wife's inviting her over, and then *she* says she doesn't want her! By Pollux, I wonder if the woman's got wind of what's in the works? On the other hand, on second thought, if that were the case, she'd have questioned me about it. I guess I'd better go inside and tow the old barge back to her berth.   735

(*Exits into his house*)

CLEOSTRATA: (*In doorway*) Well, he's finely flummoxed! What a flutter the old fools are in! Now if only that worthless, washed-out wimp of a husband of mine would happen along, I could fix him just like I fooled the other one. I'd just love to stir up a quarrel between them! And here he comes, right on cue! Goodness! Look at that solemn face. You'd almost think he was an honest man.

(*Withdraws. Enter* LYSIDAMUS, *returning from the forum.*)

LYSIDAMUS: Now it seems to my mind, really quite asinine,
   when a lover's in service to Cupid,
   with a sweetheart so pretty, to spend time in the city,
   like I've done; why it's perfectly stupid!   745

For I've wasted my time on a kinsman of mine
who used *me* as a character witness.
But I'm pleased to report, he was beaten in court.
Serves him right, bothering me with his business!

Now between me and you, it is patently true,   750
when a man asks a friend to bear witness,
It behooves him to find, if his friend's of sound mind;
send him home if the witness is witless!

(*Seeing* CLEOSTRATA)

But I'm worried I'm screwed
there's the wife, looking shrewd.
And she's heard all I said, I've a hunch.

CLEOSTRATA: (*Aside*) Indeed, I did hear—it'll cost the rogue dear.

LYSIDAMUS: (*Aside*) I'll approach. (*To her*) Well, what's up, honey
bunch?

CLEOSTRATA: I've been waiting for you, by Castor!   760

LYSIDAMUS: Is everything prepared? Have you invited our neighbor
over to give you a hand?

CLEOSTRATA: Well, yes, I did invite her over as you suggested. But
that good buddy and friend of yours, Alcesimus, was fuming with
her about something or other. He refused to let her come over
when I asked.

LYSIDAMUS: That's your worst fault! You don't know how to ask
nicely.

CLEOSTRATA: It's not the job of a wife, but the chore of a whore, to
give pleasure, *treasure*, to another wife's husband! Go invite her
yourself; I've got things to do inside that need looking after—
darling!   772

LYSIDAMUS: Well, get a move on then!

CLEOSTRATA: (*Aside*) By Pollux, I'll give him a fright, all right. I'll soon make this lover suffer!

(*Exits. Enter* ALCESIMUS *from his house.*)

ALCESIMUS: I'll just have a look to see if lover boy has come home from the forum. Fancy that old ghoul making a fool of my wife and me! Why, there he is, right in front of the house! (*To him*) By Hercules, I was just on my way to see you!

LYSIDAMUS: Same here, by Hercules! Listen, lunch meat!—Just what was it I asked you—nay—*begged* you to do?   781

ALCESIMUS: Well, what?

LYSIDAMUS: Fine job you did of emptying your house for me! Fine job of getting your wife over to our place! Because of you, me and my affair are finished!

ALCESIMUS: Why don't you go hang yourself? Didn't you tell me your very self, that your wife would invite my wife over? *Uhmmm-mmm?*

LYSIDAMUS: Why, she says she *did* invite her, but that you said you wouldn't let her come.   790

ALCESIMUS: Why, she told me herself that she didn't *want* any help!

LYSIDAMUS: Why, she just told me herself to come and *get* her!

ALCESIMUS: Why, I don't give a damn . . .

LYSIDAMUS: Why are you ruining me?

ALCESIMUS: Why, that's a blessing!

LYSIDAMUS: Why, I'll just linger a little longer.

ALCESIMUS: Why, I'd like to . . .

LYSIDAMUS: Why . . .

ALCESIMUS: Why, to do something *nasty!*

LYSIDAMUS: Why? I'll do the same. I'm going to have the last "why" today, or know the reason why!   801

ALCESIMUS: But . . .

LYSIDAMUS: That's better!

ALCESIMUS: *Why?*

LYSIDAMUS: (*Striking him*) That's why!!

ALCESIMUS: Well . . . in that . . . case . . . (*Shouting*) *why the hell don't you just go hang yourself once and for all!!!*

LYSIDAMUS: Now, how about it? Will you send your wife over to my place?

ALCESIMUS: Go on! Take her, and give yourself a fabulous flogging along with her, your own wife, and that girl of yours too!! (*Cooling off*) Go away and leave it to me. I'll send my wife along to yours right away—through the back garden.   813

LYSIDAMUS: Now there's a real friend! (*Exit* ALCESIMUS) I wonder what omen I omitted when I began this love affair. Or how I offended the goddess of Love. It's a clear case of *Venus-envy!* Here I am longing to get laid, and all I get is *de*-layed! Now what's all this unholy hubbub in the house?

(*Enter* MYRRHINA *from* LYSIDAMUS's *house*)

MYRRHINA: I'm lost! Totally done for, and dead!
My heart has stopped, my limbs are trembling with dread!
Help! Safety! Shelter! Oh, where to turn for aid?
Such things I saw inside, can scarcely be conveyed.
Bold and brazen badness! Turmoil and alarm!
(*Calling inside*)
Be careful, Cleostrata! Lest she do you harm!
The woman's lost her senses—her mind has gone astray!
For goodness sake avoid her, but snatch the sword away!

LYSIDAMUS: Now what do you suppose has frightened our neighbor
half to death, and sent her scurrying outside? (*Calls in*) *Pardalisca!*

(*Enter* PARDALISCA *onto the porch*)*

PARDALISCA: Oh! I'm lost! What is this sound I hear?

LYSIDAMUS: Look over here, will you?   830

PARDALISCA: Oh, dear Master!

LYSIDAMUS: What's wrong with you? Why are you so frightened?

PARDALISCA: I'm dead!

LYSIDAMUS: Really? Dead?

MYRRHINA: Dead, indeed! And you're dead, too!

LYSIDAMUS: (*Checking himself*) I'm dead? How come?

PARDALISCA: Oh, woe is you!

LYSIDAMUS: Woe is me? No, make that, "woe is you"!

---

*The following passage, which in the Latin text is between Pardalisca and Lysidamus,
has been altered to include Myrrhina, in the interest of making for a more lively and effective
scene. The lines have therefore been given to two foils for Lysidamus, instead of only one,
with plural forms used as necessary.

PARDALISCA: That's just what I said!

MYRRHINA: Please help me! I . . . I . . . feel faint! 840

LYSIDAMUS: Look, what's going on? Tell me right now!

PARDALISCA: Please hold me—by the waist—fan me—with your cloak!

LYSIDAMUS: You know, I'm worried about all this. Unless the two of them have been knocking it back with Bacchus.

MYRRHINA: Oh! Hold my head!

LYSIDAMUS: Oh, get hanged, and stop hanging on me! Go flog yourselves, waist, head, the lot! Unless you tell me this instant what's going on, I'll bash both your brains in, you silly sluts. You've played with me long enough! 850

PARDALISCA: Dear Master!

LYSIDAMUS: What now, dear servant?

PARDALISCA: You're too hard on us.

LYSIDAMUS: You ain't seen nothing yet! Now out with it! What the hell's going on inside? Make it snappy!

MYRRHINA: I'll tell you, just listen. (*Melodramatically*) Oh! It was absolutely horrible inside, just now! Your servant girl ran completely amok, and began carrying on in the most awful, most appalling, most un-Athenian manner!

LYSIDAMUS: What!? *Anti-attic-antics?!* 860

PARDALISCA: I'm so frightened, I can't speak properly . . . either.

LYSIDAMUS: Will you *please* tell me what happened?

MYRRHINA: I'll tell you. That serving girl that you wanted to marry off to your foreman . . .

LYSIDAMUS: Yes??

MYRRHINA: Well, inside there, she . . .

LYSIDAMUS: *What* happened inside?

PARDALISCA: She's acting like a really nasty . . . wife.

LYSIDAMUS: (*Relieved*) Oh.

PARDALISCA: Threatening to *kill* her husband!   870

LYSIDAMUS: What the *hell!?*

MYRRHINA: AAAHHhhhh

(*Faints*)

LYSIDAMUS: What now?

PARDALISCA: She says she wants to kill him. She's in there with a sword.

LYSIDAMUS: A *what?*

MYRRHINA: (*Revives*) A *sword!*

LYSIDAMUS: What about this sword?

PARDALISCA: She's got one!

LYSIDAMUS: *Mamma Mia!* Why's she got that?   880

MYRRHINA: She's chasing everyone all over the house and won't let a soul come near her! They're all hiding under tables and beds— struck dumb with fear!

LYSIDAMUS: I'm dead and done for! But what the hell's got into her?

MYRRHINA: She's insane!

LYSIDAMUS: If I'm not the wretchedest wretch alive!

PARDALISCA: You should have heard what she was saying just now!

LYSIDAMUS: Yes, indeed? What did she say?

MYRRHINA: Just listen. She swore by all the gods and goddesses, that the man she sleeps with tonight . . . she'll *murder!*   890

LYSIDAMUS: Murder *me?*

PARDALISCA: (*Innocently*) What's it got to do with you, sir?

LYSIDAMUS: (*Aside*) Damn!

MYRRHINA: Why should you be concerned about that?

LYSIDAMUS: Why, I misspoke myself. I meant to say Olympio.

MYRRHINA: (*Aside*) He's good under pressure!

LYSIDAMUS: She's not threatening *me,* is she?

PARDALISCA: Why, you're the one she hates the very most of all!

LYSIDAMUS: What for?

MYRRHINA: Because you want to marry her to Olympio. She's sworn that neither he, nor she, nor you will make it to tomorrow.   901

PARDALISCA: I was sent out here to tell you. So you can keep away from her.

LYSIDAMUS: By Hercules, I'm a goner!

MYRRHINA: (*Aside*) You deserve it!

LYSIDAMUS: (*Aside*) No old lover ever lived, or lives less lucky than I!

PARDALISCA: (*Aside*) What fabulous foolery! It's all fantasy from first to finish! Mistress and her neighbor here set the trap, and I've been sent to spring it on him!   910

LYSIDAMUS: Hey, Pardalisca!

PARDALISCA: Yes sir?

LYSIDAMUS: There's . . .

PARDALISCA: What?

LYSIDAMUS: Something I'd like to ask you.

PARDALISCA: Well, make it snappy!

LYSIDAMUS: (*Aside*) I'm so unhappy! (*To her*) Look, has Casina still got the sword?

PARDALISCA: No sir.

LYSIDAMUS: Whewww!   920

MYRRHINA: She's got *two* of them.

LYSIDAMUS: Two?! Why two?

PARDALISCA: She says one's to kill Olympio with; the other's for you.
  This very day!

LYSIDAMUS: I'm the dead-deader-deadest man alive!
  To try and save my life, I'll put on armor!
  But what about my wife, couldn't *she* disarm her?

PARDALISCA: Well, she had to be very evasive.

LYSIDAMUS: The old girl can be awfully persuasive!

PARDALISCA: That's undoubtedly true, but I'm still telling you,
  how our Casina's sworn with an oath,   931
  that she won't let them go, until given to know,
  that she won't have to marry that oaf!

LYSIDAMUS: Well, like it or not, the ungrateful slut
  will be given in marriage today.
  I won't change what's planned:
  she'll give me her hand . . .
  (*Catching himself*)
  To my *foreman*, I meant to say!

MYRRHINA: Seems you stumble a lot.

LYSIDAMUS: I'm so frightened, I'm not
  giving thought to the words that I say.   941
  (*To* PARDALISCA)
  But please beg my wife, if she values my life,
  to get Casina out of the way!
  (*To* MYRRHINA)
  And you beg her too.

PARDALISCA: And I'll beg with you!

LYSIDAMUS: Do your best, as you know how to do.
  If you hush up these scandals, I'll buy you some sandals,
  a gold ring (and some other treats too!).

PARDALISCA: Well, I'll do what I may, sir.

LYSIDAMUS: Oh, please try to
   persuade her!   951

MYRRHINA: We'll go now, without further delay.

LYSIDAMUS: Yes, go right in my dear.
   (*They exit into the house;* OLYMPIO *enters with a* COOK *and*
   ASSISTANTS)
                                          Oh! Olympio's here!
   And he's gathered a crowd on his way.

OLYMPIA: (*To* COOK) Now see to it, you crooked cook, that you keep
   these brambles (*Indicating the assistants*) of yours under tight
   control.

COOK: Why, pray, do you term them "brambles"?

OLYMPIO: Because they cling to whatever they touch; try and get it
   back, and it's gone. Coming, going, or standing still, they're
   double-trouble.   962

COOK: Oh dear, oh dear!

OLYMPIO: Aha! Now to dress myself in a fancy-pants patrician sort of
   way, and meet my master.

LYSIDAMUS: Ah, hello, my good man!

OLYMPIO: I admit it!

LYSIDAMUS: What's the latest?

OLYMPIO: You're still in love, and I'm hungry and thirsty.

LYSIDAMUS: You've come well-equipped!   970

OLYMPIO: Ah, yes! Today I intend to gorge myself on "sweet delights"!

LYSIDAMUS: Now just a minute! Don't get so uppity!

OLYMPIO: Oh, save your breath! It offends me.

LYSIDAMUS: What's this?

OLYMPIO: Standing around like this is a chore, and you're a bore!

(*Starts to go inside*)

LYSIDAMUS: (*Restraining him*) Unless you stand still, I'll more than bore you—I'll whip you as well!

OLYMPIO: (*Shaking him off, and again starting to leave*) Leave me alone, for the gods' sake. Do you want to make me retch, wretch?

LYSIDAMUS: Wait!   981

OLYMPIO: Just who do you think you are?

LYSIDAMUS: I'm the master here!

OLYMPIO: Master of what?

LYSIDAMUS: Of *you!*

OLYMPIO: I? A slave?

LYSIDAMUS: Yes, my slave.

OLYMPIO: Am I not a free man? You do remember, don't you? Don't you?

LYSIDAMUS: Wait! Stop!   990

OLYMPIO: Leave me alone!

LYSIDAMUS: (*On his knees*) I'll be your slave!

OLYMPIO: That's more like it.

LYSIDAMUS: Dear, dear Olympio, my father, my patron, I beg . . .

OLYMPIO: Now you're talking sense.

LYSIDAMUS: Yes, I'm yours. Indeed I am.

OLYMPIO: What do I want with such a knave of a slave?

LYSIDAMUS: Well then, make me over. When do we start the *res-erection?*

OLYMPIO: As soon as supper's ready.   1000

LYSIDAMUS: (*Indicating* COOK *and assistants*) Well, let them get on with it then!

OLYMPIO: (*Haughtily*) Get on inside and hurry things along! Move! I'll be in in a minute. And make sure it's a super supper, with lots to drink. An elegant and dandy dinner; none of your rotten Roman slop! Well? What are you waiting for? Be off! (*They exit inside; to* LYSIDAMUS, *who lingers*) What's keeping you?

LYSIDAMUS: They say Casina's waiting inside with a sword. Waiting to finish us both off!

OLYMPIO: I see. Well, let her wait. What nonsense! I know how to deal with a bad bargain of a woman. Go on into the house . . . (LYSIDAMUS *refuses to move*) with *me*.   1010

LYSIDAMUS: By Pollux, I fear the worst! *You* go ahead and reconnoiter. See what's going on.

OLYMPIO: (*Thinking better of it*) Look, I value my life as much as you do yours! So—*you* go in.

LYSIDAMUS: Well, if you insist . . . we'll go *together*.

(*They exit, each trying to get the other to go first. After a short pause indicating a passage of time, enter* PARDALISCA *from* LYSIDAMUS's *house.*)

PARDALISCA: They never have games at Nemea,
    nor in the Olympian arena,
    such sport of the sort as we're playing inside,
    with Master and Foreman—taking them for a ride!   1020

The whole house is in turmoil and all in a flurry,
since Master is mad to make the cooks hurry;
"Don't fidgit in the kitchen, but make haste now!
Our *tempus fugits*, so give us the chow!"

While Olympio struts in the room just outside,
clothed in white, wreathed and bright, as he grooms for his
    bride—
in her bedroom the bride's being dressed by her minions,
They're aware of a plot, but suppress their opinions!

And the cooks in their cunning are conning their master
by delaying his meal, and designing disaster;   1030
overturning the pots right into the fire,
and contriving whatever the ladies desire!

They would like if they can, to deprive him of food,
and consume it themselves, once he's gone—very rude!
I confess that the ladies eat more than they should,
they would bloat on a boatload of food if they could!

But wait! I hear the door.

(*She hides. Enter* LYSIDAMUS.)

LYSIDAMUS: (*Calling back inside*) If you're wise, my dear, you women should go right ahead and eat as soon as dinner's done. I'll consummate—*consume*—mine at the farm. I want to escort our new bride and groom there—so no one will *way-lay* her—knowing as I do the sort of unsavory characters there are around here. You two go right ahead and enjoy yourselves. (*Growing impatient*) Just hurry up and send them out now, so we can get there before dark. I'll be back tomorrow and enjoy my piece of the party then, dear.   1046

PARDALISCA: (*Aside*) What did I tell you? The ladies are sending the old boy off, unfed!

LYSIDAMUS: (*Seeing her*) What are you doing here?

PARDALISCA: Going where Mistress sent me.   1050

LYSIDAMUS: Really?

PARDALISCA: Yes sir!

LYSIDAMUS: Then why are you spying here?

PARDALISCA: *I—spy?* Not a bit of it!

LYSIDAMUS: Well, be off! Here you are hanging about when everyone else is rushing around inside.

PARDALISCA: I'm off!

LYSIDAMUS: On your way, triple-tramp! Is she gone yet? Now I can say what I want! By Hercules! A fellow in love feels full even when he's famished! (*Seeing* OLYMPIO *approaching*) Ah, here he comes now! Garland on head, and torch in hand! My comrade, ally, co-husband, and foreman!   1061

(*Enter* OLYMPIO)

OLYMPIO: Come on, flautist! (*Indicating the onstage musician*) When they bring on the bride, make the whole street sound with sweet music! (*Sings*) "Here comes the bride! Here comes the bride!"

LYSIDAMUS: How are you, my savior?

OLYMPIO: Hungry, by Hercules! And there's nothing around to savor.

LYSIDAMUS: Yes, but I'm in love!   1070

OLYMPIO: I don't give a flying flogging! You can feast on love—as for me, my guts have been rumbling for hours!

LYSIDAMUS: What makes those laggards linger so long? The more I hurry them, the slower they go. It almost seems on purpose!

OLYMPIO: Well, suppose I sing the wedding song again, and see if that gets them going?

LYSIDAMUS: Good idea! And I'll sing too, since it's a two-some screwsome!

LYSIDAMUS and OLYMPIO: "Here comes the bride! Here comes the bride!"   1080

LYSIDAMUS: By Hercules! I'm beat! I could sing until I'm flat on my back, but I'd prefer her flat on her back in the sack!

OLYMPIO: By Pollux, if you were a horse, you'd be a real champion!

LYSIDAMUS: Why's that?

OLYMPIO: Always champing at the bit!

LYSIDAMUS: (*Suggestively*) Ever fancy trying a *bit* with me?

OLYMPIO: The gods forbid! But the door's creaking—they're coming
out!

LYSIDAMUS: By Hercules! The gods are looking after me!

(*Music. Enter* CHALINUS, *disguised as a bride*, PARDALISCA, CLEO-
STRATA, *and* MYRRHINA.)

PARDALISCA: Here we go, take it slow,   1090
step over the threshold with care.
By his side, blushing bride,
keep the upper hand always and dare,

to hold sway, night and day.
Make him pamper you as his task.
Never cease, him to fleece.
Just treat him like dirt's all I ask!

OLYMPIO: By Hercules, she'll get a whopping whipping if she's
guilty of even any eany meany minimischief!

LYSIDAMUS: Shut up!   1100

OLYMPIO: I won't!

LYSIDAMUS: Why not?

OLYMPIO: That bawd is teaching the broad to be bad!

LYSIDAMUS: You'll unsettle what I've set up! That's what they'd like:
to undo what I've done.

PARDALISCA: Go on, Olympio. If it's what you want, receive your
bride from us.

OLYMPIO: (*Impatiently*) Well, go ahead and give her, if you intend
doing it today!

LYSIDAMUS: Go back inside.   1110

PARDALISCA: (*Delaying*) Just be kind to this innocent, unspoiled girl.

OLYMPIO: I will be!

PARDALISCA: Farewell!

OLYMPIO: *Go already!*

LYSIDAMUS: *Go!*

PARDALISCA: Well, then, farewell.

(*The women exit into* LYSIDAMUS's *house*)

LYSIDAMUS: Has my wife gone!

OLYMPIO: Don't worry. She's in the house.

LYSIDAMUS: Hurrah! Now, by Pollux, I'm free at last! Oh, my little sweetikins, honeykins, spring chick-chickens!   1120

OLYMPIO: Hey, you! If you're wise, you'll keep your eyes open for trouble! The girl is mine!

LYSIDAMUS: I know, but the firstfruits are mine!

OLYMPIO: Here! Hold this torch.

LYSIDAMUS: Oh, no! (*Caressing* CASINA) I'd rather hold *this* one! Almighty, mighty Aphrodite! What pleasure you gave in giving me this treasure.

OLYMPIO: (*Holding her*) Oh, your iddy, biddy, body, baby!—*What the hell!*

LYSIDAMUS: What's wrong? 1130

OLYMPIO: She just stamped on my foot like an elephant!

LYSIDAMUS: Hush up! Never a cloud was softer than this breast!

OLYMPIO: (*Fondling her*) By Pollux, what an iddy, bitty pretty titty! *Owwww!* Good Lord!

LYSIDAMUS: What now?

OLYMPIO: She hit me in the chest—it wasn't an elbow; it was a battering ram!

LYSIDAMUS: Well, why are you handling her so roughly, then? Look at me. Just treat her kind and she doesn't mind!

OLYMPIO: *Ouch!* 1140

LYSIDAMUS: What's the matter now?

OLYMPIO: Damnation! What a pint-sized power-house she is!! Her elbow almost laid me low!

LYSIDAMUS: Maybe *she'd* like to be laid low—you know?

OLYMPIO: Let's go!

LYSIDAMUS: Look lively, little, lovely lady!

(*They exit into* ALCESIMUS's *house. Music. Enter* CLEOSTRATA, PARDALISCA, *and* MYRRHINA *from the other house, somewhat inebriated.*)

MYRRHINA: Nicely wined and dined, inside! Now we can come out and watch the wedding games. By Castor, I've never laughed so much, or ever shall again!

PARDALISCA: I'd like to know how Chalinus is getting along—
(*Making a joke*) the new *male* ordered *bride* and his new husband!

MYRRHINA: No playwright ever conceived a plot cleverer than this
masterpiece of ours!   1153

CLEOSTRATA: I'd like to see the old fool come out now with his face
smashed! He's the nastiest old man alive. Not even that one of
yours who procured the place for him is worse. Pardalisca, I'd like
you to stand watch here to abuse and be amused by my husband
when he appears.

PARDALISCA: Gladly. Just like always.

MYRRHINA: You keep an eye on things here. Report to us inside
what's happening.   1161

PARDALISCA: Get thee behind me, madam!

MYRRHINA: And don't be afraid to speak up!

PARDALISCA: Shh! Your door's creaking!

(*They withdraw. Enter* OLYMPIO, *in great haste, from* ALCESIMUS's
house.)

OLYMPIO: Oh, where to run to or to hide myself from shame!
 And oh, the *scandal* that it casts on Master's name,
 and *mine!* I tremble at the shame of it and how
 ridiculous we've made ourselves appear just now.
 And this is something new for me to have to say;
 —a *fool!*—I never felt such shame until today.   1170

(*To audience*)

So listen while I tell you all, and lend an ear.
It's just as comical to narrate as to hear
the quite appalling mess I've made of things inside.

The moment that we went in there, I took my bride
straight to a little bedroom, which was dark as night.
Before the old man had arrived, I said, "All right,
get comfy on the couch." Then helped to smooth the bed,
and soon began to soothe her there, and said
a few kind words and some sweet nothings to her,
so prior to Master I could start to . . . *woo* her.   1180

I start out slowly, but am filled with fear
lest turning round I find the old man there.
To get things going and begin her bliss,
I start by asking for a sloppy kiss.
She wouldn't kiss me; pushed my hand away.
That only stiffened my . . . *resolve* . . . which stayed *that* way.

I longed to taste in haste chaste Casina's embrace,
and let the old man come in second place!
And so, I closed the door to try and minimize
the chance that in the dark he'd take *me* by surprise.   1190

MYRRHINA: (*To the women*) All right now. Let's go up to him.

CLEOSTRATA: (*Approaching*) Where is your bride, for goodness
    sake!

OLYMPIO: (*Aside*) Damn! (*Despairing*) I'm done for! It's all out!

MYRRHINA: In that case, you might as well tell all. What's going on
    inside? How's Casina? Did you find her sufficiently obliging?

OLYMPIO: I'm embarrassed to say.

CLEOSTRATA: Go right on with your story.

OLYMPIO: By Hercules! I'm so *ashamed!*

PARDALISCA: Stiff upper lip! That bit about the couch—I'd like to
    hear what happened next.   1201

OLYMPIO: It's shocking.

CLEOSTRATA: It'll be a good lesson for our audience.

OLYMPIO: It's such a scandal!

MYRRHINA: Nonsense! Why don't you go on?

(*During the following sequence, the text of which is very fragmentary, the characters may huddle to confer closely among themselves, with only the occasional word uttered aloud*)

OLYMPIO: When (*Whispers*) . . . then down below . . .

(*Whispers*)

CLEOSTRATA: Well!

OLYMPIO: . . . Wow! . . .

(*Whispers*)

MYRRHINA: What about it?   1210

(*Whispers*)

OLYMPIO: Oh *my!*

PARDALISCA: Was it? . . .

(*Whispers*)

OLYMPIO: Oh, it was just *enormous!* I was afraid she must still have a sword. So I started to investigate, and while I'm searching for the sword, checking to see if she's carrying one, I got hold of its hilt. On second thought, though, she couldn't have had a sword; the hilt would have felt cold . . .

CLEOSTRATA: (*Intrigued*) Go on.

OLYMPIO: I'm so embarrassed!

PARDALISCA: Let's see . . . was it a carrot?   1220

(*She plays charades*)

OLYMPIO: No!

MYRRHINA: (*Also acting charades, and suddenly thinking she has it*)
   A *cucumber!!*

OLYMPIO: No, it wasn't any sort of vegetable. Or at least, if it was, it
   certainly was never nipped in the bud: whatever it was, it was full-
   grown!

MYRRHINA: What happened next? In detail!

OLYMPIO: I appealed to her then by her name;
   "Little wife, don't be spurning my claim!
   By Heaven above, though I crave all your love
   for myself, I'm not *really* to blame!"   1230

   Not a word does she say, but by turning away,
   puts an end to that line of pursuit.
   Since she's in that position, I ask her permission,
   to attempt the alternative route!

PARDALISCA: (*Collapsing in laughter*)
   What a marvelous tale!

OLYMPIO: As I tried to prevail,
   I leant over to smooch with my sweet.
   But something was weird: she'd a bristly beard!
   Then she kicked me with both of her feet!

I fell flat on the ground, and she started to pound   1240
and beat me just as you discern.
Without a word more, I ran straight out the door,
to let the old man have his turn!

CLEOSTRATA: That's just *great!* But what happened to your cloak?

OLYMPIO: I left it inside.

PARDALISCA: Well, what do you think of our trick—pretty neat,
huh?

OLYMPIO: We deserve it. But the door's creaking! She's not coming
for me again, is she?

(*They all withdraw. Enter* LYSIDAMUS *from* ALCESIMUS's *house.*)

LYSIDAMUS: Oh! I burn with disgrace, and I'm dreading to face
the awful contempt of my wife.   1251
The whole business is out—and this miserable lout
apprehends it's the end of his life!

The best thing, I suppose, is to suffer the blows
that my wife will exact from my hide.
(*To the audience*)
Is there no one out there who'd be willing to share
the fate that awaits me inside?

Then I think I'll behave like a runaway slave,
since my back's for the rack in these parts.
I get beat black and blue. You may laugh, but its true!   1260
It's my folly, but by *golly*, it smarts!
I think I'd better make a run for it now!

(*Enter* CHALINUS *from* ALCESIMUS's *house*)

CHALINUS: Hold it right there, lover boy!

LYSIDAMUS: Damnation! Someone's calling. I'll go on as if I didn't hear.

CHALINUS: Just where do you think you're going, you sneaky-Greeky lover? If you want to debauch me, now's your chance! Don't you yearn to return to the bedroom? You're finished, by Hercules! Come right this way! We don't need to go to court; I've a good, strong, honest judge right here!   1270

(*Brandishing a club*)

LYSIDAMUS: I'm sunk! That fellow's going to tenderize my slender thighs with his club! It's either make tracks this way, or break backs that way!

(*Starts to leave in the opposite direction*)

CLEOSTRATA: Greetings, lover boy!

LYSIDAMUS: *Egad!!* There's the wife! Caught between the Devil and the deep blue sea! Wolves to the right of me, bitches to the left! (*Indicating* CHALINUS) Only the wolf at *this* door, has a club! I think I'd better change the proverb, by Hercules, and hope to teach this old dog a new trick.

(*Turns to face* CLEOSTRATA)

MYRRHINA: How's the secondhand husband?   1280

CLEOSTRATA: (*Sweetly*) Why dear, why are you going about in this garb? What did you do with your cane? Why, whatever's become of your cloak?

PARDALISCA: I think he lost them in lechery: *conjugating* with Casina.

LYSIDAMUS: (*Aside*) This is *murder!*

CHALINUS: Don't you want to go back to bed again? (*Throwing off his bridal attire*) *I am Casina!*

LYSIDAMUS: Go to blazes!!

CHALINUS: Don't you love me? 1290

CLEOSTRATA: Answer me now! What happened to your cloak?

LYSIDAMUS: By Hercules, wife, some maenads . . .

CLEOSTRATA: Maenads?

LYSIDAMUS: Lord yes, dear. Many maenads . . .

CLEOSTRATA: That's rubbish and you know it. There aren't any maenads anymore!

LYSIDAMUS: I forgot. Well, there may not have been many maenads, but there were *some!*

CLEOSTRATA: No, there weren't.

LYSIDAMUS: Well, if I'm not able to . . . 1300

CLEOSTRATA: By Castor, you seem nervous!

LYSIDAMUS: *I?*

(*All three speaking together*)

CLEOSTRATA: Yes, by Hercules, you're lying!

MYRRHINA: Why, how pale you look!

PARDALISCA: Why, what's wrong with you?

LYSIDAMUS: Who, *me?*

OLYMPIO: (*Joining in*) Yes, *you!* Congratulations! You're the dirtiest old man that ever was! And he's brought misery and mockery on me because of his dastardly deeds.

LYSIDAMUS: (*Frantic*) Can't you be *quiet!?*   1310

OLYMPIO: No, by Hercules! I won't be quiet! Why, you begged and egged me on to marry Casina—on account of *your* love affair!

LYSIDAMUS: (*Innocently*) I?? I did *that?*

OLYMPIO: No, Hector of Troy did it!

LYSIDAMUS: (*Aside to him*) At least he would have throttled you! You really mean to say I did all these things?

CLEOSTRATA: You dare to ask?

(*Threatening to strike him*)

LYSIDAMUS: Wait, by Hercules! If I did it, then it was wrong.

CLEOSTRATA: Just march yourself right inside. Mama will limber and dismember your timber till you remember!   1320

(*They all advance on him*)

LYSIDAMUS: *Oh no, by Hercules!!* I think I'd better just take your word for everything! But, dear wife, please pardon your husband this once. Myrrhina, beg Cleostrata! If after this, I make love to Casina—or even *appear* to *want* to do so—let alone *do* it—if I ever again do such a thing—well then, dear wife, you can just suspend me and skin me alive.

MYRRHINA: By Castor . . . (*Pauses*) I really think you ought . . . (*Pauses*) to *forgive* him.

CLEOSTRATA: (*After long hesitation*) . . . Well . . . if you say so . . .
I'll do it. And the other reason I'm willing to indulge you with
forgiveness—*this time!*—is to keep a long play from running any
longer.   1332

LYSIDAMUS: You're really not angry?

CLEOSTRATA: No, I'm not really angry.

LYSIDAMUS: Do you promise?

CLEOSTRATA: I do.

LYSIDAMUS: There's not a living soul with a more loving and lovely
wife than mine!

CLEOSTRATA: (*To* CHALINUS) Go on and give him back his cloak and
cane.   1340

CHALINUS: (*Doing so*) If you wish, I'll surrender this booty.
But, by Pollux, I've suffered acutely
For I think it's a sin to be wed to *two* men,
with neither performing his duty!

EPILOGUE

ALCESIMUS: But audience, *wait!* Learn Casina's fate.
We'll share what's discovered inside.

CLEOSTRATA: A slave no more, she's the girl from next door!
And soon, our darling son's bride.

OLYMPIO: And now it's your right with all of your might
to applaud till you bring down the house!   1350

PARDALISCA: If you do your part, you'll get a sweetheart!

LYSIDAMUS: To enjoy without telling *your* spouse!

MYRRHINA: Yet listen, because—if you curb your applause—
   you'll live to regret it, please note:

CHALINUS: *No nooky!* Instead, we'll send you to bed
   with a sodden and smelly old goat!

THE WEEVIL

(*CURCULIO*)

Translated by Henry Taylor

INTRODUCTION

The *Curculio* is, at 729 lines, the shortest of Plautus's comedies. With one exception, its ten characters are familiar stock figures, true to their specified types. The plot is simple, and its final resolution turns on the discovery that two of the characters are a brother and a sister who were separated during childhood. Set against this brew of triteness, however, is the lively pace of the play, which is varied by means of songs and "set-piece" soliloquies, as well as by the alternation of stichomythia and long expository speeches. The interruption of the Choragos (Producer, in this translation) at act 4, scene 1 is unique, and provides a powerful insight into the extent to which Plautine comedy revels in self-conscious artificiality. Finally, a few of the gags have held up moderately well for centuries.

But little of this has much to do with why I selected this play from the array that David Slavitt spread before me a couple of years ago. In the fall of 1977, I found in the May 1854 issue of *The Cultivator* a detailed and solemn letter under the headline "Experiments with the Curculio." John Parsons Jr. of Rockport, Massachusetts, had spent seven years refining his method of preserving plum trees from this pernicious beetle.

> I furnished myself with a cloth three yards by two, of the cheap white cotton, and a stick about three feet long with a piece of an old rubber shoe fastened to one end to strike the tree or limbs, if large. Equipped with these materials, and a small boy to hold two corners of the cloth, I held one with my left hand, and the other I fastened around my neck with a string. I took the stick to jar the trees in my right hand. . . . After I have gone round my trees, I open my cloth and destroy the bugs with thumb and forefinger, which has proved very effectual. . . . I send you the number of insects taken each year, from 1847 until 1853. I could

321

have told you how many I took each day if I thought it to have
been interesting, for I have day and date of every day's work. In
1847 I began operations June 1st, and ended July 14th, and
caught, on about a dozen trees, 1,421 curculios.

Parsons combines solemnity and triviality as do the didactic
poets Hugh Kenner describes in his essay "The Man of Sense as
Buster Keaton" (*The Counterfeiters*, Bloomington 1968). And like
many of those poets, he is apparently oblivious to the yoking of
vagueness and precision, as at the end of the quotation. It was
irrational and ignorant—superstitious, in short—to hope that Plautus's *Curculio* would provide very similar pleasures, and startling to
see how closely the young lover Phaedromus approximates the type.
But the play's more interesting qualities have nothing to do with this
coincidence.

Like most plays, it leaves much to the reader's imagination; its
way of doing so is to drop numerous hints that it would be more fun
to see it than it is to read it. In speech after speech, flatness lurks in
the wings, and spoken references to physical acts constantly remind
us how heavily the piece depends on performance. Though the
entrance of the main character might bring Yosemite Sam to the
mind of a modern viewer of animated cartoons, Curculio very quickly establishes his comparative subtlety and complexity.

But then the Producer enters, delivers an extensive description
of Rome, and returns the action to the players. It is a moment of
astonishing self-consciousness. The setting of the story has been
established (act 2, scene 3) as Epidaurus, but the Producer makes it
clear that the performance takes place in Rome. A completely hu-
morless and slightly dense Aristotelian might conclude that Plautus
has here gone too far in search of entertainment for a Roman audience. Is the dramatic illusion completely shattered? Not quite; it is,
rather, richly confused, in a manner with which twentieth-century
theater-goers are familiar. The Producer snatches us up out of Epidaurus and brings us back to Rome; he speaks of Phaedromus first as
a character, and in the next line as a real person involved in the
production of the play, thereby turning our perception of the Producer himself in similarly conflicted directions. The line between
fact and fancy is blurred and shifty—as it doubtless would already

have been, in a second-century Roman production. These consider-
ations are the basis of the decision to give the speech the added
artificiality of rhyme.

Following the Producer's speech, the play falls into a seesaw
pattern—approaching the resolution, then putting it off. The mon-
eylender and the pimp engage in nearly identical arguments with
Therapontigonus about their obligations to him concerning the inge-
nue, Planesium. The threat of slapstick physical violence is behind
many of the speeches; the final three scenes fulfill these expectations
in some measure, as various cuffs and blows punctuate the rapid
exposition of the plot and the reversals of superior-to-inferior rela-
tionships.

A small but noticeable difficulty for the translator is that recent
drama does not include the parasite among its stock characters,
though the type shows up here and there under various other
names. As portrayed in Roman comedy, the parasite was a semi-
professional entertainer who lived on invitations to dine. Exaggerated, insatiable hunger is a conventional trait of the character, even
when it has little or nothing to do with the story line. Because the
type-label occurs nine times in reference to Curculio, a gloss is
intruded in the first speech where this occurs.

I have taken other liberties, as translators always do, even when
they claim to have done no such thing. Chief among them have been
the decisions that the metrical subtleties of Latin verse should not
be too closely approximated, and that anachronisms are fair enough
in a mode of comedy that relies on neologism for far-fetched puns.
Sometimes the kind of verbal surprise that Plautus springs might
best be approximated by a reference to such modern phenomena as
Bag Balm and Oil of Olay. In a few instances I have simply rewritten
a gag, in the belief that the original ingredients can no longer be
made humorous. My only attempt at outsmarting the scholars is a
rendering of one of the Producer's lines; the Latin reads "uel qui ipsi
uortant uel qui aliis ubi uorsentur praebant"; it is usually rendered
"or those who themselves turn or who give others a chance to turn,"
and then described as "obscure." It occurred to me that this might
describe what we now call a fence, and I have written the line
accordingly.

The primary text for this translation is the Scholars Press edition of the American Philological Association (1981), which adds the introduction and commentary of John Wright to the Latin text as established by W. M. Lindsay for the Oxford Classical Texts edition of 1905. I have omitted none of the possibly spurious lines that Lindsay brackets, but for the attribution of speeches in the final scene I have followed the Gallimard *Oeuvres Complètes*, edited and translated by Pierre Grimal (1971).

Henry Taylor

THE WEEVIL

CHARACTERS

PALINURUS, Phaedromus's servant
PHAEDROMUS, a young man
LEAENA, an old serving woman
PLANESIUM, a young woman
CAPPADOX, a pimp
COOK
CURCULIO, a parasite
LYCO, a banker
PRODUCER of this play
THERAPONTIGONUS, an army officer

SCENE: *A street in Epidaurus. The buildings represent the houses of* PHAEDROMUS *and* CAPPADOX, *and a temple of Aesculapius. There is an altar of Venus in front of* CAPPADOX's *house.*

ACT I

Scene 1

(*Night.* PHAEDROMUS *appears, dressed as for a formal party, carrying a lighted candle. Behind him come, first,* PALINURUS, *his ser-*

*vant, and then a small procession of servants carrying torches,
wine, and food.)*

PALINURUS: Say, what's afoot, Phaedromus? What's ahead?
   Why this getup, this entourage, at this hour?

PHAEDROMUS: Where Venus and Cupid summon me, I go.
   Whatever the time of day or night, no matter
   that you've been sued, arrested, hauled into court,
   you have to go where they tell you; you have no choice.

PALINURUS: Now wait, wait—

PHAEDROMUS: You wait—on me. Don't be a pain.

PALINURUS: But this is deplorable! Sad to see,
   sad to say! You, of all people, doing the work
   your servants should do, holding your own light.   10

PHAEDROMUS: It's my candle. Sweet little honeybees
   made it, and I'll take it to my sweet little honey.

PALINURUS: Where, if anyone asks, do I say you've gone?

PHAEDROMUS: If you asked me, I'd tell you, and you'd know.

PALINURUS: And if I asked you, what would you tell me?

PHAEDROMUS: That's the shrine of Aesculapius.

PALINURUS: As I've long been aware. I didn't ask you that.

PHAEDROMUS: (*Indicating* CAPPADOX's *house*)
   And here, next door, the dearest door there is.
   Ah, you adorable door, how have you been?

PALINURUS: Greetings, O most securely latched and closed!   20
    Kept your temperature down the last few days?
    Did you have a good dinner yesterday?

PHAEDROMUS: Are you making fun of me?

PALINURUS: I? Merely because
    you inquire about the health of a wooden door?

PHAEDROMUS: Loveliest door you ever saw, I tell you, and
        discreet.
    It never whispers a single word. Silently,
    it opens as my love comes out, and keeps quiet even then.

PALINURUS: Look here, Phaedromus, you're not getting ready
    to shame yourself or your family, are you?
    Not planning an abduction, not laying a trap   30
    for some innocent—or formerly innocent—woman?

PHAEDROMUS: Nothing of the kind. God forbid!

PALINURUS: Amen to that.
    If you know what you're doing, you'll carry on
    your affairs in such a way that they can stand the light.
    Don't flash the family jewels. Preserve your rectitude.

PHAEDROMUS: What do you mean by that?

PALINURUS: Guard the jewels.
    Love whom you love, but cover your rectitude.

PHAEDROMUS: You don't understand. This is a pimp's house.

PALINURUS: Oh well, then. Buy whatever's for sale, if you can
    afford it.
  Nobody denies a man the use of the public roads;   40
  just stay off private property. Avoid
  married women, widows, virgins, boys,
  respectable youth—and love anyone you like.

PHAEDROMUS: This place belongs to a pimp—

PALINURUS: To hell with it,
  then!

PHAEDROMUS: —who—

PALINURUS: Why? Because it serves an evil
  purpose.

PHAEDROMUS: Interrupt me!

PALINURUS: Of course!

PHAEDROMUS: Will you be quiet?

PALINURUS: You said to interrupt you.

PHAEDROMUS: Fine. Now . . .
  I say not to. As I was saying, he keeps
  a young slave girl here.

PALINURUS: The pimp who lives here?

PHAEDROMUS: You've got it.

PALINURUS: Ah. I'll do my best to keep it.   50

PHAEDROMUS: Oh, bad, poor. He plans to make a whore of her,
  but she's completely crazy about me; meanwhile,
  I don't want her love for a single moment.

PALINURUS: How's that?

PHAEDROMUS: I want it always! I love her
    as she loves me.

PALINURUS: Bad business, secret love. It'll break you.

PHAEDROMUS: Oh, God, I know.

PALINURUS: Well, is she in serious training?

PHAEDROMUS: She's just as much a virgin as my sister,
    unless a few kisses have spoiled her innocence.

PALINURUS: As the saying goes, there's no smoke without fire,
    and smoke can't burn you but fire can. Furthermore,   60
    a man lost in a wheat field may find his way out:
    if you want the nutmeat, you have to crack the nut,
    so pave the narrow path to bed with gentle kisses.

PHAEDROMUS: I just told you. She hasn't slept with a man.

PALINURUS: I'd believe that if I believed in an honest pimp.

PHAEDROMUS: Well, you figure it out. Whenever she can,
    she sneaks out to see me, but before I can do more
    than kiss her a time or two, she's off again.
    All because the pimp makes my life miserable—
    except that now he's sick. He's bedded down   70
    in the shrine of Aesculapius, and praying to get well.

PALINURUS: What's he done to you?

PHAEDROMUS: One time he sets a price,
    and next time asks twice as much. He won't be straight with
    me.

PALINURUS: You're not thinking straight, either, if you believe
    you'll ever get a straight answer from a pimp.

PHAEDROMUS: There's a friend of my household, a frequent
    dinner guest, an entertaining fellow—hell, he's
    a parasite, to put it plainly, but he's in my debt for that.
    I've sent him off to Caria, to ask a friend of mine
    to lend me the money. If he fails, I don't know what I'll do.   80

PALINURUS: (*Indicating altar of Venus*)
    If you want to do right, turn right here and pray.

PHAEDROMUS: Yes, here we are! The altar of Venus!
    I promised Venus to serve her here at breakfast.

PALINURUS: You offered yourself to Venus for breakfast?

PHAEDROMUS: Myself, you, and all these others, too.

PALINURUS: She'll throw up.

PHAEDROMUS: Here, boy, give me the bowl.

PALINURUS: Now
    what?

PHAEDROMUS: You'll see. At night this door is guarded by an old
    hag
    named Leaena, who stays soaked without touching water.

PALINURUS: Hyena? Bag? The kind the Chians keep wine in?

PHAEDROMUS: Whatever the word, she's devoted to her wine.   90
    I sprinkle a little on this door, the aroma
    lets her know I'm here, and she opens it.

PALINURUS: You brought all this wine for her?

PHAEDROMUS: If you don't
   mind.

PALINURUS: Hell, yes, I mind! I hope your porter breaks his neck
   and not the jug. I thought it was for us.

PHAEDROMUS: Will you stop? We'll drink what she leaves.

PALINURUS: Splendid. Is there a river the sea can't hold?

PHAEDROMUS: Come, Palinurus, as my acolyte; approach the door
   with me.

PALINURUS: All right, then.

PHAEDROMUS: Proceed to drink, O door of my delight;   100
   drink, and kindly look upon my wishes!

PALINURUS: Would you care, O door, for olives, capers, relish?

PHAEDROMUS: Pray, send thy guardian forth unto me!

PALINURUS: You're spilling the wine! What's the matter with you?

PHAEDROMUS: Forbear. Behold, the portal of my bliss swings
   open!
Does the hinge make a sound? Ah, elegant, seductive hinge!

PALINURUS: Why not give it a kiss?

PHAEDROMUS: Quiet; let us be silent together and dim the light.

PALINURUS: So be it.

Scene 2

(LEAENA *appears in the doorway*)

LEAENA: My nose has detected the sweet bouquet   110
                    of well-aged wine;
    it calls me, and I must obey.
    Invisible presence, inaudible voice
    out of the darkness, you give me no choice
    but to follow your fragrance divine.
    Wherever it is, it's not far . . .
                        Aha, soulmate, here you are!
    Sweet grace of Bacchus, be mine!
    I'm as well-aged as you, so we make a matched pair,
                    and my love is steady and true;   120
    the sweetest perfume ever borne on the air
                    is swamp gas compared to you.
    You're myrrh to me, cinnamon, aroma of rose,
            my Bag Balm, my Oil of Olay!
    Wherever on earth the lovely wine flows,
            dig my grave there, and put me away.
    You're teasing me, teasing me. Only my nose
                    has any sweet knowledge of you:
    Come hither, I pray you, and grant sweet repose
                    to my famishing innards, too.   130
    Not here, not here, that's not it—where's that bowl?
    Let me at it! I'll tilt it and swallow it whole!
    Is this where it went?
                        It's mine, if I hold to the scent.

PHAEDROMUS: Now that's a thirsty old woman.

PALINURUS: How thirsty is she?

PHAEDROMUS: Not very. Half a keg, maybe.

PALINURUS: My God,
   this year's whole vintage wouldn't be enough
   for this old hyena. She should've been a hound;
   she's got the nose for it.

LEAENA: Please, sir, whose voice is that?

PHAEDROMUS: I'd better not hide from her. Hey, Leaena! Over
   here!   140

LEAENA: Who's ordering me around?

PHAEDROMUS: Lord of the vintage,
   blessed Bacchus, hears the drought in your throat,
   your half-asleep hawking, and comes to bring you relief.

LEAENA: Where is he?

PHAEDROMUS: Here, by this lantern.

LEAENA: Please, come a little closer, come a little quicker!

PHAEDROMUS: Good evening.

LEAENA: What's good about it, when I'm
   so dry?

PHAEDROMUS: Hold on, you'll get your drink.

LEAENA: Not soon enough.

PHAEDROMUS: There you are, sweet lady.

LEAENA: Blessings on you,
   adorable man!

PALINURUS: Pour it down the canyon, flush it down the drain!

PHAEDROMUS: Shut up. Don't insult her.

PALINURUS: I'll injure her,
   then.   150

LEAENA: (*Turning to the altar and offering a few drops as a
   libation*)
   Venus, here's a tiny bit of the little bit I have.
   Lovers always give you wine whenever they have some,
   but windfalls like this don't often come my way.

(*Drinks*)

PALINURUS: Look at the old bitch knock it back! She doesn't even
   swallow!

PHAEDROMUS: Damn, I'm stuck; I don't know what to say to her.

PALINURUS: Well, say what you just said to me.

PHAEDROMUS: What was that?

PALINURUS: That you're damn stuck.

PHAEDROMUS: Oh, go to hell.

PALINURUS: Go on,
   tell her.

LEANA: A-a-aaahhh!

PALINURUS: So? You like it?

LEAENA: Good!

PALINURUS: It would be good
   to stick you in the ribs with a cattle prod.

PHAEDROMUS: Hold it—

PALINURUS: Don't, I won't. Look, though!
   (*Indicating* LEAENA, *who has bent backward as she drains the*
   bowl)
                         The rainbow drinks.   160
   By God, I think it'll rain today.

PHAEDROMUS: Shall I say it now?

PALINURUS: What?

PHAEDROMUS: That I'm stuck.

PALINURUS: Go ahead, say it.

PHAEDROMUS: Listen,
   old woman,
   let me tell you something. I'm one lost soul.

LEAENA: And I am saved, by heaven. But what is it?
   What makes you say you're lost?

PHAEDROMUS: I can't have the girl I love.

LEAENA: Now, Phaedromus, my dear, you mustn't whine.
   You just make sure I don't get thirsty,
   and I'll take care of getting your sweetheart out here.

PHAEDROMUS: If you manage that, I'll make you a statue of vines
   instead of gold, a monument to your—heroic capacity.   170
   (LEAENA *exits*)
   O Palinurus, will anyone on earth
   be luckier than I am when she comes out here?

PALINURUS: By God, sir, a man in love and out of money is in a
   mess.

PHAEDROMUS: True, but that's not my problem; I'm sure
   my friendly parasite will bring me some money today.

PALINURUS: You're confident of grave uncertainties.

PHAEDROMUS: Suppose I cuddle up to the door and sing it a
   serenade.

PALINURUS: You're not the Phaedromus I thought I knew,
   so I won't presume to advise you either way.

PHAEDROMUS: I stand in the darkness, beautiful bolts,   180
         and my cry wells up from deep in my heart:
   I beg you, by your grace and loveliness,
         take a desperate lover's part:

   Cease to be deadbolts, turn into live bolts,
         lither than dancers tum *tum* tum tadee . . .
   Spring open, slide back, oh, let us connive, bolts,
         to bring my sweetheart out gently to me.

   But look how the latches keep sleeping, the wretches—
   whatever's holding them won't set them free.
   That's that. I see you won't help me tonight . . .   190
   wait! Sh, sh!

PALINURUS: Good God. But I'll be quiet.

PHAEDROMUS: I heard something.
   At last, thank heavens, the latches have heard me!

Scene 3

(The door begins to open)

LEAENA: Be quiet, sweetheart, don't let the hinges creak,
   or the master will know what we're up to.
   I'll dampen the hinges a bit.

PALINURUS: See how the old bitch plays doctor?
   She keeps the pure stuff for herself, and waters the door.

(PLANESIUM appears in the doorway)

PLANESIUM: Who asks that I obey the laws of love? I answer
   the summons, and pray that you appear. Where are you?

PHAEDROMUS: Here I am; if I didn't show up, my sweet, I'd
   deserve what I got.   200

PLANESIUM: My love, I don't like my sweetheart to keep his
   distance.

PHAEDROMUS: Palinurus, Palinurus . . .

PALINURUS: Why call to me at a
   time like this?

PHAEDROMUS: She's so lovely.

PALINURUS: Entirely too lovely, if you ask me.

PHAEDROMUS: I am a god.

PALINURUS: No, a man, but not much of one.

PHAEDROMUS: What have you seen—
   what will you ever see, more like a god than I am?

PALINURUS: I see an unfortunate man who has lost his head.

PHAEDROMUS: You have an unfortunate way of using yours.
    Shut up.

PALINURUS: Well, if all you want to do is stand and stare at her,
I'll have to conclude that you enjoy torturing yourself.

PHAEDROMUS: I stand corrected. This is what I've wanted all
    this time.   210

PLANESIUM: Then hold me, take me in your arms!

PHAEDROMUS: This is what I
    live for.
Your master keeps us apart, but still we meet in secret.

PLANESIUM: He cannot, he will not keep me from you,
    until death has taken possession of my heart.

PALINURUS: It's clear enough my master is a fool:
    a sane affair is fine, losing control is risky,
    and total insanity is what we have here.

PHAEDROMUS: Kings may have their kingdoms, rich men their
    gold;
    let them have their honors, heroics, and battles;
    let no man envy me, and all keep what is theirs.   220

PALINURUS: What have you done? Pledged a *pervigilium Veneris*?
    My God, it won't be long before daybreak.

PHAEDROMUS: Quiet, please.

PALINURUS: Quiet, eh? Why not go to sleep?

PHAEDROMUS: I am
    asleep. Do not disturb.

PALINURUS: Come on, you're wide awake.

PHAEDROMUS: I am sleeping, even
    dreaming, in my fashion.

PALINURUS: Look, miss, why torture a harmless man?

PLANESIUM: How
    would you like
to have your dinner snatched away while you're still eating?

PALINURUS: I give up. I can see they're equally insane,
    perishing of love; look at them tussle.
    Can't get enough of each other. Will you break it up?

PLANESIUM: No human blessing endures, as the saying goes;
    our bliss has to be spoiled by this pest.   230

PALINURUS: What's that, bitch? You, with your owl's eyes
    staring through the night, you call me a pest?
    You drunken little whore, you worthless tramp!

PHAEDROMUS: You, you dare insult my Venus? A slave, a
    whipping boy,
talk that way in my presence? Now, by God,
I'll make you flinch for that!
(*Whacks* PALINURUS *on the side of the head*)
                    That'll teach you!

PALINURUS: Help, help, Venus of owll-night vigils!

PHAEDROMUS: Can't you
    stop, you shit?

PLANESIUM: No use to hit a stone; you'll only hurt your hand.

PALINURUS: It's a disgrace, Phaedromus, a damned scandal,   240
   punching a man who tells the truth and loving a woman like
      that.
   I can't believe you've gone so far off the deep end.

PHAEDROMUS: A moderate lover is rarer than gold.

PALINURUS: And reasonable masters are ten times scarcer.

PLANESIUM: Goodnight, my love; I hear doors and people
      stirring,
   getting ready to open the temple. Tell me: how long
   must we go on this way, loving and hiding?

PHAEDROMUS: Not long; I sent my parasite to Caria two days ago
   to get me some money. He should come back today.

PLANESIUM: It's taking too long.

PHAEDROMUS: I swear by Venus,   250
   you won't be there three days before I make you free.

PLANESIUM: See to it. Before I go, another kiss.

PHAEDROMUS: Oh God, if I
      had a kingdom,
   I'd give it up for this! When will I see you?

PLANESIUM: When you get me my freedom. If you love me,
      buy me;
   no more questions. Get to work and get the job done.
      Goodbye, sweet!

PHAEDROMUS: Alone again! Palinurus, I am dead.

PALINURUS: So am I, what with beating and lack of sleep.

PHAEDROMUS: Come
    with me.

ACT II

Scene 1

(*Several hours later.* CAPPADOX *enters from the temple.*)

CAPPADOX: So. I might as well quit lying around in the temple.
    Aesculapius isn't going to bother with me,
    let alone cure me. My strength is trickling away,   260
    my sickness bloats me, my spleen is swelling up,
    and anyone seeing me walking along would swear
    I was pregnant with large twin boys. I really think
    I'm going to explode. Agh! Misery!

PALINURUS: (*Coming out of* PHAEDROMUS's *house, speaking to*
    PHAEDROMUS *within*)
    I think you ought to listen to me, Phaedromus,
    and stop worrying. You're paralyzed because
    your parasite hasn't come back from Caria.
    He's got to be bringing the money; otherwise,
    he'd have been here by now. Nothing could keep him away
    from his accustomed feed bag.

CAPPADOX: Who is that speaking?   270

PALINURUS: Who said that?

CAPPADOX: Say, aren't you Phaedromus's man, Palinurus?

PALINURUS: Now, who have we here, with a belly like a melon
and eyes the color of salad greens? The architecture
is familiar, but the decor escapes me. But of course;
it's Cappadox the pimp. I'll chat with him.

CAPPADOX: Good day, Palinurus.

PALINURUS: Greetings, scumbag. How
goes it?

CAPPADOX: I'm living.

PALINURUS: As you well deserve. But what's the
matter with you?

CAPPADOX: My spleen is swollen, my kidneys hurt,
my lungs are in tatters, my liver's in agony,   280
my heart-cords are slack, my guts are in tangles.

PALINURUS: A liver problem, probably. Yours, or one you ate.

CAPPADOX: Fine, make cheap fun of misery.

PALINURUS: See if you can survive
a few more days, while the process is at its peak,
and let your intestines ferment a bit more. Do that,
and all of you won't be as valuable as your guts alone.

CAPPADOX: My spleen has had it.

PALINURUS: Brisk walks are best for the spleen.

CAPPADOX: Quit the jokes a moment. In all seriousness,
if I tell you a dream I had last night, could you figure it out?

PALINURUS: You're in luck. I'm famous for divination. No,
really.   290
Even the prophets swear by my advice.

Scene 2

(COOK *enters from* PHAEDROMUS's *house*)

COOK: Palinurus, why are you still standing around?
   Bring me the things I sent you for, and be quick.
   I want the parasite's lunch to be ready when he gets here.

PALINURUS: Kindly allow me to interpret this man's dream.

COOK: You? You come to me for that kind of advice.

PALINURUS: True enough.

COOK: Go on; get the stuff.

PALINURUS: You, meanwhile,
   tell him your dream. I defer to an expert.
   He taught me all I know.

CAPPADOX: Just so he helps me.

PALINURUS: (*Exiting*)   You're in good
   hands.

CAPPADOX: You don't often see a pupil so respectful of his
   teacher.   300
   So, help me out, will you?

COOK: I don't know you, but I'll listen.

CAPPADOX: Last night I dreamed I saw Aesculapius
   sitting not far away. I don't think he saw me.
   He wouldn't come closer, and he even seemed to be avoid-
      ing me.

COOK: All the other gods will do likewise, clearly.
    They operate, you see, in perfect harmony together.
    It's not surprising you don't improve.
    You'd have done better to lie in Jupiter's shrine,
    since he's the one you swear by most of the time.

CAPPADOX: Look, if everybody who swore wanted to lie
    there,   310
    even the Capitol wouldn't hold them.

COOK: Listen. Go make your peace with Aesculapius,
    or your dream will come true.

CAPPADOX: Many thanks. I'll go pray now.

(*Exits into temple*)

COOK: And a fat lot of good may it do you.

(*Exits into house*)

PALINURUS: (*Reentering with kitchen supplies*)
    By the immortal gods, who do I see? Isn't that
    the parasite Phaedromus sent to Caria?
    Hey, Phaedromus, come out, come out—quick, I say!

PHAEDROMUS: (*Entering from his house*)
    What are you yelling about?

PALINURUS: Your parasite! Look!
    Down at the end of the street, running this way.
    Can you hear what he's up to?

PHAEDROMUS: Let's see.   320

Scene 3

(*Enter* CURCULIO)

CURCULIO: Heads up! Official business! Friend or stranger,
  out of the way! Clear the street, beware
  my head, or chest, or elbow, or knee!
  I'm serious. This is urgent! Of major importance!
  Nobody has what it takes to detain me now—
  no general, no emperor, no meat inspector,
  nor mayor, nor councilman, however intrepid—
  I'll chuck 'em off thē sidewalk on their heads!
  As for those Greeks in short cloaks, walking around
  with their heads covered, their clothes all stuffed   330
  with books and food baskets, runaway slaves, most of them,
  plotting and arguing, who block your path, muttering
  grave conclusions, or sit in the toddy shop
  when they've stolen some money, drinking hot drinks
  and muffling their heads, then setting out, more somber
  than sober—if I bang into them, I'll pound
  a grain-fed fart out of every one of them!
  And the slaves of dandies, playing ball in the street,
  pitchers and catchers, referees, spectators, all
  will be trampled. So stay home, and stay out of trouble.   340

PHAEDROMUS: He knows what he'd do if he were in charge.
  Servants these days are out of control.

CURCULIO: Can anybody help me find Phaedromus, my patron?
  It's urgent, I have to see him right away.

PALINURUS: (*To* PHAEDROMUS) He's looking for you.

PHAEDROMUS: Then let's
  hail him.
  Curculio! Hold up!

CURCULIO: Who's that? Who calls my name?

PHAEDROMUS: Someone who's looking for you!

CURCULIO: Ah! And I'm
  looking for you!

PHAEDROMUS: Well, my friend, it's about time! Glad to see you!

CURCULIO: Greetings.

PHAEDROMUS: It's good to see you here safely. Give me your
  hand.
  For God's sake, say something! How's my luck?   350

CURCULIO: For God's sake, how's *mine*?

PHAEDROMUS: What's the matter?

CURCULIO: My
  knees . . .
  giving way. . . . Everything's going black!

PHAEDROMUS: Good God! Fatigue, I
  suppose.

CURCULIO: Help. Hold me up. Give me an arm.

PHAEDROMUS: He's turning
  pale!
  Quick, a chair! Water! Come on, move!

CURCULIO: I'm passing out!

PALINURUS: Want some water?

CURCULIO: If there's food in it.
  Give it here, I'll soak it up.

PALINURUS: Oh, to hell with you!

CURCULIO: For God's sake, something gustatory to come home to!

PALINURUS: But of course.

(*Fans* CURCULIO *vigorously with cloak*)

CURCULIO: Hey, what is this?

PALINURUS: Something gusty!

CURCULIO: I didn't say that!

PHAEDROMUS: What do you want?

CURCULIO: Gustatory
    delights—food!

PALINURUS: Pig!

CURCULIO: I'm dying, my teeth are blurred, my tongue   360
    is bloodshot with hunger, my empty guts are worn out!

PHAEDROMUS: You shall have something immediately.

CURCULIO: Not just "something." A particular thing is better.

PHAEDROMUS: But if you knew what we have here . . .

CURCULIO: What I want
      to know
    is where it is; my teeth are anxious to meet with it.

PHAEDROMUS: Ham, tripe, sow's udder, sweetbreads—

CURCULIO: You really
    have all that?
    Probably put away somewhere.

PHAEDROMUS: No, no, served up and ready.
    We knew you were coming.

CURCULIO: Look here, don't play games with me.

PHAEDROMUS: As the girl I love loves me, I'm not lying.
    But what about what I sent you for? You haven't said.   370

CURCULIO: I haven't got anything to say.

PHAEDROMUS: You've destroyed me!

CURCULIO: Ah, but bear with me, and be revived.
    As you requested, I set out, and finally got
    to Caria; I see your friend and ask him
    to lend you money. You should be aware
    that he sends his best wishes, is truly sorry
    to let you down, wants to act as a man should
    toward a friend, and be helpful to you.
    Briefly, but in all honesty, he tells me
    he's in the same shape you are—badly short of money.   380

PHAEDROMUS: Your words are killing me!

CURCULIO: No, rescuing you—
    as I will, too.
    Well, his answer depressed me; I hated
    coming up empty. I left and went to the forum,
    where I run into a military officer. We speak,
    he shakes my hand, takes me aside, and asks
    what brings me to Caria. I tell him I'm there
    for pleasure. He asks me if I know a banker
    in Epidaurus, name of Lyco. I say we've met.
    "Have you?" he says. "What about a pimp,

Cappadox?" Turns out I've seen him; what of it?   390
"Well, I bought a girl from him, and paid extra
for some clothes and jewelry." "Have you paid him?"
"No, I left the money with this banker Lyco,
and told him that when he gets a letter from me,
sealed with my ring, he is to make sure the bearer
is supposed to get the girl from the pimp,
along with the jewelry and clothes." I'm about to leave,
but he calls me back and invites me to dinner.
My principles forbid me to decline.
"What say we go now," he says, "and take our seats?"   400
Sounds good to me. "Neither the day extend
unduly, nor abbreviate the evening."
"Everything's ready." "For us, it seems, since we are here."
By and by, we're well fed and well oiled,
he calls for the dice and challenges me to a game.
I accept, and bet my cloak; he bets his mantle,
by God, and for good luck, calls on Planesium.

PHAEDROMUS: Not my love?

CURCULIO: Hang on a minute. He throws four
    buzzards.
Not bad, but I take the dice, call on my first teacher,
Hercules of Eating Contests, and throw the royal lineup.   410
I give him a big drink, he drains it, and pretty soon
he passes out. I remove the ring from his finger,
carefully, and my feet from the couch, and start out.
The servants ask where I'm headed. "Where the well-soaked
may be comforted," I say, and when I find the door, I'm gone.

PHAEDROMUS: Well done!

CURCULIO: So far, maybe, but we've still got
    work to do.
Let's go inside and put a seal on a letter.

PHAEDROMUS: Am I in your way?

CURCULIO: First, though, ham, sow's udder, sweetbreads.
　　That's the ballast for a stomach—bread and beef,
　　a big goblet and a full pot—inspiration!   420
　　You be the writer, he'll be the waiter,
　　I'll eat and dictate. Shall we?

PHAEDROMUS: After you.

(*All exit into the house*)

ACT III

Scene 1

(*Enter* LYCO)

LYCO: Things don't look too bad. Going over my books,
　　figuring up what I have in hand and what I owe,
　　I see I'm rich, if I don't pay what I owe;
　　if I do, I'll be in the red. But I've had an idea:
　　if my creditors push me, I'll declare bankruptcy.
　　Most of us in my profession are accustomed
　　to collecting debts, but not to paying them.
　　We close accounts with our fists if we have to.   430
　　If you learn to make money, you'd better learn
　　to be thrifty, or you'll soon learn to be broke.
　　I had an idea I might buy a slave,
　　but I'd better rent one; I need my money.

(CURCULIO, *disguised as a veteran with an eye patch, comes from the house with a slave; he speaks over his shoulder to* PHAEDROMUS, *within*)

CURCULIO: I know what to do, and I'll do it right.
   I'm too full to take advice. Not another word.
   (Aside)
   By God, I did all right there! Even so,
   I left a little corner free in my belly—
   a resting place for the rest of the rest.
   (Seeing LYCO)
   Now, who's this with his head covered, praying   440
   to Aesculapius? Well, well, the very man I seek.
   (To slave)
                                                   Come along.
   I'll pretend I don't know him. Hey, you! Hold up!

LYCO: Good day, Cyclops.

CURCULIO: Are you making fun of me?

LYCO: Why, no; your sight is better than mine. You can see
   twice as many eyes in my head as I can see in yours.

CURCULIO: Sir. It was struck out by a catapult at Sicyon.

LYCO: I don't care if somebody threw an ash-pot at you.

CURCULIO: Now this one's gifted, he is; he says it as it was.
   That's the sort of catapult I usually have to dodge.
   My good man, this honorable scar was part of my payment   450
   for public service; pray do not insult me publicly.

LYCO: Then might one interest you in something more private?

CURCULIO: No sir, not I, I don't go on for such goings-in,
   in public or in private. But if you can tell me
   where to locate the man I'm looking for,
   I'll return the favor with a big, long hunk of gratitude.
   I'm looking for Lyco, the banker.

LYCO: Well, now, what would you want him for? Who sent you?

CURCULIO: I represent Captain Therapontigonus Platagidorus.

LYCO: By God, there's a name I know quite well.   460
    I filled four pages once, just writing it down.
    What do you want with Lyco?

CURCULIO: I have been charged
    with delivering this letter to him.

LYCO: And you are—?

CURCULIO: The captain's freedman, Puissant; they call me
    Pissant.

LYCO: Puissant, greetings. Why Pissant, though?

CURCULIO: Because when I go to sleep drunk, I wet my clothes.

LYCO: It would be better if you put up somewhere else;
    there's no room for a Pissant at my place.
    The man you seek, however, is I.

CURCULIO: Really? You are Lyco the banker?

LYCO: I am.   470

CURCULIO: Therapontigonus sends his warmest greetings;
    he ordered me to give you this letter.

LYCO: To me?

CURCULIO: Precisely. Examine the seal.
    You recognize it, I think.

LYCO: Certainly.
    An armed man splitting an elephant in two.

CURCULIO: Whatever is written there, he told me to tell you
   that he thanks you for carrying it out exactly.

LYCO: Stand away and let me read.

CURCULIO: As you wish,
   just so I leave with what he sent me for.

LYCO: "Captain Therapontigonus Platagidorus to Lyco,   480
   his host in Epidaurus, warmest greetings."

CURCULIO: Good, good, I've got him now, he's on the hook.

LYCO: "I hereby require that the bearer of this message
   be given custody of the girl I bought there
   with your kind assistance—and the jewelry and clothes.
   As per our agreement, pay the pimp,
   and release the girl to my messenger."
   But what about him? Why doesn't he come himself?

CURCULIO: I can explain: three days ago we came into Caria
   from India; now he's having a statue built there,   490
   pure gold, seven feet high. A monument to his deeds.

LYCO: And what were those?

CURCULIO: Monumental! The Persians,
   Paphlagonians, Sinopians, Arabs, Carians,
   Cretans, Syrians, Rhodes and Lycia, Upper Devouria
   and Lower Bibula, Centauromachia
   and Unomammaria, the Libyan coast,
   all of Hangoveria, half the nations
   of the world, to say nothing of Albania
   and the Duke University English Department,
   have fallen to him, fighting alone, in three weeks.   500

LYCO: Wha!

CURCULIO: What surprises you?

LYCO: If all those people
   were put in a cage together, like chickens,
   you couldn't walk around them in a year.
   By God, I believe he sent you; you're both full of shit.

CURCULIO: I can tell you more.

LYCO: Forget it. Come with me;
   I'll take care of the business you came to do.
   (CAPPADOX *enters from the temple*)
   And there's the very man. Good day, pimp.

CAPPADOX: Blessings on you.

LYCO: You know why I'm here.

CAPPADOX: Oh?

LYCO: Here's your money; the girl goes with him.

CAPPADOX: What about the promise I made?   510

LYCO: What's that to you?
   The main thing is, you get your money.

CAPPADOX: Some advice is better than real help.
   This way, gentlemen.

CURCULIO: All right, pimp, don't make me wait.

(*All go into the house*)

ACT IV

Scene 1

(The PRODUCER *enters. During this speech, it becomes clear that though the play is set in Epidaurus, the production referred to here is being played in Rome.)*

PRODUCER: I wonder where Phaedromus found this wonder.
    Sharp, would you say? Or merely orotund, or
    a rotunda? I doubt that I'll recover
    the clothes he rented from me; gone forever,
    though I dealt with Phaedromus, not with him.
    I'll keep my eyes peeled. In the interim,
    since we have this unusual intermission,   520
    I'll give you a brief tour, with your permission,
    of this locale, whose dens and denizens
    are pure and impure types and specimens
    of most of our native probities and merits,
    and more than our fair share of meaner spirits.
    For perjurers, you may as well inquire
    at the Assembly. The shrine of the Purifier
    attracts braggarts, and spendthrifts congregate
    at the Basilica, where they evaluate
    the worn-out whores among their seedy clients.   530
    The gastronomes pursue their greedy science
    in the market, while in the lower forum
    you'll walk among rich men of strict decorum.
    Up in mid-forum, alongside the canal,
    each would-be dandy puffs his own morale;
    above the lake the gossips dole and hoard
    their calumnies, as if they'd never heard
    malicious words applied to them. Down there
    below the old shops, moneylenders spare
    the borrower no expense. Castor's temple shelters   540
    pickpockets, con men, and like helter-skelters.

The Tuscan Alley is where the male whores gather;
you'll visit the Velabrum if you'd rather
a miller, butcher, prophet—or perchance
that double-dealer in stolen goods, the fence.
The faithless husbands with their wads of cash
go to Leucadia's. From virtue down to trash,
here is God's plenty; now that the play
is ready to resume, I'll stand away.

Scene 2

(CURCULIO, CAPPADOX, LYCO, *and* PLANESIUM *appear in the door-way of* CAPPADOX's *house*)

CURCULIO: After you, sweetheart; I can't watch what's behind me.
     The captain says her clothes and jewelry are his, too.   550

CAPPADOX: No one denies it.

CURCULIO: It's just as well to remind you.

LYCO: Don't forget, now: if this girl should prove
     freeborn, you promised my money back.

CAPPADOX: I remember, and my promise is still good.

CURCULIO: I, too, will want you to bear this well in mind.

CAPPADOX: I remember, I tell you. I convey full title to her.

CURCULIO: Am I to accept full title from a pimp,
     one of those who own no more than a tongue
     to perjure away their honest debts? You sell women,   560
     set them free, and tell them what to do, and yet
     none of them are yours; no one can cosign for you,
     nor you for anyone; of all humanity, the pimps

are about the same as bugs: flies, gnats, lice, fleas;
pesky, hateful, disgusting, no good to anyone.
No sensible man would stand near you in the forum,
since anyone who does is pointed out and slandered:
people say he's going broke, even though he's innocent.

LYCO: By God, Cyclops, you seem to know your pimps!

CURCULIO: And you, by God, are just as bad, maybe worse.   570
    At least they operate in private; in public, you
    ruin men with usury; they do it with whorehouses.
    The people have passed countless laws against you,
    but they never hold; you always find a loophole.
    Law to you is like hot water: it will cool.

LYCO: I should have kept quiet.

CAPPADOX: You've thought hard about hard
    sayings.

CURCULIO: To speak ill of the innocent is to speak ill,
    but you can hardly slander the guilty, it seems to me.
    I need no collateral from you or from any other pimp.
    Now, Lyco, is that all?

LYCO: Goodbye, farewell.   580

CURCULIO: Goodbye.

CAPPADOX: Just a moment. A word with you.

CURCULIO: Well, what is it?

CAPPADOX: I trust she'll be well cared for;
    she was brought up well and chastely here.

CURCULIO: What will you contribute toward her welfare?

CAPPADOX: Oh, hell.

CURCULIO: I expect that's where you're headed.

CAPPADOX: (*To* PLANESIUM, *who is crying*)
    What are you crying for, you stupid girl?
    There's nothing to be afraid of. By God, I have sold you well.
    Just be good, sweetheart, and go along sweetly with him.

LYCO: So, Pissant, is there anything else you need from me?

CURCULIO: Goodbye and good luck; I appreciate   590
    your generosity with time and money.

LYCO: My best to your patron.

CURCULIO: I'll tell him.

(*Exits*)

LYCO: Anything else,
        pimp?

CAPPADOX: That bit of money for the clothes, to get me through
    until things are better. Can you pay it?

LYCO: I'll pay it; send for it tomorrow.

(*Exits*)

CAPPADOX: Well, that's that;
    very satisfactory. I should go to the temple and pray.
    Imagine; I bought that girl for just one-third
    of what I just got for her, back when she was little,
    and the man I bought her from has disappeared.
    I expect he's dead. But so what? I have the money.   600
    When the gods favor a man, they do pour blessings on him.

This calls for a sacrificial ceremony;
I know better than to let these details slip.

(*Exits into temple*)

Scene 3

(THERAPONTIGONUS *enters with* LYCO)

THERAPONTIGONUS: Now hear this! This is no petty
    exasperation.
The genuine rage that drives me is the very rage
that inspired me to destroy whole cities. So,
if you're not ready to pay the money you owe me,
the money I left with you, then you'd better be ready
to end your life.

LYCO: By God, there won't be any pettiness
in the thrashing I hand you, the very thrashing   610
I deal out to those to whom I owe nothing at all.

THERAPONTIGONUS: Don't threaten me, and don't try fancy
    negotiations.

LYCO: Don't you try taking what I've already returned.
I'll give you nothing.

THERAPONTIGONUS: I figured on this when I trusted it to you—
that you wouldn't return it.

LYCO: Then why ask for it?

THERAPONTIGONUS: Tell me who got it from you.

LYCO: Your one-eyed
   servant
  who claimed he was called Pissant—I gave it to him,
  since he brought the letter, sealed—

THERAPONTIGONUS: One-eyed servant?
  Pissant? You're dreaming. I have no servant.   620

LYCO: In which case you're wiser than some pimps,
  who free their servants and forget them.

THERAPONTIGONUS: What's this, now?

LYCO: I did exactly what you asked, by way
  of your messenger, who carried your own seal.

THERAPONTIGONUS: You must be stupider than stupid, to believe
  this kind of indirect message.

LYCO: Stupid? To trust
  an ordinary message about ordinary business?
  I'm on my way. You are well and duly paid. Farewell, soldier.

THERAPONTIGONUS: Farewell, eh?

LYCO: Ill, then, if you like. I don't
   care.

(*Exits*)

THERAPONTIGONUS: Now what? What good is it to conquer
   kings,   630
  if this scrivener can make fun of me?

Scene 4

(CAPPADOX *enters from the temple*)

CAPPADOX: When the gods favor a man, it would appear
    to follow that they are not angry with him.
    After I made the sacrifice, I thought of something:
    I should get my money from the banker soon,
    before he absconds, so it will feed me instead of him.

THERAPONTIGONUS: Good day! I've been hoping to encounter
    you.

CAPPADOX: Therapontigonus Platagidorus, upon my soul!
    Because you have arrived safely in Epidaurus,
    today at my house, you shall have—not a grain of salt.   640

THERAPONTIGONUS: Many thanks, but I am otherwise engaged
    to whip your ass. You hold my assets, I believe.

CAPPADOX: I'm holding no such thing. Don't call witnesses;
    I owe you nothing, nothing at all.

THERAPONTIGONUS: How's that?

CAPPADOX: I've done as I promised.

THERAPONTIGONUS: Will you or will you not
    surrender the girl, you bastard, or would you prefer
    to surrender to my sword?

CAPPADOX: A fine sound beating
    is what I'd like to give you. Don't try to scare me.
    She has been taken away—as you shall be, if you persist
    in these insults. All I owe you is a kick in the rear.   650

THERAPONTIGONUS: You threaten me?

CAPPADOX: I'll do more than that if
    you keep at it.

THERAPONTIGONUS: What's this? A pimp trying to scare me,
    veteran of hundreds of battles? I swear
    by my sword and shield, my battlefield comrades,
    if you don't listen to me and hand over the girl,
    I'll reduce you to crumbs the ants can carry away.

CAPPADOX: I too swear, by my tweezers, comb, mirror,
    my curling-iron, scissors, and towel,
    that your bragging and posturing mean no more
    to me than the woman who cleans my privy.   660
    I gave the girl to the man who brought your money.

THERAPONTIGONUS: What man would that be?

CAPPADOX: Your freedman named Puissant, or Pissant.

THERAPONTIGONUS: Mine?
    Hold it!
    I see now. Curculio has fooled me, by God.
    He stole my signet ring.

CAPPADOX: Lost your ring?
    So here's a soldier who's lost his army.

THERAPONTIGONUS: Where is Curculio now?

CAPPADOX: In the wheat,
    doubtless,
    where you will find five hundred curculios
    instead of one. I'm leaving; hail and farewell.

THERAPONTIGONUS: Hell and fare ill. Now what? Stay here?
    Go?   670
    How could I have been so stupid? Wanted:
    Pernicious insect. Huge reward!

ACT V

Scene 1

(CURCULIO *enters, in haste, from* PHAEDROMUS's *house*)

CURCULIO: Some old poet wrote in a tragedy once
    that the penalty for bigamy is two wives.
    True enough. But this creature, Phaedromus's girl,
    is the worst I ever saw or heard of, and by God,
    I can't imagine a worse one. She saw this ring,
    and had to know where I got it. "Why do you ask?"
    "Because I must," she says, but I don't tell her.
    She tries to take it, and bites me in the process.   680
    I barely got away, damn the little bitch!

Scene 2

(PLANESIUM *enters from* PHAEDROMUS's *house*)

PLANESIUM: Hurry up, Phaedromus!

PHAEDROMUS: (*Entering just after* PLANESIUM)
                              What's the hurry?

PLANESIUM: We can't lose the parasite. It's important.

CURCULIO: Not to me. I eat what's important.

PHAEDROMUS: (*Seizing* CURCULIO)   Got him!
    Now what's this all about?

PLANESIUM: Where did he get that ring?
  My father used to wear it.

CURCULIO: Actually, it was my aunt.

PLANESIUM: My mother gave it to him.

CURCULIO: And I suppose
  he passed it on to you.

PLANESIUM: You're blathering.

CURCULIO: That's what I do; I make a living at it.

PLANESIUM: Oh, please. I beg you . . . I have to find my
  parents.   690

CURCULIO: Search me. Are they in this ring?

PLANESIUM: I was born free!

CURCULIO: Many a slave can say the same thing.

PHAEDROMUS: Now that's
  enough!

CURCULIO: I told you once; do I have to tell you again?
  I won it playing dice with a stupid soldier.

(THERAPONTIGONUS enters)

THERAPONTIGONUS: There he is! I'm saved! Ah, my good man,
  what's the action?

CURCULIO: I hear you. If you're interested,
  say three throws for a captain's cloak.

THERAPONTIGONUS: Your throws make me want to throw up.
  Give me back the money, or the girl.

CURCULIO: Money? Girl? What are you trying to pull?   700

THERAPONTIGONUS: The one you took from the pimp today,
  Grain-Bug.

CURCULIO: I took no girl.

THERAPONTIGONUS: This one, right here!

PHAEDROMUS: This girl is free.

THERAPONTIGONUS: My servant girl? Free? I haven't freed her!

PHAEDROMUS: You own her? How? Who sold her to you? Out
  with it.

THERAPONTIGONUS: I paid for her through my banker, and she's
  mine.
  You and the pimp can pay me—double from each of you.

PHAEDROMUS: You traffic in girls, and we'll take you to court.

THERAPONTIGONUS: No, you won't.

PHAEDROMUS: (To CURCULIO, *touching his ear*)
                          Will you testify?

THERAPONTIGONUS: Illegal testimony!

PHAEDROMUS: Damn you, you can learn to live without
  testi . . . mony.
  (To CURCULIO)
  But I'll ask you legally. Come here.

THERAPONTIGONUS: A slave?   710

CURCULIO: (*Striking* THERAPONTIGONUS)
There. That should show you that I'm a free man.
Now to the courtroom.

THERAPONTIGONUS: (*Striking* CURCULIO)
                            And one for you.

CURCULIO: O citizens, citizens!

THERAPONTIGONUS: What are you yelling about?

PHAEDROMUS: Why did you
  hit him?

THERAPONTIGONUS: I wanted to.

PHAEDROMUS: (*To* CURCULIO)   Come here. I'll hand him over
  to you;
  be quiet for now.

PLANESIUM: Phaedromus! Please, rescue me!

PHAEDROMUS: I shall—as I would myself. Now then, captain,
  I would like to know where you obtained that ring,
  which the parasite lifted from you.

PLANESIUM: By your knees, I beg you, tell us the truth!

THERAPONTIGONUS: How does this concern you? While you're
    at it,   720
  ask me where I got my cloak, or my sword.

CURCULIO: Mighty pleased with himself, I must say.

THERAPONTIGONUS: Get him out of here, and I'll tell you
  everything.

CURCULIO: Everything he says is nothing.

PLANESIUM: Tell me the truth.
    Please.

THERAPONTIGONUS: I'll tell you; get up and pay attention.
    It belonged to my father, Periphanes—

PLANESIUM: Periphanes!

THERAPONTIGONUS: Before he died, he gave it to me,
    as was quite proper, since I was his son.

PLANESIUM: Gods above!

THERAPONTIGONUS: And he made me his heir.

PLANESIUM: O goddess of filial love, help me,   730
    for I have been faithful to my family!
    My own brother, welcome!

THERAPONTIGONUS: How can I believe that?
    If you're telling the truth, who was your mother?

PLANESIUM: Cleobula.

THERAPONTIGONUS: And who was your nurse?

PLANESIUM: Archestrata.
    She took me to the Dionysian festival.
    We had just gotten there, and found our places,
    when a huge whirlwind destroyed the stands—
    I was so terrified, I couldn't tell who grabbed me
    neither alive nor dead, it seemed,
    and I don't know how he carried me away.   740

THERAPONTIGONUS: I'll never forget the chaos of that moment.
    But where is the man who carried you off?

PLANESIUM: I don't know. But I have always kept this ring;
    I had it that day.

THERAPONTIGONUS: Let me look at it.

CURCULIO: You're sure you ought to trust him with it?

PLANESIUM: Stay out of this.

THERAPONTIGONUS: My God. This is the one;
    I know it as I know myself. I gave it to you
    on your birthday. O sister!

PLANESIUM: My brother! It's really you!

PHAEDROMUS: It's miraculous! You are both blessed today.

CURCULIO: I think we're all blessed. You should celebrate   750
    your arrival with a dinner in your sister's honor;
    tomorrow Phaedromus gives a wedding feast. We accept with
      pleasure.

THERAPONTIGONUS: You be quiet.

CURCULIO: I will not be quiet,
    since things are turning out so well. Captain,
    give him your sister's hand. I will give her a dowry.

THERAPONTIGONUS: What sort of dowry?

CURCULIO: From me? The
      lifelong right
    to keep me fed. And I mean it, too, by God.

THERAPONTIGONUS: You do us proud. But this pimp still owes us
    money.

PHAEDROMUS: How is that?

THERAPONTIGONUS: If anyone could prove this girl
    freeborn,
our contract was that the sale was canceled.   760
So let's find the pimp.

CURCULIO: Splendid!

PHAEDROMUS: First, though,
    I'll settle some business of my own.

THERAPONTIGONUS: What's that?

PHAEDROMUS: That you promise me her hand.

CURCULIO: Why hesitate,
    captain?
    Promise her to him.

THERAPONTIGONUS: If she wishes it.

PLANESIUM: Brother, I do.

THERAPONTIGONUS: Done, then.

CURCULIO: Well done!

PHAEDROMUS: I have your
    promise, captain,
    That she may be my wife?

THERAPONTIGONUS: You have it; I have said so.

CURCULIO: And I, too, promise: you have it.

THERAPONTIGONUS: Oh, nobly done.
    But here's the pimp! My treasure chest!

Scene 3

(CAPPADOX *enters from his house*)

CAPPADOX: It's absurd to claim that bankers are bad risks.
In fact, they are both good risks and bad,   770
as I have today demonstrated. Money is not badly invested
if it isn't repaid; it is just lost. Take Lyco,
going to every bank trying to scrape together
what he owed me. I kept after him till he dared me
to sue him, which I didn't want to do: I was afraid
he might get away with declaring bankruptcy.
But his friends finally brought him to his senses,
and he pried loose my money from his own capital.
Now I'm getting home while the getting's good.

THERAPONTIGONUS: Hey, you, pimp! I want you.

PHAEDROMUS: And so do I.
                                                            780

CAPPADOX: And I want nothing to do with either of you.

THERAPONTIGONUS: Hold it right there.

PHAEDROMUS: And cough up my
money. Now.

CAPPADOX: What's my business with you? Or you?

THERAPONTIGONUS: I'll grab you at each end and stretch you out
until I can set your feet to the bowstring
and shoot you like an arrow.

PHAEDROMUS: Cute little thing!
I'll find a little dog to bed you down with,
and provide a collar for each of you.

CAPPADOX: I'll see you both rotting in jail.

CURCULIO: Grab him, send him to the rack and then to hell.   790

THERAPONTIGONUS: He won't need our help to get to hell.

CAPPADOX: In the name of the gods and decency,
   you kidnap me without sentence, without witnesses?
   For God's sake, Planesium, you, Phaedromus, help me!

PLANESIUM: Please, brother, don't condemn him too quickly.
   He treated me well and honorably at his house.

THERAPONTIGONUS: Don't thank him; Aesculapius deserves more
      thanks
   for your purity; if he had been well, the pimp
   would have got rid of you long ago.

PHAEDROMUS: Listen to me.
   I'll try to settle this. Let him go.   800
   Come here, pimp. I'll deliver my verdict,
   if you agree to abide by my decision.

THERAPONTIGONUS: We agree.

CAPPADOX: Provided, by God, you decide
   that no one gets my money!

THERAPONTIGONUS: Money you promised?

CAPPADOX: How promised?

PHAEDROMUS: You gave your word.

CAPPADOX: I take it back.
   I was born with a tongue so I could talk,
   not so I could ruin myself.

PHAEDROMUS: It's no use.
   Grab his neck again.

CAPPADOX: All right, all right!
   You'll get what you want.

THERAPONTIGONUS: Now that you're so obliging,
   answer my question.

CAPPADOX: Ask away.

THERAPONTIGONUS: Did you not swear: 810
   if this girl proved freeborn, you would return all the money?

CAPPADOX: I don't recall that.

THERAPONTIGONUS: You deny it?

CAPPADOX: By God, I do deny it.
   Who heard me? Where?

CURCULIO: In my presence, and Lyco the
   banker's.

CAPPADOX: Will you be quiet?

CURCULIO: No, I won't. I don't give a damn
   for you; don't try to scare me. He made the promise
   in front of me and Lyco.

PHAEDROMUS: I believe you.
   I will now state, so you can hear it, pimp,
   my decision: this girl is free; this is her brother;
   she being his sister, and soon to be my wife,
   give back the money. There you have it.   820

THERAPONTIGONUS: And you'll do time, if I don't get my money
   back.

CAPPADOX: You're a damn poor magistrate, Phaedromus.
    You'll regret it. And you, captain, be damned
    by all the gods and goddesses. Follow me.

THERAPONTIGONUS: Where to?

CAPPADOX: To my banker's, and to court.
    That, my friend,
    is where I settle all my debts.

THERAPONTIGONUS: It'll be prison, not court,
    if I don't get my money.

CAPPADOX: And I pray that you come
    to a bad end—just so you understand me.

THERAPONTIGONUS: Do you indeed?

CAPPADOX: Indeed, by God.

THERAPONTIGONUS: I understand my fists.

CAPPADOX: So what?

THERAPONTIGONUS: "So what?" you say? If you arouse   830
    my anger, sir, I will shut you up right now.

CAPPADOX: All right, then. Take your money now.

THERAPONTIGONUS: Good.

PHAEDROMUS: Captain, dine with me. There will be a wedding
    today.
    May it bring happiness to both of us.
    (*To audience*)
    Friends, your gratitude, if you please.

Acknowledgments

Constance Carrier's translation of *Amphitryon* appeared in *Five Roman Comedies*, edited by Palmer Bovie, published in 1970 by E. P. Dutton. Erich Segal's translation of *Miles Gloriosus* appeared in *Plautus: Three Comedies*, published in 1969 by Harper and Row, and is used here by permission.